Beyond the Western Sun

Kristina Circelli

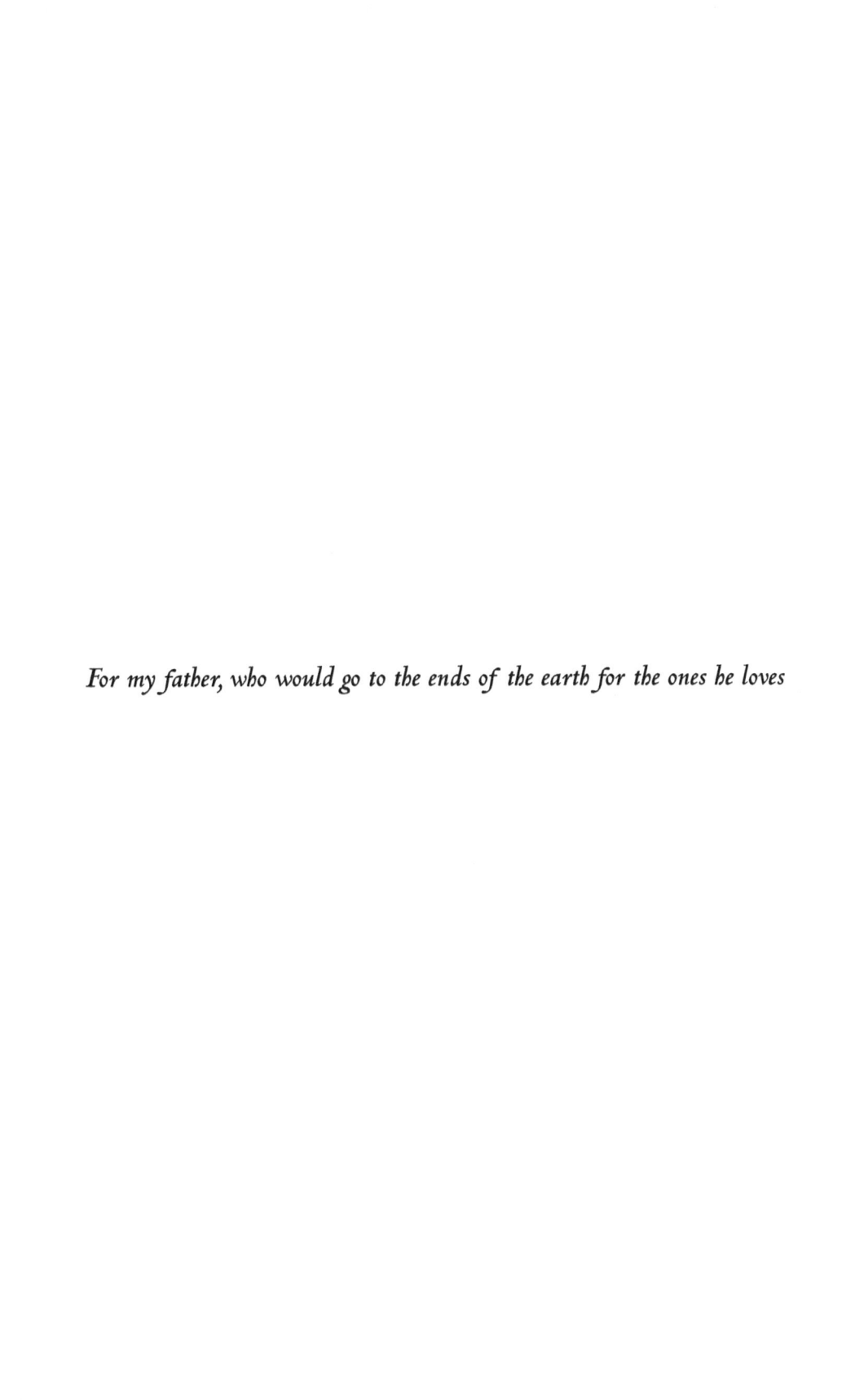

For my father, who would go to the ends of the earth for the ones he loves

Prologue

Deep in the clouded mountains, cloaked in the light of a full moon, an old man dressed in decorated tanned robes bent gingerly over a fire-pit of glowing embers, reading the wisps of smoke that circled up toward the opening of his hut. The messages of the dead formed ghastly images behind his eyes, forebodings of what was soon to come.

Orange firelight flickered around the curved walls of the deerskin hut, casting a glow around the white-haired Elder as he communicated with the future. Quiet dominated the night. Not a single sound echoed around the mountains—the animals silenced by fear and sadness, the howling wind stilled. Not even the breathing of the old man could be heard, and in his trance-like state, he seemed close to death himself.

Sitting in the shadows, a young woman watched the ceremony with haunted black eyes, waiting. The dead revealed themselves in many ways, and to the old man they appeared in the smoke that drifted up from the burning hearth. They spoke to him, trusted him, came to him in times of need. They asked him to speak to their family members, to relay their love and final words of good-bye, to pray for safe journey into the Spirit World, to protect their souls in death. In return, they helped him in his own spiritual quests. The dead acted as his spies, his partners in the spiritual realms, gathering whatever information they could find to answer his questions.

Tonight, his questions concerned the young woman, his apprentice. Something was stirring for her, something big; he could feel it deep in his bones. The girl was special, born into a world she was destined to change. She had been marked by death, promised to a fate beyond his capacity to control. One day, her gifts, her strengths, would surpass his own, and she would take her rightful place at the head of the fire.

But he feared for her, feared what the dead would reveal. Not even the Elder could predict the end to this journey. All he could sense was a recent change in the air, a rippling of the water in a still breeze. The birds stopped singing when she passed. The deer fled into the woods. Something, someone, was searching, and they were afraid.

And then, as his old brown eyes nearly hidden behind deep folds of wrinkles read the last of the dead's words, the smoke dissipated into the air and the bright red embers turned to coal. The hut fell into darkness, only a single beam of white moonlight streaming in through the opening of the roof.

"The time has come," the Elder said softly, peering through the black night at the woman, who sat with her knees drawn up to her chest, face registering no emotion. "The Land of the Dead awaits you."

Chapter 1

In the early morning light, Ian Daivya sat hunched over his drafting table, planning out designs for a new landscape installation. When he finished and was paid, the cost of labor alone would top his yearly quota, promising a nice paycheck. It wasn't every day that a brand new five-star hotel was constructed in his flourishing town of Jennsboro, North Carolina, and he secured the commission, beating out a dozen other landscaping companies for the million-dollar job.

He'd been confident from the beginning that he would win the bidding war. After all, Ian had owned his business for twenty years, working his way up from a down-in-the-dirt gardener to a corner-office landscape architect, and had the perfect eye for design. His perfect eye, along with the will and drive to work sixty-plus hour weeks, had brought him a considerable amount of success the past decade, and he had the big house and fancy car to prove it.

Right now, that fancy car was parked just outside his home office, and he took a moment to sit back in his plush leather chair and admire the sleek black design glimmering in the beautifully sunny day. The well-manicured lawn, once tended to lovingly by Ian's own hand, was now in the competent hands of one of his very first employees, who was currently on his knees hand-pulling weeds from a bed of blooming annuals in the shade of a sprawling oak tree.

Glancing over a list of suggestions provided by the hotel owner, Ian sharpened a pencil and traced a few lines, planning a rounded flowerbed that would surround the main fountain. He was thinking red and blue flowers to match the color scheme of the hotel, with some small specks of white to spruce up the entrance. Pentas maybe, or impatiens—he liked their colorful petals, even if they weren't the most durable of plants. But he wasn't worried about their durability. After all, the shorter they lasted, the more work he was guaranteed to secure. It was a gamble, assuming he would be hired to care for the entire property, but it was a gamble he was willing to take.

Forgetting the measurements of the fountain, he picked up a thick green folder his secretary had prepared for him the day before that included all the information about the hotel. Opening it, he frowned when a slip of paper and picture pinned to the flap caught his eye. The photograph was of a young, trim woman with long, flowing, curly red hair and dark green eyes accented by sparkling and shadowy gray powder. She was smiling seductively at the camera with luscious lips painted dark red, wearing black lace lingerie and sitting provocatively on the edge of a bed, leaving very little to the imagination. The woman was his secretary, Rebecca Dale, and attached to the photo was a note that read, *Think of me while you're gone, can't wait 'til you get back to the office.*

"Quite the 'thinking of you' note," Ian murmured, now certainly thinking about Rebecca.

She'd been working for him for eight months now, and while at first she was professional and eager to learn the business, she lately had become flirtatious, using every given opportunity to get close to her boss, to run her hands down his arms, lean in close and compliment the smell of his cologne. Many times, she suggested going out for drinks or catching an early dinner before heading home. While Ian was guilty of flirting back, reveling in the sexy attention of a wonderfully-figured woman more than fifteen years his junior, he was yet to take her up on any of her offers. His refusals only encouraged her temptations, making it harder and harder to resist, and he was beginning to wonder why he was even trying. He loved his wife, loved his family, but it simply wasn't the same anymore. And Rebecca was certainly willing to express her interest.

Disappointed with himself for not only thinking of Rebecca, but also of actually considering whether he would take her out to dinner first or just see what she had to offer right then and there in his office, Ian shook his head and shoved the picture and note into the trashcan. He struggled to focus on his designs.

Just as he was deciding between flowers or shrubs to plant along the main walkway, Ian's son walked into the room. Clutching a pillow and his PSP, Cole Daivya approached his father's side. At seven years old, he was the spitting image of his father, with thick blonde hair that curled slightly at the end, charming bright blue eyes, and a lanky frame. His nose seemed slightly too big for his face, but he would grow into it, as Ian had grown into his during his teenage years.

Cole yawned heavily. "Daddy? When are we leaving?" he asked, sleepily rubbing his eyes.

"Soon."

"But when?"

"Soon. Go help your mom get ready," Ian ordered without bothering to look at his son.

Cole stood looking up at his father for a moment before turning around and padding into the large, naturally-lit kitchen to find his mother. He found her at the counter, wiping up crumbs from the sandwiches she had just made. "Daddy said soon," he told her as he settled onto a bar stool and opened a juice box.

Stifling an irritated sigh, Julia Daivya, a thin and fit woman of thirty-seven, finished packing drinks into the cooler, biting her tongue as she left her son sitting at the counter and made her way through the big, open house. Once, the house had felt cozy, with family pictures hanging on the wall, toys in every corner, souvenirs from their travels decorating the rooms. Now it all felt fake, forced.

Julia made sure that everything they needed for the trip—suitcases, snacks, cameras—were by the door, then went to pressure her husband into getting ready to go.

"It's eight o'clock," she said, standing in the doorway of Ian's office. "We agreed on seven-thirty."

"Few more minutes."

"Ian, we need to get going. We have reservation times for check in."

"A few more minutes, Julia. I just need to finish the main walkway's layout."

Julia stared at the back of her husband's head, annoyed and somewhat sad. Not too long ago, she would have taken the moment to approach Ian from behind, wrap her arms around his tanned neck, playfully squeeze those well-developed biceps while hoping for a glimpse of sexy, almond-shaped blue eyes that highlighted chiseled cheekbones and a full mouth, but now all she wanted to do was get in the car and begin the long drive to the campground.

Likewise, Ian once would have taken a break from his work to run a hand through her straight, shoulder-length brown hair, gently tease his wife about her short and petite frame, maybe steal a kiss from a mouth that had never seen a tube of lipstick, but lately he didn't care about such things. Something had changed in their relationship in the past few years, an obsession with work and money taking over Ian's attention and a desperate melancholy consuming Julia's heart. She hoped this camping trip would bring them closer together, take his focus off of the hotel designs, and loosen them both up enough to have fun. It was, after all, not only a camping trip but also a family reunion, and Ian loved her family like his own, if not more.

"Ten minutes?" she asked tentatively, bracing herself for a verbal assault.

Instead, Ian only rubbed his eyes and spared his wife a second's glance over his shoulder. He couldn't be bothered to notice that her wide green eyes were hopeful yet tired. "Fine. Get the car packed up and I'll be ready."

An hour later, they were finally on the road.

Cole sat in the backseat, attention solely on his dinosaur video game by the time they pulled out of the neighborhood. He didn't notice the tension between his parents, or the fact that they rode in silence for nearly four hours. When they reached Big Creek Campground, a state-protected stretch of natural wildlife along the edge of the Smoky Mountains, the two might as well have been strangers.

After a few moments of contemplation, Ian figured out how to pitch the tent and set to work, eager to get away from Julia for awhile and have a few moment's quiet from the pressure of such silence. Without the tension of marital problems, the campground was actually rather nice, peaceful and secluded, surrounded by towering oak trees. The ground was scattered with leaves, as wooded areas usually were, and the area they had rented out for the week was an oddly-shaped oval with a spigot, picnic table, and charcoal grill. The lot next to them came with an electric outlet, which would be used by Julia's parents when they arrived. There were no other sites rented out around theirs for a good six or seven-hundred feet, so privacy was promised. With both the restrooms and creek just a quick walk away, Ian was willing to say that they had the prime location. That much he could be happy with.

At the car, Julia pulled out her camera and convinced her son to take a walk around the park. She too needed a brief escape, a chance to clear her head and walk off the stress. Julia was a proud woman, always had been, but the threat of her marriage failing was weakening her nerves.

Mother and son walked down the narrow dirt path surrounded on both sides by wild and tangled undergrowth colored in a dozen different shades of green. Being the end of March, the day was cool enough for Julia and Cole to be wearing jeans and closed-toes shoes but warm enough so that they weren't rushing back to the fire to warm their frozen bones. Julia loved the crisp weather, the fresh air. The world seemed at peace with itself.

She snapped a few pictures of a group of blue-winged butterflies perched on a fallen log, amazed when they didn't flutter away at her close approach. She turned to Cole, who was staring into the woods. "What do you think, sweetie? Aren't they pretty?"

Cole turned his eyes to the butterflies and shrugged. His mother loved nature and all animals, but the only bugs he liked were the ones that made squishy noises when he stomped on them. "Guess so. Can we go play by the water now?"

"Sure." Julia took her son by the hand and led him through a carved-out path in the woods. She enjoyed the smell of fresh blooms and crisp spring air, the sights of chipper squirrels chasing one another around winding tree branches and lively song-birds building nests for their future young. Julia loved nature, the pure innocence of it all, the beauty of a world untouched by the hands of man. It was nature, in fact, that had led her to Ian. As a struggling college junior, she had wandered into the public library one afternoon to get away from her hectic student life, turned a corner, and bumped into an attractive man five years her senior pouring his attention into a stack of books on aquatic plants.

The attraction had been instant, and for Julia, a young woman of twenty, those piercing blue eyes had been the end for her. For Ian, all it took was one smile, a smile that lit up Julia's face in a way that he could have sworn the sun shone from her eyes. At twenty-five, he was new to his landscaping business but successful enough to need help, and had hired Julia upon discovering her need for a paycheck. And from that first meeting in the library, nothing had ever been the same for them again.

Julia helped Ian build his small, backyard-business to the successful company it was today, and he supported her in her own career as a freelance photographer. Their mutual love for the environment created a strong bond between them, one that Julia desperately wanted to save, and she was willing to believe that things could be the way they used to be, if they fought hard enough. She was willing to fight. So now it was up to Ian.

Five minutes later, the winding path opened up to a river, churning with small rapids and cascading down piles of smooth rocks. Julia took a seat on a fallen tree and enjoyed the scene. She'd photographed this river for a tourist magazine three years ago and had vacationed at the campground at least four times before, but every time the scene changed. Leaves were different colors, the current moved faster or slower, animals hid in their homes or dared to venture out. It was a new adventure with every visit.

"Stay along the shore, Cole. Don't go past your ankles."

The water was bitingly icy and her son wasn't interested much in learning how to swim, so she didn't worry too much about him venturing into the water. She did, however, jump to her feet when he climbed on top of the biggest rock just on the edge of the river. "Be careful, Cole! Don't go any farther than that!"

Cole ignored his mother, curiously staring into the woods. He thought he saw something on the other side of the river, something gray and wispy that was floating through the trees. The gray and translucent thing had followed him down the path that led to the river, weaving in and out of the bushes. It looked like a little boy, but he was see-through, like a ghost. Cole couldn't tell if he looked scared or if he wanted to play, and instead of being frightened himself, he was eager to know if ghosts were real or not.

He took another step on the rock, keeping his eyes on the figure hiding behind a tree. The wispy gray boy had turned, looking over his shoulder and gesturing for Cole to follow. A mesmerizing curiosity had him moving forward again, abandoning all sense of caution, and his foot slipped on a patch of algae.

"*Cole!*"

Just seconds before he could fall into the freezing water, Julia grabbed her son by the arm and yanked him back to the shore, her heart pounding. "*Cole!* What's the matter with you? I told you not to go any farther! Do you know how *dangerous* those rocks are?"

Tears welled up in the boy's eyes. A combination of fear, shame, and embarrassment tore at him. He wasn't a very good swimmer, and the thought of falling into the cold river terrified him. He knew his dad would say that if he wasn't so afraid of the swimming pool that he would be able to swim. Cole hated it when his dad bugged him about not being able to swim, and he hoped his mom wouldn't tell him that part of the story. But, he was eager to ask what his dad thought about ghosts in the woods.

"I'm sorry, Mom. But...I thought I saw...something—over there." He pointed toward the opposite riverbank, where the gray mist had disappeared. "There...there was a ghost, I think. A little boy ghost. He wanted me to play with him."

Julia followed his finger, but saw only trees. This was Cole's first trip to the mountains, so it wasn't surprising that he was seeing things in the trees, especially considering the fact that as a toddler he'd had a strange fear of the woods. She supposed it was because rather than cartoon books and comics he'd been interested in nature stories and animal encyclopedias, and so he knew what deadly creatures lurked in the forest.

Instead of being concerned over ghosts, she hugged her son until she could catch her breath. Seeing her little boy tumbling off the rock absolutely terrified her. If she hadn't been keeping a close eye on him, he would have gone in for sure. "I don't see anything, Cole. Maybe you just saw a deer. There's lots of them around here, and they're good at hiding in the trees. That way they can escape the hunters." She pulled him to his feet and brushed the dirt off his pants. "Come on, let's go see if your daddy's got the tent up yet."

They made it back to the campground much quicker than the time it took to get to the river. Julia was determined not to speak of the incident, while Cole was eager to share his thoughts. But by the time Cole saw food at the table, he had almost forgotten about it entirely. At their site, Ian was pulling a pack of hamburgers from the cooler. The two-room tent was set up, sleeping bags and pillows already inside.

"Anyone hungry?"

"Me!" Cole raised a hand with excitement. He loved hamburgers fresh from the grill, slathered up with ketchup and pickles, and eagerly followed his mother's orders to get the rest of the lunch items from the car and set the picnic table.

Julia approached Ian's side as he began grilling. The relaxed look on his face comforted her. The brief break must have taken good care of his foul mood. She watched Cole for a moment as he climbed up on the bench and started setting out plates. A sudden gust of wind had him scrambling to recover the lost napkins and secure them with a box of cookies.

"We need to keep an eye on him," she told her husband. "He almost fell into the river."

"Why?"

Julia sighed and shook her head at the accusatory tone. Apparently Ian wasn't as relaxed as she'd thought. "He said he saw something in the woods on the other side of the river. He jumped up on the rock and before I knew it, he slipped. I grabbed him before he fell, but it scared me. Those rapids, and with his swimming......we just need to keep an eye on him."

The worry in her voice concerned Ian. He'd known her a long time, almost eighteen years to be exact, and she rarely got worked up over such trivial matters. Despite the fact that they seemed to be growing apart lately, he didn't like the tense expression spread across her face.

"Anything else happen I should know about?" Julia was quiet, wrapping a strand of hair around her finger, a nervous habit. Ian flipped the hamburgers and shifted so that he was facing his wife. He lifted a hand and rubbed her arm. "What else happened?"

The touch startled Julia. Ian hadn't shown that kind of gentle concern in awhile, and she welcomed the strange yet familiar sensation. "Cole said he saw...." she sighed again, feeling ridiculous. "He said he saw a ghost in the woods, of all damn things...the ghost of a little boy."

Rather than being worried, Ian was humored. He chuckled and turned back to the grill. "He's just a kid, Julia. That's nothing to get worked up over. Hell, I used to pretend I saw Indians in the woods when I was young so I could plan a battle. Kids see all kinds of crazy things when they want to—let their imagination run wild."

"Not our kid," Julia argued. "He doesn't make things up, and he doesn't see ghosts. If you remember, he decided at four years old that ghosts weren't real after seeing that special on the Discovery Channel. And hell, the only video games he plays are educational ones. The whole walk back he kept talking about finding the little boy and asking him what he wanted. I don't know, I'm just worried that he might actually try to find this ghost."

His wife was right, he hated to admit. Cole was a very serious, down-to-earth child. He usually chose Animal Planet over cartoons, books over his PSP, and loved to chatter on about what he learned about science in school. Talk of ghosts, monsters, fairy tales, or any other source of magic was not in his typical vocabulary.

"Tell you what," he said as he placed the cooked hamburgers on a paper plate, "if he keeps bringing up the ghost, I'll have a talk with him. He was probably just goofing around. He'll forget about it. For now, let's just try to have a decent time."

Julia relented and joined Cole at the picnic table. As Ian predicted, Cole seemed to have forgotten about the ghost and instead talked about a dinosaur show on television last night. Julia listened intently, though not able to follow the long dinosaur names he threw at her. She snuck a peek at Ian, and her smile faded when she saw that he was busy scribbling down something on a pad of paper.

Ideas for plants, she figured, just another excuse to ignore their son.

Chapter 2

The next morning Ian woke early and took the time alone to get some work done before Julia got up. It was promising to be a beautiful day, already a cloudless blue sky and a cool breeze, and if he could devote an hour or so to his business then he wouldn't have to feel guilty about blowing off the rest of the day. Or better yet, he could finish before anyone even knew he had done any work at all. He hated the disapproving stares Julia cast his way whenever he brought out his sketches, and so to avoid a potential fight, he decided to attempt to finish just the front walk of the hotel before his in-laws arrived from Georgia.

His plan was spoiled when Cole, dressed in shark-decorated pajamas, stepped out of the tent, rubbed his eyes, and sauntered over to the picnic table, sitting across from his father. He placed a thin book on the table. "Wanna see a T-Rex?"

"Not now, Cole."

"Can we eat breakfast?"

"When your mother gets up."

"Can we go to the playground and play on the swings?"

"Not now."

Cole huffed and crossed his arms. His dad was no fun at all, and never let him do anything he wanted to do unless it was about yard work. In fact, the boy couldn't remember a time when his father wasn't working. In protest to Ian's standoffishness, Cole kicked dirt up and made sure he got his shoes dirty. They were new, so he knew that getting them all scuffed up right away would irritate his dad.

Cole's foul mood didn't last long. A navy-blue truck pulling a pop-up trailer drove up in the campsite next to theirs, honking energetically. An older woman with curly gray hair stepped out with arms wide open.

"Granny!" Cole scrambled off the bench and ran to his grandmother, wrapping his arms around her neck. "You're here!"

"How are you, Sweetie?" Olivia Bard, a nearly identical, older version of her daughter hugged her grandson with a laugh. She slowly lowered herself to Cole's level and pulled a handful of caramel candy from the pocket of her corduroy jacket. He gladly accepted. "Don't you go telling your momma on me, now. I know you're not supposed to have sweets before breakfast. So where is she, anyway?"

"Sleeping."

"Well, go wake her lazy butt up!" Olivia straightened, old bones cracking, watching Cole with a wide grin. She hadn't seen her grandson in nearly six months, far too long. When he disappeared inside tent, she walked over to Ian. "And how are you, my handsome son-in-law?"

"Just fine, Olivia." Ian consented to a hug and shook his father-in-law's hand when the old man approached. "David," he greeted.

"Ian," David Bard said in return, his deep voice friendly. "You look good. Business must be doing well."

"Can't complain." Neither David nor Olivia knew of any problems between Ian and Julia, as far as Ian knew anyway, so he figured that for the moment he was safe from any scrutiny. His in-laws were very fond of their son-in-law, but the moment their daughter's heart broke would be the same moment their fondness turned to disdain, and Ian was not going to provoke that.

A retired military man, David was still strong in his late-sixties, healthy and fit with a quiet confidence that demanded respect. His age didn't seem to have caught up with him yet, for his smooth skin and sharp eyes defied the real number of years he had seen. He kept his hair cropped short, his clothes neatly pressed, and his black boots polished, looking very much the part of the Armed Forces.

Olivia, though a bit overweight and looking a few years older than she actually was, had an air of authority that matched her husband's, as she was a retired professor who was used to taking control. She too kept her gray hair short, neatly and tightly curled without any artificial coloring, and had angled wrinkles across her forehead and at the corners of her eyes and mouth. Unlike the professional dress of her husband, she chose a more casual look, wearing faded jeans, a loose lavender sweater, and ratty sneakers.

"Mom!"

Julia, fully dressed in khaki pants, a dark green T-shirt, and hiking boots, stepped out of the tent and jogged to her mother, hugging her tightly. "You're early!"

"We just couldn't wait to see you. And there was no traffic."

"You look thin," David observed, face stern. "Have you been eating right? Can you afford groceries?"

Julia let out an amused chuckle and ran her fingers through her messy hair. "Yes, Dad, we can afford groceries. And yes, I'm eating right. Don't I get a hug?" She hugged her father, though he wasn't one to show much emotion. After being released, David headed back to the truck to unpack. "Where's Lisa?"

"Oh, your sister won't be here for another day or so. You know how she is."

Julia did know. Her sister was ten years younger, but she might as well of been ten years old, in her opinion. Lisa was known to be reckless, flighty, and completely oblivious to the world around her. Blessed with striking good looks, thick blond hair that fell in waves down her back, piercing green eyes accented by high cheekbones, full lips, and a trim yet muscular frame, she often got by on appearances alone. She was supposed to arrive at Big Creek Campground that night, which meant she would probably show up sometime in the next three days. It was impossible to depend on her, but Julia loved her sister all the same. Flighty or not, she was good at heart.

"Your aunt and cousins will be here tonight. Jerry's coming tomorrow morning."

"Is he bringing the new girlfriend?"

"New girlfriend's been replaced by wife number five."

"Oh. Interesting." Love them as she did, Julia couldn't deny that her family had its faults. "Well...how about I help ya'll set up your tent."

Olivia laughed loudly, waving a hand at her daughter. "Oh, honey, that's a hoot, your father and me in a tent." Still laughing, she walked back to their truck to get her camera, and it was then that Julia saw the brand new pop-up trailer that was hitched to the back. Her father was already cranking it open. *Leave it to the Bards*, she thought with amusement, *to go camping with air-conditioning*.

While David was getting the trailer fixed up, Julia and Olivia started making breakfast. Cole stood by with wide eyes, stomach growling. They prepared bacon and eggs, and cooked toast over the grill. Cole made the process a bit faster by getting out the paper plates and pouring juice for everyone, though he spilled a good amount in the process. Ian remained at the table, working.

"He's dedicated, isn't he?" Olivia asked, glancing over her shoulder at Ian as he tore a sheet of paper off of the pad and crumpled it into a ball with a frustrated sigh.

"He's got a big commission at some new hotel going in downtown. They begin the installation about a week after we get back."

"And is he planning on having any fun on this vacation?"

Julia broke an egg over the pan and shrugged. "That's up to him."

Out of the corner of his eye, Ian saw Olivia glancing his way every now and then, and he wondered what the women were talking about, if they were talking about him, and if so, what was being said. The last thing he needed on this trip was trouble from the in-laws, or any other members of the family who would stand behind Julia no matter what. No one else needed to know their problems, and that was that. He might have to talk to his wife about keeping things to herself.

"Daddy? Can we go play at the park today?" Cole settled himself next to his father and tapped his arm. Ian looked up from his work, but before he could reply, Julia set down a large plate of bacon in front of them.

"I think that would be a great idea," she said pointedly, giving Ian a look that warned him against arguing.

Ian glanced at David, who had his arms crossed, then at Olivia, who was standing at his side. He closed his notebook and nodded, bullied into agreement. "Sure, buddy, we can go after lunch."

"Cool!"

The rest of the adults joined them at the table and began eating. The grandparents chose fresh coffee over juice, and Olivia stayed away from the bacon and butter for her toast. She had recently decided to put herself on a diet, and painful as it may be, she was going to stick to it, even on vacation.

"So how was your first day here?" David asked, folding his napkin and placing it neatly across his lap.

"I almost fell in the river," Cole announced, a tinge of pride in his voice.

"And what were you doing that close to the river, young man?"

Before Julia could stop her son, he was already telling them what he saw. "There was a ghost in the woods. A little boy ghost playing in the trees, and I wanted to talk to him. But I slipped on a rock and Mom grabbed me and made me come back to the tent. So I couldn't talk to the ghost."

At her mother's stare, Julia shrugged and lifted a hand. "He's certain he saw a ghost. I can't convince him otherwise."

"I did see one!"

"OK, Cole."

"I did!"

"OK, I believe you."

"He may very well have seen a ghost."

All eyes turned to David. Not one for the supernatural and typically excruciatingly serious, the former military man had never bothered with talk of ghosts before. Everyone was surprised by the affirmation. He took a sip of coffee before continuing. "These are very old woods, very old trees. They've seen a lot of death." His voice was serene with a hint of warning as his eyes took on a faraway expression of remembrance.

"I used to come here all the time with my father when I was a boy. There are a lot of stories about hunters, hikers, kids who wander away from their parents, who get lost in the woods and never return."

"And how do ghosts come into those stories?" Ian asked, determined to prove that his son's imagination was simply running wild.

David thought back to his teenage years when he'd spent so many hours hiking and camping with his father in the heart of Native American lore. It was one of the few bonds they'd shared, one he still held close in his memories. "There used to be a small village deep in the mountains, what was left of a band of Cherokee that had settled long before any European ever set foot in this country. I doubt they're even still here, since they were old men and women when I was a boy. Anyway, they used to tell stories about the souls of the dead. They have old beliefs about death. They say that when a person dies and is buried, they go to the Spirit World. But if the person dies and the body is never found, never buried, then their souls are left to wander the earth eternally. Some find their way to the Land of the Dead, a place for lost souls. If I remember correctly, they say it's somewhere behind the Western Sun." He looked down at his plate sadly. "I used to think about that when I saw my comrades fall during battle, and knew we would have to leave their bodies behind."

Caught up in the moment, David cleared his throat with a quick shake of his head. "Anyway, all I'm saying is that ghosts aren't such a strange thing in these parts. You never know what you'll see in woods that are home to many battles and bloodshed."

No one said a word for a long time. Julia and Ian were both thinking that now their son's beliefs would be reinforced by his grandfather's tale and they would never hear the end of it. Olivia was surprised as well, for she had never heard her husband talk of ghosts. He was a down-to-business man and not prone to imagination. Nor was he a religious man prone to spiritual creeds. The admission about old Cherokee beliefs, she pondered, must be true, at least to his understanding.

Only Cole was thrilled by the stories, because they meant he really did see a ghost. He'd never before thought they were real, but now he could actually tell his friends that he knew for a fact what ghosts looked like. They were gray, see-through, and moved like the rain.

"Enough talk about ghosts," Ian ordered then, picking up his fork. "Let's enjoy our breakfast."

Chapter 3

Later that day, Julia made sure her husband fulfilled his promise to spend time with Cole. The boy had been looking forward to the park all day, making plans about swinging as high as possible and going up and down the slide until he got dizzy. He may have been too serious for his age, but the child in him loved a good playground.

"Mom and I are going for a walk," she told Ian, who was cleaning up the lunch mess, distracted by thoughts of landscaping. "Dad's taking a nap, so now's a perfect time to take Cole to the park."

"Yeah, I'll take him."

"We'll be back in a couple hours." Julia grabbed her coat and camera. She hesitated, contemplating kissing her husband before heading for her walk, but he had already turned away. "Oh, and Ian, try to act like you're having fun with him."

Having had the last word, she joined her mother at the entrance of the site and together the two women headed down the trail, passing a few fellow campers out enjoying the day.

"Ooh, look!" Julia pointed to a doe and her fawn grazing in a patch of grass just a few yards away. "How cute." She snapped a couple pictures before the animals noticed her and bounded away into the trees. "I was hoping to see some deer. The zoo back home is putting together an article on deer populations in the wild for their monthly newsletter and asked me to supply the photos. I have a bunch of old stuff but a doe and her fawn is perfect."

Olivia offered a smile, carefully watching her daughter. She knew something was wrong. The sadness in Julia's eyes, her eagerness to get away from the campsite, the fact that she'd barely even looked at her husband, contrasted the cheeriness in her voice and were clear signs that she wasn't happy. Going on about deer and a newsletter didn't hide a thing.

"So...would you like to tell me what's going on between you and Ian?"

Julia stopped short, staring at her mother and fiddling with her camera nervously. She pretended to be inspecting the light settings. "What...What do you mean?"

Olivia cocked her head to the side and smirked, placing her hands on her hips. "Julia, I may be old, but I'm not blind. You two used to be all over each other. Now, when you say his name, you say it like it tastes bad."

Stopping by a narrow creek, Julia knelt and ran her fingers over the smooth rocks. The cold water was refreshing. "I don't know what's going on. I don't," she repeated when Olivia huffed. "Things are different lately. We don't talk. We don't spend any time together. All he does is work. He's never home."

"And you? What do you do while he's working?"

At her mother's inquisitive stare, Julia crossed her arms and smirked right back. "I'm not seeing anyone on the side, if that's what you're insinuating. Geez, Mom."

"Just making sure. But is he?"

"Not that I'm aware of. He hasn't been acting suspicious or anything, but I certainly don't trust his hussy of a secretary. That's always the case, isn't it? Big successful businessman getting off with the hot young secretary."

Olivia frowned and thought to herself that if Ian was sleeping with his secretary, then he'd better hope that she and David were far, far away when the truth revealed itself. "Do you really think he's having an affair?"

Julia paused, picking up a stone and tossing it from hand to hand. "Not really. It's just a thought in the back of my head. Paranoia, I guess."

"And are you willing to work it out?"

"If he's willing, then I'm willing." Frustrated, Julia sat on a rock that was bathed in golden sunlight and toyed with her camera. "But I don't know where to start."

Not far away, Ian kept his promise and walked with his son to the park. Cole happily skipped along, racing for the swings. The park was intertwined with tall yet thin trees that climbed their way toward the sky, canopying the playground and allowing the sun to filter through in dotted rays of light. To the west, hidden behind a tangled wall of vegetation, the river roiled with its flowing rapids and icy waves, the sounds gurgling through the leaves.

Ian sat on a bench and watched Cole switch from the swings to the slide. He chuckled when Cole slid down and landed in a patch of dirt, only to turn around and climb back up the slippery metal to do it all over again. From the top of the wooden structure, Cole waved at his father, who returned the gesture and leaned back. It was nice to watch his son, something he hadn't taken the time to do in awhile. He'd forgotten that Cole could be fun, just be a kid, not so serious all the time.

As Cole continued to slide down into the dirt, Ian's mind started to drift. He thought of work, carefully planning out different designs in his head, picturing what the hotel grounds would look like after he was finished. If he was lucky, and if the installation went smoothly, his company might be contracted to continue on as the groundskeepers. He had a few part-time men looking for full-time work, but there wasn't enough at the moment, and the hotel would be the perfect job for them.

His attention switched then to Rebecca Dale. Recently, his thoughts turned to her more and more—what she was doing at that moment, what she would wear to work the next day. Her increasingly revealing outfits were exciting, and he looked forward to her latest purchase. Those low-cut blouses, above-the-knee skirts—no, he certainly didn't mind seeing them around the office. Though nothing physical had happened, Ian had to admit that it was possible. Rebecca had given the hints, provided the groundwork, had all but offered a time and a place, and Ian was getting less and less sure what was holding him back. Julia certainly never gave him that kind of attention anymore. What was the point of marriage if husband and wife were complete strangers? No more hugs, stolen glances, smiles over silly things that happened at the dinner table. Just irritated sighs and brush-offs.

On the playground, Cole swung from the monkey bars, carefully gripping each bar as he made his way across. When he got to the other side, he reached for the rope swing then froze when he saw a shadowy movement in the trees. A chill worked its way up his spine as he squinted, wondering if the sun was playing tricks on him, or if there were some deer playing around the trees like his mom had said they like to do. Curious again, he hopped off the platform and trotted over to the edge of the woods, glancing over his shoulder at his father, who was looking off in the other direction. Briefly, he considered asking if he could go investigate, but knew that his dad would yell at him to get back on the playground. Cole could hear the river and was excited, since last time he saw the ghost on the other side of the shore, and so he abandoned any sense of responsibility and snuck away.

After a couple minutes of pushing past branches and getting his foot snagged in a thorny vine, Cole reached the river. He was a little ways downriver from his last location, and the rapids were much faster, the river wider and filled with more rocks.

And there, on the other side, was the strange gray shadow that looked like a little boy.

Intrigued by the sight, Cole stepped closer to the river. He searched for a way across, his mother's warning voice echoing in his ears. She wouldn't want him anywhere near the river. But, he argued against himself, she didn't even believe that he was a ghost, and if he could prove it to her, then that would make this camping trip the best one ever.

And so, taking a deep breath, Cole stepped out onto the slippery rocks, eyes trained on the shadow, determined to never let it out of his sight.

Back at the park, Ian mused over the idea of divorce, marriage counseling, and marriage in general. He had married Julia at twenty-nine, she at age twenty-four. They were partners in more ways than one—personal and professional, perfectly compatible, in the beginning. They struggled for years, both working hard under Ian's growing landscaping company. Around the same time Cole was born, Ian landed his first major installation at a new neighborhood development. From then on, life only got better, the days more promising, and though he'd never planned on being a father, nothing could compare to feeling he got when—

Cole.

Ian snapped back to attention, scanning the playground. It was empty, one lone swing swaying in the breeze. He leapt to his feet and ran to the slide, searching under and behind any and every block of wood.

"Cole?" he shouted, worry and dread creeping up into his throat. "Cole! Answer me! Answer me, damn it!"

When only the torrents of the white-water river answered back, Ian turned and pushed his way through the thicket, stumbling onto the riverbank. He frantically searched the water and the other shoreline, seeing nothing but endless trees. Sickness churned in his gut as he ran back to the park, racing around the trees, yelling his son's name.

But it was useless. Cole was gone.

Chapter 4

Sheriff Ray Forbe, an enthusiastic officer in his early fifties with thick gray hair, playful brown eyes, and the growing hint of a belly, adjusted his hat and approached the Daivya campsite. It was a gloomy site, the mother of the missing son wrapped in blankets in the Bards' trailer, the father sitting at the picnic table with his head in his hands, and the grandparents doing their best to hold it together for Julia and Ian while struggling not to join them in misery.

Cole had been missing for seven hours. It only took fifteen minutes after discovering his son's disappearance for Ian to report the incident to Big Creek security, and three hours after an unsuccessful search by six officers and the Daivya family, the rest of the police were called in. Eleven officers, joined by seven concerned campers, combed the woods, explored three miles of the river, and found not even the slightest trace of the boy. Now, as dusk fell and the sky darkened, there seemed to be little hope of finding him tonight.

An officer for more than thirty years in a county that ran alongside the Smoky Mountains, Forbe had unfortunately seen many children disappear. Some went missing for more gruesome reasons, but many simply wandered away and ended up being found lost in the woods a day or two later, hungry and scared. In all his years, Forbe had lost three children, and he wasn't looking for that number to bump up to four. If it took him six days, six months, six years, he would keep searching.

But it didn't look good for the child. Nights were cold and the weekly forecast called for rain. Combined with the raging river, thick forest, and a little boy's usually poor sense of direction, hope was scarce.

Forbe wasn't willing to admit this disparaging outlook to the boy's family, so when he came to a stop by Ian's side, the officer sucked in a deep breath and offered the best words he could muster.

"We'll keep looking through the night," he told Ian, who lifted his head and rubbed his tired, slightly puffy eyes. Forbe hadn't personally seen the man cry, but it was evident by the redness that he'd let a few tears escape in privacy. "Second shift just started and we've got some more men coming in a few hours. Some of the locals have agreed to help as well. We haven't found anything yet, which means that Cole could be fine, just a little lost. We're not giving up."

Ian cleared his throat. He was exhausted, angry, desperate, ashamed, and didn't believe a word the man said. "Tell me, Forbe, what is your honest opinion of finding my son?" When Forbe didn't answer, he rose and leaned against the table, crossing his arms with his eyes on the ground. "By all means, say whatever you have to say to my wife and in-laws, keep them thinking positive, but I need to know the truth. What kind of outcome are we really looking at here?"

After a moment of hesitation, Forbe finally admitted, "I don't know. Kids get lost up here all the time, usually just from wandering off in the middle of the night. And we don't stop looking until the kids are in their parents' arms."

"And when you don't find them?"

"We haven't lost a child in over eight years, Mr. Daivya. I know things don't look good right now, but I promise you that I will not stop looking."

And he didn't. Forbe kept his promise, continuing the search for two more days, through the rain, through the cold, through the desolation. And not a trace of the boy was found. In those days, the rest of Julia's family had arrived, and the reunion was put on hold as everyone aided in the search. Julia attempted to look for her son on the first day, but hopelessness engulfed her, racking her body in sobs and rendering her useless. Whatever strength she'd once had abandoned all her senses, and she was as lost as her son.

Ian returned after three hours in the woods to find his wife slumped over the picnic table. She hadn't changed clothes since yesterday morning, and had barely eaten. Her hair was unbrushed, sticking out wildly in some places, and her eyes were swollen from crying and staring vacantly at emptiness.

He lowered himself next to her and picked up a plastic fork merely for the sake of having something to do with his fingers. "Nothing yet," he said quietly, running a hand over the scruff that covered his jaw. Julia didn't answer, and they sat in silence for awhile. Officers and volunteers came and went from the campsite. Lisa, Julia's typically flighty sister, had taken it upon herself to provide food and drinks for everyone willing to help, while Cole's grandparents alternated between organizing search parties with Forbe and checking on their distraught daughter. Occasionally, one of the officers would approach Ian and ask for his account again of exactly what happened when he discovered that Cole was missing. He'd been over it dozens of times and the story hadn't changed, but the police were still hoping to catch something, anything, they'd missed before.

"You should have been watching him," Julia muttered suddenly, wrapping her jacket tighter around her shoulders.

"I was watching him."

"Then how the hell did he manage to disappear? How do kids who are being watched suddenly vanish?"

Ian didn't have an answer to his wife's accusations, so instead he placed a hand on her shoulder. Julia withdrew instantly, a look of disgust crossing her tired and ragged face. "Don't touch me," she demanded, yanking her arm away from her husband. "Cole would be here if it weren't for you."

"Julia—"

"No, don't." Julia held up a hand, an unknown strength overcoming her senses. She rose to her feet and glared down at Ian. "If you were watching him, he would be *here!* With me! Safe! But when do you ever watch him? When do you ever think of anyone but yourself? *You don't care!*"

Tears burst from her eyes and she turned away, running back to the trailer. A part of Ian wanted to follow, to comfort the woman he still loved, but another part resented her animosity. It was an accident, an honest mistake. He didn't mean for it to happen, and if the kid hadn't of wandered away like he *knew* he wasn't supposed to do then they wouldn't be in this mess.

They would find Cole. He was sure of it. They would find his son. *He* would find him, however possible. He would do whatever he had to do.

Frustrated, Ian forced his hair behind his ears and rose, starting to pace as he headed away from the campsite to escape the hate and blame. His eyes were trained on the dirt until an officer's surprised call to another encouraged him to look up.

At the edge of the campsite, a woman was approaching. Whoever she was, the officers seemed to know her, and obviously had mixed feeling about her arrival. One had taken a step forward, another a step back. Curious, Ian made his way over, stopping next to Deputies Nathan Neil and Ben Duff just as the stranger made her way to the edge of the campsite.

Ian observed the woman as she drew near. She was young, early twenties perhaps, and of Native American descent. Her long hair was sleek and black, with thick braids trailing along the sides decorated with small, handcrafted white beads. Her face was strongly sculpted—a tough jaw line, sharp nose above a small mouth, and high cheekbones accenting black eyes that completely terrified Ian. They were eyes that had seen death, torture, pain, but also life, hope, and magic. How someone so young could bear eyes so old baffled him.

He desperately wanted to know more.

The woman wore loose tan pants torn at the knees, a figure-fitting black shirt frayed at the collar with the hemline ripped off, and pieces of what looked to Ian like animal skin covering her forearms for warmth, the inner sides coated with fur. Around her left wrist was a wide band of leather, tied with sinew just above the back of her hand. Her arms, shoulders, and what could be seen of her stomach were firmly toned. Around her upper right arm was a piece of cloth tied tightly, and judging by the red scabs at the edges of the material, he guessed it was covering a recent wound. A few scratches marked her face as well—two on her left cheek and another just above her eyebrow, making her look hardened and indifferent. She was barefoot, but didn't seem bothered. A belt hitched around her waist held a small jug of water, a pouch, and a hunting knife.

Ian thought she was one of the most striking women he had ever laid eyes upon, but for some reason he couldn't identify, she scared the hell out of him.

As if drawn in by her dark aura, Ian joined the officers in greeting the mysterious stranger.

"Whisper," Deputy Neil greeted cautiously, nodding at the woman. The quiver in his voice told Ian he wasn't the only one slightly intimidated. "We were…um, we were wondering if you would show up."

"We tried to find you, but no one seemed to know where you were," Duff put in, sounding more confident and eager than his partner.

"This is Ian Daivya. His son Cole is the boy that went missing a few days ago." Neil gestured to Ian, who held out a hand in greeting.

The woman named Whisper didn't move, nor did she even look at the man. Instead, she thought for a moment and then turned to the woods. "I will search for the child," she said, her voice thick with an old, native accent. "We must go." She headed for the trees, leaving the three men behind. Duff and Neil shoved Ian in her direction.

"She meant you," Neil told him. "Go with her."

"With her? I don't even know who she is," Ian protested, not believing the woman was anything more than another volunteer, let alone a guide of sorts. "And why the hell is she named Whisper?"

"If you want to find your son, your best bet is with her. She's found a lot of missing kids over the years. That woman is…strange, to say the least, but she's got some kind of…"

"Power," Duff offered. "She can speak to things, and they speak back. She's the apprentice to old Elder Smoke Speaker, a shaman up in the mountains. He's one of the last true Cherokee in these parts...him and Whisper. Some people say she's being trained to take over as a Speaker."

"Aren't you guys a little old to be believing in witch doctors? And what does all that mean anyway? Being a Speaker?"

"It means that she can help. But if you don't go with her, she's likely to walk away for good. She hates waiting, so go." Neil shoved Ian again and he relented, jogging and pushing past branches until he caught up with her.

"Can we stop a minute?" he asked when he found Whisper kneeling by the river, mouth moving but no words coming out. "Can I ask you a few questions, like...." he trailed off when Whisper slowly turned her eyes up to him. He felt the intensity like a punch to the gut, as though he was being harshly judged. "Who...who are you exactly? And how can you help?"

In answer, Whisper stood and walked along the riverbank. When she turned away from him, he saw an intricate black design tattooed across her back and shoulders, hidden behind her shirt, and he found himself wondering what the rest of it looked like. Such an enormous marking on a relatively thin, if not muscular, woman intrigued him. Surely it had some meaning, he figured, tracing one of the lines with his eyes.

Ian shook himself back to attention to see that Whisper held a small, smooth rock she had pulled from the water. She ran her fingers over the stone absently as she watched the rapids. Ian started to ask another question, irritated by her refusal to speak, but when her lips started to move he decided to wait it out and see what happened next. This was turning into a spectacle, and despite the fact that his son was missing, it interested him nonetheless.

Almost silently, the woman whispered to the rock, bringing it close to her lips with closed eyes. When she spoke, the entire world seemed to spin. Ian took a step back, bracing himself against a tree when the wind picked up and the trees danced around them. He could have sworn that the earth trembled beneath his feet and flipped completely upside down, but nothing else seemed to move. Flabbergasted, heart racing, he watched as the woman threw the stone into the river to silence the air, then took out her hunting knife and steadily drew it across the palm of her hand. He winced as though feeling the pain himself, following behind as she sauntered along the bank, holding her hand over the water, clutching her fingers into a fist so that blood dripped into the rapids.

An offering, he questioned to himself, feeling like a fool. Blood sacrifices were for the movies, not real life.

She stopped suddenly and bent down, fishing another rock from the river. She held it for a moment in her injured hand, turning it in her palm with a look of contemplation across her face as blood coated the surface. Then she pulled a strip of leather from her pocket and wrapped it around the wound, making Ian guess that she had planned this strange ritual all along. There was a twinge of pain spread across her face, but, unknowingly to Ian, it wasn't from the self-inflicted injury. The pain was one created by what had happened to the boy, and what was soon to come.

The wind began to howl through the trees, and Ian could swear that Whisper, who had cocked her head ever so slightly, was listening to what it had to say. She stood perfectly still, statue still, her entire concentration dedicated to words he couldn't hear.

A small bird, black with a brown head, appeared from the trees and landed on a stump just on the edge of the river. It chirped a few times and caught Whisper's attention. She focused on the bird and the two stared at one another for a moment, a silent communication of words and understanding. The bird's eyes seemed to cloud, connecting with Whisper's in a moment of bonding only the two could understand. There was a soft rippling of feathers, a slight foot movement, then she nodded and the warbling creature flew back into the shelter of the canopy.

"Interesting," she muttered, then looked at Ian.

As quickly as it began, the wind faded. Whisper sized Ian up and down, waiting until he came closer to speak.

"If I told you there was a way to save your son, would you do it?"

Confused by the question, and somewhat entranced by the raspy, accented voice, Ian let out a deep breath and wondered what the hell just happened. His head was still spinning. "What...what, um, do you mean?"

"How far are you willing to go for your child?"

Now he understood. Or, at least, he thought he did. Anger began to boil in his blood as he came face-to-face with the young stranger. "What is this, some kind of game to you? What, you want money or something? You know where he is, don't you? *Answer me!*" he shouted when she merely stared at him, black eyes heavy and dark. "Where is he?!"

Then Ian made the mistake of grabbing her by the arm.

In less than a second he was flat on his back with the tip of her hunting knife pressed up against his throat. Without knowing what just happened, one hand was behind his back, the other gripping her wrist as he struggled against the blade. Her legs straddled him, her mouth in a tight line, her eyes staring without regard, and he was fully aware that even though he outweighed her in both weight and age, she could easily end his life.

"If you cross me, I will slit your throat from ear to ear," she promised quietly, calmly.

Not to be defeated, Ian glared back at the woman with hatred and fury, tightening his grip on her wrist. "Where the hell is my son?"

Whisper backed off, replacing the knife at her belt and walking over to the river, where she stood for a moment with her hands on her hips to collect her thoughts. Ian jumped to his feet, feeling his neck for any sign of injury, and found only smooth skin. Embarrassment ate at him. He, a finely-toned man of forty-two, was overpowered by a thin and spacey woman in her twenties. He would never admit it to anyone.

Suddenly surprised by a solid object flying his way, Ian caught the rock that Whisper tossed his direction, and glanced it over. There was nothing extraordinary about it, just a smooth stone, a little smaller than the palm of his hand. It was pale brown in color, splotched with dark red and a few slightly raised cracks that formed a crooked and jagged circle just a shade lighter than the rest of the rock circling the center. It may have been the one she was turning over in her hand, but he couldn't be sure. He hoped it wasn't, as that would mean that the red color was blood, and that churned his stomach a bit.

"Why…what does this…what am I supposed to do with this?"

"Keep it safe," Whisper answered.

Ian put the stone in his pocket to appease her then pointed at the woman. "If you ever pull a stunt like that again, I'll—"

"You need to understand, Mr. Daivya, that you are not in control," Whisper interrupted coolly, not fazed by his outburst. "The only power you have is whether or not you find your son."

Fighting his rage, shoving back a lump in his throat, Ian struggled for control. "Did you…do you have anything to do with Cole's disappearance?"

"No."

The simplicity of the answer surprised him. She didn't even hesitate, and though he knew nothing about her, Ian believed her. There was something about her, a strange innocence mixed in with confidence, arrogance, and dark magic that suggested lying wasn't something she was capable of. "Do you know how to find him?"

"Yes."

"Tell me!"

Whisper lifted a hand in protest. "There are two ways to find your son, Mr. Daivya. One will find him alive, the other will find him dead. How far you are willing to go?"

"What do you mean?"

Whisper cast a glance downriver, where the rapids picked up in speed. "If I tell you where to find your son, you will only find his body. He will not be alive."

His stomach clutched and his body shook. "How do you know that?"

"The river told me."

Images of his son, of his son's body, consumed Ian's mind. He fought against the pictures, refusing to believe them, refusing to believe that this woman who called herself Whisper could speak to the river. She was a hoax, a fraud, some mountain psycho who just wanted to take his money and run with it. But whether she had any information or not, he knew that in order to get information about Cole, he would have to play her game.

"How do I find him alive?"

Whisper pressed her lips together, looking Ian up and down. She wondered if he was strong enough for the journey, if he could put aside his egotism and judgments long enough to find and accept the truth. He obviously cared for his son, but had no idea how to show his affection or his concern, and he would need to learn how to do just that to save his child.

Lifting a hand to the bone necklace that circled her throat, Whisper sat on the grass and gestured for Ian to do the same. He followed her direction, his mind racing with doubt, stomach cramping with thoughts of Cole's death, heart pounding in anticipation.

"Many years ago," Whisper began, her voice quiet, "these mountains were the home of my people, the Cherokee. My ancestors walked these woods, swam this river. And now, all that is left of them are mere traces…spirits. When my people went to war with the white men, many were killed, and many of those killed did not receive proper burials." She leaned back on her hands. "When a person does not receive the proper death ceremony, when the body is not buried, the soul is forced to wander the earth eternally, unless they can reach the proper spiritual realm."

"Yeah, I know all of that," Ian said, exasperated. "Souls can't rest in peace…ghosts haunt the woods…the Land of the Dead. I get it. What does this have to do with me, and with Cole?"

"Your son is dead, Mr. Daivya," Whisper stated matter-of-factly, much to Ian's shock and grief. His hands covered his face as she continued, barely registering his pain. "And because his body has not yet been found, he is trapped in the Land of the Dead, and his soul is restless."

"Then tell me where he is! Tell me so I can find him, and bury him! What do you *want* from me?" Ian leapt to his feet desperately, pleadingly. "Why won't you tell me where he is?"

"Because there is a way to save him." Whisper also got to her feet, crossing her arms sternly. "There are ways of getting to the Land of the Dead, Mr. Daivya, and if you are willing to try, you can find him there, and bring him back here…alive."

It didn't make any sense. *She* didn't make any sense. The Land of the Dead was an old native legend. It wasn't real. It was a myth, a story. *And even if it was real*, he argued with himself, *that would be like trying to get to Heaven or Hell*. You only went there when you died, and when you did go, you certainly didn't return.

No one returned from the dead.

"If there are ways to bring someone back, then why are so many people still dead? Why don't their families try to save them?" He felt absolutely ridiculous asking such a question, and supposed it was the sheer desperation of losing his son that was making him lose his mind.

"Not many know the way there, or the way back. Or they are not willing to risk their own lives for another."

He paused while the words sunk in. "So…you're saying that if I were to some-how…magically go to this Land of the Dead, I might die too?"

"It is possible."

"Then why would I do it?"

"To save your son." Ian only stared blankly at Whisper, so she sighed and shifted impatiently, standing before him stoically. "Mr. Daivya, if the police find your son's body, my offer dies with your child. But if you choose to trust me, if you choose to believe that what I say is possible, then they will not find him before you do. You have two hours to consider my offer, and consider it alone. If you decide not to follow, then I will tell you where to find his body. If you choose to try to save him, follow that path," she pointed across the river to the west, where Ian saw a barely-discernable trail leading into darkness, "and it will lead you to your journey. Tell no one where you are going."

He stared at the narrow path overgrown with vines and verdant shrubs. His mind was racing with jumbled thoughts. "What…why two hours?"

"That is how long it will take you to reach your destination. I suggest you begin walking soon, Mr. Daivya. We do not have much time."

A moment of tense silence followed. Ian leaned over, nearly sick to his stomach. He couldn't believe this was happening. This strange Indian woman was telling him his son was dead, and deep down he knew she was right. Cole could never survive three days in the wilderness, not with these cold nights. But the idea of traveling to some mystic world of lost souls was too much for him. He couldn't fathom the idea.

And yet…he couldn't bear the thought of life without Cole. He'd often heard stories about mothers and fathers who went to the ends of the earth for their missing children, spending thousands of dollars on searches even when there was no longer any hope, traveling across the country to follow wild goose chases. It was as if logic and reason no longer existed, nothing mattered except what was missing. Life itself suddenly became a dream, and in dreams, anything was possible.

"If I did this and failed, what would happen?"

"You would die, along with your son."

"And if I succeeded?"

"Then you both live."

"And it's that simple?"

Whisper huffed. "Of course it is not that simple, Mr. Daivya. I am merely giving you an opportunity. You have two hours to decide. And you must make the decision on your own." With that, she hopped on a log that spanned the river and made her way across, toward the path she had pointed out.

"Hey!" Ian called when she was halfway across. Whisper turned. "What would you do, if you were me?"

"The Land of the Dead is a terrible place, Mr. Daivya. It is no place for a child."

And then she disappeared into the trees.

Chapter 5

Tucked away in the Smoky Mountains, in a sacred place known for many generations as Howling Vines, Elder Smoke Speaker waited.

The wind, the trees, the squirrels that jumped from branch to branch, told him that the man was close. And judging by the hesitance said to be spread across his face, he was yet to have made a decision.

The Elder built a fire just outside his hut, sweeping his long gray hair over his shoulders. His soul was heavy. His old hands trembled as he broke pieces of white sage over the flames and whispered a prayer to Creator, asking for protection, for forgiveness. He kept his back to his hut, a melancholy gloom keeping him from entering, for what was inside broke his heart.

Instead of thinking about what had happened not so long ago, he forced his mind to concentrate on the fire. The smoke thickened unnaturally, pouring up from the flames and twisting into words only the Elder could read. They foretold the man's arrival, his fears, and Old Smoke Speaker sighed heavily, rubbing his wrinkled face. He picked up another sage leaf and tore it into tiny pieces, fingers aching with arthritis. The sweet aroma drifted around Howling Vines, welcoming the footsteps of a stranger.

Ian stepped into the clearing and immediately stopped when he saw the old man sitting by the fire. He observed the figure, struck by the sight, much like he was struck by Whisper when he first saw her. The man was ancient, deep wrinkles etching his tan, rugged face, veiling his coal-black eyes. Thick, tangled white hair hung down his back, and an old leather tunic decorated with colorful images of animal silhouettes was wrapped around his brittle bones. He was staring intently at the fire, and Ian thought he looked just like Whisper—that same concentrated sense of communication with the elements spread across his face.

Unsure what to do next, and guessing this was the same Elder the officers had mentioned earlier, Ian stayed in place, shoving his hands in his pockets. He waited to be acknowledged, not out of respect for the Elder, but because he wanted more time to think about Whisper's proposition. For more than two hours now he had trudged through the woods, fighting off insects, thorny vines, and extreme doubts as to his sanity.

He couldn't believe he was actually considering it. He was actually considering going to the Land of the Dead. But he didn't even *believe* in the place, so how could he go there? Ian supposed that the only reason he was letting himself believe in such a far-fetched story was because he refused to accept his son's death. Worse yet, he knew he would never forgive himself, or be forgiven by others, if he didn't follow through on the only lead he had—two strange people who may or may not have had something to do with his son's disappearance.

But Ian didn't doubt Whisper's prophecy, for he'd known deep down that Cole wouldn't be found. Three days in the woods was too much, and with the raging river and pouring rains, there was little to no hope. But while he didn't doubt her, he also didn't want to accept it. A part of him wished to be told where to find his body, because then he would know for sure, but if they did find him, then there would be no chance of saving him, if that chance was actually real.

Cole was only seven years old, and deserved more time. And if he was already deceased, then Ian had nothing to lose. He was now as dead to Julia as her son, and he would never be able to face her, or her family, ever again. They would hate him for the rest of their lives, and nothing would ever be the same. Maybe Whisper was insane, maybe she was setting him up for some unknown crime, or maybe she was telling the truth.

It didn't matter. Ian's life was over, and if there was some incredible way of bringing his child back from the dead, then he was willing to try.

"You may join me, young man." Startled out of his thoughts, Ian cleared his throat and took a tentative step in the Elder's direction. "You have made your decision?"

Ian wasn't sure if the old man was asking a question or making a statement. He stood in front of the fire. "I don't...I don't know yet."

"You are nearly out of time."

"Until what?"

"Until the police find your son." The old Indian's voice was thickened with the same accent as Whisper, only his was rougher, throatier, and slightly harder to understand.

Ian knelt, trailing a finger through the dirt. "Who are you?"

"I am Elder Smoke Speaker, the last of my people in these great mountains."

"How do you know all of this...how to find Cole?"

Smoke Speaker lifted his head. His eyes burned through Ian, and he sensed fear, arrogance, and contempt. But at the same time, he saw grief in his face, the portrait of a mourning man torn between decisions and beliefs. "These are my ways, young man."

"Well…If I do this…how will I know what to do?"

"You will have a guide."

"Who?"

"One that Creator chose for you. One that was born so that the world may change."

"OK." Ian blew out a nervous breath, slightly irritated by the riddles, pressured by the lack of time. "Why can't my wife come with me?"

"This is not her journey."

Ian was quiet for a moment, thinking that even if he were to die on this so-called journey, she wouldn't bat an eye. The thought put a bitter taste in his mouth, and he decided that the only reason he was going through with the offer was because of Cole.

"OK," he said slowly, unsurely, to the Elder, who clasped his hands together and seemed neither surprised nor disappointed, but complacent. "What do I need to know before I go?"

Smoke Speaker stirred the fire, and dozens of embers floated up into the bright blue sky. "The Land of the Dead is a place of emptiness. It is a place of temptation, of hate, of desolation. Your nature, your devotion to the truth, your very soul, will be tested against the forces of death. You will experience pain like no other. If you give in, if you fail, you will not return to this world. You must have faith," he said when Ian drew back and shook his head, "in yourself, in your guide, and in your son."

"What if they find his body before I do?"

In response, Smoke Speaker cupped his hands over the fire, so close to the flames that Ian marveled over the fact that his flesh wasn't melting off the bone. The Elder said a few words in a language Ian couldn't understand, and the smoke began pouring up from the hearth, creeping through the old man's fingers and engulfing them both in a gray haze.

Then without warning, a strange, cold fog rolled in. It was so thick that Ian could barely see the Elder not two feet in front of him. His clothes were damp in seconds and the burning embers faded, leaving behind only thin wisps of smoke.

"They will not find your son," Smoke Speaker promised, slightly amused by the look of amazement on Ian's face. His mouth was parted in shock, eyes darting around the clearing as through determined to see something, anything, through the fog.

The Elder stood, grasping an intricately carved walking stick. "Now, Mr. Daivya, it is time we prepare."

Ian watched silently as the old man produced a small, knotted bowl carved of oak from a pouch at his side and a handful of leaves from his pocket. Smoke Speaker broke pieces of the sage with his gnarled fingers and said a prayer in his mind, then lifted the leaves to his nostrils and inhaled deeply before dropping them into the bowl.

He offered the items to Ian. "Sage," he informed the man, his old voice creating a story out of the instruction, "is a powerful medicine among my people. The white smoke cleanses the soul, purifying the body for ceremonies, for travel. Let the touch of each leaf heighten your senses, the sweet smell fill your soul, and say a prayer."

Feeling a bit foolish, Ian did as he was told and mimicked the Elder's actions, tearing the sage into tiny pieces while saying a prayer. For good measure he prayed for his son's life, then smelled the herb and thought there was nothing remarkable about doing so. Smoke Speaker took the bowl from him when he was finished, pulled a burning stick from the fire, and lit the sage.

As pure white smoke began to trickle up from the bowl, the Elder closed his eyes and inhaled deeply. *"Ha Unelanvhi,"* he prayed to Creator in a loud lilting tone that echoed off the trees, while Ian watched, mesmerized, *"elohi nvdoigaehi, galvlohi a le amequohi. Nihi hawinaditlv, a le negadv gvwadu weda."* He repeated the tune three times, his soothing voice creating an ancient atmosphere that brought back the old ways of his people, then translated for Ian, "Oh, Great Spirit, earth, sun, sky, and sea. You are inside, and all around me."

Smoke Speaker lifted a hand and wafted the smoke toward his thin, brittle body, letting the sweet gray fog roll over his flesh and cleanse his body. He cleaned himself from head to toe before turning to Ian and doing the same. Ian fought back a sneeze when the smoke blew in his face, but didn't say anything. He wasn't entirely sure what was going on, and thought it best to simply wait it out.

When the cleansing was complete, Smoke Speaker raised the bowl above his head and offered the sage to the seven sacred directions. *"Kalvgv,"* he prayed to the East. *"Wudeligv,"* to the West. *"Uyvtlv,"* to the North. *"Uganawu,"* to the South. Then, *"Galvla-ditlv, Eladitlv, Ayeli,"* to Above, Below, and Center.

For the Center, Smoke Speaker drew the sage-filled bowl to his chest, bringing the ceremony to a close. The two, one a believer in the old ways and the other a skeptic in search of a belief, were cleansed for their journey.

The Elder set the bowl down by the fire, placing a hand at the small of his aching back before getting a firm grip on his walking staff and gesturing for Ian to rise. "Our souls have been cleansed. Now we may begin."

Ian cleared his throat, wondering if he was supposed to feel different after the ceremony, and feeling nothing but cynicism. He was just seconds away from abandoning the entire thing, whatever that thing was, when Smoke Speaker started walking into the woods, leaving Ian to follow.

Smoke Speaker led Ian through the trees, limping slowly and painfully on ankles and knees swollen with arthritis. Ian trailed behind, at a loss for words as he prepared himself for what was to come. He had no idea what to expect, no idea what he was doing, no idea if he was wide awake, but hoping that this was all one horrific nightmare.

There was no distinct path to follow, so the two were forced to step over fallen trees and wrestle with vines as they walked slowly but steadily deeper into the wilderness. The further they walked, the less Ian could hear of civilization, and soon there were no sounds of society, but of nature instead. Warblers sang to one another, the river pounded against rocks, a cool breeze trailed lazily through dark green leaves. Under less unfortunate circumstances, Ian would have taken the time to carefully observe the plants, maybe take a few cuttings, learn the names of the native vegetation. Now, he kept his eyes straight ahead, wondering how much longer they would be finding their way through the thick clouds. The Elder's dwelling was already a two hour's walk into the woods, and it felt like they'd been walking even more hours in the fog.

Ian didn't have to wonder much longer. Soon the nearly invisible trail opened up to a small, crystal-clear lake surrounded by enormous pine trees. By some kind of magic, the fog didn't touch the lake, but floated around the shore, hovering inches from the ground. The sun broke through the gray in one solid beam, illuminating the lake in a thousand sparkling bits of gold.

While Ian stopped on the shore, Smoke Speaker kept walking until the water reached his thighs. He turned around with an impatient gesture. "Come."

"Why?"

"You are ready to take the journey?"

"…Yes."

"Then come."

With a sigh, Ian stepped into the lake. When the water hit his thighs, he stifled a shiver and hated the fact that his shoes would now be completely soaked for the rest of the day. "What are we doing here?"

Smoke Speaker drifted a hand across the surface, creating a flurry of ripples that glittered in the lone ray of sunshine. "The water is a powerful medium," he said quietly, his old voice soothing Ian's nerves. The ends of his long hair touched the lake when he reached for Ian, taking him by the arm. "If you wish to visit the Land of the Dead and return, water is the only substance capable of such travel."

Ian watched as the Elder lifted a knobby hand and let the clear water fall from his fingers. The tears of water descended to the surface as though in slow-motion, and Ian could swear that he heard each individual droplet touch the water.

"So…what do I have to do?"

The Elder released Ian's arm and held out his hands. "You must immerse yourself completely, to the point of unconsciousness. Then, your soul is loose, and I can direct it to the Land of the Dead."

"And what happens when I'm unconscious?"

"I am here, young man. I will watch over you. On that, you have my word. Are you ready?"

His heart pounded so hard it hurt, a fearful sensation he hadn't felt since the death of his mother when he was sixteen. He took a few deep breaths, shaking his hands when a tremble raced through them. He couldn't believe how terrified he was. Ian couldn't remember ever being this afraid. He was always in charge of the situation; he was the designer, the architect. Even now, with his son promised to be dead and his wife hating the very sight of his face, Ian resisted the Elder. With nothing to lose but his life, he still wanted control. He wouldn't admit it, but he was afraid to trust the old man, even though he was sure he could easily overtake him.

"OK." Ian blew out a breath and closed his eyes, picturing his son. He still wasn't sure that he believed in what he was doing, and couldn't explain why he was going along with the plan, but he supposed it was because of that thin shred of curiosity that wanted to see just what would happen.

He knelt down in the water, stopping just before he went under. "Anything I should know?"

The Elder stared down at him with eyes that had seen the birth and death of an entire world. "There are creatures of the Darkness you must avoid. Never linger in one place. And remember, as soon as you surface, head for the land beyond the Western Sun. Now." He put a hand on Ian's head as though to encourage him to go under.

"Wait," Ian protested, wanting as much information as possible on the off-chance that this ridiculous ritual actually succeeded. "My guide…what's his name? How will I find him?"

"You're guide's name is…*Kanegv*," Smoke Speaker answered, a tone of sorrow in his voice. "Trust your guide, and you will succeed. Now, you must go. *Kanegv* is waiting, and the Land of the Dead is no place to be alone."

Ian prepared himself, then ducked under water. To keep him from rising to the surface, Smoke Speaker placed a hand on his chest. Unsure what to do next, Ian stared up at the wavering sky, starting to feel a bit idiotic. Here he was, a grown man, floating underwater and staring up through the blurred, surreal surface at an old man he knew nothing about. And worse, nothing was happening. He felt like he always did, had the same thoughts, the same sensations. The only difference was that he was underwater.

When his last breath escaped in a flurry of tiny bubbles, Ian paused just for a moment to decide whether or not he was actually going to take himself to the point of unconsciousness. The thought only made him feel more like a fool, so he abandoned the far-fetched experiment just as his chest began to tighten. Shaking his head, Ian started to head back for the surface, only to be held in place by the Elder's force.

Confused, Ian lifted a hand out of the water to signal that he was done. He placed a firm foot on the murky lake floor and pushed up against Smoke Speaker's hold, but the old man possessed a strength he never would have imagined possible. The Elder shoved Ian deeper beneath the surface until he was tangled in the underwater ferns, and in less than a second had his cane pressed against the man's throat.

In a blind, furious panic, Ian lashed out against the old man. His fists connected with flesh, fingers desperately grasped at the wood that pinned him underwater. A blazing fire surged through his lungs, gripping his chest in a tight, painful hold of suffocation. In a desperate attempt for air, Ian gasped, sucking in a mouthful of water, choking as he kicked and splashed, fighting to get his head above the surface. He was no match for the Elder.

The sound of his own screams echoed in his head as the water mocked him, welcomed him, dragged him down deeper into the mud, into darkness. As a gray fog crawled its way across his eyes in a cold, frightening blanket of death, Ian stopped struggling, silently pleading for help, praying to be saved from this horrible mistake, from these lying, psychopathic Indians who murder for thrill.

Just before the fog engulfed him in his final moment of life, Ian managed to peer through the glazed, golden ripples at the Elder. As he faded into death, the last thought that crossed his mind was one of marvel, that an old man could drown another with such a look of calm, cool, unaffected complacency.

When his victim finally stopped kicking and squirming and his muscles had relaxed in submission to fate, Smoke Speaker released his hold on Ian's limp body and straightened, again placing a hand to his aching back. He was exhausted, his arthritic bones screaming in angry pain, but he still had work to do.

The Elder kept Ian's body beneath the water by placing a foot on his still chest. He tossed his cane close to shore, then sprinkled bits of white sage over the water. "*Unelanvhi*," he said, the fog swirling like smoke tenders up to the Great Spirit, "give him strength. He will need it."

Then he tipped back his head with closed eyes, holding his arms out to his sides. The frayed edges of the leather tunic grazed the water, his white hair lifting in the breeze as the wind picked up speed, howling across the lake. Pieces of sage spun beneath the water around Ian's body, creating a furiously spinning vacuum as the cold fog swallowed the lake in a gray haze.

Smoke Speaker turned his palms up toward the sky, and his arms trembled from an invisible weight cast upon them. Then, in a terrific burst of energy from his tired body, he slammed his hands together, the force of the blow rippling across the lake. Enormous waves crashed against one another as water exploded up from the murky bottoms, reaching high into the clouds then cascaded back down in a thick, shadowy curtain that distorted the trees behind the waves.

It was that distortion Smoke Speaker feared, for it was there that Ian would soon find himself, lost in a vague impression of the world he once knew.

Chapter 6

Aggravated and exhausted, Ray Forbe took a break at the Daivya campsite, where a large police tent had been set up to accommodate the growing number of search parties. He threw his hat to the ground and unzipped his jacket, gratefully accepting the cup of coffee Lisa Bard offered.

"Nothing at all?"

Forbe shook his head, blowing on the hot liquid before taking a sip. He looked at Lisa sadly. She was a younger version of Julia, with curly blonde hair that cascaded down her back and pretty green eyes that could make a man do and say just about anything. Her nose was just the slightest bit crooked, giving her a cute, pixie-ish appearance, and she wore old, flowered clothes that reminded the sheriff of a hippie, with a spacey attitude to match. But she was nice enough, and her love for her older sister and missing nephew was unmistakable.

"I can't believe this fog," he said with incredulity. "I've never seen anything like this."

"It came so fast," Lisa agreed, peering to her sides, then above her head. "You can barely see three feet in front of you."

"I swear," Forbe began, hating himself for what he was thinking, "it's almost like Mother Nature herself doesn't *want* us to find Cole." Lisa didn't respond, but instead stared at her hands as she warmed them around a cup of coffee.

"Sheriff Forbe." Forbe turned around, offering a smile to Julia Daivya. He gently touched her arm, and Lisa wrapped a blanket around her big sister's shoulders, hugging her tightly. Julia barely registered the affection. "Anything at all? Clothes, footprints, his PSP?"

"Not yet, but we're not giving up. We're setting up a broader perimeter, and taking the search a few more miles downriver, where the rapids open up into a smoother area. Once this fog lifts, things will go a lot easier."

She didn't believe him. "You happen to come across my husband out there?"

"No. One of my deputies said he went on a search with Whisper." At Julia's confused frown, Forbe quickly explained the nature of the stranger. "Whisper is one of the locals, one of the last few Cherokee natives around these parts. She and her mentor live up in the mountains in a place known around here as Howling Vines. Sometimes when we need help finding a missing person we look for her to come out and give us a hand."

"Why?"

"She and her mentor, Elder Smoke Speaker, have lived in these woods all their lives...know them better than anyone else you'll ever find. She can track just about anyone or anything." Forbe put his hands on his hips, picturing the young woman. "Some say she's got an ability to speak to nature. That's why they call her Whisper, because things talk to her."

"And you believe that?"

Forbe shrugged. "No reason not to. There's never been a missing person she hasn't been able to find."

Julia didn't believe a word of that kind of talk. She faced the sheriff with bitterness and scorn spread across her sleep-deprived face. "Mr. Forbe, since she's so great at finding missing people, did you ever think that she and this Smoke Speaker had something to do with their disappearances in the first place? For the recognition of finding them, or the reward money?"

"Julia," Lisa said then, attempting to comfort her older sister, "don't think like that."

"Why not?" Fighting back tears, struggling to maintain the hope that her son was still alive, but sickened by the thought of him out there, alone and scared in the fog, Julia smirked furiously. "You don't find it suspicious that this woman shows up out of the blue and suddenly offers to help? Did she even ask what Cole looks like? How old he is? Anything?"

"Well...no," Forbe admitted, "but—"

"And now she's out there with my husband. Well, isn't that wonderful." She wouldn't say it to them, but she knew that Ian was just looking for a reason, any reason, to get away from her. He'd been looking for months now, probably, as Julia suspected, so he'd have a justification for his office fling. The fact that he so willingly went into the woods with another woman without telling her only confirmed the fact that their marriage was over.

She didn't care that she was overreacting, that she was letting her fear and desperation cloud her judgment. Julia just wanted her son back in her arms, and blamed herself for his disappearance. She never should have let him out of her sight.

Just as the first bubble rose to the surface of the lake, Ian Daivya burst through the water, leaping up from the suffocating bottoms and sucking in a desperate breath of air. Instantly, he began choking, stumbling and splashing his way to the shore as though in a drunken daze. When he reached dry land, he collapsed and lay on his back, swallowing hard in between coughing fits and spitting out water. His blue eyes stared up at the gray sky in a confused and disbelieving stare of breathless life.

The world that Smoke Speaker sent Ian to was a pit of darkness, a decaying abyss of emptiness. A truly vague impression of the living world, every tree, every rock, every blade of grass, was a varying shade of black and gray, but to Ian, who was confused and disoriented from the attack, it only seemed like the mysterious fog had thickened.

After a few moments, he caught his breath and slowly crawled to his feet, dripping and shivering. The old man was nowhere to be found, which Ian thought was lucky for him, for he had plenty of ideas for revenge.

He knew exactly what happened. He remembered everything, remembered agreeing to the ceremony and to taking the journey, remembered being held underwater and blacking out. But he couldn't figure out *how* it happened. Elder Smoke Speaker was a frail old man who couldn't weigh more than one-fifteen soaking wet, and Ian was a healthy man of forty-two who exercised regularly. How could he be overpowered? Even more humiliating was the fact that the old man had the time to get away before Ian could drag himself out of the water and to his feet.

Completely embarrassed and ashamed by his own stupidity, Ian stood on the shore, gentle waves lapping over his shoes. He gathered his wits and stifled his rage long enough to find the trail that would lead him back to his campsite. All he wanted to do now was get back to his wife and tell the police to go after those scheming, murdering Indians, and get them to release Cole's location using whatever method necessary.

His chest still throbbing and his lungs on fire, Ian shoved his way into the trees. At his back was the sun, which barely lit the way as he entered the shadowy forest. The light around him was strange, a hazy, surreal kind of atmosphere that, if his eyes weren't stinging from the lake water and his mind wasn't fogged with his apparent murder, he might have found suspicious. But right now he didn't care about the fog. He just wanted to find Sheriff Ray Forbe.

In no time at all, it seemed, Ian was standing on the outskirts of his campsite. He wasn't sure how he got there; he didn't quite recall making the long trip, but supposed it didn't matter. He was tired, angry, and brain-muddled, so he didn't bother worrying about it.

He saw his in-laws' pop-up trailer in the distance, his eyes unable to make out the distinct shape. Instead, the trailer looked like it was swallowed in the fog, and, in a strange way, decaying, as though rotting away from the inside out. At the next site over stood Julia with her sister and the sheriff, and judging by his wife's body language, she obviously hated the man. Something had happened in Ian's absence, and he was going to find out what it was.

Ian started for his wife, wondering why she seemed so far away, why he couldn't quite make out her face. Her lips were moving as she spoke harsh words to Ray Forbe, but he couldn't hear her. In fact, he couldn't hear anything. The realization struck him and he spun around in a complete circle, searching for a noise, any noise.

But there was nothing, no birds chirping, no wind howling, no talking voices, only the sound of his own shoes crunching over fallen leaves, his own breath heaving in frightened gasps. Panic creeping up into his stomach, Ian ran for Julia, his feet pounding the earth like rolls of thunder across the gray sky.

"Julia!" he shouted just before he reached his wife. "Julia, I know how to find Cole!" No one acknowledged his presence. They didn't even appear to have heard him. He waved a hand in front her face. "Julia?"

Maybe she's ignoring me, he guessed. He turned to the sheriff. "Forbe! It's that Whisper woman! She *knows* where Cole is! Forbe! Go after her! *Hey!*" Annoyed by the display of disrespect, he raised an arm and attempted to slap the man on the shoulder, only his hand never connected with skin. In fact, it never reached him at all. The more he tried to touch the officer, the harder it was to even see him, let alone feel the sensation of fabric against his fingertips.

Both disgusted and shocked, Ian started to back away, shaking his head in disbelief. "What...what the hell did they do to me?" he asked himself quietly, determined to find a way out of this mess. "Julia!" He cupped his hands around his mouth. "*Julia!* Forbe! I'm here! Jul—hey!"

He spun around when a firm hand grabbed hold of his shoulder, and found himself face-to-face with Whisper.

"Are you insane or just stupid?" she spat out, releasing her tight grip. "You walk *toward* the Western Sun upon surfacing, not *away* from it."

"You." Ian's tone matched Whisper's as he took a threatening step in her direction. "You! What have you done! And why are you here?"

"I am doing what I promised, what Smoke Speaker promised. I am your guide."

"He said someone named *Kanegv* was my guide."

Whisper glared at him, and Ian got the feeling she thought he was the least intelligent man she had ever met. "I am *Kanegv*. It is my native name. It means 'Speak,' but in English I am known as Whisper. It is how the Elder decided it."

The thought of the woman being his guide repulsed him. He had nothing but contempt for the deceitful Indian woman. "I want nothing to do with you," Ian replied spitefully. She didn't react, but merely watched Julia when she burst into a fit of tears, shoving Lisa away. Ian followed her eyes, his anger fading into sorrow, longing to hold his wife. "Why can't they hear me?"

Whisper's blank stare answered his question as he pieced together the recent past, what he had prayed was just a dream, an illusion. "Because…because I'm…dead. The old man…killed me. He drowned me."

"Yes."

"Why? Why didn't you tell me? Why did you both lie to me?"

Whisper shrugged indifferently. "He did what was necessary. A man who takes his own life cannot return to the living world. Your death had to be at another's hands. Now, we must go." She tossed a bag at him, indicating that he was meant to carry it, as she had her own. "We do not have a lot of time."

Not knowing what else to do, Ian fell into place behind Whisper after casting a final glance over his shoulder at his wife, who was heading back for the trailer with slumped shoulders. He wished he could have taken the time to tell her good-bye. More, he wished he had taken the time to consider what he was doing before the witch doctor drowned him.

As he followed, he noticed that, unlike everything and everyone else, he could see Whisper in a faint hue of color. She was wearing the same torn, tanned pants but had changed from a black shirt to white tank top held together at the front by a thin strand of leather that wound its way up from a ripped hem to a low, blood-sprinkled collar. If she hadn't been wearing a deer-skin cloak that ended just below her waist, he would have seen that the thick shoulder straps crisscrossed her back. She was wearing shoes this time, a pair of sturdily-made but old boots, and a beautiful three-layer beaded necklace circled her throat.

What worried him slightly was that she seemed well equipped for their journey. The belt around her waist held two knives, a pouch with unknown contents, and what looked to Ian like bandages rolled at her hip. Strapped across her back was a bow and quiver, full of arrows, and two pouches of water. The wound on her right hand that she had made herself earlier in the day was secured with a bloodstained wrap, and she still wore the leather strap around her left wrist, which to Ian looked incredibly uncomfortable. Along with all her gear, she also managed to carry her pack, which looked identical to the one she'd tossed his way earlier. Briefly he wondered what was in them.

"Where are we going?"

Whisper stopped and waited for Ian to catch up. Her face was stoic, and her dark eyes seemed to be on a constant watch for unseen enemies. She placed a hand on Ian's arm. "You must keep up. We have a long walk ahead of us."

"Walk? Where are we going?"

The woman sighed. "To the Bridge of the Dead, Mr. Daivya, just beyond the mountains. Now, we *must* go, and remember, you must keep your eyes forward."

"Why?"

"This is a place of waiting, Mr. Daivya, a place the old people call *Agatiyv*. When a person dies, he comes here, and it is up to him to find his way to the Bridge of the Dead. Many never make it, and so their souls become lost, wandering farther and farther away from the Bridge. The longer they are lost, the more bitter they become, and when acknowledged, they will attack, attempting to drag you off your path as well."

Ian had to consciously keep himself from looking around. Out of the corners of his eyes he saw shadows moving amongst the trees, and being told that he couldn't look at them only made him all the more curious. "How do we know that Cole found this so-called bridge, and isn't lost somewhere out here?"

"He has made it."

"How do you know?"

"I have already asked."

"What do you mean?"

Exasperated, Whisper stalked over to Ian. "I have been here a long time waiting for you, and because you did not follow Smoke Speaker's directions by heading straight for the sun," she pointed behind her at the blazing orange fire in the distance, the only source of color in the otherwise monochromatic world, "we have lost time. We only have a short window until your son forgets who he is, forgets you, and can never return. I am doing my job, Mr. Daivya, and your questions only make this more difficult. Either you trust me, or you fail."

With that, she turned on her heel and headed for the mountain. Taken aback by the verbal lashing that was both humiliating and sexy when spoken through an accented tongue, Ian trailed behind, silently fuming at the woman's insolence. She would not talk to him like that much longer. Once he had his son, she would be nothing to him, and he could smack that glare of smugness right off her face.

Chapter 7

The longer they walked, pushing past dead branches and sneaking past lost souls that grasped for their arms and legs as they continued on their way, the more Whisper told him about their journey. He wasn't sure if she was telling him so much because she was bored and wanted to talk, or because it was valuable information, but he listened nonetheless.

"Our beliefs are based on the cardinal directions," Whisper explained as they began the hike up the mountain. "Life and death come from the east and the west." Squinting in the growing light, she pointed out the directions. "*Kalvgv*, the east, and *Wudeligv*, the west." She frowned as she turned her haunting eyes to the sky, her hands elegantly crisscrossing in the air as she illustrated her point. "Our beliefs say that when a person is born, the soul walks out of the rising Eastern Sun, into a new world of life, birth. When a person passes away into death, the soul walks beyond the Western Sun, to the Spirit World, or to the Land of the Dead."

He didn't like the direction the story was taking them into. "So…are you saying we're going into…the Western Sun?"

"Yes."

"But how…how is that possible?"

"How is anything possible, Mr. Daivya?" Whisper asked while continuing the walk, stumbling ever so slightly on a loose rock but catching herself gracefully. "Some things simply are."

He pondered over that as they walked the rest of the way in silence. Before long, the tree and brush-ridden landscape began to fade into a barren, flat surface with deep craters and loose rock beneath a dark sky. Looking behind him, Ian saw that they had crossed through to the other side of the mountains, and he longed to be back in the shelter of the trees. There was something about this new place that chilled him to the bone.

Ian jumped when a figure brushed past him, and out of instinct he faced the stranger. Despite Whisper's warning, he made eye contact, and almost instantly the dead soul took advantage of the invitation and lunged for his next victim.

Surprised by the attack, Ian stumbled and tripped over his own feet, his back hitting the ground hard. The figure, a young man with black eyes and rotting gray flesh that hung off his bones in a grotesque display of death, snarled and landed on top of him, clawing at Ian's face. Ian grabbed the man's wrists, amazed by the spirit's strength, grimacing when a long trail of saliva dripped from his mouth to Ian's chin. The man could only make growling noises as he fought to maim and destroy.

"Get...off...you son-of-a-bitch!" Ian shouted, kicking him in the gut and forcing him back. Ian leapt to his feet in time to block the dead soul when he reared back his deformed head and released a disturbing guttural scream, then charged. "What is *wrong* with you?" Ian yelled, throwing the man to the ground and barely registering the fact that flakes of skin burst from his body like a cloud of dust.

The soul jumped to his feet, his clothes in tatters, revealing a gaunt figure with ribs and collarbone sticking out among sunken skin. His mouth seemed two sizes too big, and when his lips parted again, black teeth barely hung from rotted gums. He released another scream and Ian prepared himself for an assault, but before the soul could attack he faltered, freezing in place for a moment before sinking to his knees, And then Ian saw Whisper. She stood behind the ghoul, a look of both anger and regret crossing her face as she leaned over and retrieved the knife she had plunged into his back.

"I told you not to look into their eyes," she said forcefully, as though reprimanding a child, wiping the black blood off the blade with a piece of buckskin. "When will you listen?"

"What the hell just happened?" Ian asked in response, touching his face and wincing when his fingers connected with exposed flesh. "Why did he attack?"

Whisper sprinkled a handful of sage over the twice-dead corpse, whispering a prayer into his ears, tenderly touching the creature's brittle hair. "This is what happens when dead souls fail to cross the Bridge of the Dead. They become lost," she told Ian, her thick Cherokee accent making everything she said sound plausible, "and forget that we are human, as they are. They begin to feel only hate and despair, and they know nothing but death. They have forgotten what it means to be human."

Ian watched as the dead soul melted into the earth, a few bits of ash-like material floating away. In seconds, the young man was gone. He swallowed hard. "What...what happens when a soul is killed...when it's already dead?"

Straightening and adjusting her bow across her back, Whisper cast a sidelong glance at Ian before lifting a shoulder. "Some say their lives exist as though never having been born at all. They are erased from memory, from stories, from existence. Others say the soul goes to a world beneath the Land of the Dead, a horrible place of endless pain, torture, and fear. I do not wish to find out. Keep your eyes forward, and follow my orders. They will keep you from learning what world lies beneath this land."

To keep her own eyes forward, Whisper reached back and pulled the long buckskin hood lined with plush rabbit fur over her head, wrapping her young face in shadows.

Together, the two continued their journey across the blackened earth, sidestepping potholes and collapsed souls. Whisper didn't appear to notice the fallen, or care for that matter, while Ian couldn't help but peek down and feel a tug of sadness for each one. Despite the sun in the distance, a sun at least two hundred sizes bigger than the one Ian was accustomed to seeing in the sky back home, there was little light. The sun cast a dim orange glow across the sky, but shadows of the souls created an aura of blackness that flowed across the rough terrain. How something so enormous and bright could create such a small amount of light baffled the man.

"So…what is this Bridge of the Dead you keep talking about?" Ian asked, a bit out of breath and wondering how that could be since he was no longer alive. It was a strange sensation, not feeling the beating of his heart, not having the urge to eat or go to the bathroom, but instead being completely empty inside. And yet, after so much walking he was winded, and a little tired.

Up ahead of him, Whisper remembered all the old stories, all the different Elders and storytellers that had ever spoken of the place. As atrocious as the Bridge was, it would be the easiest of their obstacles. "The Bridge of the Dead spans a gorge that separates the worthy from the sinned…the damned," she corrected herself, hoping Ian didn't catch her error. She worked hard at perfecting her English, but at times the wrong word slipped through. "On the Bridge is every animal that the person ever mistreated by intentionally harming, killing for food without a prayer of thanks, murdering for sheer pleasure. Those animals try to knock the person off the bridge and into the gorge, so that their soul is forced to wander the earth eternally."

"What about animals you were close to? Like family pets?"

"Those come to your side to help you across."

"Oh…and where is this Bridge of the Dead?"

Whisper stopped, turned slightly to her right, and pointed. Ian followed her finger; the discouraging sight nearly forced him backward a few steps. He did not want to go anywhere near that menacing contraption.

A gorge twice the size of the Grand Canyon cut the earth in half, sharp jagged edges slicing into the foul air. A visible blackness rose up from the depths of the chasm, a tangible dark that threatened to swallow whole any who got too close. From somewhere deep and eternal, a scream echoed off the craggy walls, the scream of a soul who failed to make her way across the gorge.

But it wasn't the gorge that took Ian's breath away. It was the Bridge, the Bridge of the Dead that caused his hands to curl into tight fists and his mouth to press into a thin line of trepidation. Thick ropes lined with the grime of dead hands and spilled blood spanned the gorge, wrapped around even thicker wooden posts at either end. Dead branches and sticks of countless lengths and sizes crisscrossed one another along the sides of the passage, hanging from the rope railing carelessly. Splintered, wooden slats served as the base for the four-foot wide bridge, and from those slats rose cracked timber that twisted its way up toward the looming black sky. Torn and tattered pieces of buckskin were sewn together with sturdy vines stripped into dozens of sinewy strings. The loose strips of leather flapped in the wind that rose from the gorge and circulated the bridge.

In front of the Bridge, only a couple yards away from the edge of the precipice, was a roughly constructed booth with no windows and a striped, slanted roof steaming slightly in the light breeze. From either side of the closed door, which was hidden behind a torn curtain, a gate that reeked of excrement and old blood wrapped its way around the building and created a wobbly circle that enclosed the entrance to the bridge, forcing the dead to walk through the hut first. If Ian had bothered to ask, he would have learned that the fence was made from old bones stripped off of dead souls, some pieces still attached to decaying muscle and flesh. All around the gate, close enough to have a clear view but not so close as to touch the gory remains of the human deceased, stood dozens of souls gathered to watch others cross the Bridge of the Dead.

Dread rose in Ian's gut, and he struggled to keep his eyes away from the souls. Beside him, Whisper drew in a deep breath to ready herself for the confrontation, then marched into the shabby construction, keeping her head low and her face concealed. After a moment's hesitation, Ian followed. When the tattered cloth dropped behind his back, he felt as though he had just sacrificed his chance to return among the living.

Inside the foul-smelling hut, two hulking, enormous figures stood side-by-side in nearly pitch-black darkness. A single white flame wavering from a gray candle in the corner provided the only light. In that dim pearly glow, the brownish gray walls that slowly oozed something thick and putrid seemed to pulsate and quiver, dizzying the air. Afraid to look at the surreal surroundings and even more surreal creatures, yet strangely intrigued, Ian lowered his head and stared out the corners of his eyes. The sights fascinated him. Whatever the walls were made of, they were alive, dripping the thick brown liquid across the floor like a slow-moving water fountain and clutching his feet when he tried to move. The candle was the only decoration, somehow mounted to the sodden walls, with stringy strands of wax descending to the ground that formed a small gray construction mirroring the Bridge of the Dead. There were two doors to the hut, the one he and Whisper had entered, and the one being guarded by the Watchmen.

Whisper nudged him forward, and Ian was face-to-face with a species of bloodcurdling creatures so revolting that even his worst nightmares would have been offended. Standing ten inches taller and hovering over Ian with boneless and fluid backs, the two identical beasts glared at their victim through watery black eye sockets with uneven gray circles in the center. They faded in and out of the background they had become a part of, their flesh loose and wavering in a nonexistent breeze. With horror, Ian watched as slimy, worm-like creatures slithered in and out of the rotting holes that pierced their slack skin.

When the dead souls opened their mouths to speak, their mouths distended and distorted their faces, translucent eyes rolling back into their heads and jaws audibly popping out of place, thin strings of flesh stretched across the gaping black hole, revealing rotted teeth.

"*Who...are...you?*" The whispery, slow, guttural voices blended together in a horrific melody that vibrated through Ian's blood. He swallowed hard, fear creeping into his throat as the creatures swarmed over his body, gaping mouths threatening to swallow him whole. "*Speak...or be cast into the darkness.*" Their arms rose and intertwined, fingers pointing into nothing.

"I...Ian," the man stuttered, taking a step back only to be shoved violently from behind by Whisper. "Ian Daivya."

"*Ian...Daivya...you seek passage...across the Bridge of the Dead.*" The creatures spun around him so fast and so blurred that he became dizzy and stumbled. "*The gods forgive... only the sacred...You...are...not...worthy....*"

Swallowing his fear, Ian lifted his head and struggled to catch the eyes of the dead souls. "I want my son back, and you won't stop me."

A strange sound suddenly filled the small room, a whirling of accusations and doubts and fears screaming from the mouths of the Watchmen, surrounding Ian in a claustrophobic cage of invisible forces. Somewhere behind his eyes he saw his son fading away into a blanket of shadows, his gray face and empty eyes melting into the background. He heard his wife's tearful sobs, her bitter words blaming him for their son's death. And, worst of all, he felt the painful reminder that he was an inferior husband, a distant father, and a selfish man. Against the wall, Whisper watched silently, eyes narrowed curiously.

"No. *No!*" Ian fought against the current, forcing his way through the force-field until he was nearly toe-to-toe with the dead souls. "I am *none* of those things! You will *not* make me feel like a failure, and you *will* let me pass to the Bridge of the Dead!"

The Watchmen dropped the cage, and the room stood still. They seemed to be considering his declaration, their glare burning through him. Ian met their stare, refusing to relent despite his heart shaking in his heaving chest. These fiends, these creatures of darkness, did not have the right to judge him, and he would not allow them to rip his soul to pieces with ignorant words.

"*Your conviction. . .will not lead. . .to your son. . . . .but to your devastation.*" Despite their words, the Watchmen moved, one on either side of the door. After only a second's hesitation, Ian swallowed his doubt, put on a mask of courage, and strode through the door. The sight that met his eyes was much like the one on the other side of the shack, and, unsure what to do, he decided to wait for his guide and gather his shaken wits.

Inside the tiny room, Whisper stepped forward without concern, her slender face cloaked in shadows by the thick hood. The creatures swarmed around her in fluid movements, happily judging her soul, measuring the courage in her heart. Their rancid breath and cold, liquefied flesh were insults to her senses, but she remained in spot, standing tall and proud, unfaltering, the corners of her mouth curving ever so slightly into a smirk of impatience and boredom.

Then, as quickly as the Watchmen had swarmed to her body to eagerly shame and humiliate her very self, they snapped back to face the woman, inquisitive scowls crossing their death-like faces.

"*Only fools. . .willingly come. . .to the Land of the Dead,*" they declared in unison, speaking quickly and harshly. "*Why?*"

Whisper's eyes only narrowed more. "*Atleisdi,*" she answered in a hushed tone that matched their own.

The word vibrated in the air, and for a moment the room was filled with a palpable respect mixed with fear and awe. The flame of the candle flickered, and the Watchmen bowed their heads ever so slightly. They let her pass, gesturing to the door that led to the Bridge of the Dead.

"*You. . .are. . .ready,*" they said as she approached the threshold. Whisper turned her head in their direction, acknowledging their approval with a knowing leer before leaving them behind to face her fate on the other side of the bridge.

Chapter 8

Unable to sleep, Julia pulled on a coat and stepped outside the tent, careful not to wake her snoring sister. She zipped up the entrance behind her and took in the sleepy campground sights. It was nearing two in the morning. The bright full moon was high in the sky, casting a soft glow around the trees. Her parents had called the search quits for the night only two hours ago, and were sleeping fretfully though soundly in their trailer. Some of her other family members, the ones that decided to stay through to the end, had pitched their tents at one of the two sites and had all turned in for the night. Only a few police officers remained awake, sitting at the picnic table beneath their own tent, keeping watch for the volunteers out searching, if they could be so blessed, for the missing child.

Julia was glad everyone in her family was asleep. She was tired of the pity, the sympathy. She knew they were just trying to help, but none of it did. And to make matters worse, Ian hadn't returned from his trip with the Indian woman. Julia wasn't worried about him getting lost, for her husband knew the woods and directions well, and if he wasn't lost, then there was only one other thing he could be doing. And she blamed herself.

She didn't really think it was Ian's fault that Cole was missing; it was simply easier to blame him. Cole had nearly fallen into the river on her watch, and she'd barely saved him from that. Children were prone to wander away, get excited when something catches their eye and curiosity got the better of them. Ian should have been watching to make sure he didn't wander off, but parents weren't perfect. Ian was all she had right now, and Julia needed him.

Deciding to finally take action, Julia strode over to the police tent, damp from the fog by the time she got there. "Officer Duff," she greeted the young man who had been a part of the search since day one.

"Mrs. Daivya," Duff, the eager, relatively new officer with a muscular frame, light brown hair swept back from his face, and wide brown eyes, returned the greeting. He blew on the hot cup of coffee he had just poured. "You should get some rest. Tomorrow's a new day."

"Yes, I know." Julia took the second cup of coffee he poured and offered to her. "That's why I wanted to see you."

"Me?"

"Sheriff Forbe said that you were the one who went looking for that Whisper woman when Cole disappeared. He said that she could help find him."

Uncomfortable because he knew where the conversation was heading, Duff shifted from foot to foot and stared into his coffee. "Yes. Whisper often helps out when someone is missing. She knows how to track in the woods. But I can assure you, Mrs. Daivya, that she had nothing to do with your son being missing."

"And how do you know that?"

"Because that's against her way. She and old Smoke Speaker live by the old ways."

"Meaning what?"

"Meaning...they believe that what they do determines the very world around them. If they do something wrong then they might throw the world out of balance. They are all about balance, and life. People go to them for healing medicines, for spiritual matters. And Whisper..." Duff shrugged, picturing the woman he'd known for more than ten years. "Whisper is just like the Elder. They aren't bad people. She's not bad. She's different, but...still great."

Suspicious, Julia angled her head to the side and stared at the young officer. "And how long have you and this Whisper been seeing one another?"

"Us?" Duff couldn't help but laugh. He set his coffee down and held up a hand. "Don't get the wrong idea, Ma'am. We're not together, nor have we ever been. I've just known her for a long time." It was true that Duff thought Whisper was the most beautiful, intriguing woman he'd ever known, and longed for her to be in his arms, but he would never act on his emotions. While he secretly loved the woman, she also terrified him. Something about her eyes made his blood run cold.

"OK, so you aren't sleeping with her, but you know how to find her, right?" Julia persisted. She didn't really care about any sort of relationship the two may have had. "You know how to find this Elder Smoke Speaker?"

"Well...yes."

"Good, then you're going to show me. My husband was last seen walking into the woods with Whisper and he hasn't returned yet. So I'm going to find him. At first light, you're taking me to them."

Leaving the officer behind in a slightly confused stupor, Julia stalked back to the tent for a few hours' sleep before her morning trek through the woods.

Ian stood on the edge of the cliff, alternating speculative looks from the deep, black pit of eternity to the lone figure about to step across the Bridge of the Dead.

From the bottomless gorge he could hear the agonizing screams of those who fell and continued their descent, hear their pleas for redemption, the careless laughter of the souls who lined the gates. Across the canyon, way off in the distance, burned the dark orange sun, the only light in a world of gray.

Whisper stood at his side, arms crossed, her thick hood having fallen back from the breeze that drifted up from the gorge to reveal a face void of expression. She didn't speak, didn't notice the screams, but instead simply watched. Her lack of concern for the dead soul about to face his fate made Ian wonder if she already knew his destiny.

At the bridge, a man stood with clenched fists. In life, a life taken away only one week ago, he had never been the nervous type. Throughout his entire sixty-three years, he had always known what he wanted, and how to get it. His confidence granted him success as a well-traveled and well-respected Ivy League professor, as well as a large family of five children and eight grandchildren, with more on the way. He'd had a large circle of friends, a cozy home, and a beautiful sailboat that some joked he loved more than his wife. In the end, it had been the boat, and the raging sea, that had taken his life and washed his body away into oblivion.

Even in death, he stood regally, as though posed before a large classroom of envious students eagerly awaiting his intellectual words. The nerves that showed in his clenched fists did not show on his face. At his feet was a pair of Dobermans, both former pets, one having died of cancer and the other dying after being hit by a car. And both, as pets, had been greatly loved and treated accordingly. They hunched and growled, ready to protect their master loyally and fiercely, and the small smile playing at the corners of the man's mouth hinted that he had nothing to fear.

He took a step onto the bridge and the smile faded, his confidence waned, when forms began to appear before him.

Ian's breath hitched in his throat as he watched. First a female deer took shape, a wide bullet wound in her side. And another, a buck, antlers removed but for two jagged and scabbed stubs. Two boars stood shoulder to shoulder, blood dripping from their mouths. Just behind them were four fawns bleeding from the necks, and a handful of birds perched on the railing. Then a furry gray cat, one front leg twisted cruelly, shimmered into sight. A flurry of rats and insects finished the challenging line of defense.

"A hunter," Whisper said quietly, "who hunts only for glory."

Ian, his throat dry, felt his heart pound for the stranger. "So…every hunter faces his kills?"

"No...only those who disrespect the sacrifices made in their name." When Ian frowned over at her, the woman, her eyes dark and sad, gestured to the bridge. "The deer, birds, and boars he left for dead, taking the antlers before the buck's last breath even left his body. He tortured them for his own joy. The cat he found lying in the grass with a broken leg, and ignored it. His time was more important than the pain of a helpless creature."

"And the rats and bugs?"

She lifted a shoulder. "Nuisances."

"How do you know all that?"

Whisper offered a nod to the doe that was gazing right at her. The innocent creature's quiet words traveled across the eternal screams to meet the woman's ears.

"They told me."

Seeing that she was intent on watching the feat, Ian swallowed the rest of his questions and turned his eyes back to the bridge. The professor had squared his shoulders and braved another few steps, ignoring the taunting, high-pitched laughter from the dead audience behind him.

Without warning, the deer charged, heads low, nostrils flared. The guardian Dobermans charged back, snarling and biting, tasting blood, wanting more. They attacked the fawns first, easily overpowering the young animals still wobbly on their legs, then took the doe down in a matter of seconds, ignoring the pounding hits they took in their sides from the buck and the jabs from bird beaks. Whisper's breath caught sharply, but she said nothing.

The cat nimbly raced past the dogs and leapt for the professor's face. Panic swept through his eyes as his arms lifted, his hands protecting him. Seeking revenge, the cat hissed and clawed, then shrieked with agonizing fury when the man got a firm hold on its body and slung it over the side of the bridge.

The deer, cat, and two birds were finished, the buck leaning heavily against the rope, panting and bleeding. Unfortunately for the professor, one of his dogs was down as well, trampled by the buck and gored by the thick tusks of the boars.

He was halfway across the bridge, stomping on the insects and kicking the rats aside, coming face-to-face with the boars, barely noticing the buck that was beginning to fade away. The two sets of eyes that stared at the man were full of hate and rage, and those that stared back at the boars were ready for a fight.

The Doberman leapt first, taking a bite out of one boar and reaching for the throat of the other. The professor ran, kicked, and fell when his ankle was caught in the mouth of his enemy. Ian winced when the Doberman yelped, convulsed, and fell silent after being struck in the side; the man was left to fend for himself. He stole a quick glance to Whisper, shocked to see the glint of satisfaction in her eyes.

She knew the professor didn't stand a chance.

It took only a few more seconds for the animals to work together, ramming the man against the rope, and hoisting him over the edge with the help of the injured buck. He screamed the entire way down, his voice fading only when the animals disappeared from the bridge into eternity.

Whisper shifted her eyes to Ian. "Let us pray you succeed."

Chapter 9

He took a few moments to collect his thoughts, calm the nerves that had leapt into his throat at the sight of the professor tumbling over the edge of the bridge. His mind struggled through its own history, searching for potential threats, desperately trying to remember any time he was cruel to the earth's gentler creatures.

Whisper stood a few feet behind him, fighting back her own nerves. She may not like her traveling companion, but she needed him nonetheless. Without him, there was no way to guarantee the success of her mission, and worse, no way to go back to fix the failure.

Needing him, though, didn't mean respecting him, and so if he took a few beatings across the bridge, she certainly wouldn't feel guilty about enjoying the view.

Ian grinned when a yipping, playful cocker spaniel came running to his side, short tail wagging excitedly as she licked her former owner's hands. "Hey, girl," he said quietly, a bit choked up at the sight of his childhood best friend. "Hi, Roxy. Oh, man, I missed you."

Roxy, who had seen Ian through his childhood years, yipped in response. She jumped up, her front paws reaching his stomach as she begged to be scratched behind the ears. He obliged her, his mind taking him back to the day when his mother had sat him down and explained that his best friend was sick. To a ten year-old, losing a dog was devastating, and he'd been furious with his parents for months after Roxy had been put to sleep. To this day, he'd refused to ever have another pet. Cole had been hinting at getting a puppy for about six months now, and every time Ian had found ways to change the subject.

But now Roxy was back, if only for a short time. And she was back to help him, to make sure he stayed safe across the Bridge of the Dead. She'd always been protective. Sweet as sugar until she felt little Ian was being threatened, and then she'd become the ultimate guard dog. Roxy had taken down the next-door neighbor's aggressive black lab, a rogue fox, and even Jimmy Henden, a fourth-grade bully.

"Let's see what I'll need protection from this time," he said quietly, kneeling down and keeping an arm around his old friend.

Ian didn't hear the sarcastic huff that escaped Whisper when the images began to form, nor did he look back to see the way her lips pressed together angrily. He was too busy calculating how the hell he was going to live through this complete and utter disaster.

He immediately recognized the three cats that sat shoulder-to-shoulder on the bridge like sentries, ears pricked, green eyes burning through him. One was all black, one white with orange patches, and the other fluffy and gray. And he knew their names—Midnight, Shasta, and Tomboy.

His sister's cats. He'd *hated* those beasts growing up. Midnight was always peeing on his shoes and Shasta shed white fur all over his clothes. They'd both died of old age. But Tomboy was curious to him, because that cat, fifteen years old and rescued from a shelter that caught fire, was still alive, roaming around his sister's house, content with being the only pet. Though he hadn't talked to his sister in about five months and knew it was entirely possible that the cat had died, he was still pretty sure that Tomboy was born of evil and would live forever.

"Guess cats really are guardians of the dead. Crap," Ian muttered, disgust curling at the corners of his mouth. Those animals would fight him to the death. As a kid he hadn't been the nicest to them, kicking them out of his way, pulling their tail because he thought it was funny. As an adult, he'd once agreed to feed Tomboy while his sister was away on vacation with her husband and three kids, then subsequently forgot about the arrangement. Five days later, he remembered and made his way to his sister's, finding the cat hungry but alive, and very pissed off.

"Crap," he muttered again when a hawk landed on the rope railing of the bridge, the same hawk that, as a teenager, he'd struck down with a stone just to see if he could. A flurry of insects scattered the bridge, as they had for the professor, and interestingly a pelican appeared just behind the cats. Ian had no idea what he had done to the bird, but wouldn't have been surprised to learn that he'd kicked sand in its face or caught its wing with a hook while fishing. There were a lot of careless things he did without ever thinking twice.

"OK, I can handle this." Ian straightened and held his head high. If these animals were all he had to worry about, and Roxy was there to defend him, he was confident he could make it across the Bridge of the Dead. He rubbed his hands together as he calculated the best way across, refusing to look over his shoulder at Whisper, worried that a single glance at her face, which he was sure was crossed with a disapproving scowl, would loosen his nerves.

"OK, Roxy, we'll run." Roxy seemed to understand, crouching low, barking twice. "We'll just run straight across. Ready?"

Ian lowered himself into a sprinter's position, glared at the three cats, his biggest threat. He took a few deep breaths, eyed the other side of the gorge, and nodded. "*Go!*"

Both man and dog lunged for the bridge. At the same time, vengeance drove forth the disrespected animals. Midnight and Tomboy leapt for Ian first, howling as they clawed at his hands, struggling to get them away from his face, biting at his scalp. Roxy pounced down on Shasta and took the cat out of the fight with a single nip to the throat. Before she could turn to help her master, the hawk bared its claws and clamped them down onto the dog's spine. Laughter erupted from the sidelines.

The yelp of pain drew Ian's hands away from his face. Midnight took the opportunity to rake his claws down the man's cheek, but Ian ignored the pain, blood dripping into his mouth, and grabbed the cat with one hand while punching the hawk with the other. The cat went sailing over the bridge and the hawk lay on the splintered wood, dazed.

Roaches and beetles crawled up Ian's legs, under his shirt, in his hair, as he grabbed Roxy and cradled her to his chest. Tomboy clung to his back, teeth latched onto his shoulder and pointed nails dug in deep. With a snarl, Ian leapt past the snapping pelican. The hook of its bill snagged his flesh, dragging across his stomach, but the bird hardly concerned the man.

He was almost there. A few more steps, that's all he needed—just a few more and he was safe. The whimpering dog in his arms drove him forward.

"Get off me, you *son-of-a-bitch!*"

With a shout of rage and desperation, Ian reached back for Tomboy, fingers clasping around the cat's neck. Tomboy fought back, curling his body around Ian's arm and kicking with his back legs. With all the strength he had, Ian rammed his arm down on the side of the bridge. When Tomboy connected with the small slab of wood he went limp, and fell into the abyss.

He'd made it. Ian collapsed on the ground, hugging Roxy as he felt the bugs crawl off his body and scatter into the darkness. Across the gorge, Whisper stood perfectly still, arms crossed, observing the scene.

Ian gently laid Roxy on the gray and cracked earth, inspecting her wounds. Deep punctures lined her spine, paralyzing her front legs. She peered up at him through watery brown eyes, feebly licking his hand as he leaned over her, petting her head as tears escaped. Her tail thumped once against the ground.

"Thank you, Roxy. You did good, girl," he whispered in her ear, knowing that the gleam in her eyes was one of pure loyalty, the devotion of a dog who loved her master unconditionally. "Thank you for getting me closer to Cole." Then, before he knew what was happening, Roxy faded away and he was left with nothing but his own blood to warm him.

The reality of his condition set in. His back stung where the shirt clung to the open wounds. His left cheek was on fire, and his arm looked like it had just seen the inside of a paper shredder. Blood soaked his clothes and was already starting to clump on his skin. He wondered if it was possible to die twice, to die again in death, because of blood loss. And for that matter, he wondered why he even had blood at all. He didn't feel weak or tired. All he felt was the worst pain of his life, a pain that brought forth anger and a sense of betrayal, as though the woman across the bridge had been planning for this to happen all along.

When he dared to look her way, he saw that she had taken her place at the edge of the bridge, but her arms were still crossed and her eyes still narrowed. She offered no words of condolence or congratulations, just a glare of repulsion.

"So what?" he shouted across the gorge, standing and lifting his mutilated arms out to his sides to challenge her, any sense of maturity shifting into a teenage need for competition. "So I'm human! No one is perfect! Not even you!" His words traveled across the gorge and reached her ears just as reinforcements came to her aid.

"Fool," she whispered, a small grin tugging at her mouth when Ian's nearly dropped to the ground.

The sight was miraculous. It was impossible. It was...beautiful. An entire army of animals lined the gorge—bears, deer, raccoons, beavers, birds, mountain lions. All stood side-by-side with pride and majesty. Their coats gleamed, eyes shining in the grayness, sturdy bodies primed for a battle that did not exist. And in the center was Whisper, the fur that lined her hood and the buckskin that clung to her body giving her an animal aura all her own. It seemed to radiate...glow. She was glowing, Ian realized, a spark of color in a world of empty hues.

The Bridge of the Dead was empty. Not even so much as a mosquito prevented her passage to the other side. And yet, as she took a step forward, her companions rushed forth, an entire battalion of spirits and guardians surrounding Whisper in a blanket of other-worldly protection.

She never took her eyes off Ian as she sauntered across the bridge. When her feet touched the earth again, she closed her eyes and whispered a prayer. The animals bowed in response before disappearing.

Whisper opened her eyes, sensing a dozen questions roaming around Ian's thoughts. "No one is perfect, Mr. Daivya," she agreed coolly, "but respect is something we are all capable of giving." To her, respect for the natural world meant praying to the gods of the earth, thanking the animals that gave up their lives so that she may live and apologizing for those she accidentally harmed, even the tiny insects that may have met their death beneath her wandering feet.

"Though," she continued, looking Ian up and down, "I am trapped with a companion who demands respect but is incapable of offering it."

Ian sighed impatiently. "Drop the holier-than-thou crap. I made it across the bridge, didn't I? And you don't have to like me, or respect me, but you brought me here to find my son. So let's go."

Whisper considered his demand. "Why did your son die?"

Ian hesitated, taken aback by the strange and unexpected question. At first he thought she was antagonizing him, but her tone was sincere. "He fell into the river and...drowned. You told me that."

"Oh...yes." She sounded disappointed as she turned. Lifting a hand, Whisper pointed to the mountains. On this side of the canyon, the sun loomed larger than before, burned brighter. "We will rest in the shadow of the cliff. We shall be safe there, and I can tend to your wounds."

Chapter 10

They made camp beneath a small overhang that ran alongside the mountain. The space was no larger than an average-sized bathroom, but the two weary travelers welcomed the sense of security. Whisper made a fire from the rotted wood of a fallen tree, and Ian marveled over the light. Expecting the fire to be orange, he had been fascinated by the white flames and black smoke. It seemed that in death, only Whisper was able to call upon the power of color.

Ian lay on his stomach, staring out at the vast open land. The earth was endless, scattered with deep potholes, jagged cracks, and scraggly trees that oozed black pus. In the shadow of the mountain, they were hidden from the light of the sun, tucked away in darkness. But what worried him most were the people, depressed bodies searching for salvation in a land of emptiness. They'd made it over the Bridge of the Dead, but were yet to find their way. He wondered if he too would be a wanderer, were it not for his guide.

Whisper was kneeling over him, gently removing the torn scraps of fabric, not at all sympathetic when he winced. She didn't say a word as she layered a foul mixture of water, dirt, tree ooze, and something dusty from one of the pouches on her belt across the wounds. He had reservations about her method at first, but whatever she was doing, it was working. The pain was subsiding, allowing his mind to think about other things, the things he'd been fighting to the back of his thoughts.

"Can I ask you something?"

Whisper frowned. She didn't want to talk to him, not to this man who had no regard for anyone or anything but himself. The only reason she was tending to his wounds was because she needed him in top form for the rest of the journey.

"Yes," she answered quietly.

Ian stared out at the traveling bodies, some leaving blood trails in their wake, evidence of their fight across the bridge. "How...why do we still have blood?"

Whisper spared a second's glance at the passing dead souls. "I do not know for sure," she answered truthfully. "Some say it is because the Great Spirit, Creator, wishes for the dead to remember who they are, and to comfort them with their human form. Other ancient stories say that it is not blood at all, but death that has entered our bodies and taken over our senses." She did not care to know which, if either, was correct. "But I sense that is not what you wanted to ask me, Mr. Daivya."

Caught, Ian sighed heavily and rubbed his eyes. "It's...it's about Cole.... How could he have survived this far? He's just a kid...how would he have known where to go? What if he's lost, back on the other side of the bridge?"

"He made it across the Bridge of the Dead," Whisper affirmed, layering strips of thin hide over his back.

"But how do you know?"

A howl in the distance troubled Whisper. She knew that sound, that cry of misery and fear. It was the sound of a soul giving up the hope of peace in death.

"Cole is...safe," she answered his question as honestly as she could. "I have asked."

"Asked who?"

Whisper waved a hand, covered with black goo, toward the vast open land. "The souls...they speak, when asked the right questions. Elder Smoke Speaker comes from a long line of Speakers. He communicates with the dead through the smokes of the earth. Fires, fogs, dusts. He taught me to communicate through the whispers that travel on the wind. I have learned the art of Speaking, but not as well as the Elder. I do not hear as clearly, or as loudly, as he, but I still hear. I have asked about the fate of your son, whispered my inquiries to those who have already reached the other side. Cole is in the Land of the Dead."

He didn't know if he believed her, or if he even wanted to. Speaking to ghosts, reading smoke, it didn't seem possible. Then again, he mused, he'd surfaced into a world of gray after an old man drowned him in a lake, a world where his hands passed through his crying wife, where angry animals tried to push dead souls into a black abyss, a world where his fate was in the hands of a young woman with a strange accent and eyes that had seen the deaths of thousands. It could have all been a dream, but if it wasn't, then he had to be prepared for the worst.

Then her words sunk in, and something she said struck a chord in him. He lifted his head and rolled to his side to ask his suddenly burning question, and was momentarily silenced by the sight that met his eyes.

Whisper had taken off her hooded cloak and fringed coat. Beneath them she was wearing a white top with straps that crisscrossed her shoulders, the back held together by a thick strand of fabric woven from top to bottom. It mirrored the front, which scooped low across her chest and was decorated with dark stitches. But it wasn't her clothing that shocked Ian. It was what he had already seen that rendered him silent, a sight that was even more spectacular in the Land of the Dead.

Black tattoos covered her skin. Circling her shoulders, down her back, and up her stomach, the intricate design wound its way across her body. Foreign letters, symbols, and places were etched out in great detail, and in between her shoulder blades was a strange spherical marking with streaks of dark red among the black. The tattoo seemed to swirl around itself, consume itself, and as Ian stared at the marking, mesmerized, he realized that it was at the center of the tattoos that traversed her body. Thin black lines exploded from the emblem, arcing across her shoulders, shooting down her spine, splitting into a language, a message, that Ian could not understand.

Despite his hatred of the woman, Ian felt himself longing to run his fingers across the markings, trace them across her fabulous body. He wanted to know what they meant, how to read the strange words, and somewhere deep in the animal side of him he wanted to know just how far down those strokes of black went beneath the waistline of her pants.

"If you have a question, Mr. Daivya, then ask," Whisper said, her back to him as she tossed a rotted log onto the white fire. Her inflected voice was accusatory rather than inviting. "Stares answer nothing."

Embarrassed, Ian cleared his throat and looked away, focusing his attention on the trees in the distance. He wanted to ask about the tattoos, but refused to admit he had been staring. "You said…you said Cole has reached the Land of the Dead."

"He did."

"Right…but, I thought…I thought *this* was the Land of the Dead."

Whisper turned and settled down beside Ian as he lifted himself to a sitting position, gingerly touching the wounds on his cheek that she had already tended to. She stretched her legs out in front of her and leaned back on her hands.

"This is not the Land of the Dead, Mr. Daivya. This place, *Agatiyv*, the place of Waiting, is merely the way there."

"Like Purgatory."

Whisper lifted a shoulder at Ian's suggestion. "Perhaps. You see, Mr. Daivya, people like us, the ones who die and never receive a proper burial, have one of three fates. *Saquu*, we are lost on the way to the Bridge of the Dead and become monsters, like the one that attacked you. *Tali*, we find our way to the bridge, but are overcome by our enemies, and so our souls are forced to wander for all eternity. *Tsoi*, we make it across, and into the Land of the Dead." She sighed, drawing her knees up and wrapping her arms around her legs. Her fingers subconsciously rubbed the leather band around her wrist as she spoke. "Those who do get a proper burial have one fate. Passage into the Spirit World."

"Which is what?"

"The Spirit World is...beautiful, peaceful, a world of light and color and love. The Land of the Dead...is dark." Whisper stared into the fire, remembering her lessons. "Those who do reach it are given a...peace...away from the fear of eternal restlessness, but are forbidden to be with their ancestors. Family...family becomes whoever you find at your side."

Ian chewed on his bottom lip, unable to imagine such a place. "Is there...is there anything good?"

"Oh, yes." Whisper nodded and glanced over at her companion. "There are intriguing people in the Land of the Dead. People with fascinating stories, endless imaginations. The people in the Land of the Dead are not like these lost souls. They are simply spirits."

Ian wasn't so sure that spirits with interesting stories made up for eternity in a dark place of nothingness. "This place is like Hell," he muttered, closing his eyes in hopes of making it all disappear.

"No, Mr. Daivya. The Land of the Dead is much worse," Whisper said in return, her quiet voice traveling the air, echoing all around them. "Given the two, I would rather be in Hell."

Chapter 11

At first light, Deputy Ben Duff followed through with Julia's instructions and led the woman through the woods. He'd told his partner, Neil, that he was simply taking Julia on a search, and made sure to leave before his boss showed up. Forbe had a way of knowing things, and he would have seen right through their fake search to what was actually going on.

As they walked silently through the woods, Duff struggled to figure out why he had agreed to take Julia Daivya to see Elder Smoke Speaker. He didn't suspect what she did, that her husband was off frolicking in the forest with the strange Indian woman, for he knew better. Whisper couldn't be bothered with such things, and that he could speak of from experience, as could many others who had been rejected over the years. Duff would even go so far as to claim that she held a strange sort of contempt for the human species. Whisper did her best to avoid people at all costs. She came to town only for absolute necessities and spoke to no one, though most avoided her anyway, and when a man dared to cross her path and suggest a night on the town, he was met with a glare of spiteful scorn that made him feel like a sniffling child being scolded by his mother for not cleaning his room.

But he didn't have an answer as to why they hadn't yet returned. It was odd enough that Whisper had brought Ian along on the search, for she typically worked alone when tracking a missing person. Duff had only been on a search with her once, and it was a day he would never forget.

They'd been searching for a five year-old boy who'd disappeared sometime in the middle of the night, likely due to wandering out of the tent in search of the bathroom while his parents were sleeping. Whisper had been called in only hours after he was reported missing, and Duff had been assigned to her side only because, at the time, she'd had a broken arm due to a nasty fall off the top of Smoke Speaker's hut and was taking precautions. She'd barely talked to Duff during the search and instead made him carry most of her things. At first he'd been annoyed, but then became mesmerized by her ways. The way she walked, the way she stared into the air as though watching a movie in the wind, the way she turned her head ever so slightly like something was speaking to her. She'd been completely oblivious to his presence until she needed something from her pack, and then only acknowledged him long enough to find whatever she was looking for.

Four hours into their search, Whisper found the boy. The child was curled up against a tree, wet and suffering from hypothermia. As they brought him back to camp he rambled on about a little girl he saw playing on the other side of the river that wanted him to play too, but by the time they reached his parents he'd forgotten the entire story.

That was the day Duff had fallen in love with Whisper, not because she found the boy, not because of the way she treated him and everyone else, but because she was fascinating. She knew the old ways, respected her heritage, and didn't need anyone but herself to survive. There was something mystical about her, something he desperately wanted to figure out. And maybe that was why he was leading Julia through the woods, because he wanted to see her again, and especially wanted the chance to speak to the Elder.

Running a hand through his damp hair, Duff marveled over the fog. He had never seen anything like it before, nothing as thick, as cold, as lasting. If he didn't know exactly where he was going, it would have been very, very easy to get lost.

"How much longer?"

Duff shook his head at the irritated tone in Julia's voice. For a woman who had been unable to pick herself up off the ground upon learning of her son's disappearance, she certainly had a bossy streak in her. He didn't know what changed in her, but he was starting to miss the basket case.

"Not long," he answered, stopping long enough to point. "See those trees up there, rising above the canopy? That's where we're going, a place called Howling Vines."

Julia followed his finger. The trees he spoke of formed a neat circle, thick vines dangling from the trunks. They didn't look too far away. "Well then, let's get moving."

She walked by the officer's side until they reached the clearing, and when they entered, the old man was waiting for them.

Elder Smoke Speaker lifted a welcoming hand, the black stone set in a silver band on his index finger glittering in the fog. "It is not every day that my woods deliver two strangers to my door. *Osiyo*, my guests." He gestured for them to sit before him. "What brings you to my fire?"

Duff and Julia exchanged a hesitant glance before lowering themselves to the ground, sitting across the fire from the Elder. Suddenly shy, Julie took a moment to observe the old man. He was...beautiful, she thought, and wished she had her camera so as to record his magnificence. Throughout her life she'd often learned about different Native American tribes, and seen old, yellowed photographs depicting tribal men and women dressed in their traditional clothing and bearing stoic expressions that told a thousand sad stories. Looking upon Elder Smoke Speaker was, for Julia, like seeing those stories unfold right before her eyes.

Smoke Speaker had tied back his thick white hair into a loose braid, a strand of white bone beads and a lone gray feather crowning his head. The beads matched those that were wrapped around his neck. He wore a tanned tunic wrapped tightly around bony shoulders, loose cloth pants, and worn moccasins. When he offered his welcoming wave, his sleeve fell back just enough to reveal a faded black tattoo accented with small circles that wound its way across his forearm.

His carved, decorated walking staff, made for and given to him by his grandfather upon his initiation into manhood, was lying next to him. In his lap was a mass of hemp, wood, and beads, but neither Julia nor Duff could make out the shape of the object.

"You are the officer who sent for Whisper," Smoke Speaker acknowledged Duff. "And you are the mother of the missing child."

"Yes…. How did you know?" Julia frowned and stared at the old man over the fire. Her frown deepened when he smiled and ran his fingers through the fire's smoke.

"The fire told me." He didn't expect them to understand, or even ask what he meant. "But it did not tell me what it is you seek to know."

Duff cleared his throat, a bit nervous. He'd only met the Elder twice before, the same day he'd gone with his apprentice on the search for the little boy, and once when his mother sent him to Howling Vines with a large gift basket at Christmas. "Mrs. Daivya's husband, Ian Daivya, went searching for their son yesterday afternoon with Whisper. They haven't returned yet, and Mrs. Daivya was hoping you could tell her where they might be."

"They have gone to look for your son."

"Where?"

"They have gone to the mountains."

Julia sighed, hating to waste time. "Sir, we're *in* the mountains."

"Yes," the Elder smiled again, "but not the right ones."

She had no idea what that meant. "When will they return?"

"When they have found your son."

She wouldn't get a location out of him. Julia wasn't sure if he was senile, or purposely being coy. She leaned forward and stared at him intently. "Mr.…Smoke Speaker, can you tell me who exactly Whisper is, and why are you so sure she can find Cole?"

Smoke Speaker thought carefully about his answer before speaking. "Whisper is my apprentice, Mrs. Daivya," he began, his old, rough voice shaking with age. "She came to me when she had barely seen five summers. I have been training her ever since she was young in the ways of our people, the ancient ways. She knows medicine, nature, the Great Spirit. She knows how to speak, to whisper to the wind, but she also knows the ways of your people. And that is how she will find your son."

His reply told Julia absolutely nothing. "Where are her parents?"

"She no longer sees her parents. They were of the last few native peoples."

"Where are they now?"

"Her mother is gone."

"And her father?"

"Her father was...terrible, a beast of a man." There was a hint of something in his voice, unidentifiable but unmistakably eerie. "I took her away from him before he could destroy her, but she still carries sadness for her mother and hate for her father's soul in her heart. For many, many moons I have tried to cure her pain, and I can only pray that I have succeeded."

She had never met the woman, but Julia's own heart broke for the girl. The way Smoke Speaker talked of her, the love in his words and the desperation for her safety, touched the mother part of her. "So you not only train her, but you raised her."

"From the time she was a child," the Elder agreed. "I saw something in her, something very special. Whisper was born into a world she was destined to change, and I am here to guide her on her journey. I taught her how to honor her culture, and how to honor those different from ours. She spent many moons learning your language, because it is important that Speakers can understand even the most unfamiliar words."

"She speaks English better than I do," Duff agreed. He'd always marveled at how Whisper could so easily switch back and forth between the languages.

"Yes." Smoke Speaker nodded in Duff's deputy. "Though she still has trouble finding the right words at times. But, Speaking is a constant journey for our people. And now, her journey is to find your son."

"Why did she bring Ian along?" Duff spoke up then. "She usually goes on searches alone."

"She brought you with her once."

There was a hint of amusement in the old man's voice, as though he could sense the officer's feelings, and Duff wasn't happy about it. "I was asked to accompany her because she was injured at the time. But she's healthy now, so why would she suddenly need help?"

"Perhaps she thought it best, considering this fog."

"But they went out before the fog," Duff argued, now suspicious.

"My apprentice knows the weather. She can sense such changes," Smoke Speaker answered easily.

Also suspicious that the Elder was hiding something behind those old eyes of ancient wisdom, Julia tried a different approach. "Mr. Smoke Speaker…have you ever lost someone?"

"Yes, I have."

"Who?"

"My daughter, Blue Feather."

"Oh." She hadn't expected he'd have a family. An old man who lived deep in the mountains with only a young woman to care for him didn't exactly scream "family man." It seemed like a lonely life, all alone in the woods. "May I ask what happened?"

It was only fair that he share his own story, as Ian was entrusting his very life to Whisper. But it stung his heart to think of his only child, so precious and irreplaceable. "My daughter was young, beautiful, full of life. She loved our animal friends, and loved children, and dreamed of becoming a storyteller." He beamed at the memories before his grin turned downtrodden. "One winter morning, she went out for a walk. Such a simple thing, a walk through the woods, something she did every single day. A terrible storm blew through the trees before she could return…and she never did."

Julia could relate to the sensation of terror and grief. "You never found her?"

The Elder pressed his palms together as though praying. "I searched for months, and when the snow melted and the ice thawed I searched again, but I never found her body. The police searched for seven days before deciding that her body must have been taken by the river, or by the local wildlife. The only trace of my daughter's death that I found was her necklace." He reached up and fingered the bones around his throat as though to emphasize his point.

"Then you understand why I *need* you to tell me where my husband is," Julia pushed urgently. "I need to be there, helping them search. I need to find my son!"

Smoke Speaker cleared his thoughts of his beloved daughter and shook his head sadly. "I do not know where they are, Mrs. Daivya. But I can offer you this." He picked up the object in his lap and held it across the fire.

Julia found herself staring at a beautiful dreamcatcher. A circle made of treated and carefully curved wood created the frame, and thin pieces of hemp spun around the casing to form an intricate web tightly woven down to a small opening in the center. Blue beads were tied to the hemp in different areas, and pieces of buckskin hung down from the wooden frame, black feathers dangling from the strands. Painted on the feathers were outlines of different animals in a variety of colors.

"The wolf," Smoke Speaker pointed to a blue outline, "for your husband. Wolf, *Waya*, is the creature of fierce loyalty. He walks his own path, but always returns to the one he has chosen to protect. And Mockingbird, *Huhu*, to help you find your inner song, and recognize your natural talents. Mockingbird shows no fear, and protects her young to the death."

Julia pointed to a drawing at the base of the dreamcatcher. "And that one?"

Smoke Speaker smiled. "*Kahnanesgi*. Spider. The Weaver of Fate, my totem. An artist always marks his creations." He gestured to the woman across the fire. "Here. This will keep your dreams safe and your sleep sound, so that when you wake you will be ready to face a brand new day."

Julia took the gift with a sense of dread. She worried he was offering the dreamcatcher because he knew her son's terrible fate. "Thank you, Mr. Smoke Speaker, but I—"

"Will need to be strong for your son," Smoke Speaker interrupted quietly. "Now, I apologize for sounding rude, but I must see to my morning nap. These old bones wear out easily these days."

Whisper let Ian sleep. Time itself was irrelevant in death, and she was in no hurry for what was to come next. It was true that the child would eventually forget who he was, which would make it harder for him to return, but she may have exaggerated the urgency to find him just a bit because she was eager to begin the journey.

Instead of gathering their packs, she stroked the fire, eyes trained on the thin trails of black smoke. She quieted the voices inside her soul, cocked her head to the side, and listened as the smoke reached for her ears.

The words were faded, as though being spoken through a wall, but Whisper recognized the Elder's voice. Smoke Speaker was reaching out to her, urgently trying to deliver a message, and while smoke speaking wasn't her gift she could still hear the whispers that made their way through the haze.

"The mother comes...her son...they search harder...suspicious...husband's infidelity...you must hurry."

Then the fire went out, cloaking them in shadows.

"So," Whisper muttered, tying back her long hair, "time does matter after all." She was curious about Smoke Speaker's charge of infidelity, but that was the least of her concerns, something to consider only when they reached the Land of the Dead.

"Mr. Daivya." Whisper reached out and kicked Ian in the ribs. She didn't care about hurting him, not after the display on the Bridge of the Dead. Ian grunted and took a few moments to rise and gather his wits.

"What?" he muttered, rubbing his scabbed cheeks tiredly.

"We must go."

They packed up their small camp quickly. Whisper pulled on her cloak, hiding her face in the fur-lined hood, and slung her bow and quiver across her back. Ian pulled on his shirt tenderly, barely noticing that the tears had been stitched up while he was sleeping. His hands and arms were stained with his own blood, and though he couldn't see it, he guessed his cheek looked worse for the wear as well.

Whisper, on the other hand, appeared refreshed and perfectly healthy. Her only visible wounds were the small scratches on her face and the slice on her palm that he'd witnessed her make at the river. How many days ago, he didn't know. Days and nights were all blended together in this place of waiting. But he did know that she certainly didn't seem too concerned with keeping him in one piece. He was beginning to wonder just what her intentions were, and if she was actually enjoying his pain.

"Where are we going?"

"To the Land of the Dead."

"How far is it?"

Whisper led him out of their camp, and together they walked along the edge of the craggy mountain, avoiding the lost souls, some that wandered aimlessly, others that headed in the same direction they did. "Just around that bend," she replied, pointing with her knife. Ian eyed the blade. He'd seen it before, when she dragged it across her palm. He hoped that she held it now only for protection against potential enemies.

As they came closer to the bend, Ian struggled to keep his eyes forward, but all he could think about was that if all of this was, in fact, real, his son had taken this very path, walked this very ground, traveled amongst these very dead souls. How could he have known where to go? Were children granted guides? And how the hell did Whisper know everything about this place?

"Whisp—"

He clamped his mouth shut, annoyed, when she merely lifted a dirty, bandaged hand to silence him. His annoyance started to fade when she crouched down and leaned against the rock, gesturing for him to do the same. "What?"

"Mr. Daivya, I need to ask you something." Whisper pulled back her hood and stared at Ian with those haunting black eyes. "Are you ready for what is to come?"

The question confused him. "Meaning what, exactly?"

"Meaning, you must prepare yourself for the Land of the Dead. You will be tested in new ways than before. The Bridge of the Dead was the first test, and the Western Sun is the second. You must be prepared."

"OK," Ian blew out a frustrated breath, a headache already brewing in the center of his forehead. "So prepare me."

Whisper touched the corner of her eye with the tip of the blade. Ian winced, fearing she was about to do something crazy. "The Land of the Dead is a place without light, without sun. And so our eyes must adjust. Do you remember what I told you about the dead traveling to the Western Sun?"

"Yeah." Ian nodded and craned his neck, trying to see the sun just beyond the mountainside. Then he snapped back against the rock when he realized her intention. "Wait a minute. You mean we have to walk *into* the goddamn *sun?*"

"Behind the Western Sun," Whisper affirmed, for the first time not humored by the look of fear spread across his face. Not even she was looking forward to the next part. "We must go the world on the other side. To prepare ourselves for the Land of the Dead, so that we may see in a world of without light, our eyes must…burn."

Chapter 12

Pain was something Ian could stand—a broken bone, collapsed lung, concussion, lacerations, an incredible sunburn after landscaping for eight hours straight; yes, he was familiar with pain. A teenage boy doesn't play three sports all throughout middle and high school without walking away uninjured. When he first began his landscaping business in his early twenties, he became well-acquainted with pulled muscles, cuts and scrapes from branches and thorns, multiple contusions, and a few broken toes and fingers here and there. Blood and bruises were as commonplace as breathing, and most of the time he hadn't known he was injured until someone else pointed it out.

But this…this would be a whole new kind of pain. Ian wasn't sure he could handle it, wasn't sure he could tolerate a pain that he wasn't able to even *begin* to fathom—his eyes…*burning*, the retina searing itself to the iris, corneas melting? A protective film, Whisper had explained, that masks the eye, blinding it to the light, opening it to the dark. His eyes teared up at the thought.

But he would do it. If walking into, or behind, the sun brought him one step closer to finding Cole, he would do it. He would experience a pain beyond imagination for his son, especially because his son had been forced to experience the same. That was a test he could pass. What worried him, though, was that if the Bridge of the Dead was the first test and the blinding rays of the Western Sun the second, then the following tests were sure to be much, much worse. And the scariest part about those unknown tests was that he had no idea what they were, but had every idea what was at stake.

"Are you ready?"

Ian shot a sarcastic glance in his guide's direction. "To have my eyes melt in the blinding light of a huge ball of fire?" He shrugged. "What can I say? The ayes have it."

After a moment of silence, the corners of Whisper's mouth tugged up into a rare half-smile. "Was that a joke, Mr. Daivya?"

"Was that a smile?"

An interesting, unexpected way to travel into the Western Sun, Whisper mused as she nodded at her companion. An enemy making her smile, an arrogant stiff cracking a joke, prefacing what may be the worst experience in either of their lives.

Rather than ponder the nature of such things, Whisper reached into the pack strapped to her back and pulled out a thin, sinewy rope. She tied one end around her waist and the other to Ian's wrist, much to his dismay.

"What's this for?"

"In case one of us falls behind," she explained, making sure the knots were tight. "We will be nearly blind until we get beyond the sun, and must help each other if one cannot make it."

"If we're blind, then how do we know where to go?"

"The Western Sun draws you in, guides you. Do not resist, and do not lose faith. I will get you to the Land of the Dead."

Whisper led the way. When they stepped out from the protection of the mountain shadows, Ian's heart leapt into his throat. He couldn't breathe, couldn't move. Terror paralyzed him.

The open wasteland stretched out before him in a dry and cracked haze of orange, turbulent winds twisting dust and dirt into an air that scalded and sparked. The ground was barren, the foul trees that rose in towers of ooze and rot seared away into bits of ash that floated with the wind. Viscous bits of tar were strung across the earth, remnants of old shoes that melted off the feet of the dead. And in the distance, the earth, heat rising in bubbling surges, gave way to the Western Sun.

The huge burning sphere arched up into the black sky, shooting crimson flames that left trails of embers across the dark. The bright, white center of the sun glared angrily, churning and pulsating and swallowing whole the wavering figures that inched their way closer and closer. Even from where he stood, Ian had to squint in the harsh light, holding up a hand to protect his vision—a futile gesture. The sun roared its presence, an almost deafening rush that pounded into his ears.

In front of him, Whisper had rolled her cloak into a tight bundle and secured it in her pack. In the light of the sun, her skin was glowing against black tattoos, the black sphere in the center of her shoulder blades mirroring their destination. Her dark hair, tied back in a tight braid, reflected the dozens of crimson hues that smoldered in the blaze. She turned, facing her traveling companion.

"Are you ready?" she asked him again, inspecting him closely. She didn't know if he could handle the Western Sun. Ian already looked like he was ready to fall over. His dark blonde hair was filthy, matted with blood and coated with a fine layer of ash, as was her own. The left side of his face was red and swollen, and although infection was not a concern in death, pain certainly was. She knew his back was excruciatingly tender, and the flesh on his forearm was in pieces. And his eyes, so charmingly blue at first, were angry, afraid, and untrusting.

"We must go."

Gathering his wits, Ian nodded and held his head high. He wouldn't let her see his fear. "Let's do this."

Whisper nodded. "Mr. Daivya, would you object to a prayer before we begin?"

He wasn't a man of religion, but right now he was open to anything that may help him through the journey to find Cole. "By all means."

The young woman closed her eyes and breathed deeply, taking in the scent of the Western Sun. When she spoke, it was in a soft, hopeful voice that floated in the wind.

"*Ulisgolvtanv ayv aisv hawinaditlv uwodu, a le ulisgolvtanv aquvsa digatoli iyuquu higowadv hia gigage a le gigesdi wudeligv.*" She opened her eyes and offered Ian a comforting nod. "*Let me walk in beauty, and let my eyes ever behold the red and purple sunset.*"

And then, bracing themselves against the harsh winds and bright rays of light, the travelers—one terrified of what was about to happen, the other depressingly accepting of a pain beyond pain—began the long walk into the Western Sun.

Sleeping soundly after the effort it took to send Whisper his urgent message, Smoke Speaker dreamed of his apprentice's journey into the Western Sun. He had many spies and aides in the Land of the Dead, as well as the world of Waiting, and none of them had reported her passing beyond the sun, or even getting there in the first place.

In his dreams, he worried. Ian was a skeptic who believed only in what he could see for himself, and Whisper was the product of a mother who could not care for her daughter and a father who cared only for himself. While they were both intelligent, strong, and brave, he feared they may be tempted by paths that led down destructive roads. The Land of the Dead was temptation manifested, where even the most courageous succumbed to their worst nightmares.

Whisper had to be close now. Images formed in his mind, enhanced by the power of his sleep, of her tending to wounds sliced across Ian's back, leading the way to the Western Sun. Even in his slumber he questioned if his visions were accurate or merely suggestions brought on by hope and faith. Either way, he knew she was yet to cross over, and her time was running out.

"*Kanegv*," he whispered in sleep, sweat beading on his forehead as his dreams took him to the magnificent sight of the Western Sun. He could feel its heat, his skin aching from the burn, his eyes tearing up with anticipation.

And there, just on the outskirts, were Whisper and Ian. Their trek was about to begin, and he could only watch until the day awakened him.

Chapter 13

Whisper was right, Ian realized, treading carefully around the cracked earth just a few steps behind the woman. There was a pull, a force that drew him toward the sun, sucking him into a gaping hole of fire. All around them, other lost souls crawled their way into the afterlife, those ahead groaning and screaming and scratching at their faces. The ones who had given up, fallen to the scorched earth, gasped for their last breaths as their flesh charred in the suffocating heat.

Ian watched only his feet, carefully taking one slow step after another. Just in front, he could hear Whisper cough when the wind increased and kicked dirt in her face. *This isn't so bad*, he thought as they made their way closer and closer. He was hot, his throat was dry, and his back was sore from the cat attack, but the Western Sun didn't seem to be threatening anything greater than typical summer temperatures and bright lights he was used to back home.

Then the first tear formed in the corner of his eye.

Ian blinked and shook his head, wiping at more tears as they began to cascade down his dirt-caked cheeks. His eyes stung, reminding him of his childhood days when he spent too much time trying to see underwater in his grandparents' over-chlorinated pool. He took another step, and his vision went blurry just as a blaze of fire flashed across his retinas. In a moment of panic, Ian grabbed the rope and tugged Whisper back against him. She spun around and slapped his hand away from her waist.

"Keep moving forward!" she shouted at him, her voice tinged with pain, and through his watery gaze he saw, with a horrific rock dropping in the pit of his stomach, that the whites of her eyes had started to...*melt*. As she glared at him with that familiar look of annoyance and hatred, her deep black irises were slowly disappearing behind thin white veils while thick, cloudy tears poured down her face. Ian knew, both by the sight and the ghastly pain pounding in his head, that his own eyes looked exactly the same.

Whisper faced the sun again and continued the journey, refusing to show any sign of agony. Ian stood, clutching his face, confused by the sensations swirling throughout his eyes, until the rope pulled at him and forced him forward. Soon, only the draw of the sun and the lead of the rope guided him as the pain in his eyes intensified to a level he never would have thought possible. The piercing white rays of the Western Sun dug into his retinas, reaching into the depths of his skull with fingers of jagged spikes that snatched away his sight. The roar of the Sun nearly deafened him.

How could Cole survive this, Ian groaned internally, his own fingers scratching at his face. This was a raw, excruciating hell beyond his own capacity to survive. He couldn't imagine a child walking across the scorched earth, his burning skin strangely cooled by the thin, waxy goo that melted down cheekbones scarred by seeping wounds crudely patched together for a journey he was never meant to take.

Ian collapsed.

He buried his head in his hands, moaning loudly, letting his fear and exhaustion overcome the drive to save his son. He was blind, terrified, desperate to wake up from what he was sure was some kind of drug-induced stupor. This wasn't real. It couldn't be. And he wasn't alone in his desperation.

The agony tearing apart her mind nearly suffocated her. Whisper struggled to breathe, to put one foot in front of the other, to swallow back the biting nausea creeping into her throat. "*Vdadisdelvdi*," she whispered, her mouth moving slightly as the quiet words crawled up the rays of the Western Sun, praying to be led quickly into safety, into *Salvation*, into the Land of the Dead. She could feel her irises detaching from her eyes, remnants trickling down her cheeks as a white film coated her pupils, and even though she had known what to expect, nothing could ever prepare even the strongest of men and women for the Western Sun.

Whisper nearly gagged when the rope suddenly went taut and dug harshly into her gut. Her legs gave out and she tumbled to the ground, striking her knees against the cracked earth. Her breath all but heaved out of her as she turned, feeling her way back to Ian with her slender fingers lightly trailing the rough and slightly frayed rope.

"Mr. Daivya...you cannot fall behind." But even as she said the words, her own body threatened to give up.

"Whisper...." He couldn't say anything more through his parched throat, couldn't ask for help, couldn't find the strength to lift himself from the fiery earth, and even in his white blindness he could sense the mocking glare of the Western Sun. He hated being so helpless, and hated even more that his arrogant, smug, and self-righteous guide was witnessing his act of shame.

"*Itsula*. Together," she whispered in his ear, her words barely making it past the crackling, popping, and roaring rush of the sun. She locked an arm around his waist, and after a moment, he responded by reaching around her back and clasping her arm.

They pushed against one another, unsteadily rising to their feet. Their breath came out in raspy wheezes, their skin beginning to tighten and peel from the heat. They followed the pull of the sun, once nearly tripping over a fallen soul that had given up his hope for eternal salvation, choosing to spend the rest of his lonely eternity on the wrong side of the Western Sun. The lost soul reached out feebly, fingers grazing Ian's ankle, mouth stretched into a ghastly silent scream, eyes only seconds away from eternal blindness. In another time, another journey, Whisper would have reached out to the fallen, helped him make the last few steps. But now, now she could not let herself worry about those she was leaving behind. There were more important matters at hand.

And then, as if their prayers had been answered, the pain began to fade.

The force of the sun changed, a sensation only Whisper recognized. She loosened her hold on Ian and gently guided him toward the narrow portal just behind the Western Sun. As the bright light weakened ever so slightly, she made out what she could only describe as the slightest of fissures in the air, a black crevice set against the burning crimson and orange that, when she reached out to touch the gateway out of Waiting, was hard and cold as stone. With the faintest of smiles, she took Ian by the hand and guided him through.

In the last, briefest moments of painful sight, the fallen and lost soul doomed to timeless misery saw the two wavering black figures disappear behind the Western Sun, and into the Land of the Dead.

Whether by the magic of the Elder's dreamcatcher or the sheer exhaustion of the week-long search for her son, Julia awoke refreshed and hopeful after a sleep free of nightmares. She rolled over and stared up at the webbed gift hanging from the top of the tent. The dreamcatcher swayed in a light breeze that drifted in through the screen window, feathers twirling around one another in an elaborate dance of pleasant thoughts.

As she lay beneath the protective craft, Julia imagined her son, remembered the feel of his hugs, the sparkle of his big blue eyes, the sound of his voice. She missed him so much her heart broke every time someone said his name, and she prayed every single minute that he was still alive.

Both her son and husband had been missing now for a week. Cole was gone because he wandered too far from a safe area, and Ian was gone because Julia had pushed him away. She could admit to her own part of the blame in this mess. The coldness she had shown toward Ian, accusing him of being an irresponsible father, completely disregarding his own feelings—it was no surprise that he had gone into the woods to search for Cole, refusing to come home until he was found. Julia could respect that, but what bothered her still was that he hadn't gone alone.

The Elder was hiding something, of that much she was sure. He knew more, or his apprentice knew more, than he was letting on, but for some reason Julia trusted him. She didn't think he was working against them or would do something to hurt her son, but she also wouldn't bet on him telling her anything. Perhaps he was just a senile old man, or maybe he was something more. Either way, he was involved, and so was Whisper.

She hadn't yet told the sheriff about her visit to the Elder just days ago. Something was holding her back, but she didn't know what. A part of her was still waiting for Ian to come back, and another part was wondering how she could be so blind and naïve. Ian had gone into the woods with a beautiful young woman and hadn't been back for nearly seven days. Julia didn't care what Duff said. Her husband was successful, attractive, and charming, and downright irresistible when he wanted to be.

After getting dressed, Julia stepped out of the tent and was immediately ambushed by her parents, who shoved a plate of bacon and eggs in her face and insisted she sit down to eat. She allowed them to lead her to the picnic table and accepted the glass of orange juice that was offered.

Olivia, who had no more tears to cry and was simply exhausted by the entire ordeal, sat down next to her eldest daughter and rested a hand on her shoulder. "The fog's not as thick this morning." She hoped her words had some amount of comfort. "Ray Forbe seems to think that's a good sign. He's got a big search party out there right now."

Julia managed to swallow a mouthful of eggs, washing it down with the juice. "Maybe they'll find Ian out there."

Olivia and David exchanged a knowing glance. They'd discussed Ian's disappearance at length, chalking it up to what they figured to be a cheating husband. The two had suspected marital problems for a few months prior to the vacation, but hadn't said anything out of respect for their daughter's privacy. Now, they both found it a little odd that Ian had gone missing as well.

David, being the skeptical and tough military man that he was, had the nagging notion that the reason why Ian had been so eager to disappear into the woods was because he knew more about Cole's accident than he had admitted to on the first day. And as soon as he got a hold of his son-in-law, he was going to find out just what was going on.

There was the unpleasant fear in the back of his mind that Cole's disappearance was not the simple case of a child wandering off and getting lost. Having grown up in the Smoky Mountains, he was well aware of the dangers these woods posed. But at the same time, he was also aware of the stories that haunted the area—stories of children being led astray by mysterious spirits, stories of tribal members' families being ripped apart by white settlers, stories of vengeance, blood, and hate.

David held onto the stories for a long time. It was hard for him to admit, but there was a part of his childhood self that had never given up beliefs in ancient ways, perhaps because as a kid his grandpa had introduced him to Smoke Speaker's own grandfather, then a respected community legend. The old man, Wind Talker, had once told David that he was meant for great things, that his people needed a true believer to lead the white man back to the old ways. On that day, he also told David of the creatures that haunted the forests, beasts that once roamed the earth and were banished to other worlds by ancient shamans.

"Stories are what take care of us," Wind Talker had said to a small group of children at a secluded powwow. David and his grandfather had been the only white guests there. "Stories are what protect our souls from harm. If a story comes to you, you must cherish it, believe in it, live it. Without stories, our lives have no direction and no meaning. Our friend *Uguna*, Badger, the Keeper of Stories, has taught us that. Badger shows us how to fight with a warrior's bravery, and so with that courage we may have the strength to fight for the tales that make up our lives."

To come across such stories, to face the legendary creatures of history, was something David had nightmares about during his childhood years. More than once, he'd been sure those nightmares followed him during his waking hours, whispering and intruding into his thoughts. He'd all but convinced himself during college to put such foolish notions away, but now, being back in the Smoky Mountains, searching for his lost grandson, such thoughts couldn't be ignored.

Tucked away in his sanctuary at Howling Vines, Elder Smoke Speaker cupped his hands over a growing fire and sighed heavily. He was tired, worried, and depressed. Keeping up the shield of fog and rain took quite a toll on his old, creaking bones, and every second he fretted over Whisper's safety. He had woken from his dream just before seeing Whisper into her passage beyond the Western Sun, and he was yet to hear word from his scouts as to her arrival into the Land of the Dead. His dreams hadn't taken him that far, and she should have been there by now.

He needed her to be there.

When the smoke began to thicken, the Elder uttered a low chant, closing his eyes and reaching out to the spirit of a woman who owed him a favor, a woman he cared deeply for, one who had been a pleasant addition into his life. When he felt her presence, and she acknowledged his own, he spoke quickly and clearly.

His message was urgent.

Chapter 14

As though being blessed by the gods, the pain in his eyes began to fade and Ian was finally able to pull his hands away from his sunburned face. He felt rather than saw Whisper standing next to him, and by the change in her breathing from labored to relaxed, he knew that she too was grateful they had just made it past the scalding fire that liquefied their retinas.

"Our eyes will adjust," she told him, releasing the tight grip she had on his arm and taking a step forward. She waited impatiently, eager to see, eager to take in the true magnificence of the Western Sun.

The sudden sensation that spread across his eyes was both soothing and irritating. A relief from the burning, melting corneas that had dripped down his cheeks, a cool, watery film coated his eyes just as a tingling began to prickle at the corners. To Ian it felt like his retinas were being rebuilt with a hundred tiny chisels, a feeling similar to his foot falling asleep and slowly waking up again, but these little hammers didn't hurt. Instead, he just wanted to blink repeatedly in hopes to speeding up the process.

And Whisper was right. As soon as they stepped through the portal behind the Western Sun, the darkness that cloaked the Land of the Dead reached out with gentle fingers and healed the charred irises, the seared sight. Their blindness was temporary, but their vision had to be restored by the powers of the dead. Sight was not the same for the dead as it was for the living.

When the prickling sensation faded and the first rays of light passed through reconstructed eyes, a rare smile spread across Whisper's bronzed and peeling face. Oblivious to Ian's questioning expression, she turned to the sight formerly at her back and stood in wonder.

The Western Sun, once so harsh and uninviting, twisted and twirled in a wondrous mix of swirling red and purple hues, the colors dark and soft and offering a comforting warmth to the weary travelers. The roar that dominated the harsh side of the towering star had faded into a quiet murmur that mimicked the sound of babbling creeks. Thin shafts of crimson light arced out from the sun, spreading across the sky in a web of protection, while lavender tints lit the way throughout a no longer barren landscape.

"The Western Sun offers beauty, as well as pain," Whisper spoke quietly, sparing a second's glance at Ian when he too stood captivated. "It is rare to find sources of both comfort and chaos. This is the only beauty that the Land of the Dead will offer us in our journey."

Before Ian could reply, Whisper turned on her heel and walked away from the sun. As she strode forward, her movements smooth and confident and irresistibly sexy, she pulled her hair over her shoulder and began to undo the tight braid. When she did, Ian realized that the round, intricate tattoo spread across the center of her shoulders was an exact replica of the Western Sun. The lines that spun out from the red and black ink mirrored the grand display of magic and marvel before them.

Like some kind of portrait, he thought, following close enough to observe what could be seen around the edges of her shirt. If he was reading it right, then they were taking a short path, symbolized by a series of dotted lines, from the Western Sun to another wavy symbol that he guessed was a body of water.

"Whisper," he started, desperately wanting to know why the Land of the Dead was tattooed on her body, "What—"

"We shall cross there," Whisper interrupted, pointing, "and enter into the Land of the Dead."

Ian followed her finger. In the distance, some ten or fifteen miles away down a slight decline on the other side of a wood patch, was a river, a vague impression of the very same water that took his son's life. But here, the trees were darker, more depressing, leaves frayed but strong, trunks thick and firm and yet to be stripped of bark. The ground was covered with dirt, small patches of wilted grass popping up here and there where the underbrush had been pushed back by thousands of passing feet. There was color behind the Western Sun, but it was faded. In fact, everything, every hue, every plant, even the sky, was washed out, as though being viewed through a screen. Ian supposed that was because he hadn't yet adjusted to his new eyes.

They walked the long barren path flanked on either side by decaying trees in silence, each reflecting over the journey thus far, the trials and tribulations they had faced. Ian tried not to think about the pink flesh torn open across his back that rubbed itself even rawer against his shirt or the skin peeling on his face. Instead, he focused on gathering his wits and wondered how in the hell he had let himself get talked into this foolish fantasy. At his side, Whisper was contemplating the next obstacle in their path. She would have to be careful here, for the river held secrets she was not yet willing to reveal.

Not a single lost soul crossed their path as they hurried along, but Whisper wasn't bothered by the fact. Many got lost in the woods that bordered the river, and because the place to cross often changed, there was no one right spot to begin the journey. But she knew where to go. She always knew exactly where to place her feet.

When they finally approached the river after a long walk burdened by their exhausted bones, the water was calm, a ways down from the rapids that slowly churned over black rocks. Gray waves gently lapped over one another, and unlike the river in the living world, this one was vast and wide, stretching for miles beneath a red-lit sky. The darkness of the world and the fog that floated across the water hid the horizon across the way.

"How...how do we get across?" He was desperately hoping she wouldn't utter the word "swim."

Whisper pointed again. "The RiverKeeper."

Somehow, in his observation of his surroundings Ian had missed the figure standing not fifty feet away. An old man forever cursed with arthritic bones, filthy clothes, and work without rest was waiting on the shore, shin-deep in the cold water. His back was bowed; long and scraggly gray hair hung in his face, with frayed and frizzy ends dipping into the surface of the river. Tattered and rotting cloth hung from his bony frame. One hand tipped with splintered yellow fingernails was gripping a worn rope, the end of which was tied to a wooden boat floating an arm's length away. The boat was strangely crafted, approximately four feet long and five feet wide with a narrow railing, two benches on either side, and a post at the back that held two oars.

When Whisper and Ian came near, the RiverKeeper raised his head to reveal a long, bulky nose, thin lips that hid two rows of black, cracked teeth, and sunken cheeks further darkened by watery gray eyes. "You seek passage to the Land of the Dead," he rasped, his voice rough and tired. "Only two may cross."

Whisper glanced over her shoulder, slightly taken aback to see a third figure standing behind them. She was rarely caught off-guard and normally sensed people's presences, and attributed the mistake to fatigue.

When the stranger moved to take one of their places, Whisper grabbed Ian by the shirt-collar and all but shoved him onto the boat, which rocked dangerously as the RiverKeeper knocked the third figure away from the wooden raft with an oar. The dead soul cried out in pain and fell to its knees, feebly reaching for the boat as it drifted away.

"Only two?" Ian asked as the RiverKeeper took his position at the back of the craft and began the long row across the water. "What about when we need to get back...and Cole is with us? What do we do with three of us?"

Lifting an indifferent shoulder, Whisper settled onto one of the benches and leaned forward, resting her elbows on her knees and gingerly touching her flaking face. "Bribery is a lucrative trade in the Land of the Dead," she answered, rubbing her eyes tiredly.

"What do you have to trade?"

"Sanctuary," was her lone reply. Subconsciously, she touched the strange pouch tied to her belt, but Ian didn't push the matter. He knew she was worn down, part of which was his own fault, and she needed the time to relax.

"The Land of the Dead was not always a place of eternal darkness," Whisper said, staring down at the fractured wood of the boat. "Our legends say that it was once a place of peace, a safe haven for restless wanderers who managed to find their way to the Western Sun."

Taking a seat across from Whisper on the uncomfortable wood, Ian set down his pack and looked around, unable to imagine a world of peace and safety. This Land of the Dead promised curses and destruction around every corner, every tree, with each step further into the dark. As the ferry across the river was likely to be lengthy, he was eager to hear the story, pass the time.

"So...what happened?"

Whisper thought about all the Elder's lessons. Some stories she'd heard from him, others from old medicine men and keepers of legends at powwows. They varied from people to people, but tended to hold the same message.

Untying the rope that connected the two, the young woman considered the best way to proceed. It was a story that had to be told, but must be told carefully. One wrong word could mean the end to their journey, and to their lives.

"Our people lived peacefully for hundreds of years," she began, her Cherokee-accented voice reminding Ian of a spiritual pillar of infinite wisdom. "Then the white man came over with hate in his heart and greed in his soul, and massacred those who treasured the land. Murder, disease, religion...you too have heard the many ways they sought to destroy our culture." Ian nodded, remembering his history classes growing up. Blankets infected with smallpox, massacres at Wounded Knee, the injustices were infinite.

"There was a family who lived in the mountains," Whisper continued softly, her eyes glazed over as if she once knew those of whom she spoke. "The man was a power-ful shaman. People went to him for medicine, for spiritual purposes, for a better crop season. His wife was known as a quiet beauty, one who rarely spoke but was kind and gentle and loved the Earth. They had a son, who was being trained in his father's craft. The family was secluded and valued their privacy, and when the white man came and demanded they leave, they fought back." *So many fought back*, she thought bitterly as the RiverKeeper listened intently, rowing hard with a heavy heart, *and so many died*.

"The woman, Gentle Heart, and child, Fighting Fox, were murdered while they slept. The man, whose name is said to have been Sun Eagle, survived the attack, but the damage to his heart and mind was too great. Sun Eagle buried his family, set fire to his home and woods, and then ambushed a village in the dead of night. He slit the throats of sixty-seven sleeping men, women, and children and burned the village down before taking refuge in the mountains." There was no sympathy in her voice for the murdered villagers, and Ian felt a chill go down his back by the tone of her voice.

"Some say Sun Eagle's souls loosened from his body, others claim he simply swore revenge on the people who killed his family. Either way, he was a powerful medicine man, and he discovered a way to follow the settlers he murdered into the Land of the Dead, and wait for them when they arrived."

She paused, and Ian frowned, trying to wrap his mind around what she said. "What do you mean, he was already there? We both had to go through absolute hell to get here. So how could he—"

"Sun Eagle had a gift," Whisper interrupted, glancing at the RiverKeeper when he scoffed, but kept on rowing. "He had ways with medicine and herbs, and with spiritual matters. Perhaps he prayed to the Great Spirit, or found another way into the Western Sun. Such a story has never been told, and only he can tell it. But he found a way to the Land of the Dead. Sun Eagle sacrificed his life to fire, burned his body on a ceremonial pyre. And he took control of the Land of the Dead."

Shifting so that she could lean back and watch the red rays of light arch across the sky, Whisper idly scratched at the skin on her arms where the heat of the Western Sun had caused it to crack and peel. Ian couldn't take his eyes off his own storyteller, fascinated by a tale he still wasn't sure he believed.

"How could he take over?"

Whisper nearly rolled her eyes at his question. Apparently, he hadn't been listening very closely. "Sun Eagle was powerful beyond knowledge, Mr. Daivya. Not even Elder Smoke Speaker can fathom his abilities. But...while we cannot understand his power, we do know his actions, and they have had a terrible effect on the Land of the Dead."

"Sun Eagle had abandoned his souls but still longed to be with his family again. His wife and child had received a proper burial and were in the Spirit World, and because he killed himself in order to follow the dead settlers, Sun Eagle was trapped forever in the Land of the Dead. Hate and evil overcame him, and he vowed to punish all dead souls so they too could join him in his misery. Some say that he consumed the moon, so that darkness was cast upon the earth, and that he swallowed the ravens, so that the dead would be left to find their own way to the Western Sun."

At Ian's confused frown, she clarified her story. "Raven, *Golanv*, was once the guide to the dead. He met the dead soul at his place of death, and brought him to the Western Sun so he would never have to wander restlessly. When Sun Eagle destroyed Raven, the dead had no one but themselves."

Whisper stopped and took a few deep breaths before continuing. "Sun Eagle became known as the Raven-Eater. In his madness, he began searching for a wife. One day, many, many moons ago, a woman was out gathering firewood for her family's dinner, and he stole her from the earth."

"He killed her so that he could have a wife."

"No." Whisper shook her head and shared a sad look with Ian. "He stole her, and locked her away. He took her from her world and brought her to the Land of the Dead, a living person in a sea of dead. Many say she is still alive, fed a special diet, because the living cannot survive on the food of the dead, and is forbidden from ever seeing her loved ones."

"And did he steal a child?" Ian asked. He waited, but she didn't answer. Instead, she slowly lifted her eyes to meet his, and her stare was knowing, reluctant, patient. There was an awkward silence, both Whisper and the RiverKeeper waiting for the realization to sink in.

"What?" Ian continued, looking from face to face and wondering why the hunchbacked old man knew the story behind Whisper's silence and he didn't. "I don't understand. Why won't you tell me if he stole a—"

And then it hit him. Ian jumped to his feet, causing the boat to lurch sideways and nearly knock him off balance. Whisper merely set her feet firmly on the floor and prepared for his fury.

"You...you're saying that this raven-eating psycho has my son?" Ian shouted, pointing into the distance. Whisper sat forward and let Ian fume. "My son is *dead* because some other kid was murdered more than two hundred years ago? You have *got* to be kidding me!"

Ian paced the narrow length of the boat, avoiding the RiverKeeper's gaze. Nausea was creeping up his throat, his stomach was in knots, and his heart had all but stopped.

If his guide was right, and her stories were accurate, then Cole was in the company of a vengeful spirit that demanded death.

"But wait." Ian spun around and pointed at Whisper, who recoiled slightly and waited for him to put the rest of the pieces together. "You knew he wanted a child. You knew all along. You knew the reason why Cole was missing...but you said he was dead." Whisper's brow furrowed at the statement. "What if this Sun Eagle took Cole alive, like he did his wife? Then we don't have to worry about finding him before his body is found. Right?"

"No, Mr. Daivya...no. Cole is dead," Whisper affirmed. "Yes, the Raven-Eater did take him. Yes, I knew. I have known for many years of his plan. He has tried to take children from the mountains for many moons. The mountains were his home, and so that is where he searches. For the winters before I came to him, Smoke Speaker took on the burden of rescuing the children the Raven-Eater attempted to trick into death, and then he trained me. Raven-Eater is a trickster, luring children into the woods to meet their end. He will not take them alive, as he did the woman, because he desires an heir. The heir to the Land of the Dead cannot be of the living. He craved a living wife, however, for the feel of a warm body, the touch of a pulse, some semblance of the one he lost."

"OK." Ian could accept that. "But if you were able to find all the other boys before they died, why couldn't you find Cole?"

"It was too late for your son, and so I offered you a way to save him."

"OK." He could accept that as well, and though he wasn't feeling any better, Ian sat back down and ran his filthy hands through even filthier hair. He took a few moments to calm his nerves, and was glad that his guide was so even-tempered. She balanced him out. She hated him, but balanced him nonetheless. "So...Cole's...the Raven-Eater...I don't know...I guess....Hell, can I ask you a personal question?"

"Yes."

"Why don't you like me?" The question came out wrong, making him sound like a seventh-grade boy in puppy love with the cute girl from homeroom, and embarrassed him completely.

Whisper observed the man curiously. "Why do you think I do not like you, Mr. Daivya?"

Ian huffed and gave Whisper a fatherly look of sarcasm. "Oh, please. You refuse to say my first name, you treat me like a pile of dog crap you just stepped in, and besides the fact that we're here for my son, you seem to want nothing to do with me."

Toying with a strand of sleek black hair, the tattooed young woman pressed her lips together and found it interesting that her traveling companion would even bother to ask such a question.

"I do not call you by your first name, Mr. Daivya," she began coolly, "because you are my Elder, and I was taught to respect my Elders. Only Elders that are friends are called by their first names. However, while I respect your place as my Elder, I find it hard to respect you as a person, or as a father."

"Why?"

Whisper thought back to the first time she met Ian Daivya. How long ago that was, she didn't know. Two days, two weeks, two years, time was different in the Land of the Dead. "Do you remember when we searched the river, the first day in the woods?"

"When you sliced open your hand?"

"Yes." Whisper glanced down at her hand, gently touching the thin scar spread across her palm. "When I asked about the fate of your son, I was met with conflicting answers. Some, the whispers that traveled the wind from the Land of the Dead, guided me here. Others spoke of you unkindly."

"Others like who?"

"A tiny creature came to me, Mr. Daivya, known as the cowbird, a black bird with a brown head, a bird that looks to others to raise its young, leaving its eggs in the nests of another to be reared at the cost of the stranger's offspring. The cowbird is representative of abandonment, the need to face responsibilities. It speaks to your failures as a father, as a man, and as a respectable human being. You have much to prove, Mr. Daivya, if you wish to save your son."

Ian blew out a breath. If he'd thought he was embarrassed by his question, then he didn't know what to call the emotion created by the answer. No one, not even his wife, had ever made him feel so small, and the fact that he actually felt bad slightly angered him. He didn't like that Whisper had that kind of power over him, could make him question himself. Oh, yes, he would prove whatever he had to prove to the woman, and she would learn to respect him.

Whisper understood Ian's silence to be that of uncertainty, shame, and resentment, just as she had expected. But she couldn't be bothered by his emotional shortcomings. There were bigger things to worry about.

"May I ask you a personal question, Mr. Daivya?"

"Go for it."

"Why did your son die?"

Ian sighed and lowered his head. He didn't see the way the RiverKeeper paused just long enough to shoot Whisper a warning glare, and didn't see her smirk and narrow her eyes in response. "Cole was always a curious kid, always had lots of questions and if you didn't give him an answer he liked, he'd go off and find it on his own. He swore up and down he saw a ghost the first day we arrived at the campground, and my guess is he went looking for it when we were at the park." He never would have thought Cole would go on a ghost hunt, but then again, he didn't really know his son all that well.

"He must have fallen into the river. He's not a very good swimmer, and is afraid of the pool we have at home. I'm not sure why. But I guess it doesn't matter. If what you said is true, then he didn't stand a chance anyway. That Raven-Eater was determined to get him."

When he was finished, Whisper nodded slowly, chewing on her bottom lip. She could feel the dry, blistered skin on her face crack with each movement, and was pleased that Ian's flesh was worse than her own. "Well then, Mr. Daivya, I suppose the matter is settled." She lowered herself to the floor of the small wooden ferry, lying back and placing her coat behind her head. "You should rest. The river is the only peaceful part of our journey."

Although he wanted to ask why she didn't seem pleased with his answer, Ian relented and leaned back against the railing. He wasn't going to argue with the need to rest.

Chapter 15

Somewhere deep inside the magnificently sinister mountain of winding halls and dark caverns that housed the Raven-Eater and his infinite army, Cole Daivya sat huddled against a grimy wall, clutching his skinned knees to his chest and shivering.

He wasn't cold, though. He was terrified.

It was his fault he was there, trapped in a small oval room filled with old bones and smelly piles of black goo. He was in that room because he had misbehaved, had sassed the two guards who were hurting his arms when they carried him up the stairs to the tower, but he had been brought to the tower because he hadn't listened to his mother and father.

It was supposed to be an adventure, searching through the woods for the ghost he was absolutely positive he saw. If he could prove there were ghosts at the campground, then he could have believed in them, and done research on them when he got home. He loved research, and learning new things. The ghost had been there, just beyond the edge of the playground, and since his dad wasn't paying attention, it had seemed like a good time to go on his adventure. The ghost, a little boy ghost that laughed and danced and played in the fallen leaves, led him to the river, where he floated across the water and beckoned for his new friend to follow.

Cole was afraid of the water, but the rocks had formed a path across the river that looked easy to navigate. Plus, it didn't look too deep, so if he fell then surely he could have made it to the shore. But his foot slipped, and he had plunged into the icy water. The shock of the cold had stolen his breath straight from his lungs, and his head dunked underwater. Beneath the surface, frantically clawing at water, Cole had felt his body rushing down, slamming against rocks and logs. His leg jammed in the crevice of one rock, his body trapped under the surface. He remembered looking up through the waves to see the blurred image of the ghost staring down at him sadly, and suddenly pain and fear overcame him, and he lost the fight.

Then he surfaced into a world of gray, and nothing was the same ever again.

Two figures that Cole thought looked like the bad guys from *The Lord of the Rings*, except they were taller with black skin that oozed white pus, were waiting for him. Without speaking, they each grabbed one of Cole's arms and dragged him away, ignoring the boy's screams, his cries, his desperate questions and pleading wishes to go home.

Without stopping, they marched across the Bridge of the Dead and into the Western Sun, oblivious to his agonizing wails as his eyes melted. And then, when on the steps of the Fire Tower, Cole had found the strength and courage to kick one of the guards in the shin, and trip the other. His actions did not go unpunished.

Picking himself up off the floor, Cole dusted off his hands and wiped at his eyes and tear-stained cheeks. He wanted to go home. His clothes were dirty and torn and his shoes had fallen off a long time ago. His hair was caked with dirt and he was covered with scratches. But he didn't care what he looked like. He just wanted to be with his mom and dad again.

What frightened him the most was that he didn't know where he was. He remembered falling into the river and wondered if he had died and this was where people went when they were dead. But if that was the truth, then where was everyone else? Besides the two guards, Cole had only seen one other person, and the man who came to the doorway of the dungeon room filled the boy's nightmares and turned his blood to ice.

The terrible man stood in the doorway for only a short time before nodding. "He will do," he had said, his voice so deep and booming that it sounded like thunder rolling across the black sky. Then he had disappeared, and the guards stood watch so that he couldn't escape.

Dragging himself over to the lone window no bigger than a box of crackers, Cole peered out at the vast, strange land. He was high above the ground, looking down on treetops, small mountains, and the edge of a valley. Animals that Cole couldn't identify were wandering about, and villages filled with people were spread all around way off in the distance. He longed to be with those people, but any sign of life was so far away that he doubted anyone ever came close to the tower. They were smarter than that.

Suddenly the door opened, and Cole's knees buckled in fear. He braced himself against the wall, eyes widening when a woman stepped through.

"Hello, my son," she said tenderly, her voice calm and soothing and reminding the child of the classical music his mother liked to play. She kneeled down in front of him. "My name is Gentle Heart. I am your mother."

Cole stared at the woman with disgust. She was pretty, with long black hair filled with beads and feathers that hung down to her hips, soft brown eyes, and a kind smiling mouth. She wore a tan dress with red stitching across the front and down the sides, and her wrists, neck, and ankles were decorated with glorious jewels. But he didn't care that she was pretty, or that she looked nice.

"You aren't my mommy," he spat out violently. "My mommy has green eyes and brown hair and doesn't wear dresses. You're a stranger."

Gentle Heart smiled sadly, understanding his hate. "My little Fighting Fox, I am your mother now. You must accept that."

"No! And my name is Cole! Cole Daivya!"

She once had another name as well, one that she fought hard to keep. But in time she was defeated, and Gentle Heart became her soul. "Sweet child, this is your life now. Behave, my little Fighting Fox, and you will be rewarded."

Instead of answering, Cole crossed his arms and stepped away from the stranger. He didn't want to listen, and Fighting Fox was a stupid name anyway. Who wanted to be a wimpy little fox? He wanted no part of it.

Gentle Heart rose and offered the boy a bundle of cloth. "These are for you, a gift. I hope you'll like them. I will come back later with food."

Cole waited until the door closed behind her, then kicked the clothes across the room.

It seemed like a lifetime before they reached the opposite shore. Whisper slept the majority of the way, lost in a dreamless sleep free of the worries that burdened her shoulders when awake, but Ian was cursed with restlessness. He couldn't get his mind off of Cole, off the story of Sun Eagle or Raven-Eater or whatever he was called now. More, he still couldn't figure out how he was even there, on a ferry being oared across the river by an ancient, gray-haired man with rotted teeth.

When they were within mere feet of the shore, the RiverKeeper slid down into the dark water and pulled the craft through the mud, steadying the boat so that his passengers could exit safely. Whisper waited until Ian had stepped onto the shore before rising. She stretched, gathered her packs, and turned her eyes to the old man when she passed.

"Why are you here, *Kanegv?*" The RiverKeeper's hoarse question was more accusatory than curious. "There is no hope in the Land of the Dead."

Whisper glanced over her shoulder at Ian, who was watching them intently but far enough away to miss what was being said. "There is always hope, RiverKeeper," she replied softly, "for those who demand it."

"You know I cannot ferry him back across the river. There are rules in the Land of the Dead, *Kanegv.*"

"We all have a price, RiverKeeper." Whisper leaned close and shifted so that her back was to Ian. The black clouds appeared to float down and cast her eyes in gloom, shadowing her face with an evil aura when she met his stare. "Yours has been named before."

The RiverKeeper curled his lips in a callous sneer, his homely face contorting into a visage of conniving comprehension. "What could that miserly man possibly have to offer?"

Lifting a finger to her lips to illustrate the need for secrecy, knowing she could trust his silence only because he would want the offer for himself, Whisper lowered herself so that she was nearly nose-to-nose with the cursed old man.

"He will be carrying with him the blood of the half-breed."

Her quiet, slowly-spoken words filtered through his ears and brought back memories of a promise made to him so many years ago. The RiverKeeper's brooding black eyes lit up, widening just enough to show his interest. He turned and sloshed through the mud and water, climbing back onto the ferry with cracking bones. When he had settled in his place, gripping the splintered oars tightly, he offered a final look at Whisper.

"Perhaps there is hope after all, *Kanegv*...for those who demand it."

Whisper watched the RiverKeeper until he had disappeared into the dark fog, praying to Creator that the bribe would be enough, and believing it would be. Approaching her side, Ian attempted to read her lips, as the whispers passing them were unable to reach his ears.

"What did you say to him?" he asked, gazing through the fog at the blurred outline of the ferry. The RiverKeeper gave him the creeps.

"I secured passage back across the river."

"Why would you need to do that?"

Whisper shrugged, not in the mood for another history lesson. "The RiverKeeper ferries souls to the Land of the Dead, Mr. Daivya. He is bound by the law of the Raven-Eater to keep the souls from returning."

"Then how do we get back?"

"We all have a price," she repeated, "even in death."

Chapter 16

Taking a deep breath and mentally preparing herself, Whisper shouldered her pack, secured her bow, and headed away from the river. Ian, again irritated by her frustrating coyness, fell in step behind her, touching a finger to his scarred face. His wounds were healing fast, and he hoped that was because injuries healed quicker in the Land of the Dead instead of the alternative, that they had been there a lot longer than it seemed. The thought of Julia being left all alone, searching for her son, wondering where her husband had gone, was too much to bear.

Then again, he mused, she probably thought he had gone into the woods with Whisper for some quality alone-time with the beautiful stranger. That was more like Julia, to assume the worst about her husband, and that fact lessened some of the guilt about leaving her to fend for herself. As far as he was concerned, he wouldn't have to sneak away into the woods if she showed any interest at home.

The woods opened up into a spacious clearing, trees and underbrush cut back in a lengthy and wide rectangular shape. Crudely made constructions, some in the shape of huts and others taking on an appearance of old-fashioned longhouses, lined the edges of the clearing. Thick logs were tethered together with strong straps of sinew, topped with dried fronds, the ends of which flapped quietly in the light breeze. Windows and doorways were cut out of the wood, covered by pieces of cloth. The houses were spaced just far enough apart to allow room for vegetable gardens in between each one—food gardened by the dead and meant only for the dead to eat. At one end of the clearing was a fenced-in patch of grass, where creatures that Ian couldn't identify were grazing contently, and at the other end was a small but clean pool of water, where three women sat washing their clothes.

The ground was pure dirt without a hint of grass, and as he walked across it, Ian heard, for the first time since he had died, a sound that was both eerie yet welcoming—that of a child's laughter. He turned to the source and watched a little girl no older than five race around a fire pit while a small gray dog chased after her. Sitting in the doorway of a hut, dressed in a long, faded dress, was a young woman with short blond hair, smiling as she kept an eye on her daughter.

Had he asked, Ian would have learned that they had been violently murdered by a serial killer seventy-three years ago, their bodies buried deep in the earth behind a junkyard in rural Texas. Had he of gotten close enough, he would have seen the savage scars across their throats and chests. Not having received the proper burial, they were cursed into the Land of the Dead, forever separated from their family. But they had found a new family here, among men and women who understood their pain and loneliness, and the longer they resided in that clearing, the more they all came to see one another as their own blood, traces of their old life drifting away.

This was a village of dead but happy souls. They walked freely and calmly across the plaza, tended to their gardens, chatted amongst friends. There were no obligations to fret about, no schedules, simply all the time in the world. For Ian, idle time was boring, useless, and frustrating, but these souls seemed to enjoy the freedom away from the stresses of the living.

"*Kanegv!*"

Whisper turned, the briefest of smiles flashing across her face as she embraced the woman who approached. "Annabelle," she greeted, holding the older woman by the arms and touching her forehead with her own. They took a silent moment to themselves, each recalling memories of life in the living world. It was rare to hear her true name spoken so lovingly, and Whisper enjoyed the sound.

"It has been too long." Then she moved so that Ian could meet her. "Mr. Daivya, this is Annabelle, a close friend of Elder Smoke Speaker. She used to live in town, and made sure we were cared for during the rough winter months."

Ian shook Annabelle's hand when she offered it, his mind going over the chances of meeting with a dead soul Whisper and the Elder knew in the Land of the Dead. Slim to none, was his guess, unless something fishy was going on.

The woman looked trustworthy, though, and kind, if not a bit frumpy. She was short, with close-cropped brown hair, a large smile, and almond-shaped eyes. The thick buckskin dress she wore didn't do much to hide her wide hips and thick legs, and her bare feet were filthy.

"Scuba-diving," Annabelle said when Ian merely stared.

"I'm sorry?"

"I made a silly mistake, and it cost me my life. I went scuba-diving without a partner and ran out of air before I could make it back to the surface. The last thing I remember is thinking about my dear, sweet husband and how I'd never see him again."

Annabelle wiped at a tear and sniffled. "I was only thirty-eight, Mr. Daivya, and I wasn't ready to go. But I haven't forgotten my loved ones, including the Elder and this little firecracker over here." She playfully ran a hand through Whisper's hair, and Ian was shocked when his guide let her do so.

"How long has it been, *Kanegv?*"

"Seven years."

"That long?" Annabelle still remembered her old life as freshly as if she had just died yesterday. Unlike the others, she refused to let go, and it saddened her to think that she had been away from her loved ones for seven years. And unlike other dead souls, she was yet to find peace with her death. "Well...no use being bothered over such things, right? Whisper, I have a message from the Elder. He says it is urgent."

The relaxed look on Whisper's face tightened into one of distress. "What does he say?"

Annabelle hesitated, casting a sidelong glance at Ian. "The Elder wished only for you to hear the message." Whisper nodded. "Ian, my home is just over there, the one with the little clay pot outside the door. You may set your things inside, and have a bite to eat."

It bothered him that he was being deliberately kept out of the loop, but there was no sense arguing, and Annabelle waited until he had ducked inside her home to continue. She faced the young woman she had known for nearly fifteen years, not at all fazed by those dark eyes and intense stare.

"Smoke Speaker says you must hurry," Annabelle said quickly. "He says that he fears his age is catching up with him, because he cannot hold the fog much longer. I'm not sure what that means, but hopefully you do."

The news fell like a jagged rock in the pit of her stomach. "...Is he safe?"

"Yes, but he says that Ian's wife is suspicious, and that he fears the police may come back. He says you must finish your journey as quickly as possible, Whisper, because there isn't much time. Not as much as you both thought."

"Did he mention the safest route to get there?"

"Yes." Annabelle reached out for her friend's hand. "He says he will do his best to provide you with guides along the way, but you must travel west, through the Weeping Forest and find a woman there from the Deer Clan who will be waiting for you. He didn't know her name. Whisper...you must go to the base of the Fire Mountains. And cross the Barren Plains."

Inside the hut, Ian lowered himself to a floor made of thin but tightly-woven vines that had been flattened for comfort. Clay pots decorated with pictures of animals and nature were stacked in each corner, but the tree-log walls were bare. Along the wall adjacent to where Ian was sitting was a small straw bed, and a hole had been cut out in the center of the hut's roof to allow for smoke to pass through. A fire hearth had been built in the middle of the floor, where a clay bowl filled with a mushy green substance was cooking. It looked disgusting and smelled like a mixture of turnip greens, fresh fish, and cabbage, but it made his mouth water.

Suddenly ravenous for the strange concoction, Ian leaned over the bowl and stirred the green pottage with the wooden spoon resting next to the hearth. He remembered something Whisper had said about food being different for the dead, and she must have been right, because he never would have even considered eating whatever was in the bowl when he was alive.

"Crota."

Ian turned to see Whisper and Annabelle duck into the hut and fasten the cloth door on a hook behind them. "I'm sorry?"

"It's called Crota." Annabelle picked up three wooden plates and spooned generous helpings on each. "Our vegetables here are a bit different than you're used to."

"Obviously."

"Eating is a necessity in life," Whisper offered her own bit of information as she accepted the plate from her old friend. "In death, it is a luxury, even in this dark place. The dead do not need to eat, but it does give one a sense of humanity. That is one thing the Raven-Eater has not yet taken away."

Cautiously, Ian lifted the bowl and sniffed. His stomach growled in response. He didn't hear Annabelle's pleased laughter when he devoured the food, and thoroughly enjoyed every bite.

When dinner was over, Annabelle rose to her feet and gathered the plates. "Well, you two, I'm off. I'll be visiting with my friend just across the plaza tonight. Have a good night."

"You do not need to leave, Annabelle."

"My dear, this hut is barely big enough for me, let alone three grown people...and you two need your rest. And Whisper, could I have a word with you?"

Whisper followed Annabelle out of the hut and guided her behind the home, where they could have a bit of privacy. "What is it, Annabelle?" she asked, concerned by the sad look on the woman's face.

Annabelle shuffled from foot to foot. "Whisper, I wanted to ask about…well, about my Joe. He must be…almost fifty now." She sighed heavily, remembering her beloved husband. "He was so good to me, Whisper. He made me so happy. I laughed every day with him."

"You were a wonderful couple."

"Yeah, well…"Annabelle took in a deep breath. "I was just wondering…and I probably shouldn't even ask this…but did Joe ever remarry?" She knew it was a terrible question, for if the answer were in the affirmative she surely would be miserable for the rest of eternity. Whisper only frowned and lowered her eyes to the ground. She didn't want to answer, didn't want to break the heart of a woman who was so good to her and Smoke Speaker.

"Whisper? He did, didn't he? Whisper, you can tell me….did he?"

"No, he never took another wife," Whisper said quietly, shaking her head slightly, regretting what she was about to say. "Annabelle…Joe passed away two years ago. He was hit by a car on the way to work. He is…he is in the Spirit World."

Whisper wasn't prepared for Annabelle to drop to her knees at the news. She stood before her old friend, startled, as the distraught woman began to weep, covering her face with dirt-stained hands. Grief racked her body as she rocked back and forth.

"My Joe," she cried softly in between sobs. "He…was…so young…I always hoped…prayed…we would meet here." Through a glaze of tears, she peered up at the young woman who had never been known to shed a single tear. "I'll never see him again, will I? I'll never see my Joe?"

Although she didn't completely understand love and all the emotions that came with it, Whisper could feel the pain that vibrated off the grieving woman in tumultuous waves. It was a deep pain, one that clutched her heart and filled her head with confusing murmurs that spun around one another in a bewildering dance of sensation. It was too much for one person to bear, and the whispers in the dark that slammed against one another inside her head was enough to make her press a hand to her forehead and squeeze her eyes shut in defiance of the emotions.

"Annabelle."

Whisper shook her head to clear her confused mind and lowered herself to her friend's level, resting a gentle hand on her shoulder. "I can offer you a place in the Spirit World, so that you may be with your loved one."

Annabelle sniffled and raised her head. Hope and guilt tore at her. "I…I can't ask for that, Whisper. That gift is not meant for me."

"It is mine to give, and I choose you," Whisper replied softly but firmly, relieved when the grief swirling in her head began to fade. "You were kind to me in the living world, and kind to Elder Smoke Speaker. I have never forgotten all you did for us, and now the favor shall be returned."

A place in the Spirit World was something Annabelle could not imagine. Seven years in the Land of the Dead had stripped her thoughts of any spiritual world greater than the place of dark skies with a red and purple sunset. But Joe, Joe she remembered. Her dreams were filled with images of his tall, lanky frame, his thick brown hair that curled at his ears, his bright green eyes that sparkled in the sun. And his voice, so deep with just the slightest hint of a southern accent, met her ears every morning in greeting. He had been her entire life.

Annabelle watched as Whisper reached down and untied the pouch at her waist. Faith, something she hadn't felt in a long, long time, tingled in her belly. She listened closely when the young Cherokee woman whispered a prayer, but couldn't comprehend the meaning. Annabelle had learned some of the language from the Elder, but not much more than a few phrases here and there.

"*Kanegv*." Annabelle stopped her by closing a hand over Whisper's own that was clutching the pouch. "You must tell him the truth."

"He will know…when the time is right."

"Whisper…." Annabelle wanted to argue, to emphasize the importance of honesty, especially when lives were at stake. But she stopped when Whisper reached into the pouch and produced a pinch of gold dust. Her eyes widened at the sight of such brilliant, sparkling color that shone against the dark of the Land of the Dead.

Whisper lifted her hand, offering Annabelle one final smile. "*Didayolihvdvgalenisgv, unalii*."

"Goodbye, my friend," Annabelle whispered back, closing her eyes. "*Wado*."

Just as a light breeze traveled in from the east, a sign of new life for the deceased, Whisper blew the golden dust over Annabelle. It shimmered and flickered across her body, surrounding her in a cocoon of pale light. The dead soul shimmered life, an essence of redemption and sanctuary, as her feet rose from the ground, lifting her in a golden sphere. And then she disappeared from the Land of the Dead.

"You're welcome," Whisper answered to the air, her lone reply traveling the wind.

When Whisper returned to the hut, Ian's face was full of questions. She turned her back to him to avoid his gaze and instead settled down onto Annabelle's straw bed.

She wasn't tired, but the incredible sensation of feeling Annabelle's grief and hearing her agonizing thoughts weakened her soul, and that was something that had never happened before.

"Everything alright?" Ian asked cautiously.

Whisper laid back and covered her eyes with an arm. "We will rest for a short time, and then continue."

He hated her answers. Just about every one she offered told him absolutely nothing, and he wasn't sure if that was simply how she was, or if she refused to tell him anything because she held no respect for him.

It may help, he thought as he spooned another bowlful of Crota, *to get to know her a little*.

"So…why do you live with Smoke Speaker?"

Whisper lifted her arm just long enough to shoot Ian a cautious glance. "What do you mean, Mr. Daivya?"

Ian swallowed a mouthful of the delicious food and hoped that when he returned to the living world he would remember the splendid taste. "I mean, why don't you live with your parents?"

"My father treated me terribly."

"What about your mom?"

"She was weak."

"Oh…so where does the Elder come in?"

"He took me away when I was young, and brought me to the mountains where I would be safe."

She spoke without any emotion, he thought. She didn't seem affected by her past, or concerned about being taken away. Either she had accepted being an orphan long ago, to parents who may or may not have been dead, in prison, or searching for their lost daughter, or there was something she wasn't telling him. Regardless, Ian felt for her. It was unfair for a child to be forced to grow up without the guidance of a mother and father, or at least one of the two.

"Do you remember your mother?"

"A bit."

"Any siblings?"

"No."

Her cryptic, nonchalant answers told him she wasn't well-accustomed to small talk. Ian observed her for a moment. Lying on the bed with her face half-covered, she didn't move a muscle. The only sign of life was the rise and fall of her chest as she breathed. Her black hair was spread all around her, pants ripped at the knees, boots muddy. Her forearms and shoulders were covered with scratches that matched his own, evidence of their venture through the woods. With her arm lifted and a hole torn into the side of her shirt along her ribs, he saw the word *Gohiyudi* inked in her flesh.

Ian finished the helping of Crota and set the bowl aside, lying down next to the warm fire and placing a bulky blanket beneath his head. "So…you got a boyfriend back home? Husband…Girlfriend?"

Whisper scoffed, slightly amused. "No."

"Any prospects?"

"No."

"Too busy saving little kids from a raven-eating bastard, huh?"

Baffled by his sudden interest in her life, Whisper uncovered her eyes and rolled onto her side. Ian was peering back at her with what she judged to be genuine interest, and she was willing to speak freely with the man if he was willing to forgo arrogance.

"Some things are not meant for everyone, Mr. Daivya. Love was not meant for me."

She said it matter-of-factly, so Ian knew it wasn't a declaration made for pity. "Why would you say that?"

Whisper shrugged indifferently. "Love clouds the mind with matters of the heart. I vowed to become the Elder's apprentice, and so I must remain focused."

"Yeah, but…doesn't that get lonely?"

"Loneliness is for those who refuse to see the world around them, Mr. Daivya. My life has not been empty. I have had the Elder, and friends like Annabelle. I have the creatures of the earth, those who accept who and what I am without prejudice."

It sounded like an excuse to Ian, and there was something in her voice, the slightest hint of wistfulness, that made him think she was lying even to herself. He knew that every woman wanted to be loved, no matter who raised them, what future they were being trained for, or their ability to speak to the wind, and this one was no different.

"Well, I think you're missing out," Ian said in a tone reminiscent of a father speaking to a daughter. "You should be open to love. Love makes your life worth living."

Whisper's eyes narrowed at his hypocrisy, but her irritation was soothed by his genuine concern. "If you have been granted a life filled with love, Mr. Daivya, then you should cherish it, and fight for those who hold your heart."

She was calling him out, and he knew it, but because he refused to admit defeat he merely waved a hand in her direction. "You're still young, Whisper. You have plenty of time. Hell, I've got a guy who works for me about your age, good guy, working through med school. I'll have him give you a call."

There was sadness tugging at the corners of her heart, but she ignored it and lay back down. "You should rest, Mr. Daivya. We have quite a walk ahead of us."

Chapter 17

This time they would get answers.

Sheriff Ray Forbe, Deputy Duff, and Julia and her sister stalked through the woods to Howling Vines. The men were determined to uncover the truth behind Cole's disappearance, while the women were devising a plan of their own.

The two camps, the police on one side and the family of the missing child on the other, had subconsciously divided themselves over the past few days as suspicions intensified and hope waned. The police had decided that Ian Daivya and Whisper were accomplices in the death of Cole Daivya, while Julia had come to suspect that they were off on a search mission of their own, with the Elder leading the quest. It had been two weeks since Cole disappeared, and many of the volunteers had given up and gone home. The police and local townspeople had done their best to keep the story quiet, as none wanted the national media sniffing around for a lead, but once Forbe formerly declared Ian a suspect, he knew all hell would break loose.

When they reached Howling Vines, the clearing was unoccupied. The fire, set in a stone hearth, was burning low with a cooked rabbit propped over the heat, and the hide that covered the opening to the hut was fastened shut. Everything was still and quiet, eerily so.

"Elder?" Forbe strode over to the fire, where the Elder usually rested. "Smoke Speaker! We need to talk!"

"You need not shout, Mr. Forbe." Forbe spun around as Elder Smoke Speaker stepped out of his hut, letting the hide fall into place behind him. His voice was heavy with sleep; he stretched as he came over to the foursome. He sat at his fire and stoked the embers with a long stick. "What may I do for you?"

Forbe squatted and glared at the Elder over the fire. "I want to know everything you know about Cole Daivya."

"The missing child?"

"Yes, the missing child," Forbe answered impatiently. Julia and Lisa backed away, not wanting the sleepy Elder to think they were any part of the officer's rant. "I want to know where Ian Daivya and Whisper are, where they went, why they went there, and what you know about the child's disappearance."

"I know what your workers have told me."

He didn't believe the old man. "Where is your apprentice?"

Smoke Speaker sighed. "I have not seen Whisper since the day she took Mr. Daivya into the woods." Even though he was telling the truth, he could read the disbelief in Forbe's face. "If you see them, please tell Whisper that she is needed. My garden is suffering in her absence."

Forbe muttered a curse to himself, not at all amused by his attempt at misdirection. "Elder, this isn't a game. If you can't tell me where Whisper and Ian are, and if you can't produce any evidence that they had nothing to do with Cole's disappearance, then I have no choice but to put them on my list of suspects."

A flicker of anger sparked in the old man's eyes. "You would accuse *Kanegv* of murdering or kidnapping a child? A woman who has saved your officers from the troubles of several missing children over the years? For all my apprentice has done for this community, you would disgrace her good name to cover your own incompetence."

"This is not about her name, Elder. This is about the life of a little boy."

Smoke Speaker ignored Forbe and turned his furious glare to Duff, who was standing a few feet behind his boss. "And do you also feel this way, Mr. Duff?"

Hesitating, Duff shuffled his feet and cleared his throat nervously. He'd never seen the Elder angry, didn't know he was even capable of such ferocity. "I...yes, sir, I do."

"Hmm," was all Smoke Speaker said in reply.

Irritated, Forbe straightened and put his hands on his hips. "Elder, I'm going to need to search your home and these grounds."

"No."

"Excuse me?"

Smoke Speaker tossed a handful of herbs into the fire, and white smoke billowed up from the embers. "I may be an old man who holds on to old ways, Mr. Forbe, but I am not a foolish old man who holds on to foolish old ways. I know my rights, and I do not give you permission."

"Fine." He all but spit the word out. "I'll be back, Smoke Speaker, and I'll be back with a warrant."

"Until then, Mr. Forbe." The Elder got a little kick of pleasure out of the sheriff's frustration, but he was troubled by the words of the other. "Mr. Duff," he called quietly, waiting until the younger man turned around. "I pray that you find peace with your betrayal."

Rendered speechless, Duff couldn't meet the Elder's eyes, and instead started his walk of shame out of the clearing. Forbe started to follow. "Mrs. Daivya, let's go."

"That's all right. I'm going to stay here for a bit."

Forbe stopped and glared at the woman. He was in no mood for games. "Mrs. Daivya, it isn't safe for you here."

Julia stood her ground. "We're fine, Sheriff. We'll be along shortly, I promise."

After Forbe had stalked out of the clearing, still muttering beneath his breath, Julia faced the Elder. "I have some questions for you."

"Are you of the same mind as the men?"

"No."

"Then please, join me." Julia and Lisa lowered themselves to the ground on the other side of the fire. Smoke Speaker set the rabbit on a wooden plate and began to remove the meat with knobby fingers.

"Elder, this is my younger sister, Lisa Bard." Julia hoped to gain the Elder's trust by showing her love for family. "She has helped out a lot these past couple of weeks."

"Elder," Lisa greeted with a charming smile that her older sister recognized as flirtatious and playful. She ran her fingers through her long hair and batted her lashes. "Your necklace is beautiful. I bought one from an old woman about four years ago at a powwow in Oklahoma. She made beautiful jewelry."

Few things truly ruffled Smoke Speaker's feathers enough to raise his temper, but her words pierced his heart. "My people have been forced to sell their crafts to feed their families, and few who purchase them respect their true value."

Lisa wasn't sure if the Elder was scolding her or simply making a statement. "I can promise you that I respect its value. I've been going to powwows for years. Your culture fascinates me. I've even been thinking about what I'd like my Indian name to be."

Smoke Speaker lowered the rabbit and regarded Lisa with a cool stare. "You do not choose your name, Miss Bard. An Elder grants a name to he or she who is deemed worthy of such an honor. Those who claim their own names are imposters, and shame my culture with their disrespect."

Thoroughly humiliated, feelings hurt, Lisa clamped her mouth shut and stared at her hands. She didn't know what she had done to provoke his abhorrence, but she vowed not to say another word.

Julia too was shocked by the treatment, but a part of her rejoiced at having the chance to witness her flighty and conceited sister getting put in her place. Everyone else had always fawned over her, and finally one man wasn't immediately taken by her false charms.

"Elder Smoke Speaker, Lisa has nothing to do with why I'm here." She thought it best to now separate herself from her sister. "I want to help you."

Putting his anger aside, Smoke Speaker focused on Julia. "With what, Mrs. Daivya?"   Julia nervously wrung her hands together. "Could you give us a few minutes?" she asked Lisa, who rose and walked off in a huff. The Elder didn't mind at all that she was upset. "Elder...these past two weeks have been more than I can bear. At first, I was so frantic over finding Cole that it was easy for me to write off Ian's disappearance as him having an affair, or just up and leaving like he usually does when we fight. But now...I'm not stupid. I know that Cole couldn't have survived this long, not in this weather, in these woods. He's just not old enough or strong enough to know what to do. But we haven't found anything, and that still gives me hope. But Ian...." Her head hung low as she pictured her husband. "Something just isn't right. I don't believe he's lost, not Ian. He knows the woods better than anyone, grew up in them. And I don't think he just left me. I spoke to our house sitter this morning and she says no one has been there, and Ian had a big meeting yesterday with a new hotel account. He loves his business. He wouldn't have missed that meeting."

Smoke Speaker listened patiently, and when she finished, he reached over the fire and touched the top of Julia's head. "He did not leave you," he comforted her softly.

"How do you know? You know where he is, don't you?" She sensed the Elder's reluctance to reply. "I won't tell Forbe, or anyone else. I don't agree with the direction their search is going. Between you and me, please tell me where my husband is."

He trusted the woman. Sheer desperation would force her to keep her word. "Your husband has gone to find your son, Mrs. Daivya. He left, knowing he was risking his life, to save him."

"Why didn't he bring me?"

"This is not your journey."

"Why did your apprentice go with him?"

"To ensure his success."

She was confused, encouraged, and suspicious. "Elder, did Ian or Whisper have anything to do with Cole's disappearance?"

"No."

"Was he kidnapped?"

"No."

"Why won't you tell me anything more?"

Smoke Speaker offered her a plate of meat. "You must have faith in my ways, Mrs. Daivya."

Julia swallowed a small piece of rabbit and set down the plate. "I can't have faith in a person who hides the truth. I'll find out what you're hiding, Elder, and my son better be alive."

That night, the Elder slept fitfully amidst frightening nightmares. In his sleep, he fought off the evil that walked the earth, searching for the daughter he lost so many years ago—she was there in the distance, reaching out for him, begging and praying for her father to find her in the snow.

But the faster he ran, the farther away she moved, her tears black against pale cheeks. Thunder rolled across the dark sky, and the dead rose from the depths with spindly fingers, grabbing him by the ankles, dragging him down to join the eternally restless.

And there in the distance, a lone white figure emerged from the mountains, growling and snarling and waiting for the chance to devour his daughter. Bunching its muscles, the beast leapt, and his daughter's screams echoed throughout the Land of the Dead.

Smoke Speaker woke in a convulsion of distress and terror, his old heart gripped in pain. Grief filled his soul for the child he lost, the child he could not save. Eighteen years ago, he had failed her, and now, eighteen years later, he still dreamed of that terrible journey into death.

But this one had been different. Despite his panic, he knew that in this dream he was being sent a message, and he had to warn his apprentice. She now had more to fear than the betrayal of the living world.

Whisper wasn't exaggerating, Ian thought as he panted his way through the woods, when she said they had a long walk ahead of them. They had been traipsing around wide trees, thick underbrush, soggy grounds, and thorny vines for god-knows-how-long and all Ian wanted to do was soak in a hot tub or lie down for a long massage. He loved nature, loved it enough to make it his career, but if he got through this mess alive he had half a mind to find a new job altogether.

The Weeping Forest, as Whisper had called it just before they entered, was appropriately named. Thick, dark drops of liquid dripped from the canopy like a light rain, staining their clothes and flesh. The forest showered them mercilessly, making their trek sticky, foul, and depressing. It was forever crying, forever tarnished.

"Where are we going? I'm getting a little tired of the woods."

Whisper stopped to untangle her pack from a gooey branch. Her fingers came back coated in a black, tar-like substance that she wiped on her pants. "There is a lake not far away. We will camp there and come up with a plan for the rest of our journey."

"Our journey where?"

"To the Fire Tower, the home of the Raven-Eater."

The home of the Raven-Eater was the last place he wanted to go, if the stories about the spirit were accurate. But if Cole was there, then so be it. "And where is this Fire Tower?"

"In the Fire Mountains, the core of the Land of the Dead. From there, the Raven-Eater can watch over all of his prisoners."

"Oh. Wonderful. Why is it called the Fire Tower and Fire Mountains?"

"Some say the Tower was built from the evils of Land of the Dead souls, and so it is a place of sin. Others say the Fire Mountains were once nothing but flames, and the Raven-Eater found a way to contain them within rock. There are no longer any fires, but the Fire Mountains are extremely hot, unbearable in some places."

As much as he wanted to know more, Ian was hesitant to ask. Sometimes ignorance was bliss, and the more he knew, the less likely he was to trust his own courage. The entire journey was starting to sound like the plot from some low-budget sci-fi film, as far as he was concerned.

They continued silently but quickly, sticks and leaves crunching beneath their aching feet. When the wind decided to swell up with angry gales and pound through the trees, the thorny branches whipped at their arms and faces, slicing easily through flesh. Whisper's hair, having been twisted into a tangled mass, was tied back in a messy braid, and Ian tried hard to keep his head down and still see where he was going.

A growl to his right made him freeze in his tracks. Ian immediately crouched low and ducked behind an enormous shrub. Whisper, who had also heard the menacing sound, joined him, lowering one dark green leaf just enough to find the source.

"What...what are they?" Ian whispered, revulsion in his voice as he stared at the beasts. There were two of them, two foul creatures hunched over a rotting carcass. Bearing a distant resemblance to mules, only lower to the ground with two-toed hooves tipped with curved claws, the beasts snarled and barked as they bit into the fallen animal with jagged yellow teeth. Their long, knotted fur was encrusted with old blood, leaves, and slimy mud, their ears flattened against bald heads, mouths dripping with saliva. A pungent odor secreted off their bodies worse than that of the carcass. One was larger than the other, its kinked tail longer, legs thicker.

When Ian looked closer, he could see that it was greedily chomping on the thickest part of the carcass, while the smaller one was chewing on the bones already stripped. Sensing their presence, the smaller beast lifted its head, and looked directly at the intruders. Its black lips pulled back into a vicious snarl, revealing two double rows of razor-sharp yellow teeth.

"Mr. Daivya, we must move on. It is not safe here."

Ian didn't object, and gladly snuck away from the beasts. He wasn't interested in being their next meal, and hoped they were too weak and focused on their measly meal to follow them. He couldn't get the image of the rotted meat being torn apart by razor-sharp teeth out of his head, and in a panic-induced craze he frantically looked over his shoulder and behind every tree to make sure they weren't being followed.

Finally, the Weeping Forest gave way to a meadow of tall grasses that reached just past Ian's thighs and gently blew in the wind. Just beyond the meadow was a small lake. The water was clear and clean, a welcomed sight from the gloom of the trees that leaked pus.

They washed the black goo from their clothes and bodies in the lake, kneeling on the shore beneath the red-streaked sky. Crimson from above and violet from the ground reflected in the lake, sending shimmering dots of light across the meadow.

"It's kind of nice here," Ian commented, running a hand through his wet hair. "Is it not nice?" He changed his mind when Whisper sent him a sarcastic glance.

"Do not be fooled by your surroundings, Mr. Daivya. Few things in the Land of the Dead are what they seem."

He didn't see how a meadow with a clean lake and soft colors could actually be a cesspool of evil, but he wouldn't argue. Instead, he helped Whisper make a fire at the edge of the woods and prepare a meal with supplies she had taken from Annabelle's hut. He wasn't so sure about the food Whisper called Spana, made of mushed yellow leaves, a watery reddish meat, and lumpy gray sauce. Like the Crota, it looked disgusting, and like the Crota, it tasted delicious.

After the meal, they both rested by the protection of the fire, which burned bright and white with thick black smoke. Whisper, fighting sleep, lay on her side and stared at the smoke, eyes reading the wisps as they circled into symbols and pictures. The Elder was reaching out to her.

"*Temptation,*" she read to herself, straining to decipher more in her state of half-sleep, wishing she had had more time to learn the art of smoke speaking, and he the gift of whispering. "*Love. . .the beauty of. . .water. . .beware the Trickster.*"

On the other side of the fire, Ian watched Whisper watch the smoke. He knew that look in her eyes by now, that faraway gaze that told him she was seeing something beyond his own capacity to perceive. When her eyes closed, he figured that whatever she was reading in the smoke wasn't too important, and soon fell asleep.

Chapter 18

He awoke to the sound of splashing water.

Lifting himself to his elbows, Ian peered around their small makeshift camp, blinking the sleep from his foggy brain. He saw Whisper at the lake, kneeling down as she washed her hair in the clear waters, running her slender fingers through the long, sleek strands. She had changed from her filthy clothes into a fitted buckskin dress that made her look like a charming, innocent woman he just happened to pass by on the path to the Raven-Eater. She was barefoot, her toned legs glistening with violet water drop reflections. He had imagined her to have a great body, and he was right.

When she sensed his stare and turned, Ian rose to his feet and walked toward her. She ran her hands down her hair, wringing out the water, and met him almost halfway. Something had changed in her eyes, a refreshing glint of happiness and youth, and he thoroughly enjoyed the way those eyes now regarding him as he approached with both caution and complete abandon. He even enjoyed the way she stopped just a couple feet short, making him take the last few steps.

He didn't bother to speak, to ask permission to run his hands up her muscled yet feminine arms, to cup her chin in his landscape-calloused palm. It was obvious to them both that it was time to put aside their differences, join together if even for just one night. After all, they were in the Land of the Dead, where myth, legend, lore, and desire came to life.

He touched her damp hair, curling a strand around his fingers, gently drawing her face up to his. He had imagined what those lips felt like, tasted like, and now what he had dreamed was his very own reality.

Ian leaned down, eager for her touch, her mouth. But just when he should have met those luscious lips, he was greeted with empty air instead. Startled, he took a step back, eyes widening at the sight of Whisper standing before him with an arrow aimed in his direction.

"You would dare to touch another," she accused, her voice reverberating in the wind, echoing in his mind. "You…are…*unworthy*."

And then she released the arrow.

The shot shattered his dream into a thousand pieces, shocking Ian out of sleep and nearly to his feet. His heart pounding, he glanced over at Whisper to see that she was still resting soundly, and guilt instantly racked his heart and soul. She was his guide, half his age, and he was married. They had no physical or emotional relationship, purely professional. He had no business dreaming of her. And yet, part of him was disappointed that the dream had taken such a foul turn. To know the feel and taste of her body, even in sleep, seemed like an opportunity too good to pass up.

The familiar splashing sound that had first intruded his dreams suddenly met his ears again, distracting him from his thoughts of Whisper. Through the purple haze he saw a small figure slowly moving around in the lake, creating smooth ripples that gently lapped on the shore. This time, he knew it was real. Making sure Whisper was still asleep, he quietly rose to his feet and walked down to the lake, keeping careful watch on the figure.

As he edged his way closer in the eerily quiet night, he saw that the figure was an animal, and stopped cold. The last thing he wanted to do was get too close to another of those foul beasts. Only...this one didn't look so foul, or evil. This one was white as snow, with smooth fur, bright gray eyes, and a curious face. It was knee-deep in the water, and to Ian looked like a wolf of sorts.

The majestic creature turned its sleek head in Ian's direction, eyes shining in the purple light. Mesmerized, Ian crept closer, watching the creature closely, and the wolf moved in unison with his steps. The large animal was gorgeous, a magnificent display of nature, with fur that glowed in the red and purple lights and a streamlined form that boasted strength and perfection.

Then, as Ian's breath hitched in his throat and his heart beat wildly in both wonder and anxiety, the wolf started to change.

The transformation began with a bright flash that startled the sleepy man. The brightness faded to a slow, spinning whirl of shimmering whiteness, the wolf rising to its hind legs in a fluid, slinky motion. But suddenly, it wasn't a wolf anymore.

Smooth fur melted slowly into creamy flesh, the long snout pulling back into a small yet elegant nose above full red lips, thin limbs stretching into finely-toned legs and slender arms. The wolf rose gracefully from the water, gently lifting from the lake in a slow circle as flowing tresses sprung forth from the sparkling fur and wafted in a nonexistent wind, before setting back down on two exquisitely crafted feet.

When the white wind spun its final swirl and disappeared into the waters, a woman stood where the wolf once was.

Her beauty astounded Ian—a perfect face, with high cheekbones, a soft jaw, dark gray almond-shaped eyes that were welcoming and kind, and long, lustrous, pearl-colored hair that fell down her back in a tumble of loose curls. A perfect body—curves in amazing places shown off in a white dress that blended beautifully to her skin, with a slit almost to her hips, revealing legs that could have been sculpted by the artistic geniuses of Florence. And then she smiled a perfect smile, wide and loving and inviting.

Slowly, she strolled out of the water, bare feet moving silently across the shore as she came to the man who couldn't take his gaze away. "Ian." She spoke with a voice that inspired music and laughter, a sound that lilted and echoed in the air. "I have been waiting for you."

"Who...what...I...." He felt like a thirteen year-old boy with his first crush, stumbling over his words at the sight of the beautiful woman, a beautiful woman who had just spun out of the shape of a white wolf. He didn't question her origin, for of all the sights he had seen in the Land of the Dead, she was quite far the best. By now, he was willing to accept just about anything. "Who are you?"

The woman reached out and gently ran her fingers through Ian's hair, taking a step closer so that her body was nearly touching his. "I am the one you dream of...the angel you pray to...the love that fills your soul."

Captured by her voice, Ian found himself lifting his hands to her hips, relishing the touch, and inwardly cursed himself for doing so. He shook his head. "I love another woman, my wife...and this...this isn't right." But he kept his hands where they were, and didn't move back.

"Ian." She smiled again, tilting her head seductively and kissing the corner of his mouth. "In the Land of the Dead, desire is never wrong." She molded herself against him, arching her back when his hands traveled up her spine.

His brain was muddled and foggy, barely able to put together a decent sentence. The mystifying woman was right. He wanted her; she was the one he dreamed of, and he didn't question it. He instantly desired this sexy stranger, the beautiful mystery whose fingers pressed into the firm muscle of his arms and shoulders with admiration and yearning. There was something familiar about her, the way she smelled, the way she moved, the way she needed the touch and feel of his body. There was something familiar about the way he wanted her, the reluctance to pull away, the guilt of savoring the sight of those luscious lips, the craving to pull her curvy hips against him.

Rebecca.

He had a brief moment of epiphany. The woman who was all but melting in his arms was the image of his secretary, but with ivory hair that concealed her true identity.

He broke free of his captivation long enough to hold her back at arm's length and look her up and down.

"Who the hell are you?" he asked again, trying hard to fight the desire.

"I am who you want me to be," she answered smoothly, running her hands up his arms. "You worked hard in life, and are being rewarded with the chance to live your dreams. Ian, I give myself to you."

"And when I go back to my wife?"

The woman laughed, the sound filling Ian's head with clouds. In one stealthy move she spun around and pressed her back against his chest, wrapping his arms around her. She laid her head back against his shoulder and nuzzled his throat. "Ian, in the Land of the Dead, all we have is right now. If you return to the Land of the Living, you will have no memory of this place, or your actions. Let yourself have the moment. You have earned it."

She began to move in a swaying rhythm, a slow and seductive dance. Ian moved with her, considering her words. He was being given the chance to live his desire, a desire that racked him with guilt and insecurity when alive, a desire that he deserved to have fulfilled. He was a man faced with a stunning, willing woman, and he had the opportunity to act on his temptations without facing any ramifications when the journey was complete.

Pouring his attention into the exotic beauty, Ian entered into the alluring dance, taking the woman by the hand and spinning her into a circle before letting her fall back gracefully into his arms. She peered up at him adoringly, batting her long lashes and tipping up her chin with invitation. Never before had a woman looked at him with such trust, such worship, such complete, unconditional love. And he wanted to explore every last inch of her warm body.

"If you have been granted a life filled with love, Mr. Daivya, then you should cherish it, and fight for those who hold your heart."

Whisper's words came crashing into his head. Startled by the intrusion, and contemplating where they came from, he stopped just before his lips touched her neck.

"Ian." The woman's voice was strained, as though desperate for his kiss. "Do not let me go. Give me your heart."

But he couldn't. Julia's face appeared behind his eyes, her smile, her laugh, even that look she got in her eyes when he did something to irritate her. She was the one for him, his light and joy. Julia, for all their bad times, still held his heart.

"No." He set the woman on her feet and took a step back. "Even if I don't remember, I'll know right up until the moment I get back, and I can't live with that."

"But you won't live with the memories, Ian. And until they fade away, you will feel my touch with every breath. You will be strengthened by my heart and soul. That is my promise to you."

Ian slapped her hand away when she attempted to touch his cheek. "I don't care. Look, you're beautiful and yes, very sexy, but I...I can't do this."

Her eyes narrowed, pearly hair blowing around her face as the wind began to pick up speed. "I understand. It is because you want another. The one who leads you farther into the Land of the Dead."

It took him a moment to realize who she meant, because the notion itself was absurd, despite his dream. "What? No...I have no desire to be with Whisper."

There was a flash of something dark and sinister across her pretty face, a contorted and violent mask hidden behind the creamy complexion and bright eyes that made him take a step back. "So you would risk your life for the deceit of another," she spat out viciously. "For the unworthy, and for the half-breed who—"

Her words cut off in a choke of shock and pain. She stumbled, clutching her abdomen, and Ian looked down to see an arrow sticking out of her stomach, dark blood staining the skin-tight white dress in a growing red circle. He could do nothing but stare, freezing in place and choking on his words as he struggled to figure out what was happening. With a pleading look of desperation, the woman fell to her knees, and it was then that Ian saw Whisper standing at the edge of the woods, bow still raised.

"Oh, Jesus." He looked back at the woman in time to see her body jerk and convulse, then slowly transform back into its original form.

"Coyote," Whisper muttered when she approached, kicking the lifeless form with a sneer. She leaned over and retrieved her arrow. "Beware the Trickster."

"What?" Whisper raised her head. Ian was gaping back at her. He couldn't believe she had just killed someone again, and he witnessed it happen right in front of him. "Beware the what?"

Whisper pointed with the bloody arrow. "Coyote," she repeated. "Coyote is a Trickster spirit. He is sent to distract people from their quests, and lead them astray. Some say that it was Coyote who convinced the Raven-Eater to consume the moon, claiming that in doing so the Raven-Eater could cast the living world in eternal darkness. But Coyote secretly wished for his wife, who was still of the living, to be able to see him, as the dead are only visible to the living in a place without light." She cleaned her arrow with a scrap of leather and shook her head. "But in consuming the moon, they released an evil that spread throughout the Land of the Dead instead of affecting the living world. In the Land of the Dead, it is likely that Coyote is a servant of the Raven-Eater."

"Sent to distract us?"

Whisper regarded him with a sarcastic smirk. "Not us, Mr. Daivya...you. I was informed of the Trickster. I should have warned you, but I did not think he would strike so soon." After a final, disapproving glimpse down at the already-decaying body of Coyote, Whisper led the way back to the protection of the fire, where she returned her arrow to the quiver.

"So that woman was sent to...what, tempt me?"

"I told you that the Land of the Dead was full of obstacles, Mr. Daivya, that will test your worth as a man and a father." Whisper held the arrow up in the light of the fire to make sure it was clean. "If you succumb to any, such as the temptation of the Coyote, then you fail." She placed the arrow in the quiver before returning her gaze to Ian. "But you resisted, in the end." There was a congratulatory hint in her voice, and while he knew she wouldn't actually say the words, it was enough to read it in her face. It wasn't enough, though, to erase that fact from his mind that he had fallen for a trickster spirit whose primary form was a coyote and who was referred to as *he*.

He would have to swallow his pride to admit that he had nearly taken the bait, but not today. The shame was still too new, and stung a bit too much, so he tackled another issue that Coyote had raised.

"The woman said I was risking my life for someone who is deceiving me," he said coolly, not taking his eyes off his guide, who didn't acknowledge his words. "I can only guess that she meant you. So, what kind of deceit is she talking about, and who is this half-breed?"

Now Whisper did recognize his words. She sighed and moved so that she was sitting Indian-style, facing Ian. He got the feeling that he was in for another lesson.

"Coyote was right," she admitted frankly. "I did not tell you about the half-breed. It was not necessary for you to know, until the time was right."

"Well, I'm telling you that the time is right now. So talk."

Whisper bit back a sharp retort. She hated being ordered around. "The half-breed is the child of the Raven-Eater."

Ian frowned and crossed his arms. "But you said he took Cole to be his son, to make up for the one he lost."

"He did." Whisper nodded, toying with the frayed laces of her boots. "You see, Mr. Daivya, a child was born to the Raven-Eater and his wife, one a spirit and the other a living woman in the Land of the Dead. The child was born half-spirit, half-alive… a half-breed. The Raven-Eater believed the child would be his heir, until a prophet foretold his destruction. The prophet said that the half-breed would have the power to destroy its creator, its father, and would do so to take the throne of the Land of the Dead. As one would expect, he ordered the half-breed to be put to death, and began his search for a son in the living world."

"So why would the woman bring up the half-breed, if the child is dead?"

Picking up a thin stick, Whisper began to draw in the dirt. "There are many legends about the half-breed. Some say that the half-breed was killed as an infant and buried beneath the Fire Mountains, but others say that the half-breed was taken away and hidden from the Raven-Eater. Some believe the child was taken to the living world, some believe that a powerful magic was cast so that the child may be reincarnated into the body of a living child to one day return for revenge, and others believe that the child never left the Land of the Dead, and will destroy the Raven-Eater when the time is right."

"And what do you believe?"

"I believe the half-breed is here, in the Land of the Dead."

"And how do you expect to find it?"

Whisper cocked her head to the side and lifted the stick from the earth. "Find, Mr. Daivya? I already know."

"You—how do you…" His voice trailed off when the truth rang loud in clear in his head. "You think Cole is the reincarnated half-breed? Are you *insane*?! My son is not some half-spirit, half-human beast. He's a little boy who was murdered by an ancient, psychotic shaman!"

Whisper didn't reply for a moment. Instead, she finished her drawing in the dirt, and only when it was complete did she respond. "These worlds work in mysterious ways, Mr. Daivya…ways we are not meant to understand. But we are given clues along our paths to destiny."

"Clues like what?"

"Like the mark of the half-breed." She gestured to her drawing, and Ian looked down to see the mark displayed in the dirt—a crooked circle, with five dots in the center, and a V-shaped symbol at the base. There was nothing spectacular about the design, but it haunted him nonetheless.

"So…but Cole doesn't have that mark. He doesn't even have any birthmarks."

"The mark of the half-breed is visible only to the dead."

Of course it is, Ian thought sarcastically. "OK…so if Cole has that mark, then he… he is the half-breed who can destroy this Raven-Eater. God." He blew out a heavy breath and buried his head in his hands. It was too much, too much information and knowledge. Their journey was getting so much more complicated than he'd ever anticipated. "How would he destroy him?"

"The…prophecy…" Whisper took a few seconds to think about the word, wondering if it was correct, "says that only the child who has been accepted into the arms of the Raven-Eater can destroy his power, by taking a piece of his spirit body and burying it in the Land of the Living."

He was beginning to put the pieces together. "So you knew from the very beginning that all of this wasn't just about finding my son. It was about killing the Raven-Eater."

"In a way." Whisper stared down at the mark in the ground. "I cannot guarantee that our legends are correct, Mr. Daivya, and I cannot guarantee that your son has been accepted by the Raven-Eater. I have fought for many years to keep him from stealing the soul of a child, because when his family is complete, he will raise up his army for war with the living. I do not know what would happen should he be destroyed, but I can only pray that the Land of the Dead is not destroyed with him."

Her deceit burned his blood, and even though he'd known all along that she wasn't telling him the whole truth, he still wanted to throttle the woman. "How do you know all this?"

"Do you know the story of the Bible, the story of your origin?"

Ian peered through the purple haze at the young woman. "Of course I do. I was raised with it."

"As was I." Whisper nodded and pulled on her jacket as the temperature slowly began to drop. "This is my heritage, Mr. Daivya, my story of origin. It is the way I know. Stories have been told about Water Beatle and Buzzard for many moons."

"So…no Adam and Eve, huh? No Tree of Life and big flood and hanging on a cross?"

Whisper cocked her head, curious. "How interesting it is that people are willing to believe in a man who turns water to wine, cures blindness, and rises from the dead, yet say that the stories of my people are nonsense and myth."

It was true, Ian silently agreed. He believed in God, and before crossing beyond the Western Sun would have brushed off Whisper's ways as childish...nonsense, as she said. He got the feeling that she had bared the brunt of many such brush-offs. "So what is your origin?"

Picking up her bow to tighten the string, Whisper let her people's creation story form in her mind. "In the beginning, Mr. Daivya, the earth was a great island suspended in the air by the four cardinal points. This island hung above a land of pure water, a place where people could not survive, and where animals were yet to thrive. But soon the island became crowded, and so Water Beetle went down to the ocean to search for land. He dove deep into the water, and brought forth mud to the surface. This mud spread across the surface of the water, but it was still too soft for people to live." *Such a tiny creature,* Whisper thought, *with such large accomplishments.*

"Now the earth was dry and flat, but soft. So the people sent the Great Buzzard to search for hard land. Buzzard flew for many moons, and found nothing. Eventually he began to tire, and he flew lower to the ground. The tips of his wings struck the ground, and where they did, great valleys were formed. When he lifted his wings, mountains rose up with them. Now the earth was dry and people came down from the island to live, but it was dark. They created the sun, and when they could see, they found their new land was empty of plants and animals."

"So they created plants and animals? How?"

His genuine interest pleased her. "No, Mr. Daivya, such things cannot be created out of air. The people discovered that there was another world beneath theirs, and the only way to reach it was by the waterfalls that fell from the mountaintops." Without realizing it, Whisper lifted her hands high and brought them down as though traveling the waters in her mind. With her animation and slow way of speaking, Ian could only think that the woman was a born storyteller.

"They could only enter this world with a guide, one who would share their plants and animals. When the people's new world had plants and animals, they were told by Creator to pray for seven days. As each day passed, the people and animals and plants began to fall asleep, until they reached the seventh day. Only Panther and Owl remained awake, and so they were given the gift of wisdom, and sight in the darkness. Because they can see, they can prey on the other animals that fall asleep."

Whisper absently wiped a hand across the symbol of the half-breed marked in the dirt as she thought about the rest of the story, her story of creation. "The problem that arose then was that the people could not reproduce, and their village was dying. So man struck woman with a fish and told her to have a child, and she did." Ian laughed at that, covering his mouth with a dirty hand, and lowered his head to avoid Whisper's angry glare. "Women gave birth every seven days, until they had too many people, so Creator made it so a child would be born only once a year...And that is the origin of my people."

To recover from his momentary lapse of laughter, Ian nodded and forced a serious expression. He could tell Whisper was offended, and wondered what he could say to make it right. The story was certainly colorful, as was that of his own creation. "That's quite an origin. More interesting than my own....How does it end, according to your people?"

Whisper lay back and stared thoughtfully at the sky. "It depends on who is telling the story."

Chapter 19

In his dungeon of a bedroom, Cole sat against the wall, picking at the fringes of his shirt. After wrestling with the idea of changing into the new clothes the strange woman brought him, he had finally decided to slip them on. His old clothes were filthy and smelled like, in his opinion, rotten poop. And even though he hated to admit it, he liked the animal designs that were sewn onto his shirt and pants, and the clothes were really comfy.

But even though he had broken down and donned the clothes of a dead boy, Cole promised that he would never call himself Fighting Fox.

Cole closed his eyes and thought of home. He pretended that this was all a dream, and that when he woke up, his mom and dad would be ready for a day of canoeing and barbecues. And when he woke up, he was going to ask if he could have a puppy. A chocolate lab that he would probably name Ghost, because even if the little boy ghost made him die, it was still a really cool adventure.

Plus, he had to admit, the food was awesome. He especially liked Boomie, something slushy and white that reminded him of his mom's homemade grits. The lady named Gentle Heart brought him a bowl twice a day. The more he ate it, the less he could even remember how real grits tasted, but that was fine by him. And the more he saw Gentle Heart, the less he could remember of his own mother's appearance. He didn't like that part, but wasn't sure what to do about it.

The clinking of a key in the door lock had Cole jumping to his feet and folding his arms across his chest defiantly. He would show anyone who crossed his path that he was angry, not scared and confused.

Gentle Heart stepped into the room, carrying a tray filled with sparkling stones. "Hello, my sweet Fighting Fox. Did you sleep well?"

"I never sleep."

The beautiful young woman smiled and set the tray on the floor. She was pleased to see that he was wearing his new clothes. "You look very handsome. One day you will grow into a very fine young man."

Despite himself, he liked the compliment. He edged a bit closer to the tray, peering curiously at its contents. "What are those?"

"These belong to you, my strong Fighting Fox. With these, you will become an amazing warrior." Gentle Heart pushed the tray in Cole's direction, then stepped back and waited.

After a few moments of eyeing the strange but pretty stranger suspiciously, Cole walked over to the tray. Child-like excitement filled his heart as he knelt down and wrapped his fingers around the shaft of an emerald-encrusted dagger. The handle was crafted from bone, with smooth edges lined in green stone. The blade was made from a flattened stone sharpened to an almost paper-thin edge.

"That belonged to the Raven-Eater," Gentle Heart said quietly. "His great-great-grandfather was a legendary Trader. He traveled the Great River and visited many tribes in his long life. He traded a rare white buffalo hide for this blade, and became the richest shaman in our people's history. It is said to hold power."

"What kind of power?"

"The kind that turns a boy into a man."

In that moment, Cole desperately wanted to be a man. A man could play video games past seven p.m. A man could eat whatever he wanted for dinner. And most importantly, a man could beat up the bad guys.

Gentle Heart smiled. "Your father, the great Raven-Eater, will be pleased to know you like your gifts."

Cole made a face. "My daddy's name isn't Raven-Eater. His name is...his name is...."

He couldn't remember. He could kind of picture his parents, but their faces were getting blurry in his mind.

Watching the boy struggle to remember his father's name, Gentle Heart felt a part of her soul sadden. She too once had another family, another life that was taken away. And for a long time, she had fought against forgetting, refusing to give up her old identity. But after awhile, their faces faded away, and she was left with mere impressions of her former life. She was stripped bare of her old memories, whether by magic or time, and the Raven-Eater was her entire world. She loved him now, belonged to him, and couldn't imagine an existence anywhere else. Here, she had wealth, status, and power. She had a husband who ruled the world.

Gentle Heart reached out to the boy. "Come, my little Fighting Fox. I'll show you to your new room."

After a moment's hesitation, Cole took her hand.

After facing the Trickster spirit, Whisper and Ian walked around the lake and prepared to re-enter the Weeping Forest on the other side. Whisper, deciding that there would be no more breaks, no more chances to be caught unaware, was going to push Ian to move as fast and as hard as he possibly could. She knew he was used to laboring long hours beneath a hot sun for his landscaping business, but she would introduce him to a brand new kind of work.

"So, back into the Leaking Forest."

"Weeping Forest."

"Yeah, I was just kidding." He needed to help her acquire a sense of humor. "How much farther through the woods?"

Whisper pushed back a thick branch, fingers already sticky with the black substance that dripped from the treetops. "The Weeping Forest spreads far across the Land of the Dead," she answered, glancing up at the sky through the canopy. "There are villages throughout the forest, dead souls who have forgotten that they once had better lives. They will help guide us through."

"Or kill us," Ian muttered beneath his breath, not convinced that the villagers would be eager to help. He didn't trust anyone or anything anymore, not even Whisper. For all he knew she was just another Trickster waiting to seduce and kill him. "This place gives me the creeps."

"Many believe the Weeping Forest is…haunted, as the white man says."

"Haunted?" Ian glanced around incredulously. "How can a place of dead people be haunted by more dead people?"

Stepping over a fallen log, Whisper touched the trunk of a wide, gooey tree with her fingertips. "There is a story my people have told for hundreds of years," she said as she broke off a piece of bark. Sticky black pus oozed from the new crevice. "It tells of an ancient creature, a beast that disguises itself as a tree and feeds on the bodies of young women."

"What kind of beast?"

She knew how he would react, but Whisper placed the bark in her bag, in case she needed it for a future magic, and provided her companion with the answer. "The Giant Inchworm."

Despite himself, Ian grinned, his first real smile since arriving in the Land of the Dead. "A worm?" It was so ridiculous, such an incredibly funny image of women running from a worm, that he felt a laugh bubbling up from his gut. "Are you serious? A tiny little worm?"

"They were not always so tiny, Mr. Daivya," Whisper replied coolly, not at all amused by his lack of respect for her culture. "The Giant Inchworm, *Ustahli*, was once a great creature, with a massive body and strong limbs. *Ustahli* was a proud creature and believed he owned all the land. He lived in the mountains and disguised himself as a tree, so that villagers could not tell him apart. He fed off the bodies and souls of young women. One day, after deciding they had lost enough women, the village Elders met and came up with a plan. They made villagers out of rocks and built a great fire, and the men left for a false hunt." Whisper inspected a tree as she passed, and Ian found himself doing the same. "*Ustahli* was fooled, and grabbed a rock, thinking it to be a woman. His surprise caused him to stumble into the fire, and the more he moved, the more badly he was burned, until all of his limbs were scorched from his body. Finally, all that was left were mere inches, as we know him today."

Ian picked at a piece of bark, satisfied when it didn't retaliate. "Well...then, why is the worm feared in the Land of the Dead, if it's only an inch long?"

"Because in the Land of the Dead, *Ustahli* lives in his true form."

"Huh." Ian considered the story for a moment. "So then I guess that means that all the Cherokee stories come to life in the Land of the Dead."

"Many stories live in the Land of the Dead," Whisper corrected him. "My people are not so arrogant as to believe that our way is the only way."

She was taking a dig at his own people, and he knew it, but decided to let it go. Instead of starting an argument, or saying something that would only fuel her animosity toward him, he pretended to examine the trees. "So how can you tell a tree from the giant worm?"

"The trees don't eat you," a voice said from behind.

Both Ian and Whisper spun around, startled by the intrusion. A young woman stood just a few feet away, chocolate-hued hair in tangles, clothes muddy and torn, face ashen, and dark eyes tired. She looked beaten down, worn and faded by an eternity in the Weeping Forest. In her hands was a scratched wooden bowl filled with a gooey gray substance.

The woman dipped her hand into the bowl and slung a string of slime on the ground at Ian's feet. He jumped back, immediately angry. "What the hell was that for?"

"So *Ustahli* will not detect your scent."

"I thought he only ate women." His tone was sarcastic and condescending.

"*Ustahli* does not discriminate when hungry," Whisper answered, stepping over the slime and over to the woman. She reached into the bowl and rubbed the goo over both hands like it was lotion. "Did the Elder send for you?"

"Yes, *Kanegv*," the woman said vaguely, using Whisper's Cherokee name. "He reached out to me in my sleep, and invaded my dreams. He asked me to guide you through the Weeping Forest, to the Barren Plains."

Whisper nodded while Ian muttered something beneath his breath about another crappy place with another crappy name. "How do you know the Elder?"

The woman frowned and shook her head. "I...I do not remember."

"What is your name?"

"My name is.....

Whisper pressed her lips together, somewhat sad by the stranger's loss of memory. Being a part of the Weeping Forest for so long had overtaken her mind, pushing away the memories of her living life and replacing them with the sorrow of a dark eternity. Whisper could only guess how she knew the Elder, but judging by the markings on her upper arms, she came from the Cherokee, and likely met Smoke Speaker at a powwow.

"You are Deer Clan, of the Cherokee?" she asked, pointing to the markings. The woman glanced absently at her tattoos. "So I will call you Fawn."

"Fawn," the woman repeated carelessly. "Yes, I am Fawn."

With little regard to Whisper or Ian, the newly-named Fawn walked away from the dilapidated village in the distance. She started down a narrow path, sprinkling the earth with the gray goo.

"Are we supposed to follow?"

Whisper shrugged, hoping the Elder knew what he was doing when he asked Fawn to be their guide. He may not have known how far gone she was by now. "I suppose. Keep within the boundaries of the Element."

"The what?" Ian asked as Whisper fell into step behind Fawn.

"The Element," Whisper repeated. "It is a mixture that only the dead can create from the herbs that grow in the Land of the Dead. It is used to cover scents and protect against enemies."

"If you say so." He obeyed, but wondered how a drop of thick liquid could keep away a hungry beast. *Then again*, he thought in amusement, *they're worried about some stupid worm.*

They continued through the Weeping Forest silently, dodging thorny limbs, wiping the black goop from their bodies as the leaves dripped, until the path disappeared in a tangle of fallen trees and jumbled shrubs.

"Now where?"

Fawn reached down and produced a long blade from the fold of her skirt. A solid three feet of metal with an edge that looked like it could slice a hole through thin air, the makeshift machete terrified Ian, mainly because it was in the hands of a spacey, unpredictable dead soul. She started hacking at the vines and branches, throwing them thoughtlessly behind her so that Ian was forced to duck out of the way.

Whisper stood back with crossed arms, eyeing Fawn sardonically. They would never get through that mess of woods. She was more than willing to go around rather than hack her way through, but the strange woman didn't seem aware of any other route. She would tire herself out within minutes, and then they would have to wait for her to rest before continuing on their way.

They might have stood there for hours waiting for Fawn to make even a dent in their path. No matter what they said, what alternatives they suggested, no matter what they did to help, Whisper knew this road was not meant to be walked.

"Fawn, there are other paths," she said, not moving in order to avoid being struck by a flying branch. Fawn didn't hear, and instead kept cutting. The machete whirled through the purple air, catching the light as she lifted it above her head. "Fawn."

"What the hell is wrong with her?" Ian stared at Fawn with both curiosity and irritation. "It's like she isn't even there."

"She is not with us," Whisper replied. "She has been in the Weeping Forest for so long that it has become a part of her. The Elder must have misjudged the strength of her mind."

Ian sighed. That was just what they needed, some crazy woman holding them back. "Great. So what do we do now?"

"We try to bring back her mind." Whisper took a tentative step forward. "Fawn, that is enough. Fawn...*Fawn!*"

"Damn it, woman, listen to us!" Ian stepped in front of Whisper, just far back enough to avoid the swinging blade. "Fawn, I said—*what!*" he shouted when Whisper grabbed his arm.

"Listen," she said quietly, holding up a hand to silence him. Her eyes narrowed and traveled to the treetops.

"Listen to what?"

"Listen!" The urgency in her voice convinced him to do just that. He turned his attention toward the trees, and heard the suspicious sound. A strange, haunting groan was working its way around the forest, similar to the sounds of oak trees creaking in a heavy wind storm, and the dozens of voices that traveled the sudden breeze reached her ears in a panicked song of warning. "He is coming."

"Who?"

"The—Fawn? Fawn?"

Ian looked over to the underbrush. Fawn was gone, the machete lying on the ground, abandoned. Dread curled in his gut. "Where did she go? Whisper, where did she—oh, God, she's…."

He could do nothing but point up to the trees. Whisper followed his gaze and her knees nearly buckled when she saw the young woman gripped in the gnarled, four-fingered hand disguised as a branch. Her mouth was open in a monstrous display of torture and pain, blood dripping from the corners as her eyes pleaded for help.

With a nauseous moan of terror, Ian saw the four jagged tips of grimy fingers that were pierced through her back and stomach, gripping the woman in an ironclad hold as her feet kicked and her hands clutched at the one that held her hostage. Blood seeped down from the trees, spotting the ground at Ian's feet and smearing across his cheek when he wiped at his face.

"What do we do?!"

Whisper spun around, desperately searching the trees. She looked for one, just one, that was different, that was posing as a part of nature, but could find only bark and leaves.

"*Ustahli* is here," she said pressingly, grabbing the wooden bowl at her feet. She pulled the gray mixture from the bowl and spread it in a circle around her and Ian, then used what was left to smear across his chest and face.

"Whoa, whoa, what are you doing?" he protested when she continued to coat him. The Element reeked, offending his nostrils and nearly making him gag.

"Protecting you," Whisper answered, wiping the Element on his hands. "*Ustahli* cannot track your scent with the protection of the Element. He already knows we are here, and will not stop tracking us until we are caught. I need you alive, Mr. Daivya. Do not move from the circle."

Then she jumped over the gray ring she had made.

"Wait! Whisper, stop!"

He didn't step out of the circle for fear of being attacked, either by the creature or by Whisper for not following her orders, and instead watched with wide eyes and a pounding heart as she plucked the machete up from the ground and gripped it with a steady hand.

"Whisper, now is not the time to be a hero!"

"Is it the time to be a coward, Mr. Daivya?" Her icy tone, mixed with the Cherokee accent that made everything she said sound important and mysterious, embarrassed him despite his panic. "*Ustahli* does not offer mercy."

Whisper tightened her hold on the handle of the blade and trained her ears toward the wind. The creatures of the forest, the souls of the dead, would reach out to her, aid her in the fight. They told her where the *Ustahli* stood, where he waited, and the exact moment he went to strike.

In one swift movement, Whisper dropped to her knees and arched backwards just as the fast and spiked limb of the *Ustahli* swept across the air and reached for her throat. The claw grazed her chin, easily slicing though flesh. Barely registering the shallow cut, she rolled to the right just in time to dodge a claw that slammed into the ground only inches from her stomach. The earth cracked and wet clumps of dirt burst up from the impact, showering over Whisper as she spun around to dodge another attack.

He strikes from the East, the voices in the wind told her, and she leapt to her feet, swinging out with the machete and connecting with the limb that grasped for her, cutting cleanly through muscle and flesh. The scream of the beast pierced the air, burning into Ian and Whisper's ears, and in a spasm of pain, the *Ustahli* dropped its victim.

Fawn fell to the ground and landed hard on her back. Whisper, who had again lowered to her knees at the sound of the scream, crawled over to the woman and searched for any sign of life, but she was too late, and there was no time to mourn.

Ian watched as Whisper straightened and stepped over Fawn's lifeless body, holding the machete like a sword with her head slightly turned to the side in a pose he recognized as listening to the wind. He glanced around, unable to tell tree from enemy, branch from limb, and so instead kept his attention on Whisper, silently praying for her safety. He needed her alive so much more than she needed him.

"Where are you," she whispered, flexing her fingers on the handle. She scanned the trees again. *Ustahli* had to be hiding in the cluster just to her left, she was sure of it, and so she observed the bark, the roots, the leaves, the canopy. Black bark lined the trunks, with branches that arced out across the sky, leaves seeping the tar-like substance. The air was still, the sky gloomy, casting the trees into the shadows and silence.

But only one tree breathed.

"*Osiyo, Ustahli*," Whisper greeted, and pushed forward with the machete.

"Whisper!"

Ian couldn't help the shout that escaped when a limb slithered across the ground and wrapped around Whisper's ankle, jerking her off her feet.

Her breath flew from her lungs as she fell flat on her back. The arrows strapped to her shoulders scattered across the ground. When the limb started to drag her across the ground, she slapped at the tree-bark arm attached to her ankle with the blade. Free, she tossed the bow aside and prepared herself, risking a sidelong glance at Ian, who was clenching his hands into fists nervously. She was secretly pleased that he hadn't moved from the circle.

Bracing herself, Whisper moved forward, keeping her eyes on the tree she believed to be the *Ustahli*. She leapt when another limb swept at her feet, landing solidly, her stare never faltering. That was the reason why the *Ustahli* was so hard to kill—people lost concentration. In the Land of the Dead, the men and women of the Weeping Forest could not focus, could not think through a plan of attack, and so they perished one by one, like Fawn. The *Ustahli* was not prepared for Whisper, though, and did not expect her skill.

The *Ustahli* attacked suddenly from the west, knocking Whisper off-balance and sending a shooting pain through her right shoulder. She responded by waving the machete above her head in an arc, connecting with solid limb, and smirking at the wail that sounded through the air.

The beast moved in a shuddering motion, pushing past the trees and snapping them in half as it shoved its way closer to Whisper, whose black eyes widened at the impossible sight.

Standing as high as the tallest tree, with a torso as round as the widest trunk, the *Ustahli* loomed over Whisper, staring down with watery gray eyes and a mouth of jagged teeth. Its dark brown body, made up of thousands of veiny scales covered with slime and dirt, undulated and heaved. More than a dozen appendages protruded from various outlets, three of which had been cut in half by his enemy. The creature's low, hoarse moan echoed around the woods, thundering in her mind and causing her heart to shudder. The *Ustahli* was powerful, and likely didn't even know his own strength.

The eye in the center of his stomach, the wind said as it blew past her ears. *His weakness is your strength.*

As the beast edged closer, leaving behind a thick trail of slime, Whisper dropped her weapon and grabbed her bow from the ground, knocking a single arrow. She would only get one chance. Her eyes narrowed in concentration as she scanned the beast's gullet, then down his stomach, watching for that one small spot unprotected by rock-hard scales.

"There you are," she whispered, and released the arrow.

The guttural scream that rocked the woods roared through the trees, forcing Ian to cover his ears with a low moan of pain. Whisper's hair blew back from her face as the rotten stench of blood and guts pierced her nostrils. She didn't give the beast the pleasure of showing the incredible pain behind her eyes, and she moved only her head to watch when the *Ustahli* shuddered and stumbled and came crashing through the trees, landing inches from where she stood.

Ian leapt from the protective elemental circle as the *Ustahli* slammed to the ground, narrowly missing being torn apart by the creature's sharp limbs. Staring down at the beast incredulously, Ian absently wiped at the Element that clung to his skin in sticky strings and took in the amazing sight.

The *Ustahli's* body was more than five feet around, sleek and gray with dark circles indenting its body in giant rings from head to toe. Thin, veiny flesh moved in tune with its shallow breathing, remaining limbs feebly reaching out for help.

As he moved around the head of the beast, Ian crouched down and peered into the watery black eyes only as big as his fists. Hate glared back at him, and he had the fleeting thought that it was a look Whisper had long since perfected. Huge holes on either side of its head, which Ian took to be ears, made up for the lack of sight. They were covered with a translucent film that retracted at the slightest bit of noise.

"You sure are good at killing," he commented, glancing over at Whisper, who was rubbing her injured shoulder.

"Your time to kill will come, Mr. Daivya," she warned in response.

"No...I could never do what you do." He shook his head and almost sneered. "I'm not a killer."

Whisper unclenched her teeth and settled the insulted rage in her heart. "No... perhaps you do not yet have the courage to do what is right."

Ian didn't answer, but instead stared back down at the *Ustahli*. With an arrow in its gut, it no longer seemed threatening. In fact, he kind of felt bad for it, and supposed it was the landscaper/naturist side of him that hated to see a creature so beneficial to the environment as the earthworm shuddering in pain and death.

Watching the blood ooze from the wound, he knew that he was nothing like Whisper. Murder was not something that came so easily to him, and it didn't take courage to see what was right and wrong.

Ian jumped when a hand suddenly clamped down on his arm. He spun around and faced Whisper, who was gripping her bow tightly.

"We must go, Mr. Daivya," she said urgently, fingers digging into his muscle.

"What's the hurry? The thing's dead, isn't it?"

"The *Ustahli* cannot die in the Land of the Dead. It can only be slowed," she replied, casting one final glance at the beast she had shot through the stomach before retrieving her arrow. "We will head west as quickly as possible. The *Ustahli* will not be disabled for long."

With that, she grabbed Ian by the arm, and together, they plunged into the woods.

Chapter 20

Just before daybreak, Julia and David hiked through the woods without a single break in stride until they reached Howling Vines. The distraught mother had turned to her father for support, guidance, and a tough helping hand. David, a career military man, knew how to get information out of people. The thought of interrogating the Elder excited him, gave him a fresh kick in his step. Ever since his retirement, he had missed the thrill of combat.

"Here we are," Julia said as they entered the clearing, lit only by the glowing embers in the hearth. The fog, illuminated with an orange glimmer, cast an eerie light around the circle. She turned to her father. "What should we do?"

"Go for the direct approach." David wasn't going to waste time, and decided that a surprise ambush was the best line of attack. Squaring his shoulders, the retired colonel stalked over to the small hut and yanked back the deerskin curtain. "Smoke Speaker!"

Emptiness echoed David's voice back to his ears. The hut was empty.

Julia peered over her father's shoulder, disappointment coiling in her stomach at the sight of the vacant bed. She'd been expecting and hoping the old man would be asleep, so they could startle him into telling the truth.

"Where do you think he is?"

"Maybe the trees told him we were coming."

David sensed the sarcasm, and turned to his daughter to silence her with a stern glare. "Be careful who you mock, Julia."

Julia regarded her father with a cynical glare. "Please, Dad, since when did you become superstitious? I thought military men were supposed to be tough and real."

"Some things deserve respect. I just never bothered to tell you those things because I didn't think you cared."

David slowly lowered himself to his knees, wincing at the cracks and pops as he peered beneath the bed for anything that might serve as a clue to the Elder's whereabouts or guilty actions. He wasn't willing to get into an argument with his daughter, especially over a culture she didn't understand. After all, he'd grown up hearing old stories from his grandfather, who had been close friends with a Navajo Elder from the western plains. Although the stories varied from the Cherokee legends that dominated the North Carolina mountains, they were similar and fascinating enough to capture his attention. A military man he may be, but there was still something about the Native American spirituality that enthralled him, called to him. All these years later, he still had dreams of old Wind Talker and his people.

But he'd never shared those stories with Julia. As a child, she was more interested in science, toys, and boys. The souls of the world were never her area of interest.

Ignoring her father's strange comments, Julia rifled through a stack of clothes, reaching between the folds of scratchy rags and soft hides. Her fingers touched the edges of something hard.

"What's this?" she muttered to herself, pulling out a thin, buckskin-covered pad of parchment. The papers were tied together with frayed hemp, and covered with a slate of wood carved into an intricate tribal design that circled around what looked to Julia like an owl.

While her father continued to rummage around the end of the bed, shuffling through stacks of clay and woven baskets, Julia gently lifted the cover of the book.

The portrait of a young woman stared back at her with haunting black eyes. Sketched onto the parchment with thin charcoal lines, she peered at Julia as though seeing straight through to her soul. Long black hair lifted in an invisible wind and disappeared into the edges of the paper. Her mouth was relaxed, but there was a hint of something in her eyes that suggested a deep, internal sadness.

Mesmerized by the portrait, Julia turned the page. This time she saw the woman from head to toe as she leaned over the riverbank and peered into the water. A bow and pack of arrows were slung across her back, and a knife was secured at her waist. Even in the charcoal drawing, Julia could see the toned muscles in her arms and the scratches across her cheek and shoulders.

This was Whisper, the Elder's apprentice. Julia was sure of that fact. This was the woman Deputy Duff was secretly in love with, the one her husband had joined for a mysterious trek through the woods. She was beautiful, mysterious, poignant, confident, and exuded an unnerving sense of danger. Julia got the feeling that trouble followed this young Cherokee apprentice wherever she went. Or maybe she just went looking for it.

Prying her eyes away from Whisper, Julia turned her attention to the next picture, and nearly lost her breakfast when she saw the image of her son standing on a rock in the middle of the river.

"Jules?" David rose and placed a hand on his daughter's back when she gasped and lifted a hand to her mouth. Unable to reply, Julia handed him the book of drawings with a shaking hand.

"Oh…no," David whispered, thumbing through two more pictures of Cole, one of which depicted the boy waist-deep in the water, staring at two black figures on the shore, and the other showed the child gripping an intricately carved dagger.

"He knows what Cole looks like," Julia managed to say through the sobs that were stabbing through her heart. "He knows, Dad. He knows what happened to my little boy."

David gripped Julia's trembling hand, gently kissing her fingers. He desperately wanted to offer her comfort and soothing words, but he needed to see more. He had to know.

Julia couldn't tear her eyes away from the drawings as her father turned one page after the next. She unwillingly watched a running narrative of her son's disappearance, her husband's journey, and Whisper's unfailing guidance. Ian stood before a terrifying ghoul with a gaping mouth, then at the base of a bridge with three cats blocking the way; Cole stared defiantly at a gorgeously dressed Indian woman who held a bundle of clothes, his young face determined to show hate and fury; Whisper leaned over Ian as she dressed wounds across his back, while he winced at the touch.

"Ian," Julia whispered, reaching out to the image, drawing back her hand when they came to a picture of him holding a fascinating woman. Rage and disappointment surged through her blood, until she saw the arrow through the woman's stomach.

David's lips parted in amazement when he came to the last page, a terrifying drawing of a beastly worm towering over Whisper, who was lowered into a warrior's stance as she held a machete out at her side. At the edge of the page was Ian, standing in a gray circle.

"It exists."

She wasn't sure if he was talking to her or to himself, but Julia's curiosity got the better of her. "What exists?"

"The Land of the Dead."

"The what?"

"The Land of the Dead," he repeated, the realization of what that meant slamming into him like a wall of bricks. "Ian has gone to the Land of the Dead to save Cole." He shook his head, gripping the book to his chest. All the old stories were real. Wind Talker had been right. And the nightmares, the images that haunted his thoughts as a young boy….

"The Elder's apprentice led him to the Land of the Dead. They know how to save Cole."

Julia shook her head. "What…what do you…you're saying that Cole…." She collapsed to the bed, tears streaming down her cheeks as she choked on the painful words. "Dad…did they kill him?"

"I don't know." David's hands balled into fists as the notebook dropped to the floor. It wouldn't make sense to kill the boy only to save him, but with these people there was no telling what they were capable of, what tricks and secrets they may have up their sleeve. "But I plan on finding out."

From the edges of Howling Vines, Smoke Speaker hid. He'd barely managed to escape into the thicket of forest before they arrived, and for the first time in many years, he was frightened.

The Elder was an old man, his heart and soul weakening with each passing day. The strength it took to keep up the fog, to hide Cole Daivya's body from the police, to keep watch over Whisper in the Land of the Dead and send her messages, was too much to bear. And now, having to hide himself as well, he was finding his ancient body more and more exhausted.

Only an hour before Julia and her father arrived, Smoke Speaker had been awakened by the panicked chirps of Grandfather Bluebird, who was perched just outside his hut. His message was urgent, warning the Elder of enemies on the trail to Howling Vines. They were furious, Bluebird said, urgent, and one, the man, was willing to hurt the Elder in order to get answers.

Knowing there was nothing he could say to Julia that would appease her, nothing but the truth, and that he was not yet willing to admit, Smoke Speaker decided to hide. He rose from the bed, old bones cracking with each movement, wrapped a ratted cloak around his frail body, and hurried into the woods. No sooner had he settled behind a two hundred year-old oak tree than Julia and David marched into the clearing, shouting his name as they burst into his home.

He'd waited patiently, and when he saw them leave with his journal in hand, he was pleased. Now they would know the truth, as much as they needed to know, without forcing him to betray his apprentice. Let them see his drawings, show them to the police. Let them come back with their guns and their hate. Their ways were no match for him. Smoke Speaker had the entire forest, the mountains, on his side. With one word, one message on the tendrils of smoke, he was protected. His enemies would never reach him.

In Howling Vines, he was safe. He only wished he could say the same for Whisper.

Chapter 21

Ian had expected Whisper to be light on her feet, but he wasn't prepared for the race through the forest. Whisper dodged trees and logs with ease, navigating around thorny vines and branches without so much as flinching when they scraped against her skin. Ian did his best to follow in her footsteps, fighting against the urge to look back over his shoulder as the *Ustahli* crashed through the woods in pursuit.

After what he deemed a two hours of running and jumping and panting, the giant beast ended his chase and went back to prey on the lost souls of the village. Whisper slowed to a trot after being sure he was gone, and stopped completely when they reached a tiny clearing.

"What's the plan?" Ian asked between pants, hunching over and resting his hands on his knees. He was secretly pleased to see that Whisper too was breathing heavily, still favoring her aching shoulder.

Whisper stared through the trees, searching for any sign of the *Ustahli*. The Weeping Forest was silent, eerily awaiting their return. But they were headed west, away from the forest, into a land much more dangerous.

"The Barren Plains," Whisper answered quietly. "A world without mercy…only hate."

Of course, Ian thought bitterly. "So what's up with this Barren Plains place?"

Whisper chewed on her bottom lip, a rare sign of nerves. Her fingers were quickly untying the knife from her belt. She handed the machete to Ian. "Some say that when the Raven-Eater followed his victims into the Land of the Dead, he buried their rotting corpses in the Barren Plains." She turned her black eyes to Ian. "He cursed the land, so that they may rise only to join his army.…Now, only those who serve the Raven-Eater dare to cross the Barren Plains."

With those final words, Whisper reached out and drew back the floral curtain to reveal their most perilous journey yet. Ian sucked in a breath and dared to follow Whisper's gaze.

A vast, open land stretched out for miles, cloaked by the treacherous dark sky, lit only by the purple and red lights that arced across the clouds. Trees, shrubs, and grasses were not to be found. In their place was a dry, dusty ground covered with loose dirt.

When they took their first step onto the Barren Plains, Ian made out tunnels of risen dirt that crisscrossed the ground. Whisper was careful to avoid them, stepping over each mound as though she respected the formations.

"What are those?"

"Only one creature braves the wrath of the Raven-Eater," Whisper answered. "A species so full of evil and revenge…vengeance…" she corrected herself, hating the fact that her second-language vocabulary had failed her at such a moment, "that it lives only to destroy lives. For that, the Raven-Eater allows its presence."

"What is it? The Giant Cockroach?"

Whisper's eyes narrowed; he felt the punch of her glare deep in his gut. "The more you mock my traditions, Mr. Daivya, the less progress we make."

Ian held out his hands in surrender. "OK, sorry. So what is it?" He followed his guide as she continued to make her way across the Barren Plains. Not a single sound accompanied their travel, but the silence screamed danger.

"Many moons ago," Whisper began, her voice seeming out of place among the quiet, "a man loved a woman who despised him. She would not take his hand in marriage, and his love for her consumed him. He could not eat, could not sleep, could not live. He would not live without her." Braving the consequences, she reached down and grasped a handful of dirt, letting it fall through her slender fingers as she walked on.

"The man went to the *Utlav*, a creature who greatly desired to be the matchmaker of souls. That night, the *Utlav* burrowed beneath the woman's longhouse and stole her heart while she slept." Whisper's hand drifted to her chest as she spoke and gently tapped her heart. "The *Utlav* took her heart to the man and told him to eat it so that she would be his forever. And so the man ate her heart."

Ian found himself intrigued, and was annoyed by the fact that he wanted to hear the rest of the story. "So what happened then?"

Whisper sighed disappointedly. "The woman awoke with a strange desire to be with the man. She could not resist the feeling, and so she went to the man, and they were married."

"Happily ever after, huh?"

She heard the sarcasm in his voice, but didn't address it. She wasn't finished yet. "The other men at the village were suspicious of the match, because the woman hated her husband. They knew her love was the work of an evil magic, and only one creature lived with the desire to join hearts."

"The *Utlav*."

"Yes." Whisper was so pleased that Ian actually remembered the name that she didn't bother correcting his terrible pronunciation. "They found him, and chased him underground, where he stayed for fear of being murdered by the angry villagers. But he continued to steal the hearts of women, out of vengeance and spite, and was never caught because he learned to use the earth as his sanctuary. In the Land of the Dead, the *Utlav* seeks revenge for his prosecution. He pretends to help, while leading his victims into a trap. And *that*, we will use to our advantage."

Ian ran a hand through his dirt and grime-caked hair. He knew where this was going. "So the *Utlav*...it's a mole, right?"

"Yes, Mr. Daivya."

"So...they're as annoying in the Land of the Dead as they are in real life." He wanted to kick one of the mounds like a child enjoying knocking over ant hills, but resisted the urge. After seeing the Giant Inchworm, he had no desire to instigate a fight against Mole. "Do you think they know we're here?" He frowned when Whisper's eyes took on a strange glint and the corners of her mouth tugged just a hint. "Why are you looking at me like that?"

Then, with dread in his gut, he watched as Whisper drove her fist straight into a loose mound of dirt.

"What...what are you doing?" he asked as she pulled away handfuls of dirt, her fingers stained black, until a small hole opened up in the earth. "Should you be doing that? Why are you just announcing yourself to this thing?"

"Mole already knows we are here, Mr. Daivya. He senses the vibrations of the earth."

"Then why taunt him? Seriously, why bring him here if the damn thing gets his kicks by ripping out women's hearts? Whisper, hello? Anyone there?" He waved his hand in front of the woman, who was on her knees in the dirt staring at him like he had just lost his mind.

Ignoring his questions, Whisper lowered herself until her lips were even with the level of the ground. She whispered to the *Utlav*, commanding his presence, demanding his help. When she was finished, she moved her head slightly to the side, and listened.

"Do you hear anything?" Ian couldn't help but ask. Her expression was one of anticipation, annoyance, and dread. "Well?" He lowered himself to his knees, keeping a close eye on the strange, enthralling woman. He longed to know what it was she felt, what connection she had to the spirit world, what made her so unique. "What do you hear?"

"I hear your voice in my ear, Mr. Daivya," Whisper commented, barely moving. Ian took the hint and backed away. A sudden rumble beneath the earth knocked him off his feet, but Whisper hardly noticed. Instead, she leapt back just in time to avoid the piercing claws of the *Utlav* as he popped up from the earth.

From behind, Ian watched in silent shock as a brown, round creature the size of a football crouched on the ground, then rose to its thick back legs and stared at Whisper with small, beady eyes that were heavily clouded over. Its spindly hair was standing on end, a low growl emerging from deep in its throat as its long, opaque nose sniffed the air.

"Grandfather Mole," Whisper said so quietly that Ian couldn't make out the words, "we need your help."

The *Utlav* responded only with a slight head movement and twitch of whiskers, but Whisper could hear the messages of deceit that traveled the rays of the creature's inner sight. *We are your humble servants*, they said kindly. *Let us assist you on your journey.*

Whisper was not to be fooled by his kindness, but pretended to be pleased by his words. She smiled, and if Ian hadn't of known she was just as deceitful as the *Utlav*, he would have thought she looked grateful.

"We seek safe passage through the Fire Mountains," she whispered, gesturing toward the black distance. "We ask for a guide to protect us from the Raven-Eater."

As you wish, my Queen. Mole bowed his head, closed his eyes, and disappeared into the earth.

"Where is he going?" Ian asked when the ground stopped shaking, indicating the *Utlav's* distance.

Whisper's eyes narrowed as they followed the trail that led straight into the Fire Mountains. "To inform the Raven-Eater of our presence."

A ferocious storm tore through the living world, pounding the Smoky Mountains, lifting trees from the ground and raising the river waters past their shores. At the campsite, Julia and her family found refuge in the Bard's trailer. At Howling Vines, the Elder rested in his hut without worry of the storm's dangers.

Howling Vines was protected from floods and falling trees by the magic of his ancestors. His father, grandfather, and grandfathers before that were powerful men, each of whom consecrated Howling Vines with chants and charms that fortified the clearing and made it a sanctuary for the ill, the lost, and the frightened. Smoke Speaker's father had been a healer, his grandfather a medicine man, and his great-grandfather a warrior blessed by the gods. Now it was up to the Elder to maintain his family's legacy.

He slept fitfully, his dreams consumed by images of Whisper's death. He saw her walking the Barren Plains, preoccupied by thoughts of the Raven-Eater. He saw that look of distracted concentration in her eyes, the one he had always warned her about. She had lived in her thoughts as a child, oblivious to the world around her. Many times he had to shout at her during their lessons to regain her attention, and more than once he was forced to slap her across the face in order to break her from her thoughts.

That was why he had named her *Kanegv*. It was a command within a name, ordering her from her thoughts while connecting with her as a person. A command to Speak, to whisper, to break free of the chains of thought and rejoin him in reality. Her intense focus on spirit worlds and battles brought her into an entirely different existence, as though she was able to transcend the living world into a brand new life.

For that reason, he knew she was guided by Butterfly, *Kamama*. *Kamama* was the only creature able to pass from the living to Spirit World, and back again. It was said that *Kamama* was responsible for the balance of nature, which meant the tiny and colorful beauty carried the weight of the world on its wings.

And so Smoke Speaker also knew his apprentice was born to change the course of the world. She was the embodiment of nature, the epitome of power. And now, she was about to sacrifice her life for her thoughts.

In his dreams, the Elder screamed at the young woman, shouting for her attention. But it was no use. Not even Ian could stop what happened next, the fury of the Raven-Eater, the deceit of Mole, the choking arrival into death.

Smoke Speaker awoke in a fit of sweat and tears. His heart raced, his blood ran cold, his fingers aching from the tight grip they had on the edge of the bed. The images of Whisper's black, vacant eyes and purple throat haunted him. Silently he prayed, begging the gods for their mercy, for their protecting hands, as the storm raged on outside.

When a bright flash of lightning lit up Howling Vines, Smoke Speaker rose from the bed and peeked outside. In the pouring rain, fierce winds, and rippling puddles, the fog was gone. When the storm passed, there would only be humidity and rainbows in its place.

At this point in the journey, Smoke Speaker no longer had the strength to hold the fog. He had failed Whisper, and now she was walking straight into her death.

Chapter 22

Whisper and Ian kept to the outskirts of the Barren Plains, where the tracks of the *Utlav* were less frequent and the light a bit brighter. Ian was always one step behind his guide, looking back over his shoulder, fingers tightly wrapped around the handle of the machete. Whisper's relaxed walk and stoic expression suggested tranquility, but the hold she had on her knife shouted caution. She was braced for an attack, but wasn't watching for one with every step she took. She had better things to do.

In the silence, Ian took the time to observe the Fire Tower, which was approaching faster than he would have liked. It was a castle he could have imagined only in his nightmares. Cold black steel twisted and turned to form looming towers that arced up toward the sky. Huge peaks tipped with flaming spikes warned any trespasser of impending danger, while windows barred with soiled slabs of wood prevented any prying eye from looking in, if one could ever get close enough to do so. Eight towers made up the mansion of murder and hate, rising from solid walls that wrapped around what he supposed to be a dry and decaying courtyard of sorts. It was blocked by an enormous gate decorated with dark red stones that glittered in the bare light. The land around the Fire Tower was damp and black, seeming to blend with the steel that was buried deep in the ground for strength against enemy battles. Large rocks surrounded the Fire Tower, further securing the building from unwanted visitors.

Ian wondered where the Raven-Eater found the steel to create such a wide and massive structure, but supposed it didn't really matter. All that did matter was the fact that each turret, doorway, and eave that made up the Fire Tower was sharp, dangerous, and solid as stone. No one could scale those jagged walls, climb across slanted roofs spiked with metal nails, or sneak up on what he guessed were guard dogs that leapt from the small, dark entryways at every nook and cranny.

Worse, even more so than the jagged walls and looming turrets, was the heat that radiated off the Fire Tower. True to its name, the Tower pumped heat from its every square inch, a heat that was visible in the dark light. It wavered across the Fire Mountains, fingers of it reaching their way through the Barren Plains. Ian could feel touches of heat as they walked closer, reminding him of long, hot days beneath the sun as he labored in a customer's yard. This heat wasn't as suffocating, but it was uncomfortable nonetheless. He could only imagine what inside the Fire Tower felt like.

As she led the way toward the Fire Mountains, Whisper thought back to the Elder. She hadn't received a message from him in awhile, and for that reason, she knew he must be tired, must be wavering in his steadfast ability. Smoke Speaker was an old man, and this journey was too much for his body. As a child, she'd never thought she would see the day that Smoke Speaker lost his strength, his power. He was always a leader, always the majestic teacher, the father she never had.

Whisper barely remembered her parents, her home among her people. At times she saw them in her dreams, a beautiful mother with lost hope in her eyes, and a menacing father who cared only for gratifying his own desires. Her mother had done her best to shield her daughter from her father's hate, but Whisper nevertheless had her father's detestation spread across her back. It was a scar Smoke Speaker had long since covered with the black and red Western Sun that swirled between her shoulder blades, a scar that ached with every passing moment, a scar that told the story of the day her father tried to kill her.

She didn't remember how Smoke Speaker got her away from the man who could not control his rage, and didn't care to. All that mattered to her was that she stayed true to the Elder.

"Do you hear that?"

Ian's voice broke Whisper from her thoughts. She stopped, turning just enough to exchange a glance with her companion. "Hear what, Mr. Daivya?"

A sudden explosion of wind knocked Whisper off her feet, throwing her onto her back. Her throat tightened, and she clawed at the invisible fingers clutched around her neck as all the air disappeared from her lungs.

For five long seconds, Ian watched, dumbfounded, as Whisper writhed on the ground, feet kicking, eyes wide with fright and confusion, mouth gasping for air. He had no idea what to do, or what was happening. The woman looked like she was having a seizure, and he was at a loss for both words and actions.

Then the creature appeared, shimmering out of thin air. A ghastly woman formed, with long, knotted white hair that twisted around gnarled shoulders, full black eyes wide with murderous intent, and a warped body hidden beneath a ragged, flowing cloak that swirled around her like a tornado.

Ian reacted the only way he knew how. He reached out with a solid right hook, and was blown back ten feet by an invisible punch, head connecting solidly with the ground.

Fighting the burning fear in her chest, the dizziness in her head, the panic in her heart, Whisper grasped for the witch. Anger surged through her, mixing with fear.

When her foot connected with her adversary's gut, the hold on her throat loosened just enough to let in a quick, refreshing breath.

Screaming with rage, the witch lifted Whisper from the ground with strength unknown to human power. As Ian struggled to clear his head and regain full consciousness, Whisper fought the black cloud covering her eyes as she gasped for breath. Her feet kicked the air, eyes squeezing shut as her face darkened to a frightening scarlet shade.

Elder, she prayed silently, searching for his guidance, for his strength, as the witch lifted her higher off the ground, an evil laughter piercing her ears and bringing forth a thin trickle of blood.

This had never happened before. She had never been caught unaware, never been forced to fight so hard for her own life, never felt the incredible pain of her throat constricting as her lungs burned and strange, gargled noises escaped her lips.

In her final effort, Whisper reached up with what might she had left, and plunged the thin blade of her knife into the witch's wrist.

The night sky erupted with a horrific wail, a furious scream that echoed for miles. The witch reared back, throwing Whisper to the ground, landing on top of her. Black blood spurted across the earth, filling Whisper's eyes, blinding her. The witch slammed her good hand into Whisper's face, snarling in a foreign tongue as saliva dripped from cracked lips that hid rotted teeth.

Before she could regain composure, Whisper felt the fingers wrap around her throat again, slippery with blood but tightening nonetheless. She grabbed for her knife, picking up dry dirt instead. Her heart beat wildly as she struggled against the weight of the witch, barely feeling the jabs to her ribs, the lacerations across her neck and shoulders from sharp nails. Her world was fading, her fight losing power. Her mother's image flashed behind her eyes, a tormented look of desperation spread across her face.

Then she disappeared into nothingness.

Silently, smoothly, Ian rose from the ground. Dark red blood dripped down his cheeks, anger flashing from his eyes. The whirling tornado of cloth and power had diminished, replaced by a visible fury that vibrated in the air. It was a fury that matched what was pumping through his blood.

In one swift, fluid movement, overcome by a dark rage that pulsed through his veins and dug deep roots into his heart, Ian lifted the machete above his head and swung down hard. The blade split through the witch's back like a boat through murky waters. Before Ian could even react to what he'd done, she vanished in an explosion of black dust.

For a moment Ian merely stood in place, staring at the cloudy air. He marveled at the sensation of murder, the thrill of triumph, the fear of becoming just like his guide. Then, ignoring the strange bitter taste in his mouth that formed in response to the cloud burst, he dropped to Whisper's side and frantically searched for signs of life.

"Whisper? Whisper, can you hear me?" She responded only by choking and gasping for air. Ian gently lifted her head, brushing sweat and dirt-caked hair away from her face. He grimaced when he saw the ugly bruises across her throat, the blood dripping from her ears. "Breathe, Whisper, you can do it. Come on."

Wheezing in a breath and spitting out a mouthful of dirt and dust, Whisper reached up weakly and wiped at her eyes. The witch's black blood was sticky and thick, and felt like a mix of tar and oil as she struggled to free her vision from the gooey mess. Ian helped, mopping up the blood with the end of his shirt until he could see the whites of her eyes. He pretended not to see the fear, because he knew that would only embarrass her. Instead, he blotted the black smudges on her temples and cheeks and grinned.

"It's a good look for you," he commented, helping her rise to a sitting position. "The whole raccoon mask made out of crazy lady blood."

Despite the searing pain in her throat and the fire in her chest, Whisper nearly grinned. "A witch," she said in response, her agonizing vocal cords throbbing as she spoke. "A restless spirit…spy…for the…Raven-Eater."

With the combination of her strange accent and hoarse voice from the strangling, Ian didn't understand a word she said. "Don't try to talk. Just take it easy for a second." He was pleased that she followed his command by lying back down and getting her breathing under control. Her bottom lip was bloody, her right cheek purple and swollen, and judging by the hand she had clutched on her side, her ribs were bruised and possibly cracked.

Whisper lifted a hand to her bare but bruised throat. "My necklace," she said fretfully. "Where is it?"

Ian glanced around until he saw the beaded necklace that had been ripped off by the witch. He retrieved it and handed the hemp-string bones to Whisper, who quickly fastened it in its proper place. The bright white bones and beads looked out of place against the purple bruises and black blood. "So," he commented thoughtfully, "I guess you're not as invincible as I thought."

The statement irritated Whisper. She sat up, glaring at Ian through slightly-blurred black eyes. "I am still alive, am I not, Mr. Daivya?" Her voice was surprisingly cool and collected, even though her neck and shoulders were covered with multiple contusions, some of which surrounded deep lacerations, and her ears were still ringing while blood dried on her lobes. But she couldn't be too angry with him, for even she was surprised by her weakness.

"You proved yourself a warrior," she complimented, glancing down at the blood-covered machete. Ian smiled proudly in response then helped her as she attempted to stand. Her knees buckled once when her ribs shouted their protest, but she ignored the pain. Once she was sure her balance was restored, she rubbed her neck and ran a slightly-shaking hand through her hair. "Now you must prove yourself a man."

Rather than be insulted, Ian laughed to himself and shook his head. The woman just had her ass kicked and she was still as arrogant as ever. The blood smudged across her face made her look like a masked bandit, and her attitude certainly matched the appearance.

Whisper took a few hobbling steps forward, determined to be the strong, unwavering guide she knew she was. He stared at her back as she walked away, slow and limping. Her shirt was torn, claw marks shredding the material. Through those holes he could see the rest of that fascinating tattoo, the wavy lines that surrounded primitive trees, the jagged lines that looked like mountains, and there, in the center of one long black strip, the word *Ayohuhisdi*.

"Whisper." Ian picked up the machete then jogged until he caught up with his guide. "What does that word mean? The one on your lower back?"

Whisper turned, surprised to see the shreds of blood-splattered cloth. She took in a deep breath, fighting the pain in her chest. "It is no concern of yours, Mr. Daivya," she answered raspily. "Your concern lies with your son."

"My concern lies with the truth." He was mad, and his fatherly, alpha-male tone reflected that. "Don't forget that I just saved your life."

Whisper stalked up to Ian until she was right in his face. "And I thank you. But I too have saved your life, Mr. Daivya, so now our souls are at peace with one another."

She had him there. The woman, despite being the reason behind his death, had kept him safe throughout their journey in the Land of the Dead. So he caved and backed off. "Fine…then at least answer me this. Why was that psycho trying to kill you?"

In response the sky erupted with ear-splitting wails that had Whisper and Ian cringing and gripping their heads. Swirls of black spun around them, circling the pair and forcing them back-to-back. Ian's hand tightened on the machete handle, while Whisper grasped for her knife only to find it missing. She glanced to her left to see it lying on the ground where the witch had attacked just moments ago.

"You got to be kidding me," Ian muttered when the sulfur-smelling spinning stopped, and six evil spirits stood in its place. "Family reunion, huh?"

They resembled the witch killed by his own hand—the same scraggly black hair, flowing and translucent rags hanging from bony bodies, pale skin that flashed with images of bone and blood. Their faces were twisted into grimaces of hate, sharp teeth flecked with brown spots and saliva eagerly awaiting a taste of enemy flesh, sunken and hollowed eyes wide with anticipation of a fight. They stood with their gnarled hands out at their sides, taking small steps forward toward their next victims.

"Are you ready, Mr. Daivya?"

"Ready?" Ian repeated incredulously, shouting over the wind as it picked up and threw dirt in his face. He lifted the machete. "What the hell are we supposed to do?"

"Fight."

He could feel her back tense against his. He spared a second's glance over his shoulder to see that she had no weapon. "What are you going to fight with?! Take the machete!"

Whisper lowered herself slightly, glaring at one of the spirits and silently goading him into a confrontation. "No, Mr. Daivya, I have other ways."

Before he could ask just what those ways were, the first spirit lunged.

On reflex Ian lifted the machete in front of his face, and the witch exploded on contact. A whoosh of black dust swarmed over him, clogging his ears and eyes. But just as he was marveling over how easy the kill had been, a set of razor-sharp claws dragged its way down his shoulder and across his chest. When they reached his throat, Whisper spun around and grabbed hold of the witch's wrist, twisting the arm and snapping the bone clean. The scream of pain echoed throughout their minds, but before the witch could move Whisper had pulled an arrow from her quiver and slammed it down into its eye, yanking it out just as the spirit vanished in a cloud of darkness.

"Four left, Mr. Daivya." She was panting, but he could still sense the thrill exuding from his guide. She lived for this kind of danger.

As though driven by some sort of primal competition, Ian released a guttural scream and launched himself forward, right in between two snarling and spitting spirits. At the same time, Whisper pushed off of him and went hand-to-hand with the third and fourth, dodging the daggers with a grace born out of need and desperation. She kept her eyes trained on those weapons, arching back to avoid a slice to the gut. She felt a hand wrap around the back of her neck and she grabbed for the witch, her fingers grasping cold, hard hair. She yanked down, feeling the spirit's hot breath on her throat while the other shifted the dagger in its hand, poised to cut her open from navel to nose.

Just as it was lowering the blade, Whisper stomped the earth. The ground erupted in a flurry of dirt at the spirit's feet. A flash of brown and fur lashed out and sucked the spirit into the narrow hole. Leaving Mole to devour his prey, Whisper spun agilely from the witch's hold and dropped to her knees, sliding across the ground to her knife. The witch followed, shrieking and flying with a speed not humanly possible. As it leapt with arms reaching for her throat, Whisper lifted the blade and sent it straight into the spirit's heart.

Just feet away, Ian was struggling through his own battle. He had fought them off for as long as possible, knocking one to the ground and battling sword-to-machete with the other. His body showed the signs of his fight—shallow lacerations across his chest, deep cuts in his forearms and upper thigh, bruises on his face. His ears burned with the spirits' screams and his head felt as though a freight train had just run through it.

With one last push, Ian kicked the witch in the shin then lashed out with the blade, burying it in the spirit's neck. Rather than a burst of air, this one died slowly, melting to the earth in a pool of black, steaming blood. When it was gone, Ian stood over the spot, satisfied.

Then he heard the shriek behind him. Spinning in a circle, losing his balance, Ian could do nothing but watch as the dagger came down toward his chest.

Out of the corner of his eye Ian saw Whisper move. Less than a second later, her knife pierced through the spirit's back, and it disappeared with a look of shock on its face.

Free of the fight, the pair took a moment to collect themselves and catch their breath. Whisper picked up her knife and held it tightly, ready for more unwelcome visitors, while Ian took a seat and tended to his wounds.

Whisper watched him, noting the look of both anger and pride spread across his ragged face. "Oh no, Mr. Daivya, you are not a murderer at all." She said it slyly, wiping a spot of blood from the corner of her mouth. There was a hint of satisfaction in her voice.

"I'm not like you."

"Are you convincing me, or yourself?"

Ian hesitated, looking over his shoulder at the bare ground. Not a trace of the evil spirits remained but for marks in the dirt from their feet. And they were gone because he had killed them. Or at the very least, sliced them open and sent them into whatever world awaited those who died their second death.

He avoided Whisper's haughty gaze and shrugged. "Believe whatever you want. I know who and what I am. But what I don't know is why those witches were after us and wanted to kill us."

"Because *Utlav* did his duty. He aided us during the fight because I asked him not to, and he sent word to the Fire Tower because I asked for his secrecy." Whisper looked off to the west, toward the Fire Mountains, as she wiped away the blood from her ears. Her stare shifted to Ian. As always, he felt saddened and terrified by her eyes, and wondered what it was she had seen through her years that gave them such age.

"So what does that mean?"

Whisper's lips curled into an evil smirk. "They know we are here."

Safely tucked away in his new room, Cole bounced from foot to foot and jabbed at invisible bad guys with his freshly-sharpened spear. One of the guards outside the door had shown him how to rub the blade against a special rock to grind it down to a point, and ever since then, the boy hadn't stopped practicing his hunting skills.

I'm gonna be the best hunter ever, he told himself, pretending that his enemy, the giant buffalo, had just fallen to the ground. He pumped his arms in victory. *Raven daddy will be proud.*

He paused then, frowning. The scary Raven man wasn't his father. But...who was? He couldn't remember his real father's name. He knew he had blue eyes, and that he worked outside, but...what else? All Cole could see when he tried to picture his father was the Raven-Eater.

Oh, well. Cole shrugged his shoulders and went back to hunting practice. He wasn't too concerned with who his father was anymore. Here, wherever "here" was, he got awesome food, lots of awesome toys, and a huge awesome room. The woman named Gentle Heart had even given him a shaggy black dog that he named Ghost. He couldn't remember why he liked that name, but it fit his new pet, who was quiet and liked to sneak up on people.

Cole was so consumed by his pretend hunt that he didn't hear the fierce wail that echoed through the Fire Mountains from the direction of the Barren Plains. But even if he had, he wouldn't have bothered to care. There were strange noises all the time. Sometimes they sounded like people crying, sometimes like wolves howling. Sometimes he couldn't figure out what they were. The noises used to scare him, but now he was used to them. He didn't even jump into defense-mode anymore when someone started to open his door.

The door was opening now. The guard appeared in the frame. He was tall and well built, with thick black hair, dark eyes, a strong chin, and even stronger cheekbones that signified his Navajo heritage. A long scar, accented by several smaller wounds, was spread across his left cheek, trailing down his neck and shoulder. It was that wound that killed him, a wound he was forced to wear even in death. His face could have been friendly, but a guard for the Raven-Eater never smiled.

He wore buckskin pants carefully stitched by Gentle Heart's own hand, with three solid red stripes just above the right knee that showed his acceptance into the Fire Tower. His shirt was one made for a warrior, fringed at the end with red beads, slit at both shoulders to reveal thick black tattoos, and decorated with a blood-red bird silhouette design that spread across his chest to announce that he was under the protection of the Raven-Eater. His beautiful clothing was accented by the leather bands wrapped around his wrists, the white bone beads in his hair, and the small black circles that lined his cheekbones.

Cole once feared this man, named Hunting Hawk. Now, he was his friend. He thought of them as cousins of sorts, since they both proudly wore the Raven-Eater's mark. Hunting Hawk displayed his on his clothing, but Cole's had been burned onto his upper arm.

He'd been terrified when Hunting Hawk and three other guards held him down and lifted a red-hot metal rod from the fire. When the metal touched his flesh, he'd screamed and kicked one of the guards in the stomach, but the grip on his wrists and legs only tightened. These burns were to show Cole's acceptance by the Raven-Eater, they'd explained, to announce to the Land of the Dead that he was protected by Greatness.

The boy's arm now boasted that protection with three straight lines stacked on one another in increasing lengths.

"The Raven-Eater wishes you to see something," Hunting Hawk said, his deep voice booming into the room. "Come with me."

Cole set down his spear and followed the guard through the Fire Tower, glancing around excitedly when they walked outside. He hadn't been allowed outdoors since he first arrived, getting only glimpses from his window. The vast openness of the world surprised him. There was so much land, so many mountains and plains and dying trees, but no houses. He wondered where everyone else lived.

He saw the Raven-Eater in the distance. The Guardian of the Dead no longer scared him and he was getting used to his frightening appearance, but he still was nervous about speaking to him. Cole was glad the Raven-Eater was far away, standing at the edge of a cliff as he stared down at the Barren Plains.

"Great things are happening, Fighting Fox." Cole still didn't like being called Fighting Fox, but didn't feel the need to say anything. The guard, though, wasn't pleased by the look on the boy's face. It meant he still remembered his past life.

Gentle Heart too refused to give up her memories, in the beginning. Hunting Hawk supposed that was because the Raven-Eater took her while she was still alive. Only a living woman in the Land of the Dead could act as the guardian's proper wife, warm and real with beauty that never faded, but being alive meant she still remembered. The Raven-Eater had taken care of that, though, clouding her mind with thoughts of him, and him alone. She fought them at first, and eventually gave in.

His magic also made sure she stayed young forever. His son would age only as quickly as the Raven-Eater allowed, a body able to grow in death because of the guardian's great magic. With a wife devoted to him, and a child trained to one day take over his kingdom, the Raven-Eater's family was restored, just as they were in the living world. Cole's mind would strengthen, his knowledge would grow, and the guardian's wife would be there to answer his every beck and call.

The Raven-Eater no longer trusted Gentle Heart to give him a proper heir. She failed him once, producing a hideous child born only to destroy him, and it would not happen again. He had destroyed that abomination, and his children would now be taken from the Land of the Living.

"The world is changing," Hunting Hawk asserted to Cole, his voice shaking the boy's soul. "The world is the Raven-Eater's to command. Soon, his army will rise and make war with the living. Our world will consume theirs, and both the living and dead will be cast into darkness." Then he pointed, and Cole followed his finger to the Barren Plains that sat at the base of the Fire Mountains.

Through wide, amazed eyes, Cole watched as the earth shook and rumbled in the distance. Bodies buried deep in the ground emerged, shaking off dirt as they slowly rose, turning to face the Raven-Eater. They were his loyal followers, forced into servitude by their own greed and malicious actions. Now they would be ordered to destroy the world they tried so hard to perfect.

"Together, Fighting Fox, you and your father will take over the Land of the Living, and will rule both worlds."

Chapter 23

The day was crisp and clear, the bright sun shining down from a cloudless blue sky. It seemed that finally, after a month of incredible and mysterious fog, nature was giving Sheriff Ray Forbe a break. By this point, he believed Cole Daivya to be dead, but he would find the boy's body if it was his final task on earth.

The Elder's testimony, as they were now calling the sketches Julia brought back from Howling Vines, was being treated as evidence toward Smoke Speaker and Whisper's guilt in the child's disappearance. To physically call them murderers was too much of a stretch for him right now—he'd known Whisper since she was six years old and she'd never caused harm to any one or thing—but he couldn't ignore the facts.

His plan had been to bring Smoke Speaker in for questioning, but he and his deputies had run into a new kind of problem. When his officers had gone to collect the Elder, they had encountered an entire brigade of animals and insects blocking their path. The creatures formed a circle around Howling Vines, everything from bears and mountain lions to rattlesnakes and hawks. Tranquilizer guns had been brought in, but to no avail. They were chased off before any break in the line could be made. The sight was amazing and awe-inspiring, but frustrating nonetheless. Even Forbe was surprised by the Elder's power and influence.

The media, having finally caught wind of the boy's disappearance, was having a field day with the story. Reporters were throwing out speculation after speculation, dubbing Smoke Speaker and Whisper the "Cherokee Killers" and accusing Ian of having an affair with the beautiful apprentice. Some even went so far as to question Julia's competence as a mother and wife, blaming her for her son's disappearance. All the negative press had forced the owners of Big Creek Campground to ask Forbe to move his headquarters elsewhere. Now, they had set up camp at the nearest hotel, and were working round the clock.

With the good weather, volunteers had rejoined the search and were currently combing the woods. Julia and her parents were out with them, while her sister was helping keep the deputies fed. In Forbe's opinion, the young hippie was more interested in flirting with Deputy Duff than finding her nephew.

For the thousandth time, Forbe flipped through the journal. Whether by the Elder's magic or his own exhaustion, the pictures seemed to be alive, reaching out to him, guiding him through Whisper and Ian's journey. If he were to believe these pages, then the two were in the Land of the Dead. He recognized the Bridge of the Dead from stories his father told him, stories he'd heard from the Elder himself. But if they were in the Land of the Dead, then that meant that Whisper and Ian were no longer alive, which could only mean that Smoke Speaker killed them, and probably Cole too.

As she walked through the woods, peering behind every tree, every bush, Julia kept one thought in mind. She didn't believe in the Land of the Dead, but was starting to believe that the Elder drew those pictures specifically for her, to throw her off track. But he wouldn't make a fool out of her.

They were nearing the river. She could hear the water trickling in the distance, and couldn't help but remember their first day at the campsite when Cole slipped and nearly fell off the rock. Call it a mother's intuition, but she felt that the river, more so than the Elder or Whisper, contributed to her son's death. She could no longer deny the fact that her son was dead, and supposed it was pure adrenaline and a lingering yet suppressed denial that kept her from breaking down. Her focus was on finding his body, and maybe then she would let herself grieve.

Ian was no longer her concern. Her husband had been distant and emotionally gone for longer than she could remember. Now he had abandoned her during the toughest, most devastating time she would ever face in her life. She'd seen the drawings, him holding a gorgeous woman, and she couldn't deny the fact that wherever he was, he was with Whisper. So now, Ian was forgotten. All Julia wanted was her son, and she had to make an enemy out of her husband in order to block the horrific feelings of despair that formed when she thought of her marriage.

"We'll find him," Olivia said, as though reading her mind. She was panting; her knees ached terribly, but this was the first clear day they'd had since Cole went missing and there was no way she was going to waste it on complaints.

"I know," Julia said determinedly, the thought of Smoke Speaker's journal sparking a renewed fire in her heart. "Today's the day. We're—"

Suddenly the world....pulsed. Julia and the others froze, staring to their sides as the woods shook and the leaves rustled in a fresh blast of wind. It was over in a second, but no one could rid their bodies of that rumble of terror rushing through their blood.

"What the hell was that?" Julia asked, gripping her father's arm. "What just happened?"

Smoke Speaker knew exactly what was going on.

His heart leapt in his throat, his knees buckling, forcing him to the floor of his hut. Even though his animal friends protected him from the police, he now knew their efforts were all in vain.

A new danger was taking over this world.

The dead had been disturbed, forced from their eternal resting places to join the Raven-Eater's war. Soon they would emerge from the Western Sun, bringing their curses with them. And worse, the searchers were nearly upon Cole's body.

If he is found...if he is buried, Smoke Speaker thought, frantically building a fire in the middle of his hut with shaking hands, *then we fail. Our world ends. Whisper...you must HURRY.*

As the smoke rose to the roof, the Elder reached out to the last dead soul that could help them. *Old friend,* he prayed, sending out his message as quickly as possible, *our last hope lies with you.*

In just seconds he got his answer. *I do this, old man,* the voice said in return, *and my debt is paid. I have no loyalty to you.*

Chapter 24

Whisper and Ian had just reached the bottom of the Fire Mountains when the ground shook and a sinister feel corrupted the air. They spun around and watched in horror as rotting hands and decomposing corpses pushed and groaned their way through the surface of the earth.

Dread rose in Whisper's gut. The dead souls stood before her, standing perfectly straight on shaking knees with their arms at their sides. They stared ahead with empty eye sockets, quietly breathing through tongueless mouths—the Raven-Eater had their eyes and tongues removed as a part of their eternal curse.

These were the men who killed the Raven-Eater's family, who murdered the real Gentle Heart and Fighting Fox. These were the women and children of those men, slaved into eternal service and damnation because of the sins of their husbands and fathers. But they were also the souls the Guardian of the Dead had recruited for his army, thieves and rapists he had ripped from the Spirit World, suicidal serial killers bent on destruction. The sight of such an army rising was both heartbreaking and terrifying.

"What are they doing?" Ian whispered, the words trembling from his lips.

"Waiting for orders," his guide answered, gripping the knife at her belt. "The Raven-Eater is preparing for war."

"With who?"

Whisper turned her ghostly eyes to Ian. "The living."

Before Ian could stutter out another question, a shout from above caught his attention. Both he and Whisper glanced up, and while he took a step back in fear at the sight, she merely grinned her wicked grin.

The line of soldiers marched down a well-worn path faster than Ian ever would have thought imaginable. Spears, knives, and arrows were drawn as the guards neared, their faces marked with black smudges, their hair drawn back tightly and secured with bone pins at the napes of their necks, which were beaded with sweat. Ian was positive they were going to kill them, but Whisper didn't seem concerned. In fact, she seemed eager for their arrival.

Sure enough, Whisper moved forward when the guards approached, not at all concerned by their fierce faces or blood-stained weapons. She feared no one.

Whisper untied the pouch at her belt and held it up as the guards approached. The contents shimmered through the leather, curiously catching their eyes. "I offer free passage into the Spirit World for any who aid us on our journey."

For a moment no one said a word. The guards stood poised with their arrows raised high, Whisper braving their wrath and holding the mysterious pouch up, Ian staying a few steps back with his arms crossed cautiously, afraid to look any of them in the eye. In the background, the dead souls waited for their orders.

Finally one man lowered his weapon and moved forward from the line of guards. He was tall, with thick black hair tied back in a bun and secured with thin bone pins. His face was scarred, evidence of his years warring with enemy villages, shadowed by wide tattoos that circled down his neck. Pants patched up with thick layers of leather hid toned legs, but his arms, chest, and shoulders were completely exposed to the harsh winds of the Fire Mountains. He was heavily muscled, with tattoos and scars that intertwined with one another. Whisper didn't recognize the markings, but then again, she didn't know much about the symbols of the Plains tribes. They had no connection to her own people, in her opinion. But they were intriguing nonetheless.

So, she has a heart after all, Ian mused despite his panic. He noticed the way her gaze lingered as she looked him up and down, and even though her expression was one of disgust and courage, he knew her well enough by now. She never looked at anyone that long, not even in hatred. And he doubted she even realized what she had done. After all, she herself claimed she wasn't capable of love.

"Who are you?" Whisper demanded to know, lowering the pouch and holding it to her stomach as though worried he would try to steal it.

"Hunting Hawk," the man answered, his voice so deep and menacing that Ian's breath was nearly taken away. "How is your offer possible?"

Whisper turned her head slightly, but enough so that everyone knew she didn't want Ian to hear her reply. Hunting Hawk gestured to an overhang far enough away from the group, then signaled to his men to watch Ian while he was gone.

For the first time during her journey, Whisper followed someone else. She stayed behind Hunting Hawk as they approached their meeting place, keeping a close eye on him in case he attempted an attack. Instead, he merely turned, crossed his arms, and waited.

Whisper eyed him curiously, wondering why he was so willing to talk rather than kill. Perhaps the promise of the Spirit World was greater than the wrath of the

Raven-Eater. "Do you know who I am?" she asked, tucking the pouch into her belt and holding her head high.

Hunting Hawk smirked. *"Kanegv,"* he answered, taking a step closer. "Our spies know everything."

"Do they know how to pass into the Spirit World?"

"Do you?"

Insulted, but determined not to show it, Whisper produced the pouch and opened it just wide enough to reveal the sparkling contents. She watched Hunting Hawk as he leaned over and peered into the leather bag. The gold glimmer reflected off his tanned skin. Although she despised anyone willing to give up their eternal souls for the Raven-Eater, she couldn't help but take in his scars. She respected scars, respected their story. She had hers; Smoke Speaker was marked by his life. And now she was considering giving Hunting Hawk a new one for his arrogance.

"My Elder is a powerful shaman," she said, closing the pouch. The golden glow disappeared into the darkness. "He has traveled far, and met many along the way who have shared their secrets. I offer passage into the Spirit World, but demand your assistance in return."

Hunting Hawk matched her haughty tone with his own. "Suppose I simply kill you, and take the magic myself."

"Without the prayer, you will not reach the Spirit World."

There may have been a prayer, but Hunting Hawk doubted it. He knew the woman was a master of deception. No one could reach the Fire Mountains through honesty. She obviously was hiding the truth from her traveling companion, who was desperately trying to hear their conversation.

Still, he was amused by her self-assurance, and interested in her offer. "The Raven-Eater has ordered your death. Trespassers on his land are not accepted, especially during times of war... What do you wish in return for this gift?"

The corners of Whisper's mouth turned up to form her plotting, conniving grin. "In exchange for your passage, and the passage of your men, I ask for one thing." She glanced over her shoulder at Ian, who was staring right at her, then turned her eyes back to Hunting Hawk.

Ian was not going to like what happened next.

Julia stood on the bank of the river, hands on her hips as she stared out across the water. It was a lost cause, in her opinion. The incredibly thick, almost magically destructive fog over the past month had limited police attempts to search the river. With almost zero visibility and the danger of sharp rocks, fast rapids, and sudden drop offs, even the most experienced river guides weren't willing to risk the currents.

Now the air was crystal clear, and the river was waiting. Sheriff Forbe was insistent that they scour the waters, but Julia was skeptical. Even if they found Cole's body, it would be unrecognizable, something she never wanted to see. But she doubted he would be found. After so many long days of searching, so many long hours crying over her lost son and husband, Julia had resolved the issue herself. In her mind, Cole was taken by a sadistic killer, an evil man who haunted the woods. Forbe and the other deputies had shared stories of other missing children over the years, children Whisper and Smoke Speaker had managed to find. The cases were all too similar to ignore the connection.

Bottom line, Cole would not be found.

"Forbe!" Deputy Duff shouted suddenly, thigh-deep in the river and bracing himself against a rock to fight off the current. Dread dropped like a rock of fire in Julia's gut as she watched the sheriff race over to the bank. David and Olivia froze in place, barely able to breathe.

The three of them stood back, unable to move as four more deputies entered the water, staring down at something hidden behind a rock. Pushed forward by a strange force of motherly nature and a fearful curiosity that had to be satisfied, Julia edged her way closer, ignoring her mother's desperate pleas to stay behind. David reached for her arm, but she brushed him off, waving an absent hand in his direction.

She had to know. She had to know what they were looking at, what was causing that deep crease in Forbe's forehead, that look of misery in Duff's eyes.

Her feet moved silently over fallen leaves and twigs. Everything else disappeared; all sounds faded into nothingness. Life was only a dream, and nothing existed except for what was found in that narrow tunnel of vision that led straight to the river.

One of the officers tried to hold her back when her shoes touched water, but Julia couldn't be stopped. Later, she wouldn't remember shoving the man to the ground or tripping over a rock and busting open her knee. She wouldn't remember the bitter cold of the water, the strength of the current. All she could focus on was the water, seeing past the rapids.

And there, at the bottom of the river tucked between two thick boulders, was the wavering blue image of her son's T-shirt.

Chapter 25

Ray Forbe marched through the woods, stomping across logs and loose dirt, shoving branches out of his way. This time, when he reached Howling Vines, he wasn't leaving without Elder Smoke Speaker.

Cole Daivya's body had been found shoved so tightly beneath a crevice that it had to have been done by a human hand. It was possible that the strong currents had somehow managed to push him against the rocks over the past month, but Forbe wasn't stupid. Cole was put there on purpose. The only reason they even found him was because Duff had been standing at just the right angle downriver looking in just the right direction at the one second the rapids parted long enough to reflect the bright blue color of the boy's shirt. And even then the Deputy hadn't been sure that he actually saw something. Plus, they were so far away from the place Cole disappeared that it didn't seem likely he'd of traveled such a distance, yet another reason why the sheriff was so sure Cole was murdered.

But that wasn't the main reason Forbe knew Smoke Speaker was behind the boy's death. After a month, Cole's body should have been destroyed by the elements. But when they pulled him out of the water it looked like Cole's exterior body had been preserved the entire month he was dead. The sheer impossibility of that fact caused the police to demand a full investigation and autopsy to determine how exactly that happened.

Or maybe Cole hadn't been dead since his disappearance, but was killed just days before they found him. That was another thought rolling around in Forbe's mind. Either way, someone was taking the blame.

As expected, Howling Vines was empty, so quiet and still that it seemed abandoned. He didn't mind. Taking a seat on a hand-carved chair, Forbe leaned back, stared at the empty fire hearth, and waited.

Smoke Speaker was no fool either. He knew Sheriff Ray Forbe was out for his blood, and didn't need his animal friends to tell him first. The river spirits informed him when the boy's body was found, and less than five minutes later the Elder was on the move.

He found sanctuary at the lake in which Ian took his last breath, the lake Smoke Speaker had recently named Whisper's Waters. Few people knew of this location, and so he was sure that he had enough time for Whisper to either succeed or fail before he was caught.

The Elder stood knee-deep in the water, gripping his innately carved staff and balancing himself in the thick mud. All around him was quiet. Black crows watched him from the treetops, eyes wide and accusatory. A fox sat on the lake shore, tail tucked around her legs and head cocked slightly to the side. Up above, an owl soared silently through the trees, rustling not so much as a single leaf. They were there to observe the ceremony, regardless of whether or not they approved.

Such silence didn't bother Smoke Speaker. In fact, he welcomed it. This was a solemn time, a time for respect and sacrifice.

He stared down at that sacrifice now, two young people who had given up their lives for a greater cause. One had died so his son could live, the other had chosen destiny in eternal darkness. No one in this world would ever know what they had done, but if they succeeded, everything would change. Neither the living nor the dead would ever be the same.

One month ago Smoke Speaker had anchored Whisper and Ian's bodies to the bottom of the lake by securing heavy rocks to their waists. For one month they had been lying in the mud, Whisper's long hair swirling in the water, Ian's blue eyes still half-open in shock. The Elder knew ways to preserve their bodies, as he had done with the boy to confuse the police when they found him, but with these two it didn't seem necessary. Instead, he had only half-preserved their bodies just for his own peace of mind. Luckily, the ripples and lake grasses shielded his view from the toll of thirty days of death.

Lowering himself to his knees, the Elder reached out and placed a hand on Whisper's heart. The water came up to his chin, and he shivered from the cold waves. This was the only way he could reach her now, by speaking to her soul. He couldn't return to his camp, and it was too dangerous making a fire here, where people may see the smoke rising above the tree tops.

He could only pray she understood his message.

Chapter 26

When Ian opened his eyes, dried black mud patched to a thick ceiling filled his vision. The ground was hard, cramping his back as he stretched out the kinks in his neck. Dark gray drops of liquid dripped all around him, much like the Weeping Forest had done, while ugly red bugs crawled over his legs.

In a spasm of panic, Ian swatted the creatures away and leapt to his feet, spinning in a complete circle. Instantly dizzy, he touched the side of his head, surprised when his fingers came back bloody. Slowly, the events of the past day came back to his memory.

He remembered watching Whisper closely as she spoke to the guard, trying to read her lips but unsuccessful in his attempts. That look of calculating deceit had worried him, and he'd had a feeling of dread, knowing that something terrible was about to happen. The guard, a man named Hunting Hawk, had stared at Whisper as though amused by her tough façade, then his eyes darkened. When Whisper glanced Ian's way, the fear set in.

In less than a minute, it seemed, Hunting Hawk made a gesture and Ian's arms were yanked behind his back and he was struck across the head before he could even stammer out a protest. And now he was waking up in some hot, stuffy dungeon of a room where his feet stuck to the floor and the only light came from a thin, barred window in the corner.

Following the red and purple beam, Ian saw Whisper lying on her side in a shallow layer of muddy water, her back to him. From across the room, he couldn't tell if she was breathing. Slowly he crept over, craning his neck as he strained to see her face, which was hidden behind tresses of black hair caked with dirt and blood.

"Whisper?" Ian knelt down in front of the young woman, frowning as he gently brushed the hair away from her face and inspected her condition. A trail of blood from her nose had dried on her upper lip, and a dark purple bruise had formed just above her right eye. Her arm was marked with impressions of hard, rough hands, and he turned it over to make sure the blood caking the skin wasn't from a laceration. The wide band of leather tied to her left wrist was stained dark red, and when he wiped away a patch of drying blood on her inner arm he saw a small tattoo he'd missed before. This one was a symbol of sorts, two triangles on top and bottom of a jagged square, with a black diamond in the center. There was no time to wonder what it meant, though, especially when his mind was more concerned with the fact that all the weapons on her belt were gone.

A red bug crawled up her thigh, and he brushed it off before shaking her again. Her skin was slick, glistening with a thin layer of sweat. "Whisper, wake up." The fatherly side of him crept back up, the part that worried over a cold, dreaded an emergency. He never would have thought the tough young woman was capable of being captured. Her strength must be waning, her steadfast determination dissipating into the darkness.

"Hey, there you go," he said gently, when her eyes opened slowly. "How's your head?"

Groggy and slightly confused, Whisper rolled over onto her hands and knees, cringing at the pain searing across her forehead and throbbing in both temples. When she'd demanded Hunting Hawk make their capture look genuine, he'd certainly listened. Her hand went to the pouch at her belt, and she wasn't surprised to find it missing. Not that it mattered, though, for the gold dust had done its purpose.

"What the hell happened?" Ian asked, scratching dried blood from his cheek, mildly irritated that he had traded one wound—the cat scratches from the Bridge of the Dead—for another. "Why are we here? And what was in that bag?"

She couldn't tell him the entire truth, so she racked her pulsing brain for an answer. The truth was that Mole had deceived them in the Barren Plains, which she had expected. The Raven-Eater had sent the witches to kill them, but they killed them first. Guards, led by Hunting Hawk, were then likely ordered to cut off their heads and bring them straight to the Raven-Eater, again something Whisper had anticipated. She had prepared for that by arming herself with adequate leverage—passage into the Spirit World. After all, the Raven-Eater was not one to take prisoners. He had neither the time nor the desire to deal with them, so she had to guarantee their capture, rather than their destruction. The gold dust ensured the guards wouldn't be punished for their disobedience—they would be long gone before the Raven-Eater knew what they had done.

Their capture had to be authentic, though. No one could simply walk into the Fire Tower, and she couldn't tell Ian that she had planned their imprisonment. He wouldn't understand, not yet.

"The guards were sent to kill us," she said honestly, the only truth she was willing to give. "I offered a bribe, for them to keep us alive in exchange for passage into the Spirit World. They kept us alive and took the passage. The Raven-Eater would have them killed for bringing in prisoners, and so they escaped before he could find out what they had done."

He could have guessed that much. "So…your bribe worked, kind of." He glanced around with a frown. "So, where are we?"

"The Fire Tower."

"The…" Realization and understanding suddenly set in. "This is the Raven-Eater's home?"

"Yes."

"Then this is where Cole is?"

"It is likely."

Excitement crept into his gut, and Ian couldn't help but smile, despite his condition and surroundings. He was close, so close. His son was somewhere nearby, waiting to be saved.

Whisper ignored his grin and managed to pull herself to her feet. She sighed and lifted a hand to her head, gritting her teeth in pain. They were nearing the end of their journey, but this was only the beginning of her fight.

She walked over to the only barred window in their dungeon room, peering outside. They were high up, probably in one of the actual towers. Through the narrow hole she could see the Weeping Forest, the Barren Plains, and parts of the Fire Mountains. With the red and purple lights soaring overhead, the sight was almost picturesque, except for the army of dead souls still awaiting their orders on shaking legs too bony and rotted to carry their weight for long.

Ian came to her side, stomping on a pile of slimy creatures. He looked out across the Land of the Dead, his joy in finding Cole disappearing into depression. It was so gloomy, so disheartening.

"What's that?" he asked, pointing to a mass of people in the distance. They were walking in groups, clutching their personal belongings close to their chests, heads hung low. Every so often one of them would stumble and struggle to pick themselves up again. Even from the tower he could hear the children crying, the women weeping over their lost loved ones. The men were lean and weak, struggling to keep a strong lead but tripping over their own feet. "What are they doing?"

Whisper stared at them for a moment, then averted her eyes. "Walking the Trail Where They Cried."

Her answer, so soft and thickly accented, made no sense to him. "What does that mean?"

"The Trail of Tears, as the white man says." Whisper lifted her arms to the window ledge and rested her chin on her hands. "They are the men, women, and children who died on that walk, forced to suffer their massacre for eternity."

He couldn't watch such horror. "Another gift from the Raven-Eater?"

"Yes. Although he is of Cherokee heritage, he blames our people for not being strong enough to stand up against the white man. He believes that those who died on that walk deserved their fate, as they did not fight back like he did."

Sickened by the window's views, Ian lowered himself to the floor and leaned against the wall. Exhaustion racked his body, whether from the head injury or simply the culmination of his entire journey. He wanted nothing more than to hold his son in his arms, kiss his wife, spend an entire year doing nothing but making them laugh, and showering them with the love and attention he had been hoarding for himself lately. He missed his wife's laugh, the sound of his son's young and inquisitive voice.

"It's so quiet," he said, immediately feeling stupid for the comment. "I mean...ever since we've been here, there's no background noise. No people talking, no singing, no birds chirping. I used to hear birds all the time at work. I miss that."

Whisper had turned her attention back to the Trail of Tears. Nostalgia filled her soul at Ian's words as she watched her people struggle to continue their walk. She too missed the sound of birds. "Do you know why the birds sing, and the butterflies are silent, Mr. Daivya?"

"No." Ian looked over at Whisper, once again desperately wanting to know what that word on her back meant. "Why?"

She took in a deep breath, taking in the sights of the Land of the Dead as she held back a cough brought on by the boiling air. She lifted her wet hair off her neck to cool her skin. "Many moons ago, Creator was watching the children play. He was saddened by the Elders, who were watching from their seats, too old to join their family in games. So he decided to conceive a creature that grew younger as it grew older, from a wrinkled worm to a smooth, winged soul...*Kamama*, the butterfly."

"*Kamama*," Ian repeated, figuring by the way Whisper touched the tattoo on her upper arm that the symbol meant Butterfly.

"Butterfly soon became the favorite creature of the world. So beautiful, so colorful, with wonderful songs that inspired dance and love, everyone treasured this new creature. But the birds were jealous. They believed that the gift of song belonged to them, that their voices deserved to be heard, and that it wasn't fair for Butterfly to be beautiful, young, and full of music."

As she spoke, Ian pictured her story in his mind. He imagined a village, with children dancing around swarms of rainbow-printed butterflies and blue jays, cardinals, and mockingbirds watching sourly from the treetops.

"The birds went to Creator and stated their case, claiming that Creator made Butterfly too perfect. He had given song to birds first, and now had taken away the gift that made them special. Creator agreed, and took song away from Butterfly. That is why they are silent today."

"Huh." He didn't know what else to say. Whisper seemed to truly believe the legend, and he didn't want to offend her any more than he already had on their quest by stating his own disbelief. Besides, she didn't seem to be finished.

"Some say that the butterfly is the symbol of transformation and everlasting life. It is said that if you have a secret wish, you can capture a butterfly and whisper your wish to it. Because they have lost their voice, your wish is safe, and when you release the butterfly it will carry your desire to Creator, the only one able to understand the thoughts of butterflies. By setting the butterfly free, you restore the balance of nature, and so you are worthy of having your wish granted."

Whisper shifted then, bracing her bad shoulder against the wall as she looked across the room at Ian, then said, "Butterfly is my Spirit Guide."

Ian paused, eyes narrowing. It seemed like she was trying to tell him something, or, at the very least, offering a story that revealed some secret. But he didn't understand. The woman wasn't a butterfly. Crazy, that was a possibility, but a butterfly? Not a chance in Hell.

"OK." He blew out a breath and rose to his feet. "Well. . .I have two questions for you."

"So ask them, Mr. Daivya."

"My first one is why is the butterfly your Spirit Guide?"

Whisper considered the question with a small smirk. "A Spirit Guide is not given or assigned, Mr. Daivya. They simply are. They are inspired by your character, your heart, and your soul. And your second question?"

"What does that word on your back mean? *Ayohuhisdi?*" When her face darkened, he knew he had struck a nerve. The fact that she was so unwilling to tell him only reinforced his suspicions. "What aren't you telling me?"

"Mr. Daivya, some things are not—*Ah!*"

Whisper crashed to her knees when a fiery fist of flames gripped her heart. Her body convulsed as she clutched her chest, her breath coming out in heaving gasps. Ian hesitated, shocked at the outburst and not knowing what was happening.

Searing pain pumped through her blood, traveling in surges up her neck, slamming into her brain. She clutched her head, screaming as explosive waves crashed against one another. Then she heard the Elder's voice urgently invade her thoughts and project a violent eruption of images on the screen behind her eyes.

She saw herself standing on the riverbank, watching from a distance as the Raven-Eater claimed his last victim, the one who would finally cross beyond the Western Sun. She saw the boy tumble into the water, frantically gasping for air, his foot catching on something and dragging his body beneath the rapids. She saw her own hands securing the limp body between two thick boulders deep in a swirling eddy.

Then the world shifted, and a strange fog covered the land. Men and women were combing the woods with huge flashlights and rescue dogs sniffing for tracks. Julia filled her vision, the distraught mother confronting Smoke Speaker, flipping through a journal, stomping through the woods. Her face was contorted with grief and fury, fear and determination, hate and hope. This was a mother who would give up her life for her son, a woman who would never give up.

Kanegv, the Elder's voice ripped into her thoughts, *I fear I am weakening. . .I fear I have failed you. Hurry. You must hurry.*

Without warning, the fog lifted and she was back on the river. The sun shone down beautifully and the water sparkled in the light. She couldn't hear Ian's frantic questions or feel his hands on her shoulders. All she could focus on was the river, the churning of rapids, Julia's desperate struggle on the bank, and the deputies pulling Cole's body from the water.

The vision faded, replaced by black dungeon walls. The pressure in her head lessened and her heart finally returned to a regular pace. Taking a moment to catch her breath, she stayed down on her knees while Ian continued to ask what was happening.

"They have found your son," she said shakily, still holding her chest. "We have little time left."

Chapter 27

Julia's foot shook as she waited for Ray Forbe in his office. The sheriff had called her only an hour ago, requesting her presence at the coroner's, but she didn't have the strength for that just yet. Pulling her dead son out of the water, then having to identify the slightly bloated body, took every ounce of life out of her. Her heart was ripped into a thousand pieces, her eyes were permanently swollen, and her lips were scabbed from thirty days of nervous chewing. It was hard to believe that only yesterday Cole had been found.

She didn't remember much of yesterday afternoon. There were flashes of the day's events, her father's voice urging her to stop, Duff's look of utter depression, a flicker of blue reflecting in the sunlight. And Cole's eyes…Ian's eyes…the spark of joy and childhood completely washed away. There was no going back from that, no reason left to live. She had lost her son, her husband, and her will to continue. The only thing keeping her going was her parents' support. Even her sister had gone home, claiming she couldn't be around the sadness any longer. As far as Julia was concerned, Lisa was also dead to her. She couldn't take the flightiness anymore, the selfishness. Lisa was a spoiled flirt, and wasn't worthy of Julia's love.

"Hi, Julia." Forbe entered his office slowly, closing the door behind him. Today he truly felt his age, and he would have done anything to avoid a confrontation with Julia Daivya. "Julia…I'm not sure how to say this." He sighed and sat down at his desk while the woman across from him merely shrugged. She was beaten down, and he knew it. "The coroner…he has no explanations."

Julia looked up at that. "What do you mean?"

"I mean…" Forbe held up his hands in exasperation. "He can't explain what happened to Cole. We originally thought that because of his appearance, he hadn't been killed until a few days before we found him. But the coroner, Dr. Hessy, seems to think that Cole was killed a month ago, according to the autopsy. On the outside he looks like he was gone only a few days, but on the inside…."

She didn't understand. "Then why didn't he look like it?"

"No one knows. There are ancient…ways," he felt like a moron for saying it, but it had to be revealed, "that are passed around the few remaining tribal members along the Rockies—beliefs about preserving bodies for ritual purposes…thing like that."

When Forbe fell silent, Julia scoffed and felt nothing but derision. "It doesn't matter, Sheriff. It doesn't matter that no one could find my son in time. It doesn't matter that your Dr. Hessy can't do his job right. It doesn't matter that my husband has abandoned me. And it doesn't matter what stupid beliefs you have about tribal shaman. All that matters is that Cole is dead." The hatred in her voice was tinged with sorrow. "I'm taking him home and giving my son a proper burial. He deserves that much."

She desperately wanted to rush out of the office before her tears started flowing again, but Forbe stopped her at the door. "Julia, there's more."

"What!" she shouted, silently pleading for all of this to be some horrible nightmare. "What more could there *possibly* be?!"

The sheriff loosened his grip on the angry, distraught woman and crossed his arms. Julia shrank back, looking small and timid in the harsh light of his office. He worried what she may do to herself when she got home, after Cole was buried. A part of him knew that there was no life left in her, and with no life, there was a very big possibility that she would cause a great deal of harm to herself.

Regardless, it was better that she heard it from him, rather than see it blasted across the six o'clock news.

"Julia…Ian has been listed as the prime suspect in Cole's murder. A manhunt has been issued to find him and bring him in." If his words registered with Julia, it didn't show in his eyes. "If he tries to contact you in any way—"

"Ian stopped caring about me a long time ago," she cut in coolly. "He proved that the day he walked away with that Cherokee hussy." She cocked her head to the side sarcastically. "How about you start a manhunt for her too?"

"We have." Forbe nodded. "We already brought Elder Smoke Speaker in. We found him sitting at a lake about thirteen miles from Howling Vines. He's in one of our holding cells if you'd like to speak with him."

A strange, eerie expression crossed Julia's face. "I have nothing to say to that murderer. Let me know when I can take my son home, then I'm done with every last one of you."

From his cell, Smoke Speaker heard every word Julia spoke. There was terror, anger, sorrow, hate, and, worst of all, a lost will to live filling her words. The woman was crushed, spiritually, mentally, emotionally, and he couldn't fault her for her feelings. But at the same time, it was necessary. Cole was a vital part of this war, as were Ian and Whisper. This was the burden Julia had to bear for the sake of the world. If his apprentice succeeded, all her pain would be erased. She would never remember this misery. Smoke Speaker hoped for the end to her pain, but he prayed for Whisper's success more.

The Elder didn't care that he was now imprisoned, blamed for Cole's murder even though he had never even laid eyes on the boy. After all, if Whisper failed, everyone in the Land of the Living would be a prisoner to the Raven-Eater.

The Raven-Eater's war had been a long time coming. The Elder's spies in the Land of the Dead had kept him well informed, though the one thing they couldn't tell him was why the Guardian of the Dead waited so long. He was a powerful man, much of his magic strengthened by the fear of his people, and his army was waiting in the Barren Plains. Some said he was gathering the greatest collection of souls the dead had ever known, a brigade of assassins and rapists, serial killers and psychopaths. Other soldiers were forced into serving, the men, women, and children the Raven-Eater blamed for his family's death so many years ago.

Others claimed the Raven-Eater was biding his time, waiting for the perfect moment to strike, when the living world was at its peak, when all the tribal Elders who may have the power to stop him were dead. Smoke Speaker was one of the last, along with only a handful of others across the globe, who could have ever banded together to strip his powers and destroy him forever. It was too late for the Elders, and so Whisper was their last chance. As Smoke Speaker truly believed, she was born into a world she was destined to change. This was her destiny, to save the Land of the Living from eternal darkness.

And so he could face the rest of his time behind the depressingly grim bars, if it meant giving Whisper more time to succeed.

Chapter 28

Ian paced the dungeon floor, occasionally shaking the door or window bars in a desperate escape attempt. Whisper, still recovering from Smoke Speaker's incredible message, rested in the corner, bathed in purple light. Their time was limited, and it was up to her to figure out what to do next.

"Are you gonna help or what?" Ian asked angrily, kicking the thick wooden door. He'd already tried picking the lock, to no avail. "You're supposed to have all the answers, aren't you? Or maybe all you have is secrets."

Bothered by his accusation, Whisper rose and stalked over to her traveling companion. She was tired of his complaints, of his distrust, of his outright hatred of her beliefs. "My answers have kept you alive, Mr. Daivya, and my secrets—"

"Alive?" he repeated with a shout. "*Alive?* When the hell was I alive here in the wonderful Land of the Dead? You're goddamn Elder *murdered* me!"

"You made the choice to die, Mr. Daivya," Whisper replied coolly, her dark eyes flashing.

"No, I did not make that choice. I chose to save my son," Ian corrected.

"And in choosing your son, you chose death."

"Which neither of you told me. Yet another secret."

"You know nothing," Whisper spat out, the bruise around her temple darkening her face even more than it already was. "Your words mean nothing. I have brought you here to save your son, and yet you regard me with disdain. I do not owe you any truth."

"Oh, you owe me the truth, woman." No longer fearing her wrath, Ian grabbed the young Cherokee apprentice by the arm and slammed her against the wall. "*What* is going *on?!*"

"Shall I come back another time?"

Ian released Whisper and spun around in a fit of fury. A woman in her early twenties stood in the doorway, beautifully decorated with gems, colorful feathers, and ornately sewn clothing. "What do you want?"

"My name is Gentle Heart," she said softly, taking a step into the room. Ian considered shoving past her until he saw the shadow of a guard just outside the door.

Whisper's anger evaporated into awe and compassion. She knew this woman, recognized her face. Smoke Speaker spoke of her often, drew her often, dreamed of her often. This woman was one reason why she was in the Land of the Dead, and despite being pressed for time, she couldn't take her eyes off of her.

As if in a trance, Whisper pushed herself off the wall and walked closer, each step slower than the last. The Elder's drawings were so accurate, yet none could capture her incredible beauty, her innocence, that light behind her eyes that shone despite being trapped in the Fire Tower for so many years. But this woman, this beauty before her, was not always called Gentle Heart.

"You went by another name once," Whisper replied as she unclasped the bone necklace around her throat. Gentle Heart smiled and merely shook her head. "You lived in the forest, with your father, a powerful shaman."

"Young woman, I—"

"Until one day you were taken," Whisper interrupted, continuing her story, never taking her eyes off the Raven-Eater's wife. "The Raven-Eater made you his bride, made you forget who you truly are." She stopped in front of Gentle Heart. "He made you forget your true name…Blue Feather."

Gentle Heart frowned, staring at the necklace Whisper held out.

"What is this?"

"This belongs to you," Whisper answered, placing the necklace in her hands, relishing the touch with reverence, then crossing her arms when Gentle Heart lifted a hand to her throat.

"I only have room for one."

Whisper eyed the necklace, curious about the black hair braided around thin bones. White feathers trailed from blue beads, painted with images of crows. The necklace was beautiful, and she wanted it.

"Is that your hair?"

Gentle Heart chuckled. "Oh no, this was made for me by my husband. His hair shows that I belong to him."

Whisper already knew that, but she needed to hear the words to know for sure. "My gift comes from your father…from Elder Smoke Speaker."

Ian couldn't conceal the rage that instantly spread across his face. So, Whisper wasn't here for his son. She suckered him into dying so she could save Smoke Speaker's daughter. And if he found out she killed his son to get him here, he would tear her apart with his bare hands.

"You lying bitch," he muttered, pleased that she heard him. "So this is what you've been hiding. Did you murder Cole too?"

Whisper turned on her heel while Gentle Heart stared down at the necklace. "Your son died because of forces I could not control. Perhaps you know one of them... Perhaps *you* can tell me why he died."

He didn't know what answer she was looking for, but ultimately it didn't matter. "Why the hell do you even need me?"

"Only a child protected by the Raven-Eater can strip him of his powers." Whisper all but spit out the words. "I did not kill your son, but I need his help, your help, to kill the Raven-Eater."

"The Raven-Eater," Gentle Heart said suddenly, looking up from the bones. "He wishes to speak with you."

"Why?"

Gentle Heart turned toward Ian. "It seems many of his guards have disappeared, and since they know better than to take captives alive, he assumes you have something to do with this matter."

Gentle Heart led the way, followed by Ian, Whisper, and finally, two remaining guards armed with spears, bows, and arrows. As she walked, Gentle Heart fingered the necklace, her mind going over the captive's words. Blue Feather, Smoke Speaker, the names sounded so familiar. And the jewelry, she could swear she remembered the feel of the cool bones against her throat. Who was this stranger, bringing her a necklace and telling stories of a past life, of her husband taking her from the living world? Was it possible she was speaking the truth?

Second in line, Ian struggled to keep his fury in control. He now fully believed that Whisper had something to do with Cole's death, and she certainly was to blame for his own. She had lied to him from the very first word, and now she expected...what? For him to believe anything else she said? He had never despised anyone as much as this woman. All he could actually expect from her were tall tales, far-fetched stories, and a mouthful of deceit.

Whisper kept her eyes on Gentle Heart, nearly smiling at the vision. Smoke Speaker loved this woman dearly, and prayed to Creator for her safety every night. Together, they had planned her freedom, but first, she would have to recover her memories. Whisper was more concerned with that than with the horror she was about to face, though her nerves were slowly beginning to twist into a knot in her gut. She knew that if they faced the Raven-Eater now, it would be the end for them. They would never find the boy, Blue Feather would never be free, and the living world would be taken over by death and despair. She had to do something.

Dropping down, Whisper spun around and swept a leg across those of the two guards. They crashed to the floor, cursing, but before they could fight back Whisper grabbed a knife from one of their belts, leapt on top of them, and plunged the blade into their hearts one after the other.

Whisper was covered with blood before Ian even turned around. He was a bit sad to admit that he wasn't surprised how easy it was for her to kill, or even how fast. But, he also had to admit, the girl knew how to get the job done.

Without hesitating, Whisper rose and knocked Gentle Heart to the floor, then wrapped a hand around her throat. "Where is the boy?"

Gentle Heart struggled against Whisper's grip, but the woman was too strong. Fear filled her eyes. "What boy?"

"Where is he?!" Whisper tightened her hold until Gentle Heart relented and pointed to a door just down the torch-lit hallway. The young apprentice glanced at the closed door, and then slammed a hand into Gentle Heart's head, rendering her unconscious. Before rising, she snatched the hair-braided necklace from her throat and secured it at her waist. "Let us get your son," she said to Ian, who had already forgiven Whisper long enough to see how the hell she was going to make up for her lies.

Whisper and Ian wasted no time running down the hall and shoving open the heavy door. When they stepped inside the room, brightly lit with white-flame candles, they saw a child who resembled the boy once known as Cole Daivya.

Cole, who had been playing War with tiny figures made of dried mud, looked up and eyed his intruders suspiciously. They looked familiar, and he felt a strange tugging inside his body for the dirty, bloody man, but he wanted them out nonetheless. "Who are you?"

"Cole," Ian whispered, taking a step forward. His son looked so different, so... regal, in a white-feathered headdress circling blonde hair that had grown incredibly long in the past month, a buckskin tunic ornately stitched with animal patterns and Cherokee symbols, and expertly crafted moccasins tipped with beaded tassels. His face had three small circles painted at both temples, and his wrists were decorated with hair-braided bracelets.

"Cole, it's me...It's—" Ian froze when Cole's small hand moved instinctively to a large dagger at the edge of the table. "Cole, what are you doing?"

"My name is Fighting...Fox," the boy said slowly, unsure of his reply. "You aren't supposed to be in here."

Ian shook his head, confused. "What....what?" He turned around to face Whisper, who was standing back with her arms crossed, waiting. "What's going on?"

"Make him remember you," Whisper said softly, keeping her eyes on the boy. She didn't trust the grip he had on that blade. "His mind is not completely gone. But he has been protected by the Raven-Eater."

"How do you know?" Whisper merely pointed to her arm, then to Cole's. Ian followed her finger to see the three lines burned into his skin. They were still red and inflamed, and the sight caused his blood to boil. Someone had seared his son's flesh with a mark that represented hatred and darkness. "I'll kill whoever did that to you."

"Make him remember."

"I'm working on it!" Ian yelled, then lowered himself to his knees. "Cole, you know me. I'm your father, Ian Daivya. Your name is Cole Daivya. Remember?"

"My name is Fighting Fox."

"No, you're Cole Daivya. You love dinosaurs and science and learning about dogs. We went on a camping trip, and you fell in the water."

"I don't like camping," the child answered, his face haughty. "And I don't like the water. So I'd never fall in."

Ian felt his heart flutter at his son's disbelieving words. "Cole, you have to remember. We were camping, and we went to the park. You thought you saw a ghost earlier in the day, and so maybe you went to find him."

"Ghosts aren't real."

"You were tricked, Cole." Ian took a step closer, holding up his hands when the boy lifted the dagger again. "The...the Raven-Eater kidnapped you." He felt foolish saying the words, but they had to be stated.

Cole stared at Ian through narrowed eyes. "My name is...Fighting Fox. The Raven-Eater is my father. Why would he kidnap me?"

"Because he's a bad man."

"You're a bad man!" Cole took a swipe at them with the dagger, forcing the strangers back three steps. A growl came from the corner, making the two intruders immediately aware of the large black dog that had just risen to its feet. "Go away!"

Ian sighed and glanced up at Whisper, careful to watch the dog from the corner of his eye. "What do I do? How do I even know this is really Cole, and not just another one of your tricks?"

"He bears the mark of the half-breed," Whisper answered. "He is your son."

"What mark? Those three lines? Anyone could have that."

With a snarl, Whisper marched forward. The dog lunged, but she merely grabbed the beast by the fur and all but threw it against the wall. It fell to the floor with a whimper and stayed there, licking its wounds. When Cole raised his dagger and threatened to use it, she merely lifted a booted foot and kicked him hard in the wrist. Cole dropped the weapon with a cry, bringing Ian instantly to his feet.

"Hey!" he yelled as Whisper yanked Cole around by his shirt and grabbed for his collar. The boy shouted in protest, trying to kick the woman he believed to be an attacker. "I'm gonna—"

Then he froze. Whisper had lowered Cole's shirt just enough to reveal the brown mark in the center of his shoulder blades, a jagged circle with five dots in the center, and a slight V shape at the base. "That's impossible."

"Nothing, Mr. Daivya, is impossible."

"But...how?"

"In death, the truth is revealed."

While the two exchanged words, Cole shifted his attention to the strange woman holding his shirt. She looked so familiar, but...why? Where did he know her from? Did she work for the Raven-Eater? Was she a friend of Gentle Heart? And why was she fighting with the strange man who looked just like him?

"You're the lady from the river," he said suddenly, tilting his head to the side. "When I was playing...you...you were the lady by the water."

Silently, Whisper released the boy and stepped back. She had known this moment would come, and was waiting for it. She could only pray it didn't slow them down.

"What do you mean, Cole?" Ian asked, upset by the grimace his son made at his true name. "When were you on the river?"

Cole shrugged. "I don't remember. But I remember her." He gestured to Whisper, who again had crossed her arms; a haughty, though slightly nervous, expression had crossed her face. "Remember? I...I couldn't breathe, and you...you watched me."

"And the truth is revealed," Ian snarled, advancing on Whisper. "You wanted him to drown, didn't you? You stood on the shore and let him die, because you needed him to get me here! Didn't you!" Whisper didn't move as he approached, but instead only glared at him through those stoic black eyes. Her self-righteousness only fueled his rage. "All along! All along you were the reason behind his death! This is *all your fault!*"

In a blind fit of fury, Ian slammed his fist into Whisper's jaw.

The moment his hand connected with flesh he felt guilty. It was the first time he had ever struck a woman, but his anger didn't allow him to care as Whisper tumbled to the ground. She clutched her chin, staying down long enough to give Ian the time he needed to rear back again. "Is that what that word means on your back?" he shouted, lifting a foot to her ribs and knocking her down when she tried to rise. She grunted quietly, spitting blood. *"Huh? Does it mean murderer!"*

Then Whisper did something he never would have suspected.

She began to laugh.

As she rolled onto her hands and knees, blood dripping from her mouth, Whisper laughed, gasping in pain when her ribs refused to allow deep breaths. The very idea of his words, his arrogance, his presumptions, it was too much. Ian Daivya was the most ignorant man she had ever known, and refused to learn from his mistakes. There was nothing else to do with that but laugh.

"What's so funny?" Ian demanded to know. "Does it have something to do with that word? What does it mean?"

"Why…why did your son die?" Whisper asked between chuckling breaths, wiping a string of blood off her chin.

"What does that have to do with *anything*? I am *so* tired of you asking me that! You *know* why he died! You were *there!*" Frustrated and irate, Ian pounced on Whisper, grabbing her by the throat much like the witch had done. His fingers matched the bruises left by those of the gnarled, possessed woman, the first person he had ever murdered. "Did you kill my son? *Answer* me!"

Whisper grinned, her teeth red. "No," she replied truthfully, and for some reason, he believed her. "But I did not save him."

His grip tightened. "Why not?"

"I need you both."

"You're not getting a damn thing from either of us. I'm gonna kill you right here and now."

"So you are a murderer, Mr. Daivya."

"I'll make an exception for you."

"Dad! Stop!"

Shocked, Ian released Whisper and spun around to face his son. Cole had removed his headdress and was standing just behind him, clutching his hands together. "Cole?"

The boy pressed his lips together, slightly confused. Whether by the shock of his father's rage or the power of Whisper's memory, he remembered his past life. Indecision tore at him as he struggled to decipher the truth behind his two lives. Was he a little boy who loved to read about dinosaurs, or was he the son of a great leader, training to take over a new kingdom? Both seemed like such real possibilities.

"Cole? Do you know who I am?"

The boy pressed his lips together, remembering the camping trip and his mother, not Gentle Heart, grabbing him from the rock, his grandmother sneaking him candy before breakfast, the ghost on the other side of the river. Was that real, or was the Fire Tower his home? "I...there was a ghost...and he...he tricked me. The lady...she said...she said she would help you save me."

Ian looked back at Whisper, who was on her back and had risen to her elbows. Thick, dark red blood stained her shirt. Then he grabbed his son into a tight bear hug. To his delight, Cole hugged him back. "I missed you so much, Cole."

"Can we go home now?"

"Absolutely." As soon as the word left his mouth, a rumble echoed through the Fire Tower. "What was that?"

"The Raven-Eater knows something is wrong," Whisper spoke up from behind, slowly rising. "We must go now."

Ian gathered his son into his arms and didn't bother to help Whisper to her feet. "You're not off the hook."

"No, but you will trust me long enough to get you out." He wasn't sure if that was an insult or a statement, but he let it go anyway. "Stay behind me, and do everything I say."

She's certainly quick to forgive, Ian thought, but wouldn't have apologized even if they had the time. Whisper could have saved Cole, could have prevented this entire trip from happening, but as always, she was calculating. He still didn't quite understand her end goal, but whatever it was, he didn't care. From now on, it was all about using her to get the hell out of the Land of the Dead.

Whisper led the way out of the room and down the hall. She was limping slightly, occasionally wiping her face and slinging blood to the floor. Apparently, Ian considered, he'd hit her harder than he meant to. Cole clung to him with a death grip, fingers digging into his shoulder. His memories restored, he was terrified and desperate for his father to save him.

As he followed his guide through narrow, dimly lit passages, down slick steps, around sharp corners, Ian marveled at the fact that she led them through half-closed eyes, as though she was listening to inaudible directions and reading a map in her mind.

She seemed to know exactly where she was going, and he silently thanked her for getting rid of the guards at the base of the Fire Mountains, however the hell she did that.

When she stopped, holding up an arm, Ian caught a strange movement across her back reflecting in the wavering torch lights. He didn't know if he should be sickened or awed over the red lines pulsing through her tattoo. For the three seconds they stood in place, he stared at the movement before he realized just what he was looking at—a map. It was a map of the Fire Tower, of the Land of the Dead, and those red lines were telling Whisper where to go. But how was it possible? The thought racked Ian's mind as the race through the stale-smelling, golden-lit hallways continued. This entire time she had been led by a tattoo, a tattoo that spoke to her...whispered to her.

Despite everything he'd been exposed to in the Land of the Dead, he couldn't accept that.

"Oh, thank God," Ian muttered when they burst outside. The light was brighter now, though he didn't know it was because the Raven-Eater was on the hunt for his missing captives. The wind had picked up as well, whipping Whisper's hair around her face and making her look like a beautiful, though incredibly bruised, angel of death. Once outside, Cole began to cry, frightened by the strange noises that he knew were coming from the Raven-Eater's army.

Suddenly Whisper slammed a hand into Ian's chest, shoving him back against hard rock. A black horse erupted from a chasm deep in the Fire Mountains and landed right where he had been standing.

"Where the hell did he come from?"

"A friend," Whisper answered, as though that explained everything. She gestured to Ian. "Get on."

Chapter 29

Cole Daivya's body was arranged to be transported back home by police escort. The media frenzy was yet to die down, and Julia tried her best to fend them off as she prepared to return home. Olivia would drive her back, while David had elected to stay behind to take care of the final details. In less than three days, Cole would be six feet underground.

Dr. Hessy had determined the autopsy complete, with no real answer as to Cole's death. On the outside, it looked as though Cole had only been dead a few days. On the inside, the body was a mess. Partially decomposed, yet not enough to figure out when the boy actually passed away. At his best guess, Cole died either the day of his disappearance or shortly thereafter, and because there were no physical signs of trauma, his final determination was that the boy died of drowning. His lungs at least had evidence of that. The preservation of his body was a mystery, and after conferring with five other doctors, no one had any clues. And Smoke Speaker wasn't talking.

The hunt for Ian and Whisper had spread from North Carolina to the surrounding states. Police, FBI, and volunteers were combing every nook and cranny for the alleged murderers, while reporters soaked up the limelight with outrageous claims of extramarital affairs and sacrificial rituals. Julia ignored them all, while Forbe was forced to answer probing questions on a daily basis. Personally, he didn't think Ian or Whisper would ever be found. She was too swift and sneaky to be caught, if she was even still alive. Plus, Forbe wasn't so sure the Elder hadn't done something foul to them.

The only person sure of anything was David Bard. He knew, without a doubt, that Smoke Speaker was innocent. How he knew, he couldn't say, but he was planning on getting to the bottom of his instincts.

Ian eyed the black horse cautiously, frowning over the beast's matted coat, wet nose encrusted with snot and blood, mouth dripping thick gray saliva. The horse stomped and shook its head, black hair shaking in the breeze. The reins jingled, biting into the creature's mouth and head, and the saddle sat heavily upon its back.

"You're joking right?"

"We do not have time for questions." The urgency in her voice prompted Ian to shift Cole to one arm and use the other to hoist himself onto the horse. Whisper grabbed the reins and led the horse away from the Fire Tower, just as a horrifying scream burst from the mountain tops. Ian glanced over his shoulder to see the dark figure of the Raven-Eater staring down at him. His guards missing, he could do nothing but watch as his captives escaped. Watch, that is, and aim carefully with the bow and arrows that had been stripped from Whisper's back. To kill a foolish woman with her own weapons was a justice that filled his heart with pride.

Whisper dodged the first arrow, having heard its nearly silent whistle as it glided through the air. It struck a rock, mere inches from her head, and shattered into a dozen pieces. Panic began to creep into her bones, and she struggled to brush it off as the ground began to rumble, signifying the terrible fact that the army was on the move. But this was the moment she had been waiting for, training for. This was the reason why she had dragged Ian through the Land of the Dead, and she was not going to let the threat of a murdered army slow her down.

"We must hurry," she whispered to herself, her grip tightening on the reins as she raced to the edge of the Fire Mountains. When they reached the outskirts of the Barren Plains, Ian surprised Whisper by lowering a hand.

"Get on."

Whisper paused, then shook her head. "*Soquili* will take you all the way to the River Keeper," she said, pressing herself up against the horse when another arrow threatened to take her life. The air thickened then, swirling around them angrily with an almost humid desperation, as the sky filled with clouds of reds and purples tumbling together furiously. All around them rocks crashed from the sides of the Fire Mountains, one striking Ian in the shoulder.

"The RiverKeeper will take you back, for a price," Whisper shouted above the wind, taking them further into the Barren Plains and keeping her eyes on the Raven-Eater, who was advancing on them quickly. "You must then travel back to the Bridge of the Dead, and face the Watchmen!" She dragged her hair out of her mouth and spat out a thin stream of blood. It dripped down her chin, but she hardly noticed. "Then head into the Western Sun!"

"*Whisper!*" Ian grabbed her by the arm and would have leapt off the horse had Cole not screamed for him to stay. "What are you talking about?!"

"You must go back to the lake!" Whisper yanked Gentle Heart's necklace from her belt and shoved it into Ian's arms. "You must die to live! When you surface, bury this necklace in Howling Vines. It is the only way to stop the Raven-Eater!"

"But—wait! Whisper, *wait!*" He didn't understand what was going on, but when she thrust the reins into his hands, he realized that she wasn't planning on going with them. The fact bothered him, as he still despised the woman yet there was a part of him that nonetheless wanted her to live. "What are you doing? We can't do this without you!"

"You have to, Mr. Daivya! There is no other way!"

"Come with us!"

At the invitation, Whisper paused just long enough for Ian to see the regret pass through her unforgettable ebony eyes. He watched as she untied the leather band around her left wrist then held up her arm.

"I cannot return to the Land of the Living," she said, and Ian had to strain to hear her over the wind. "I took my own life to be here, Mr. Daivya, and I intend to stay. Everything we have done has been for this moment. This is the way it must be."

Confusion, anger, sorrow, desperation, all tore at him as he stared down at the thick, raised scar slashed across her wrist. He didn't get it. Why would she commit suicide? Why would she take her own life, when she could have saved Cole's from the very beginning?

Whisper used Ian's stunned silence to her advantage. Just before the Raven-Eater descended upon them, she lifted a fist high into the air and offered her traveling companion and his son one final nod. The slash across her wrist looked rougher and painful in the purple lights. "Thank you for your company," she said earnestly. "Take care of your family, and yourself." Her hand uncurled then just as the Raven-Eater lifted the bow for a final shot and his army began the march across the Barren Plains.

"And Ian," Whisper said suddenly, almost as an afterthought. He turned for one last look at the most incredibly mysterious woman he had ever known. "Please tell Smoke Speaker...I said good-bye."

Then, with a furious strength that surprised even herself, she uncurled her fist and lashed down her arm, slapping the horse across the rear.

The horse took off with a grunt and stomp, and Ian hunched over with Cole bound tightly in his arms. When the wind picked up dust and threw it into his eyes, he looked back to see the blurred vision of an arrow plunging deep into Whisper's chest.

Chapter 30

There was a foreign scent in the air, a strange combination of death, magic, and dangerous foreboding. The average person was immune to its stench, but Smoke Speaker struggled to fight back the gags that racked his body. He knew that smell, recognized its danger, what it meant.

The Army of the Dead was on the move, steadily marching toward the Land of the Living. The closer they got, the more powerful the scent. The Elder prayed to Creator every minute, begging for more time. He now had no way of knowing where Whisper was, what was happening in the Land of the Dead, where the dead soldiers currently were. It would take them some time to reach the Western Sun, as the dead souls raised from the Barren Plains, those eternally cursed for their sins, moved steadily, but at little more than a brisk walking pace. That much Smoke Speaker knew to be true, just as he knew that a sudden mass invasion of the Land of the Living could potentially destroy the world forever, leaving nothing for the Raven-Eater to rule but a vast land of black ash. Ian and Cole could return safely because they would surface through the same medium in which they died—water, the most powerful of spiritual transports. The Army, on the other hand, would simply burst through one realm to the next, and such an eruption of worlds had to be done slowly, slyly.

Smoke Speaker was planning on enjoying what little time he had left in this world. He stood on his bed in the tiny holding cell and stared out the small barred window. The stars shined brightly against a black sky. He let their brilliance fill his closed eyes, savoring the light as it traveled through his soul, warming his heart.

"Watch over us, good men," he whispered, then opened his eyes. "*Osiyo*, Deputy Duff."

From just outside the cell, Ben Duff shuffled his feet and wondered how the old man knew he was there. It looked to him like Smoke Speaker was completely enraptured by the night sky, rather than the happenings of the sleepy police station. Duff had been one of two left at the station for a few hours now, and it was too much to resist Smoke Speaker's draw. He had always admired the man, and was fascinated by his ways. "Hello, Elder."

"Mr. Duff...do you know why the stars shine down on our people?"

The deputy wasn't sure if Smoke Speaker was luring him into something or being genuine. Either way, he was curious. "Why?"

The Elder smiled, resting an old, wrinkled hand on the window ledge. It was rare for him to share his people's stories with the white man, and ancient law dictated that such stories could only be heard upon invitation. Smoke Speaker was inviting Duff to listen because he knew the man loved Whisper, had fallen for her the moment she filled his vision. Duff didn't believe Whisper was guilty, despite his siding with Forbe, and that loyalty went a long way with the Elder.

"Many moons ago, Mr. Duff, seven young boys spent their days playing a traditional game, rolling a stone across the earth and chasing it with a curved stick. Their mothers did not like this, because the boys neglected their chores day after day, and so they collected stones, boiled them, and told the boys to eat them for dinner, if they love this game so much."

Duff scoffed, immediately wishing he could take it back when the Elder shifted slightly. He hadn't meant any disrespect; he was simply imagining his own mother saying such a thing. "Sorry."

Smoke Speaker focused again on the stars. "The boys were very angry with their mothers, so they went to the village center and danced the sacred Feather Dance to pray to the gods to teach their mothers a lesson. Soon, they danced so long and so hard that their feet began to lift from the earth, and they rose higher into the night sky." The Elder's wrinkled hand lifted as he spoke. "The mothers tried to save them, but only one could reach. She pulled so hard that the boy struck the ground and sank beneath the surface."

The deputy grimaced and looked down at his hands. Obviously, this wasn't a happy story. When the old man paused, taking in a deep breath, he feared the tale was over, and wanted to know what happened. "What about the other six?"

Smoke Speaker hid a smile. *So*, he thought with amusement, *we have a believer.*

"The young boys danced into the sky, where they remain today. Our Cherokee people grieved for them, and the mothers cried over the earth where the one boy vanished. Soon, a tree began to grow, until it rose into what is now known as the Pine. The Pine, Mr. Duff, is made up of tears, and cherishes the bright lights of the night sky. And that is why we have the stars, officer, because of the sacrifices young mothers were forced to make."

"Like the sacrifice my daughter was forced to make?"

Both Duff and Smoke Speaker spun around, surprised by the question. The Elder nearly tumbled off the bed, but caught himself in time to step down carefully and face David Bard squarely, bravely, and proudly.

David stood behind the two with his wide arms crossed. He didn't bother explaining that the guard on front desk duty had let him in, warning him with a stern lecture not to cause any trouble. He wasn't here for trouble, he was here for answers.

The veteran walked up to the cell and slammed a hand against the bars. "Was my grandson sacrificed to your stars?"

Smoke Speaker would not lie to the distraught grandfather. He too knew what it was like to lose a loved one. And besides, he no longer had anything else to lose. "Your grandson was sacrificed so that our world may survive."

David hesitated. He'd been expecting a runaround answer, some kind of riddle. "What do you mean?"

"A war is coming, Mr. Bard, a war that will end our world and enslave our people to the Guardian of the Dead. Your grandson's death means that we have a chance to fight back, to live."

David knew many of the old stories, but couldn't remember ever hearing anything about a war. The Raven-Eater's war had never come up in legends, nor had any tale about a child saving the day. And Cole…how could one young boy play such a large role?

"Ian," he said suddenly, glaring at the Elder, taking in his long, tangled white hair, tired black eyes, and deep wrinkles that signified many, many years on Earth. "Ian has something to do with this, doesn't he? And your apprentice?"

Smoke Speaker nodded slowly, his old bones screaming and pleading for him to rest. He could only hope the pain didn't show on his face. "Whisper and Mr. Daivya have gone to the Land of the Dead to rescue the boy, and kill the Raven-Eater. Their success is vital for our survival. If they fail, we will die, and none of this will matter anymore."

For some strange, unexplainable reason, David believed the Elder. Smoke Speaker may have been crazy, disillusioned, but he knew he truly believed what he was saying.

Blowing out a breath, and hating himself for what he was about to say, hating himself for who and what he believed, David uncurled his fists and rested his forehead against the cool bars. "OK…so what can I do to help?"

Whisper awoke with a rough cough that sent sharp spears of pain through her chest and back. An agonizing cry escaped her lips as she clutched the open wound with shaking hands, blood seeping through her fingers. Weakly, she glanced down to see the dark red circle that stained her torn buckskin shirt. The arrow that shot her lay disregarded on the floor. It was her own arrow, and if she hadn't been in so much pain, Whisper would have fumed over the idea of being taken down by a weapon she crafted with her own two hands.

Instead of raging, all she could do was lie on her back and struggle to breathe. She felt her souls detaching from her body, her spirit draining, and prayed to Creator for the strength to carry on.

The last image playing behind her black eyes was of Ian and Cole shooting off across the Barren Plains, Ian clutching the reigns and hunching over to maintain his balance while the Army of the Dead began their long march to the living world. She remembered the look of surprise and confusion across his face when she told him she wouldn't be going with him, and for some reason, she regretted letting him down.

Whisper supposed that for all his faults, for all his disrespect, she had grown fond of Ian Daivya. He was a decent man at heart, and she hoped that they would succeed not only for her sake, for Gentle Heart's sake, but also for his own chance to rebuild his family.

She had known from the moment Smoke Speaker began their training that her destiny was to die fighting the Raven-Eater. For years she studied the ways of her ancestors, practiced their magic, waited for the moment until she was finally ready to strike. Waiting meant having to rescue countless children lured into the wilderness by the Guardian of the Dead. While saving them helped strengthen her tracking and survival skills, with each rescue, she only further realized the Raven-Eater's power and determination.

Finally, Smoke Speaker announced that Whisper was ready. She was ready to fight, ready to kill, ready to save his daughter from the Raven-Eater's powerful hold. When Cole Daivya went missing, he ordered his apprentice to track him, wait until he died, then secure his body far down the river so he wouldn't be found. Burying him was not an option, as that would mean the boy was lost forever in the Spirit World. No, they needed him in the Raven-Eater's care, and needed his father to bring him back to the Land of the Living. That meant preparing her body for death, sharpening her prized blade in the light of a burning fire, sliding it across her wrist, and watching without emotion as thick blood dripped to the ground just moments before Ian stepped into

Howling Vines, all the while knowing that in killing herself, she was contributing to the murders of Ian and Cole Daivya.

It was deceptive, it was dishonest, it was evil, and she would have done it all over again if it meant stopping this war and saving Blue Feather.

Chapter 31

For what seemed like days, Whisper lay on the floor of the filthy Fire Tower room in spasms of the worst pain she'd ever experienced. Not even when the Elder had tattooed the map for the Land of the Dead across her back, when her ankle snapped beneath the weight of a fallen pine tree, or when she sliced her own wrist with a flint-sharpened blade had she felt an agony quite like this. But she would suffer through it, had to suffer through it, to accomplish her mission and fulfill her destiny. She got through the pain by remembering that nothing else mattered but her destiny—not Ian, not the child, not even Smoke Speaker. She had easily deceived them all to get this far, and now it was her time to rise to the top.

Heavy footsteps outside her dungeon room had Whisper struggling to a sitting position. She grit her teeth together as the fire ripped through her body, but managed to pull herself against the grimy, black-caked wall. The footsteps neared, getting louder and heavier, until they stopped just outside the closed door.

And then he entered.

In her state of half-delirium, Whisper didn't realize that her eyes widened instead of narrowed, that her lungs sucked in an involuntary breath of nervous air, and that her hands instinctively curled into fists. Her heart beat wildly as she took in the magnificently frightening sight of the Guardian of the Dead.

His thick, menacing frame filled the doorway, lit from behind by the fire torches that lined the hallways. Dark shadows were cast across his rugged and worn tattooed face, while golden highlights reflected in his long black hair that reached to his waist, with tresses tied in thick braids and adorned with dark blue feathers. He glared across the room at his victim through fiery black eyes set beneath a wide, deeply lined brow that shouted his eternal rage. A thin white bone pierced his left nostril, while long white scars trailed across cheeks, tattooed with Cherokee symbols representing a lifetime dedicated to war and revenge. His ears were likewise decorated with bone piercings that dangled white feathers and square-shaped beads that just touched the tops of his broad, muscled shoulders.

Trailing from those shoulders were arms as thick as the dead oak trees lining the Weeping Forest. His enormous hands were rough and calloused, evidence of his many years farming, building, and battling enemies. In another life, perhaps in his time of living, he may have been considered handsome. But now, after being hidden away in the Fire Tower for so long, letting hate, vengeance, and an unquenchable thirst for blood fill his soul, his inner repulsiveness was reflected on a face that met the world with an eternal scowl.

But what truly struck Whisper, despite the fear creeping into her heart, were his incredibly ornate, beautiful clothing. His broad chest was wrapped in a thick buckskin tunic gorgeously decorated with blue and white beads, braided fringes, and animal shadows. The collar was slit in half at the base of his throat, tied together by thin straps of sinew. His pants matched the shirt, expertly stitched by a careful hand. Adorning his wrists were three bracelets crafted with twisted leather straps intertwined with feathers and beads.

"So you are the one who destroyed my guards," he spoke suddenly, his deep voice thundering across the room, rattling Whisper's eardrums. "So small and pathetic." She shook her head slightly when his words caused a brief but powerful dizzy spell. When she didn't answer, he took a few steps closer, keeping his eyes trained on the prisoner, reveling in her painful misery. He was keeping his captive alive for three sole reasons.

One, she was to blame for his missing guards, and he wanted answers.

Two, his son was now missing as well, and he wanted him back. As powerful as the Raven-Eater was, even his spies seemed to have disappeared from the Land of the Dead. With his army on the move, he was needed here, at the Fire Tower, to direct his soldiers into battle with the living. It pleased his black, rotted heart to know that the ones who had taken his family's lives were now under his control. They would be his slaves until he decided to free their souls, which he would never do. They didn't deserve mercy.

And three, he enjoyed her pain. He had used her own handcrafted weapon to take his enemy down, and he knew by the widening red stain on her chest that she was near death—a second death, in the Land of the Dead. When she passed, her memory would be erased from the living world and her soul would face the eternal depths of a world reserved for the greatest of sinners and forgotten names. Not even he knew what horrors waited for those unfortunate enough to die their second death.

But before she died, she would speak.

"You," he growled, kicking Whisper hard in the shoulder. She tumbled to the ground, biting back a pained shout when his foot connected with the area injured in her fight against *Ustahli*. "Who are you? Why have you come?" She had strange power, this beautiful, mysterious, captive, and that displeased him. The fact that she made it this far, with a white man no less, was both curious and maddening. "Before you die, prisoner, you will answer my questions."

Despite her injuries, her burning chest, throbbing jaw from Ian's punch, scratchy throat from the witch's scaly hands, Whisper huffed sarcastically, rising to her hands and knees. "I owe you nothing, Raven-Eater. Not even death."

Outraged, the Guardian of the Dead slammed a hand on Whisper's shoulder and lifted her completely off her feet. "We shall see," he snarled in response, then dragged her out of the room.

As he exited, the Raven-Eater turned to the last guard left at the Fire Tower, his own personal guardian. "Hunt her companion down, kill him, and return Fighting Fox to me."

Julia entered the coroner's office, her father one step behind. The determination that once filled her step, the last determination to bury her son and get this nightmare over with, was gone, replaced by pure emptiness. After she returned home, after she lost her son for good, she didn't know how she would move on, or if she even wanted to. There was no life without Cole, and she feared living with the memories of his death, of Ian's betrayal, of her husband's possible involvement in the murder of a seven year-old boy.

David sat down next to his daughter in Dr. Hessy's waiting room. They were there to make the final transportation plans for Cole's body. Julia thought she would be leaving tomorrow, but David knew otherwise. After speaking with Smoke Speaker at the jail, he no longer knew what was right and what was wrong, but he did know that he believed enough in the stories his grandfather used to tell him to trust that look on the Elder's face.

Plus, David never thought that Ian was capable of murdering his son, like the police were now claiming—cheating on his wife, yes, but killing, not a chance. So the only reason he was missing, in David's mind, was because he was doing something about Cole's death. And whatever he was doing involved the Elder's apprentice, whether that involved actual traveling to the Land of the Dead or not. If there was a chance, no matter how small, that Cole could be saved, then David was determined to take advantage of it.

Dr. Hessy entered, interrupting his line of thought. The doctor was a small, timid-looking man with thin arms, a gaunt face, and graying hair. Wide glasses sat atop a long nose, hiding his dark blue eyes behind thick frames. He seemed nervous to approach

Julia, who didn't bother to rise. She was tired of showing respect to people who could no longer help save her son.

"Mrs. Daivya, I don't know if you've been informed yet, but the F.B.I. have decided to prolong the case a few more days."

Julia did rise at that. "Excuse me?"

"An agent came in yesterday." Dr. Hessy picked up a form. "I was given this. Apparently they are not satisfied with the results and have asked me to conduct another series of tests."

David recognized that look on Julia's face. It was one from her teenage years, when she was about to explode with all her frustrations, all her rage, all her pent-up aggression. She was typically pleasant, but didn't hold her anger well.

As she began lashing out at the meek mortician, David let his thoughts trail back to his conversation with Smoke Speaker. He briefly wondered if he truly believed in the old man, or if he simply chose to believe because he desperately wished for Cole to come back to life. Either way, he could feel the internal wrestle between his heart and his head deep inside his soul, the military man arguing against such nonsense and the boy he'd once been begging for a return to the ways that fascinated him.

"What can I do to help?" David had asked. He would never forget the expression on the Elder's face. It was one of torment, desperation, and hope. *"What is going on?"*

"They need more time," Smoke Speaker had replied, closing his eyes as though believing that such a thing would not happen. *"They are so close, but have so far to go. If the child is buried, he can never return to the Land of the Living, and neither can Ian. You must find a way to keep the child in this world."*

And so David went to the sheriff, pretending to be furious over his feeble and ineffective attempts to solve Cole's case. He demanded to speak with one of the F.B.I. agents that had been sniffing around the woods during the investigation, and claimed he wanted more answers. It took some work, but he got both the agent and the sheriff to agree for more testing.

More time. How much time was needed? The testing would only go on for three more days, and then Cole would be returned to Julia. And when they were back home, it wouldn't take long for the boy to be buried. David had one final idea, and it tore his heart apart.

He knew that when his plan was put into action, and Smoke Speaker's words proved false, Julia would never forgive him.

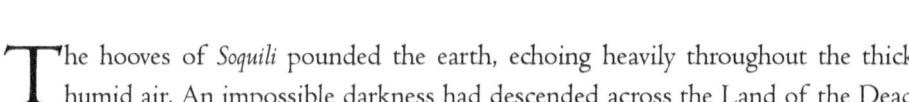

Chapter 32

The hooves of *Soquili* pounded the earth, echoing heavily throughout the thick, humid air. An impossible darkness had descended across the Land of the Dead, starting to cloak the red and purple sunset in the distance.

Ian kept his eyes on that sun, the Western Sun. That was his destination, where he and Cole would find their salvation. Even as the dust was thrown into his eyes, Ian's focus never left the huge orb of tumbling hues. He clutched his trembling son to his chest, legs cramping as they gripped the sides of the black horse. The speed of the beast was unbelievable; they crossed the Barren Plains, crashed through the Weeping Forest, sped through clumps of wandering lost souls. Both Ian and *Soquili* paid the price for speed, as they were covered with dozens of scratches, beaten down by exhaustion, and desperate for a break. But *Soquili* was cursed with obedience—he would run until he reached their stopping place. The Raven-Eater had long ago bestowed a powerful magic upon him, one that forced him to run until his hooves bled, until his lungs burned, until the mission was accomplished.

As he clutched both horse and boy, Ian reflected on Whisper's last words. The young woman had slit her own wrists to reach the Land of the Dead, knowing she would never return. She had willingly given up her life so Cole could live. But...why?

And she had called him by name. This entire trip, she had regarded him with a cool, icy glare and a constant "Mr. Daivya," which always sounded full of disdain. Yet when speaking her last request to him, to tell the Elder good-bye, she used his first name. Had she finally reached some level of respect for him? Or was she so rushed, so frazzled for once in their escape, that she had experienced a mere slip of the tongue?

It didn't matter, because either way, he had left her behind. He would never forgive himself for leaving Whisper alone in a strange, evil place with the Raven-Eater rapidly descending upon them. And the arrow...in his final look back, he had seen the arrow that struck her down, blood bursting from the impact. The young, mysterious woman he believed to be so strong and invincible had tumbled to the ground, left to the wrath of the Guardian of the Dead.

The regret and hatred he felt toward himself mixed with relief and anticipation when the river came into view. It was only seconds before *Soquili* skidded to a halt, nearly throwing its riders to the ground.

Ian climbed off the horse's back, feet landing solidly on the rumbling ground. He looked over his shoulder to see the Army of the Dead somehow gaining ground. The closer they got to the Land of the Living, the more their pace quickened, and they walked in straight lines a mile thick, rotting flesh hanging off cracked bones, torn and ragged clothes flapping in the increasing wind. Some, those who had died fighting, carried weapons; others had only their hands for war. But their lack of weapons didn't matter. In the Land of the Living, they couldn't die, couldn't be killed. They would take over one murder at a time.

Just ahead of them was Hunting Hawk, the Raven-Eater's last guard. He was one of three of the Raven-Eater's guards who hadn't taken Whisper's bribe, for reasons of his own. He had plans in the Land of the Dead, and wasn't prepared to leave just yet.

Hunting Hawk rode his own horse, appointed to him by the Guardian of the Dead himself. Not quite as fast as the *Soquili* Ian rode, he nonetheless flew across the earth, determined to reach Ian before he launched across the river.

Not wasting any time, and desperately hoping to avoid a fight against the Raven-Eater's guard, Ian dragged Cole off the horse and raced to the riverbank, where the RiverKeeper was waiting.

"So you return," the RiverKeeper sneered, greedy saliva dripping from the corners of his cracked lips. He held out an old, deformed hand. "Give it to me."

Heart racing, sweat dripping into his eyes, Ian grabbed for Cole, who was staring back at Hunting Hawk and the approaching army through wide, terrified eyes. "What?" he panted, fear creeping through him that they may not make it onto the boat in time. "Give you what?"

The RiverKeeper's eyes narrowed and his hand clutched into a fist. "I want what was promised to me!"

"What? I don't..." Ian looked around, as though Whisper would magically appear to once again save the day. The RiverKeeper was glaring at him with hungry greed spread across his face. Dark water lapped against the shore as the wind picked up. "I don't have anything!"

"You have *everything!*" the RiverKeeper shouted, shaking his fist in Ian's face. "You carry the blood of the half-breed! It was promised to *me!*"

"The..." Ian's voice trailed off when he realized what he meant. The blood of the half-breed, the mark on Cole's back.

The RiverKeeper wanted his son.

Whisper grunted as she was dumped at Gentle Heart's feet. The gaping wound in her chest screamed in defiance, dark red blood seeping to the stone floor. Gentle Heart took a step back, swallowing hard with nerves. This strange young woman had rattled her, stating odd yet somehow familiar claims of her true name, of her alleged father, of a beautiful necklace that used to be hers. She had that necklace wrapped around her wrist now as she struggled to regain her memories.

"What have you told my wife to make her so afraid?" the Raven-Eater demanded to know, kicking Whisper in the shoulder. "What lies have you brought to my home?"

"I bring no lies," Whisper choked out through a mouthful of blood. She spat the thick liquid at the Guardian of the Dead's feet, pleased when a scowl crossed his homely, deathly terrifying face. "I bring only salvation, from the Elder Smoke Speaker."

The Raven-Eater knew that name, and it burned through him like two thousand fires. He had stolen the man's daughter many years ago, not for vengeance, not for hate, but because Blue Feather, now Gentle Heart, was the most beautiful woman he had ever seen, the only one who ever resembled his lost wife, and he wanted her for himself. The man had tricked him once, infiltrating the Fire Tower with a false face crafted by strong magic. He had posed as a guard, tried to steal Gentle Heart back to the Land of the Living.

And he had failed, as the Raven-Eater's magic was far greater and he had already destroyed her memories of her past life. Smoke Speaker returned to his world before his guards could capture him.

"How do you know that name?"

"She is his apprentice," Gentle Heart spoke up, surprising herself. "She knows him well. He trained her in the old ways."

"Why?" The Raven-Eater lowered his enormous body to his knees, peering curiously at his dying captive. Her face had paled, her eyes were tired, and she was starting to shiver from the cold. "Why have you come to steal my son? What is your mission? You will tell me before I kill you, and before I kill your companion."

Ian and Cole's faces flashed behind her eyes. She prayed to Creator to keep them safe, even in the Land of Darkness, where He had little reign. "You have cursed those in Death, and seek to destroy the living. We are here to kill you."

At that, the Raven-Eater laughed, a booming, hoarse laugh that thundered into Whisper's ears so fiercely that she covered them with shaking hands, despite her will to stay strong.

"Kill me?" he snarled, slapping her hard across the face. "No one can kill me."

With a desperate burst of energy, Whisper rose unsteadily to her feet, nearly knocking Gentle Heart over in the process. "There is one," she replied coldly, bracing herself with a hand against the slimy wall. "There is one who has the power to strip your magics, to destroy you."

"I killed that abomination years ago," the Raven-Eater sneered. "The half-breed is dead. Your Elder is a fool, sending a woman to find a half-breed who no longer exists."

Whisper grinned, her white teeth stained red. "Are you sure about that, Raven-Eater?"

Chapter 33

Instinctively, Ian moved Cole behind him, sheltering his son from the selfish hands of the RiverKeeper, whose lips were smacking with anticipation. The groaning and shuffling sounds of the Army of the Dead were rapidly coming upon them, and Ian could hear Hunting Hawk's approach in the pounding of horse hooves.

"You can't have my son, old man," Ian growled, pointing a finger at the boat. "But you will take me back across the river."

"*Kanegv* promised me the blood of the half-breed!" the RiverKeeper shouted in response, spit flying from decaying gums. "Only the blood of the half-breed will secure your passage across the river."

Having only seconds to make up his mind, Ian nodded and kneeled down next to his son. "OK, relax. What if I cut his finger, and give you a few drops of blood? You can't have his life. I'll kill you before you kill my son."

The RiverKeeper sneered. "I want the blood of the half-breed."

Frustrated and annoyed, Ian spun Cole around and pulled down his fantastically-designed shirt. The glorious mark between his shoulder blades reflected in the fading red and purple light. "Here, see? He has the mark of the half-breed! Now take us across the river, damn it!"

Gentle Heart wrung her hands together as her husband picked his captive up by the throat and tossed her carelessly against the wall. Despite her will to be strong, Whisper cried out in pain, fighting back tears. She didn't bother to get up this time. Instead, she stayed on her stomach, focusing on her labored breathing. There was little life left in her.

As she watched the dying woman, Gentle Heart ran her fingers over the gorgeous bone necklace. It was familiar to her, and she could remember the feel of the cool beads against her skin, the many compliments her friends and family gave her on its beauty.

And Smoke Speaker.

Suddenly her past life came flooding back to her—her father, the famous Cherokee Elder, a magical man who helped anyone in need and never asked for anything in return.

He was a gentle soul, one who loved nature, who respected the ways of all people. She recalled her long walks through the woods, cherishing the natural glory of the earth, reveling in her friendly relationships with animals. She got her name from Grandfather Bluebird, who sang her into the world even as her mother passed from it. And her mind pictured the day her happy life was destroyed by the dark shadow stalking her through the forest, snatching her from everything she ever knew and loved.

That was the day she learned to believe in evil spirits, and gave up childish notions of knights in shining armor. No one ever came to save her but her father, who risked his eternal soul for her safe return. But his journey resulted in him returning to the Land of the Living without her, leaving her behind to suffer her own eternity with the creature of hate who forced himself on her at his own whim. This was her life now, filled with people and places she had not grown up around, and the necklace brought back the memories of a time when happiness surrounded her every day.

And this woman, this Whisper…did she know her too? Gentle Heart had to discover the truth behind her mysterious journey.

Before the Raven-Eater could resume his attack, Gentle Heart raced over to the fallen woman and helped her roll over onto her back. Whisper grit her teeth together as she moved, glancing over at the Guardian of the Dead as he crossed his thick arms and glared down at his wife.

"What do you think you are doing, Gentle Heart? Get away from my captive! She is mine to destroy."

Gentle Heart cradled Whisper's head in her lap, pressing a hand on her wound. Blood oozed between her fingers. "I know this woman," she whispered with a frown. "But I don't know how." She brushed the young Cherokee woman's hair back from her sweaty face. "She's dying."

"As she deserves," the Raven-Eater answered with a crooked, satisfied smile. "She has little life left." He crouched down and grabbed her by the chin, forcing Whisper to look at him. "Before you die, prisoner, you will know that my guard has captured your companion, slit his traitorous throat, and regained my son." He straightened and cast a scorned look down at Whisper before heading for the door. "So much for your half-breed saving your precious Land of the Dead."

Whisper didn't know what to believe, but she was a master of deceit and knew better than to believe a captor. The Raven-Eater wanted her to die her second death with the knowledge that she had failed, and that was something she refused to believe…even as she succumbed to the pain.

The RiverKeeper stepped down from his boat and stalked over to Ian. He leaned over, bones cracking with the effort, and peered at the mark on the boy's back, a jagged circle with five dots in the center, the mark of the half-breed.

He straightened and peered at Ian through accusing eyes. "What sort of treachery is this?"

Ian frowned, again looking over his shoulder at the approaching Hunting Hawk. "What? Whisper told me this was the mark! She said Cole was the half-breed!"

"Did she?" the RiverKeeper asked, again leaning over. "Did she say that, exactly?"

Ian struggled to remember her exact statement, and came to the realization that the words of Cole being the half-breed never actually escaped her lips. She said she believed the half-breed was already here, in the Land of the Dead, but…she had never said she thought Cole to be the one. But why would she lead him to believe that his son was the half-breed if it wasn't true?"

As Ian searched his memory, the RiverKeeper licked a bony finger and drew it across the boy's mark. A brown smudge was left where his finger touched skin. "A trick," he snarled, pushing Cole toward his father, "as I suspected."

Ian clutched Cole by the shoulders and took in the smeared sight. "I…I don't understand," he stammered. "If Cole isn't the half-breed, then who is?"

The dark, damp room was silent as Whisper's last breath passed through her lungs. The Raven-Eater was at the door, ready to go after Fighting Fox, ready to take over the Land of the Living now that his enemy was no longer a threat.

As Gentle Heart took one final glance down at those haunting black eyes before they closed, she suddenly realized why they were so familiar to her. "I know you," she whispered again, tears streaming down her cheeks. "My daughter."

The Raven-Eater froze, one hand on the doorframe. He turned slowly at those two terrifying and angering words. "What…did…you…call…her?" His question was a slow, low, terrifying growl.

Gentle Heart laid Whisper's head on the ground softly, her heart ripping in two as she ran a hand down her long black hair. "My daughter," she repeated quietly, remembering that frightening moment twenty-three years ago when she realized she had given birth to a girl. A half-breed, part living, part dead, the only creature with enough power to destroy the Raven-Eater.

"The half-breed is *dead!*" the furious Raven-Eater shouted, slamming a fist against the wall. "I ordered her death! I *ordered* her to be destroyed!"

"No," Gentle Heart whispered, both sorrow and joy tearing at her souls. "I saved her."

"You saved her," he repeated, crossing the room in three long strides and grabbing Gentle Heart by the throat, much like he had done to Whisper only moments ago. "You defied me?" He couldn't believe her insolence. She had been such an obedient wife all these years, giving him everything he wanted, everything but a son. And now she revealed her deceit, the ultimate betrayal.

"You will die for your treachery."

"Put her down."

The Raven-Eater dropped Gentle Heart in surprise when the rough, accented voice met his ears. He turned to see Whisper standing behind him, gripping a spear that had been hanging on the wall, his own weapon. Genuine shock and confusion raced through him, rendering him speechless as Gentle Heart crawled over to the wall for protection.

Whisper narrowed her black eyes and bent her knees slightly, preparing for an attack as a strange sensation of power filled her body, a feeling she was yet to understand. The wound in her chest no longer seeped blood, but her clothes and skin were stained with the reminder of her death.

And dead, she now was.

For twenty-three years she had waited for this moment, trained for this moment. For twenty-three years she had dreamed of the day she would take her rightful place at the throne of the Fire Tower. And now she finally had the chance to fight the man who gave her the scar between her shoulder blades, the scar Smoke Speaker couldn't stand to see and had insisted on covering with a representation of the Western Sun.

Swinging the spear around in preparation for their fight, Whisper spoke the only two words that could ever fill the Raven-Eater with fear.

"*Osiyo*, Father."

Chapter 34

"Whisper."

Ian's heart sank into his stomach. His guide, the mysterious woman with haunting eyes that had seen so much he did not understand; had been the one they sought the entire time. And she had promised her blood to the RiverKeeper.

"I...I don't have her blood," he told the old man, holding out his hands helplessly. "I don't know what—"

Then his mind raced back to the day he first met her. They had walked to the river, where he watched her whisper to the wind, where he first found out that Cole was trapped in the Land of the Dead. In his mind, he watched her drag the tip of a knife across her palm, drip blood into the water, then fish out a rock with, he just realized, the mark of the half-breed. She turned the rock over in her hand, coating it with her blood, tossing it to Ian.

"*Keep it safe,*" she had instructed.

Ian's hand flew to his pocket as he silently prayed for the rock to still be there. With relief, his fingers touched the small, cool stone, and when he pulled it out he hoped that it still held her blood.

Another test, he thought with some amusement. A test to follow direction, to trust in his guide enough to do such a seemingly unimportant thing as keep a rock in his pocket.

Ian held out the stone. "But...I've been in the water since she gave this to me," he said regretfully. "Her blood may have washed—"

"It never washes away," the RiverKeeper cut in as he grabbed the stone from Ian's hand. "It binds to that which she gives power. With this, I am free to live again. I am free of this curse, and will live again with my family."

While Ian pondered over the idea of this coarse old man ever having a family, the RiverKeeper hurried back to the boat and gestured for Ian to do the same. They pushed off from shore and were just out of arrow range when Hunting Hawk reached the river edge. Ian watched with both relief and terror as the guard threw his bow down angrily, stalking the shore for an alternative path across.

They rowed silently for some time, the RiverKeeper dreaming about his new life soon to come, Cole sleeping on his father's lap, Ian trying to make sense of what was happening. All around them, water gently lapped against the edges of the boat, soaking

Ian's shoes. The wind was getting stronger with each passing gust, and the Western Sun seemed so much farther away now than when he was crossing the Barren Plains. A trick, he thought, another deception, this time from a different source.

"So…Whisper is the half-breed," Ian mused to himself, his voice barely above a murmur. "So that means Gentle Heart is her mother, and Smoke Speaker is Gentle Heart's father…and that means…Smoke Speaker is Whisper's grandfather." He laughed incredulously, partly in shock over the realization. "She's not his apprentice. She's his goddamn granddaughter."

"We have waited a long time for her to return."

Ian lifted his head. "What?" he asked the RiverKeeper, who was looking right at him as he rowed with skinny, wrinkled arms. "Return?" Then he remembered the Elder's words. *She was born into a world she was destined to change.* Smoke Speaker never said her world of birth was that of the living. "You knew her when she was young?"

The RiverKeeper huffed and shook his head. "You have much to learn, Mr. Daivya."

"So enlighten me."

"Very well." He nodded and peered into the darkness toward the Fire Mountains, now disappearing into the distance. The Army of the Dead was like a black fog lining the horizon. "The Raven-Eater stole Blue Feather from the Land of the Living many moons ago, when she had seen but four and twenty summers. It was then that his reign darkened, and he began building his army. Once he was born a son, his family would be complete, and he could take over the living." He paused for a breath, remembering stories of the day Blue Feather arrived. Her screams had carried across the Land of the Dead for many miles, for many days. Then they stopped suddenly, cut off as though she had been struck down, and the next time any dead soul laid their eyes on the woman she had been clutching a squirming child to her breast.

"Smoke Speaker dedicated his life to saving his daughter from the Raven-Eater, and asked an old friend, one of the last Cherokee men in the mountains, to get him to the Land of the Dead."

"But I thought if you killed yourself, you couldn't return."

The RiverKeeper grimaced, irritated by the interruption. "He did not take his own life, Mr. Daivya. His friend killed him at a time he did not expect, and guarded his body so it would not be buried. The Elder crossed into the Land of the Dead, disguised himself as a guard, and entered the Fire Tower to save Blue Feather."

"A father saving his child from the Raven-Eater," Ian commented. "I can relate."

"No, young man, you cannot."

Ian narrowed his eyes at the insult. "And why not? I'm here with Cole, aren't I?"

"The Elder went alone, not knowing what dangers were before him. And he faced a decision worse than any you will ever know."

"Like what?"

The RiverKeeper sighed, thinking back to Smoke Speaker's journey. "Blue Feather bore a daughter, and lied to the Raven-Eater about the infant. He believed his child to be a son for five summers, until Hunting Hawk discovered the truth and revealed her deceit to the Guardian of the Dead."

"The Raven-Eater was furious, and tried to kill his child by throwing her from a tower window. But *Kanegv* is the half-breed, half-dead, half-alive, and was born with a power far greater than the Raven-Eater. She survived, but for a scar between her shoulder blades."

"The mark of the half-breed," Ian whispered, rubbing a finger over the smudges on Cole's back. "She led me to believe that Cole was the half-breed so I would help her get back to the Fire Mountains, back to her mother. But…how did she escape?"

A howl in the distance had the RiverKeeper pausing in stride. He looked over both shoulders worriedly before continuing his story. "The Raven-Eater ordered his new guard to kill the child, and burn her body."

"The Elder."

"Yes," the RiverKeeper affirmed with a nod. "Smoke Speaker went to retrieve the child, and to save his daughter. But only two can cross the river, so said the RiverKeeper during that time, as there must always be a RiverKeeper. So he told Blue Feather to take *Kanegv* and run. He would take her place in the Land of the Dead. Blue Feather refused, because she knew that the Raven-Eater would hunt her down, and destroy the Land of the Living to get her back. She gave her daughter to Smoke Speaker, and asked her father for one final task, to raise her as his own. And so he took the child back with him, and taught her his magic, so that she would always be able to speak to the earth."

The pieces fell into place for Ian. "So Smoke Speaker left Blue Feather behind and brought Whisper back and raised her, and trained her to one day come back and kill the Raven-Eater…her father. And the Raven-Eater no longer trusted his wife to give him a son, so he began stealing them from the living world. And Whisper saved them until she was ready to return. She let Cole be taken, so she could return."

"Only a child protected by the Raven-Eater can strip his magic, by burying a lock of hair in the Land of the Living." The RiverKeeper pointed to Gentle Heart's necklace tucked into Ian's pocket. "But someone must stay behind to kill the Raven-Eater."

Then he released a heavy breath. "Smoke Speaker has never forgiven himself for leaving Blue Feather behind. He lives his life with one purpose, to kill the Raven-Eater, so that *Kanegv* can take her rightful place as Guardian of the Dead and Blue Feather can be freed. The Land of the Dead is desperate for a righteous ruler of justice."

"But..." Ian frowned as he thought of something, "if Whisper is half Blue Feather, and half Raven-Eater, then wouldn't that mean that she's part good and part evil?"

"Yes." The RiverKeeper blew out a breath. "The Elder has worked for many moons to teach her to walk the Red Road, to cast out the darkness hidden behind her eyes. The Raven-Eater will always be a part of her, but Smoke Speaker has also taught her good."

Ian wasn't so sure. Whisper was callous, rude, and quick to fight. She could lie without batting an eye, bleed without showing pain, kill without a moment's remorse. She helped him save Cole only to reach the Fire Tower. Everything about her was deceitful.

"She is capable of good," the RiverKeeper said suddenly, as if reading Ian's thoughts. "Her actions here may have been dishonest, but in the living world she was full of charity and giving. She dreamed of her mother often. We are lucky that she has returned."

"How do you know all this?"

The RiverKeeper was silent for a moment, wondering if he should answer the question. He had nothing to lose, and everything to gain with the blood of the half-breed, and decided Ian could handle his words. "Because I am the man who killed the Elder. I watched him die, and I watched him reenter the Land of the Living holding a child. Three winters later, I died in a snowstorm, and the Elder promised me the blood of the half-breed in return for my assistance."

The revelation didn't surprise him—very little surprised him now. "So why didn't you say something when we crossed the first time?"

"A long time has passed. I did not recognize her until the end."

The final image of an arrow plunging into Whisper's back flashed into his mind. "It doesn't matter anyway," he said, his heart sinking into his stomach.

"We failed. The Raven-Eater shot her in the back just as I left. There's no way she could survive that."

The RiverKeeper grinned then, revealing a row of rotted teeth. "Only the living part of *Kanegv*, what living parts remain in the Land of the Dead, can die. Death is where her power lies."

Chapter 35

Ian rested with his head in his hands as the RiverKeeper rowed steadily across the dark waters. Gradually, the sounds of the Army of the Dead faded, and nothing existed around them but waves and wind. Cole kept a sharp eye out while his father slept, peering into the blackness, terrified that the Raven-Eater would grab him out of nowhere and bring him back to the Fire Tower. He clutched Ian's leg for security.

The RiverKeeper reveled in his thoughts while rowing, thinking about how he would enjoy his new life. The blood of the half-breed, the one guided by *Kamama*, was good for one wish, one secret desire that would be carried to Creator for granting.

His wish was for his family. He wanted to see them again, wanted to feel the warmth of his wife's skin, wanted to watch his daughter grow up into a beautiful woman. Both the love of his life and the little girl he never got to know died during childbirth, devastating him.

But now, now was his chance to experience the life stripped from him so many years ago. He knew that the Raven-Eater's army was advancing on the Land of the Living, bent on its destruction, but he believed in Whisper, believed in her abilities, and knew she would succeed. Even as a child there was something special about her...eerie, yes, but mysteriously special. She had a power not even she understood, a way to connect with both the living and the spiritual world that transcended everyone's capacity to comprehend, including the Elder. Smoke Speaker once told him that only in her death would she experience all that she was capable of, a death that could only happen when her living soul was taken from her in the Land of the Dead. Judging by Ian's earlier words, the Raven-Eater had already unknowingly done just that.

The RiverKeeper shifted when Ian awoke with a start. Using the moment to his advantage, Cole crawled into his father's lap and buried his head in his shoulder, silently wishing for his mother. Ian looked around, momentarily confused before his journey came rushing back to his memories—the Barren Plains, the Raven-Eater, his guide's deception from the very beginning.

He took out Gentle Heart's necklace and stared at the sleek black hair braided around beads, feathers, and some kind of gray material. It really was a beautiful piece, holding more magic than he would ever know or understand.

"It's so dark," he muttered to himself, peering up at the sky with a frown. "God, I miss the sun."

"She is a beauty."

Ian turned to his raft captain. "She?"

The RiverKeeper nodded. "Mother Sun," he replied when Ian merely shrugged. "The white man has no appreciation for our great earth."

"So teach me. Whisper told me every other friggin' story."

He doubted that, but continued nonetheless. "Mother Sun and Father Moon once lived side-by-side in the sky, watching over their children. Our people never knew darkness or light, only a unique combination of the sun and the moon that cast them in a perfect glow. Then one day Father Moon saw a beautiful young woman walking through the forest. She was the daughter of a chief, and was wanted by all the village men."

Sounds like a chick flick, Ian thought, but said nothing.

"Father Moon disguised himself as a god in man's form and met her in the woods. She fell in love with his charm and handsome face, and lay with him. Mother Sun discovered her husband's infidelity, and warned him that there would be consequences, should it happen again." The RiverKeeper imagined the fight as he spoke, giving Mother Sun a gorgeous, glowing face much like his wife's. "Father Moon ignored his wife, and lay with the woman again, and so Mother Sun left. She traveled to the other side of the world, casting the people in darkness. "

"Kind of like the Land of the Dead," Ian commented, but the RiverKeeper ignored him.

"Soon, the people began to suffer. Their crops failed, their health weakened, and their village moral declined. The threat of chaos was in every living soul's eyes. The Elders begged Father Moon to find Mother Sun and return her to the sky, and so he left on the journey. But Mother Sun was not to be fooled. She ran from her husband, and he chased her. They traveled around the world, always twelve hours apart. He chases her still, and that is why we now have the days and the nights."

"Because the moon is chasing the sun around the sky," Ian finished.

"Yes."

"Huh."

The RiverKeeper eyed his passenger. "It is interesting that your journey is through the darkness, Mr. Daivya. The dark is a symbol for deceit, infidelity, and arrogance."

Ian couldn't help but take slight offence of the man's jab at his personal life. But how would he know about his consideration to take his secretary up on her offer? Or that there were problems in his marriage? Perhaps Whisper had said more than he realized during their first trip.

"Yeah, it's interesting," was all he would say in regard to the RiverKeeper's comment. "And I'm looking forward to getting back into the light."

"Tread carefully, Mr. Daivya. Now is not the time for wandering thoughts."

With that, the boat hit shore.

Chapter 36

Whisper slowly circled the Raven-Eater, hands gripped tightly on the finely-crafted spear. It was an artistic masterpiece, that weapon, one that was made especially by her enemy with a talented hand that carved intricate figures in the thick wood. And now she was going to use it against him, just as he had done with her own arrow. The gloomy tower room, darkened with gray slime and black tar that dripped from the roof, encouraged her attack, welcomed it.

As she carefully placed one step after the next, her eyes never leaving his face, she marveled at the power swelling within her. Smoke Speaker had warned her of this power, warned her against its manipulation. Magic was tricky, with a mind of its own. Only in the Land of the Dead, he had explained, would she realize her true potential. And only in the Land of the Dead would her true nature be revealed. Whisper had little say in the makeup of her genes, so the Elder acted as an influential voice in how she used what was gifted to her body and soul.

She was constructed of equal halves of good and evil. The Elder worked for many moons to teach her to walk the Red Road, worrying that she would be corrupted in death, when he was no longer there to offer his guidance and words of wisdom. But Whisper was strong. She knew what she wanted, and how to get it. She knew the difference between good and evil, the dangers of magic. More importantly, she knew what everyone expected of her, and what she expected of herself. Ultimately, neither her grandfather nor her father could influence her souls.

And what she wanted right now was the tip of the spear pierced through the Raven-Eater's chest.

Gentle Heart clutched her hands together as she watched father and daughter square off. Always a shy and timid woman, she wouldn't dare intrude on this fight, a battle that was twenty-three years in the making. It stunned her to know that not only was her daughter alive and full of power, but that she was barely younger than her own self. She couldn't feel like a real mother knowing she wasn't there all those years, knowing she would never be someone to look up to.

Something inside Whisper urged her forward, lifted the spear high, and struck forward with strength unbeknownst even to her. The Raven-Eater spun sideways, dodging the strike while lashing out at the woman, but the whispers within his attacker led her into another strike, instructing her where to step, where he would step, and where he was most vulnerable. The whispers spun around them in a visible dance of sensations, bursting with each stomp, thickening with each turn of battling bodies. They guided Whisper, lifted her limbs when the Raven-Eater lashed out, pointing the weapon in the right direction. The Raven-Eater's foot connected with her ankle, knocking her off balance, and she steadied herself with a furious shout that echoed off the grimy walls. Grunting with the effort, Whisper broke free of the magic that surrounded her mind and leapt toward the Guardian of the Dead. He struck out with an enormous fist, clipping her on the side of the head.

Whisper stumbled as the Raven-Eater crouched into a position of attack. She took but a second to banish the pain, and abandon her senses to the murmurs that pounded at her soul just as her enemy raged forth.

The spear plunged into the Raven-Eater's chest, piercing through flesh and bone, blood spurting across the wall in an arc of black goo. Whisper nearly gasped, shocked by the connection, by how easily the blade slid through his body.

"Wound for wound, Raven-Eater," she spat out, lifting a bloody hand to her chest and smirking when the Guardian of the Dead staggered back. Then her lips parted in surprise when he merely laughed and removed the spear, tossing it to the side. He staggered slightly, but stood tall nonetheless.

"Tell me, half-breed," he said with his rough, terrifying voice as blood seeped from the corners of his mouth, "have you come to kill me, or to join me?"

Whisper paused, half-poised for a second attack. His question both interested and confused her.

The Raven-Eater used her hesitation to his advantage, silencing Gentle Heart's protests by lifting a threatening hand. "You cannot kill me, half-breed, and I cannot kill you." He pointed to the gaping wound in the center of her chest, one that had shocked him at first, but now that he knew the reason behind her survival, it made sense to get her on his side. "My power and magics protect me from a second death. But you have a power even I do not know. You know my thoughts, my intentions, while I cannot read yours."

He was right, Whisper realized. The murmured thoughts rumbling throughout her mind were his own inner voice, and the more she concentrated on them, the more she could understand their messages. And what worried her was that he was being genuine. There was no deceit running through his head, she thought, as she stared at the man who gave her life, the dead soul bleeding black blood and glaring at her through eyes filled with hate. He knew he couldn't kill her, and so rather than make her his enemy, he wanted her on his side as his partner, his apprentice. He was calculating, but not deceptive.

"Soon my army will take over the Land of the Living," he continued, taking a brave step closer to Whisper. "All souls living and dead will be my slaves, penance for their massacre of my people, of your people. Join me, and the Land of the Living is yours to command. I will rule the Land of the Dead from the Fire Tower, and you will have your vengeance on the living world who scorns your heritage. You are, after all, my rightful heir."

Authority and control surged through Whisper as the Raven-Eater's words came to life in her mind. She saw what he saw, two worlds joined together by darkness, one world of dead and living souls existing beneath the hands of rulers with a craving for eternal existence. The dead walked where they pleased, the living suffered and waned beneath a constant moon. She would have the power to do with the living world as she wished, whether to let people exist in peace, as they did now, or to enslave them to her bidding.

The Raven-Eater nodded when Whisper gave him a look of approval and grinned. He reached back and produced her machete from the folds of his cloak, tossing the weapon to Whisper, and then gestured for her to follow. "Come, half-breed. If it is my kingdom you desire, I shall give you your own to rule."

"*Kanegv!*" Gentle Heart found her voice as the two headed out the door. "Do not do this! You are not like him! Please, I beg you, as your mother—"

"I have no mother," Whisper interrupted harshly, barely looking over her shoulder. "I live only for myself."

Julia stared at herself in the mirror, debating even a feeble attempt at improving her haggard appearance. Today was the day she would make plans for Cole's burial, which meant that in less than three days, her son would be six feet beneath the ground. It would be a small, quiet funeral, with select family only. She would do her best to keep the media from finding out. The last thing she was willing to deal with were the scum smearing her family's name in the papers.

With a sigh, she tossed her unopened mascara tube onto her dresser and stepped out of her room, heading down the hall to the guest bedroom. "Are you almost ready?" she asked her mother, who was perched on the edge of the bed. Olivia didn't answer, but instead continued staring at the floor with a look of regret and sickness on her face. "Mom? What's wrong?"

"Nothing, Sweetie," Olivia answered quietly, biting back a sob, hating herself for going along with her husband's evil plan. "I'll be ready in a moment."

"Meet me downstairs." Julia chalked up her mother's attitude to sorrow and hurried downstairs, where her father was waiting. "Are you ready to go? We have to meet the funeral director by four."

"Yes." David held a hand to his stomach, sickened by what was about to happen. It had taken hours of internal struggles for him to reach this point, and he now knew it had to be done. For Smoke Speaker, for Ian, for Whisper. For Cole. "But...I need to show you something first."

"What?"

"I...I think there's a leak in the bathroom. Let me show you."

He took his daughter by the arm and led her to the downstairs guest bathroom. It was a small, fairly updated room with modern fixtures and an antique claw-foot tub. There were no windows, so the light was a bit harsh on the eyes. "It's by the toilet."

Irritated by the interruption, and by the thought of having to call a plumber, Julia lowered herself to her knees and peered behind the toilet. She touched the floor, feeling nothing but dry tile. "I don't see anything wrong, Dad." She straightened, surprised to see that David had stepped out of the bathroom. "What are you doing?"

"Please forgive me for this, Julia," David said, then slammed the door and immediately locked it from the outside. He had reversed the locks while Julia slept the night before.

Stunned, Julia did nothing but stare at the closed door for a moment. Then she reached for the knob, finding it locked, and couldn't comprehend the situation. "What are you doing?" she shouted angrily through the door. "Unlock this goddamn door!"

"I can't," David answered. "There are bigger things happening here, Julia. I can feel it inside me. I have to help. I don't know how I know, but I feel that this is right."

"What are you talking about?" She slammed a palm on the heavy wooden door and rattled the handle. "Let me *out!* I have to meet the funeral director!"

David wiped away a tear and rubbed his wide, strong hands over his tired face. "I can't let you do that, Julia."

Pure shock and confusion silenced her. What was happening? Was she dreaming? Why was her father acting like this? What was he planning?

Whatever it was, he wouldn't win. She would find a way out.

Julia yanked open the medicine cabinet, surprised to find it empty. She looked beneath the sink to see that everything had been removed. There was nothing to throw, nothing to use as a weapon. In a fit of rage, she thrust back the shower curtain, eyes widening at the sight of a full stock of food and drinks.

Her father had stacked at least a week's worth of dry food and beverages, along with a cooler of items. Everything from chips and cans of Coke to sandwiches and pre-cooked pasta meals met her eyes. Blankets and a pillow were set next to the food. Clearly, this was planned.

"Son-of-a-bitch," she muttered, only able to think that her father was a part of Cole's disappearance. Why else wouldn't he want her to bury her son? Julia picked up a bottle of water and threw it against the wall. It clattered to the floor without damaging a thing.

"Mom!" she yelled, slamming a fist against the door. "Mom! Please! Let me out!" Her voice broke then, and she gave into the tears, slumping against the door. "Please let me out," she whispered, sinking to the floor.

Just outside, David leaned against the wall and said a silent prayer of forgiveness. If he was wrong, and the facts were clearly against him, then his relationship with his family was over.

David couldn't stand his daughter's frantic shouts, her tearful pleas, but it hit Olivia the hardest. She buried her head in her hands in the upstairs guest room, silently wondering if her heart would stop beating from the stress and depression of what she was doing. She was betraying her daughter, and for what? For her husband? For a foolish legend that may or may not be true?

For whatever reason she was going along with the plan, it was too late to back out now.

Chapter 37

There was only one last bit of power left in Smoke Speaker to give Whisper more time to stop this war. If David Bard stayed true to his word, if Ian stayed true to his son, and if Whisper stayed true to her destiny, then he could offer them just enough time to win.

Up to this point, their success depended on how well Smoke Speaker had trained Whisper, and how much help he could provide along the way. Now, it was entirely up to her, and the power within her souls to walk the Red Road that her ancestors had carved with their own hands.

The pull of the Raven-Eater was strong and steadfast. It had been tugging at her souls since the moment the Elder brought her into the Land of the Living. The darkness had shadowed her black eyes, clouding her vision, impairing her judgment. As a child, it was too tough a burden to bear. For years Smoke Speaker fed her herbs and powerful mixtures meant to bind the evil blood that pulsed through her veins. He taught her good, righteousness. And he succeeded.

Like her mother, Whisper came to love nature and animals. She respected their spirits, what they had to offer the world. She believed in balance and harmony, and was willing to bleed for the protection of the natural world. People came to her for help, for treating illnesses, for prayers of good fortune, for advice. Though she never personally connected with any of them, she was always willing to extend her hand in assistance, even if she kept her words to a minimum.

But now, he was not there to guide her through the deceptiveness that ruled the Land of the Dead. He could not offer his advice, teach her life lessons based upon his own experiences. He couldn't stand between his granddaughter and the beast who once tried to take her life as she faced her most difficult task yet.

Smoke Speaker knew what would happen. The Raven-Eater would try to kill Whisper, until he realized who she was. He would know then that he couldn't destroy the half-breed, even if Whisper didn't, and so he would change his tactics, trick her. The Raven-Eater would ask her to fight for him, join him as a ruler. And that part of her still dominated by his bloodline would awaken once again.

For all his training, all his education, Smoke Speaker couldn't prepare Whisper for the power that released itself in her souls upon death. He could only pray to Creator that she was able to resist its pull toward the darkness.

Because he had faith in his apprentice, his granddaughter, he would do this one thing for her. He would trade his life for more time.

He didn't know what his sacrifice would mean for the future. If Whisper succeeded and time went back to the day of Cole's death, then the Elder wasn't sure his life would be restored. Perhaps he would survive the journey, or his body may lie in waste until stumbled upon by an unlucky traveler or hungry animal. Either way, Smoke Speaker's life was no longer his to bear, and he welcomed the unknown.

Standing at the window, the Elder cast one final look at the beautiful stars above, the boys who had danced and danced until they became one with the night sky, then lowered himself to the thin mattress. This jail cell couldn't contain the abilities Creator had bestowed upon him so many years ago, gifts handed down from grandfather to father to son. He had power within him, a power that rested peacefully, dormant, until called upon during one moment of desperate need. It was a power that reached out to the spirits that made up the earth, acknowledging their glory while asking for their help.

Lying on his back with his hands folded across his heart, the Elder reached out to the generations of Speakers that filled his family tree, the ones who made up every bit of his soul and fed him the power to speak through smoky tendrils. He would draw on what bits of magic they left behind in the living world to slow time down. This magic was in every tree, every rock, born in every person. It manifested itself in the orbits of the earth, in the rising and lowering of the sun, and in the hearts of those who knew what power truly ran the currents of the world. By drawing on that magic, melding it with his own power, Smoke Speaker could give Whisper one last gift for her triumph.

No one would know what was happening, though they would feel sluggish and perhaps a bit confused, as their minutes stretched to hours, their hours to days. But Ian would have more time to reach the Western Sun before the boy was buried.

It had to be done now. Smoke Speaker could sense the impending approach of the Army of the Dead. They were getting closer, and with each step, their evil ripped into the Land of the Living. The clouds had already darkened, stars already faded, plants already wilting. The signs were subtle but to the trained eye, and the Elder knew exactly what to look for.

With no thoughts of regret, and with the image of his beautiful daughter in mind, Smoke Speaker released the last bit of his life into the forces that made up the Land of the Living.

Ian wasted no time in plucking Cole up from the raft and stepping back onto solid ground. The Army of the Dead was getting closer, and the last guard of the Raven-Eater was already far ahead. If he could see that far, Ian would have known that Hunting Hawk had forced his horse into the icy waters, the splashes reflecting swirls of red and purple lights that drifted into the sky.

"Run quickly," the RiverKeeper ordered, nearly shoving Ian backwards with his oar. "*Kanegv* has but one gift left for you."

"What—" Ian started to ask, only to be silenced when the old man turned his back. Though his head was screaming at him to run toward the Western Sun, his heart was drawn toward the RiverKeeper, who was staring down at the stone covered in the blood of the half-breed.

In his mind, the RiverKeeper made his wish. He let his thoughts fill with images of his beautiful wife, ideas of what his daughter would have looked like as a young woman. They were both so lovely, and loved him dearly, loved him as he used to be in the living world. His wish was simple, to be with his family again in the Spirit World.

Having made his desire known to Creator, he released the stone into the river.

Ian watched through wide eyes as the water rippled from the stone, ringlets surrounding the old man in spinning circles that vibrated and pulsed. The RiverKeeper merely smiled—a peaceful expression Ian had never known. Then, with no elaborate show, no fancy departure, he merely disappeared. Who would man the boat now was a question he didn't have time to consider. But there must always be a RiverKeeper, and had Whisper of told him the story, he would have learned that the next unfortunate soul to pick up the oars would be cursed with the eternal duty.

"Good luck, old man," Ian murmured, then turned on his heel and began the long race through tangled woods to the Western Sun. He dodged boulders, fallen trees he didn't remember being there last time. Cole clutched his neck, whimpering in his father's ear, quietly crying over and over again that he wanted to go home. Ian was already panting, constantly struggling to catch his footing. Besides the deep cracks and loose rocks that lined the ground, Ian wasn't used to running while carrying a seven year-old. The RiverKeeper's words reflected in his ears, *Kanegv has but one gift left for you.*

What gift, he thought, sucking in a deep, hot breath. *She's no longer here.* Whisper was dead. No one could survive that arrow through the chest. He didn't care what the River-Keeper said; no one magically died a second death only to live once more. And worse, she died because he left her behind. *So what could she have to give?*

He didn't have to wonder long.

A piercing cry from up above startled Ian into stopping dead in his tracks. The sound reminded him of the witch that burst from thin air and nearly suffocated Whisper to death. He wouldn't let that happen again.

But this time there was no witch. This time that shrill scream came from an enormous eagle soaring above him. Its wingspan was at least the length of his house, with feathers of brilliant gold. A bald eagle, Ian realized when the giant creature swooped down, and starting coming for him.

"Oh...God."

With his heart in his throat, and Hunting Hawk somehow already more than halfway across the river, Ian released a long stream of terrified curses and struggled to figure out how he was going to outrun this incredible beast in a land where hiding places were few and far between. He was too far away from the patch of woods. There was nowhere to run, nowhere to duck into, nothing to do when the eagle shifted positions, bearing down with talons wide open. In a last ditch effort to avoid being ripped apart by the razor-sharp claws, Ian leapt to the side, hoping to confuse the animal.

The eagle merely announced his annoyance with a harsh shout that nearly made Ian's ears bleed, then reached out with an enormous foot and grabbed both man and child from the earth.

Ian fought against the beast, pounding his fists against the hard flesh that wrapped around shiny black talons. But he was in a tight hold, and could barely move. In fact, the eagle's toes were wrapped around his back and legs so that he was almost in a sitting position, with his arms locked to his chest and, therefore, safely locking in Cole.

Do not fight Eagle.

"Whisper?"

Ian craned his neck, swearing he could hear his guide's voice coming from the creature as they rose into the night sky. He half expected to see her riding the eagle's back. Then he felt something, a warm kind of tingle that reverberated through the bird's blood and spread to Ian. It was a message, whispered to Eagle from the Land of the Living before this journey ever even began, a message that traveled from the creature's heart, through its soul, and transferred into Ian's unsuspecting mind.

Eagle is my last gift, Mr. Daivya, Whisper said inside his head. *Eagle is majestic, a warrior for Creator against the Raven-Eater. He will take you to the Bridge of the Dead.*

"Then why didn't he take us to the Fire Tower?" Ian muttered to himself.

As if having anticipated the question, Whisper gave the answer. *Only Eagle defies the Raven-Eater, and so he is cursed. Eagle must only fly away from the Fire Tower, and into the Western Sun, where he begins his eternal journey again.*

So he can't fly enemies to the Raven-Eater's front door, Ian concluded. It made sense, in the twisted way that everything in the Land of the Dead made sense.

He could relax, though, and that was all that mattered to him. So he held his son as tightly as possible and hummed a made-up song that lulled them both to sleep.

Chapter 38

It was a sight she had seen often in her dreams, a view she had longed for as a child, one she felt incomplete without. This sight came to her in visions, as it was a part of her very core, what made up the Raven-Eater and, therefore, what made up half of her soul.

They stood atop the Fire Mountains, overlooking the Land of the Dead. Whisper kept her place two steps behind the Raven-Eater, staying focused on him should he choose a sudden attack as they watched the Army of the Dead advance on the river. But the longer she stood there, taking in everything that would be hers, the more she realized that she had nothing to fear. There were many suggestions of hate and vengeance swarming about the Raven-Eater's mind, but the dominating thought was that he could not kill her, and so he would use her to build his kingdom in the Land of the Living.

It gave Whisper a dark kind of thrill to know she couldn't be destroyed. Smoke Speaker had explained it once to her, informing her that when the living soul bonds with that of the dead, it creates an impenetrable force that shields the body from harm. A half-breed could bleed, could feel pain and hunger, could cry, could suffer every human emotion, but couldn't die. The living half could pass into oblivion, but the death side would live forever, even after the body had withered away from old age. Only in the Land of the Dead would a half-breed live on in the same body in which it died.

The Elder had called this a curse, but as Whisper felt her strength build, her eyes sharpen, her mind fill with a power she had never known before, she knew it was a gift. Being the half-breed gave her the power to do as she wished—to change the world as she saw fit.

And no one could stop her.

Whisper took three steps forward, stopping at the edge of the cliff. From behind, the Raven-Eater kept a close watch on the half-breed that was his daughter. He was drawing her in, sucking her into his world of domination, and succeeding because she was, indeed, half his. But he was still cautious of her motives, and of her power. He had tried to kill her once because of what pulsed through her blood, as it wasn't the little girl he had once feared. It was the woman she would grow up to be.

That woman was here now, and it was up to him to defeat whatever good the Elder had managed to stain her with.

"What is your purpose here, half-breed?" he asked with his harsh, deep voice that cackled in the dry air. Whisper didn't answer, but merely stared forward, watching the Army of the Dead begin their walk across the river. The Raven-Eater crossed his arms. "You removed my guards, and my son, for what reason?"

"Your guards do not serve me, and would not even if I ordered it," Whisper replied, sparing her father a stolid glance. "And so they are of no use."

"And my son?"

"He has no place in the Fire Tower." She felt that truth deep in her heart. Cole Daivya was not meant for the Land of the Dead. His soul belonged in the light. "His return to the Land of the Living restores the balance between our worlds." It was a balance disrupted by a living child being taken from his life without having breathed his last breath. Being taken too soon, ripped away from an unfulfilled life without just cause, threw the harmony of nature into a mix of chaos. For the survival of the Land of the Living, the Raven-Eater's chosen child had to be rescued.

With the balance restored, her debt to the Elder for saving her from the Guardian of the Dead was fulfilled. She owed him that much, penance for his intense training and bravery in facing what lie beyond the Western Sun. Now she was free of that burden.

Such words coming from the half-breed, a creature bred to deceive, did not pacify the Raven-Eater's doubt. He held out a hand. "Prove your allegiance, half-breed," he ordered, a bright white flame forming in his palm.

Whisper stared at the fire, which hovered just centimeters from his flesh. In time, she would learn to use her new skills, and could do so much more than that. "In what way, Raven-Eater?"

But then her mind tapped into the thoughts that reverberated off his soul. She saw what he saw, the path to the Western Sun consumed in flames, Eagle struck down, Ian and Cole tumbling to the ground, flesh burning as they struggled through their race. They were almost to the Bridge of the Dead, and the Raven-Eater wanted their journey to end in a red blaze.

She turned her eyes, filling with power as her pupils dilated and irises darkened to an even deeper shade of black, back to the Raven-Eater. "To kill Eagle is a great offense against Creator."

The Raven-Eater's scarred mouth twisted into an evil grin. "You are no longer under his control, half-breed. To kill Eagle means your loyalty to the Great Spirit has come to an end."

The thought interested her. No longer bound by Creator's rules, free to worship the spirits of her choosing, eternal wandering no longer a fear. Whisper stepped closer to the fire, taking in a deep breath and letting the magic granted to her in death work without boundaries.

Feeling only the slightest of regrets at what she was about to do, Whisper blew into the fire.

Just as Ian was letting himself enjoy the relaxing ride in Eagle's thick talons, the entire world erupted into a searing sphere of fire. Huge balls of pure flame poured from the sky, slamming into the ground and filling deep cracks with bright red rivers of fire and brimstone. In this land of black and gray nothingness, the incredible orange and red hues stung his eyes while burning his flesh. Trees just below his feet burst into red ash, and before he could wonder why they weren't flying higher, Eagle released a painful shriek tinged with torment.

Ian looked up to see Eagle's wings laced with orange flames, flames that licked their way closer and closer to their prey. Unable to fly, Eagle struggled to lower his cargo to the ground, but collapsed mid-air when the fire consumed his body.

The three crashed to the ground, Ian and Cole rolling across the scorched earth, dodging burning rocks and pitted lava. When they rose, both were marked with the scars of their fall, Cole with a black burn across his cheek and Ian's arms charred with pink rashes. Eagle landed hard, skidding only a few feet before coming to a stop. Holding Cole close to his chest despite the burns that laced his throat, Ian raced to his flighted companion, falling to his knees. He couldn't leave such a majestic creature there to die.

Eagle merely looked up at Ian with apologetic eyes, eyes that urged him to continue on, to leave him to die. Sacrifices must be made, Ian thought he could hear, and sometimes sacrifices are made at the cost of others.

Not knowing if he was moving by his own free will or by Eagle's last power, Ian rose and spun around, searching for the Western Sun. His search was fast, as the Western Sun loomed ahead of them with a menacing glare that made Ian's knees buckle. The red and purple sunset didn't look so beautiful anymore; instead, it was like a warning of danger if he chose to pass through.

But there was no other way, and so he sucked in a deep breath, glancing behind him to see the black cloud that was the Army of the Dead marching through the fire, and Hunting Hawk far ahead of them, just about to pass Eagle's burning body. Ignoring the searing pain as his skin blistered and his clothes stuck to the burns on his back, his mind thought back to his first passing, when Whisper felt her way across the sun to the sliver of a portal that cut through thin air.

After a few moments, his fingers touched the delicate edge and he slipped through, leaving the Land of the Dead behind just as a wall of flames hurled toward him.

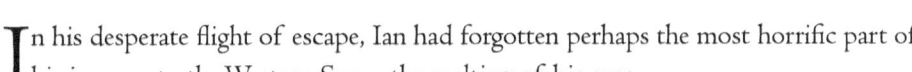

Chapter 39

In his desperate flight of escape, Ian had forgotten perhaps the most horrific part of his journey to the Western Sun—the melting of his eyes.

As he stood on the other side of the Land of the Dead, finally free of the blistering fire that had erupted amidst unsuspecting travelers, Ian was blind. Only a white cloud met his vision, and when Cole whimpered, kicking his father in the stomach when he struggled in panic, Ian knew that he too couldn't see.

But they had to move forward, and to do so they would have to fight the pull of the Western Sun. It was twice as strong for Ian as he carried both himself and his son across the hot earth, and each step was slow, lethargic, and painful. Yet as he moved, hearing the grunts and moans of the fallen all around them, his eyes began to cool. A sensation even stranger than the melting began as his eyes congealed and slowly formed. He imagined his retinas being reconstructed, reattaching to the cornea, giving him back his bright blue irises. It was a wonderful sensation, if not eerie and a bit uncomfortable, feeling as though he had opened his eyes underwater.

And then the familiar sight of a land littered with fallen souls met his vision, fuzzy as it still was. Thankful for his sight, Ian continued his journey, hunched over to protect himself from the fierce winds, concentrating only on keeping himself on two feet as the pull continued to work against him. Looking ahead, he could see the edge of the Western Sun's grasp, the place where Whisper had attached herself to him and ordered him to move. But it was so far away, so far from salvation, so far from relief.

Ian nearly tripped over a fallen corpse that was wasting away into ashes. Righting himself, he momentarily contemplated making Cole walk because he was so off-balance before chastising himself on such stupidity.

The force of the Western Sun was incredible, pulling him two steps back for every three forward. His feet dug into the ground, toes cramping as they curled around what was left of his shoes. A shout of extreme effort and determination escaped his lips, his hands gripping Cole by the shoulder and waist as he fought to move his legs, heavy with extra weight.

To combat the Western Sun, Ian leaned further forward, blinking rapidly as his eyes finally settled and his vision completely cleared. But a sudden hand clamping across his ankle had him crashing to his knees, kicking at the scorched black arm reaching for him and his son. The dead soul was groaning and foaming at the mouth, empty eye sockets peering at nothing as they stared straight at Ian—after so long a time before the Western Sun, not even getting his distance could cure his blindness. With a ferocious snarl, Ian kicked the fallen corpse in the face and freed his foot, crawling to his knees.

"Daddy! Hurry!" Cole frantically jabbed Ian's shoulder, pointing behind them. Ian looked back to see Hunting Hawk burst forth from the Western Sun, arm raised, horse panting as saliva dripped from its crusted lips.

"God help me," Ian muttered, struggling to his feet but tumbling back to his knees beneath both the weight of his son and the force of the Western Sun that was determined to suck him back in. At least four feet of track marks scarred the earth before him where he had been dragged back after being grabbed by the dead soul. There was no way to move, no way to escape the wrath of the last guard of the Raven-Eater as he raced closer and closer, the Western Sun barely affecting his stride.

Cole screamed in terror when he saw the familiar guard, burying his head in Ian's shoulder when Hunting Hawk lifted his bow and knocked a deadly arrow. Panicking in his immobility, Ian crawled on his hands and knees in a blind escape, disgruntled shouts echoing across the land as he was heaved further and further back, closer and closer to Hunting Hawk.

Dirt and grit clogging his eyes as he looked over his shoulder, the roar of the Western Sun nearly deafening him, Ian could only think that after all this, after so much pain and doubt and struggling, he had failed. Hunting Hawk released the arrow, and Ian could only close his eyes and wait.

A grunt behind him had Ian jumping and spinning around to see a second rotting dead soul collapsing to the ground. She held a jagged blade made of stone that fell from her fingers as black blood gushed from the arrow's wound. An assassin for the Raven-Eater, Ian wondered, or just another lost soul searching for salvation?

He didn't have time to find the answer, though, for before he knew what was happening Hunting Hawk had closed in, reached down, and grabbed Ian by the shoulder with a strength not humanly possible. His feet dragged on the ground as the guard carried him across the bright orange earth, not speaking a word but instead merely staring straight ahead through eyes still adjusting to the light. Ian grabbed Hunting Hawk's wrist and fought back, not realizing until the guard dropped him at the base of the Western Sun's pull that he was helping, not harming.

"Hurry," Hunting Hawk ordered, pointing in the direction of the Bridge of the Dead. "The Army of the Dead will soon pass, and your world will be destroyed."

Confused, Ian picked himself up and gently set Cole down. Cole clung to his father's leg, peering suspiciously at the guard. All around them, dead souls continued to pass, some dropping before they could reach the Western Sun. "I don't understand," Ian said through a mouthful of dust. "I thought you served the Raven-Eater."

"I serve my own purpose," Hunting Hawk replied indifferently. It would have taken too long to explain that he served the Raven-Eater only to save his soul from eternal wandering, and now that the half-breed had returned, the Land of the Dead could be restored. While time was a luxury in death, it was now something that could not be ignored. "Cross the Bridge of the Dead, and return to the waters of your death. You and your son must drown before you can return. When you surface, you must head for Howling Vines. The Elder will know what to do from there."

"And what will you do?" Yet again, he felt the guilt of leaving behind someone who had the chance of life, but was returning to death to save him and his son. That and it slightly annoyed him to know that the entire time he was running from a man who was only trying to help.

"The half-breed faces corruption," Hunting Hawk answered, his deep voice hoarse in the harsh wind. "The Land of the Dead depends on her salvation. I will fight off the Army of the Dead as long as I can so you have time to reach the lake. But I can only fight on this side of the Western Sun, where I am free from the Raven-Eater's reign. Now go. You do not have much time left. "

With that, Hunting Hawk steered the giant beast back into the Western Sun, leaving Ian to face the rest of his journey alone.

Chapter 40

Olivia had given up on David's outlandish plan, and refused to be around him any longer. Just that morning she packed her things and gave her husband an ultimatum—to release Julia, or lose his wife. Now she was on her way home; David had made his choice. He believed in his actions, believed in the Elder, and knew that if Ian and Whisper succeeded, none of them would ever remember any of this horrible, heart-wrenching time. Something had taken hold of him, and he was steadfast in his conviction. It had taken everything in his power to get Olivia to leave without finding a way to free their daughter, and he feared that if Whisper's mission failed, then she would wither away from the guilt and self-hate of what she had let happen, what she knowingly left behind.

David and Julia sat on opposite sides of the bathroom door, both leaning against the thick wood listening to the other breathe heavily. Julia had abandoned her escape attempts—hands raw from pounding the wood, fingers scabbed from picking at the hinges and edges of the doorknob. Her cheeks were stained from thick tears, and her heart was torn between hating her father for what he was doing and grieving for his inability to accept his grandson's death. David had already explained his reasoning behind his actions, and while Julia didn't believe in such foolishness, her father was steadfast in his belief. She knew her father well, knew that when he believed in something he never backed down. But what she couldn't understand was how a man so devout in his military creed could put so much faith in mystical nonsense.

As she rested her back against the door, Julia toyed with a framed picture of her son. Cole was happily hugging a goat he had bonded with at a small spring festival. The goat was chewing on the collar of his shirt, Cole laughing as he clung to the animal. It was one of her favorite pictures, one she would cherish forever. For all her father was doing to her, she was happy that he had included the photograph in his stock of supplies.

On the other side of the door, David could hear his daughter sniffling. He closed his eyes, feeling more sluggish than ever before and not knowing why. Every movement seemed to take incredible effort, and it seemed like the morning was lasting forever. If he had known of the Elder's last action, he would have thus known that his heartbeat had decreased, less blood pumping through his body, the sun rising and lowering slower. The three days Julia had been locked in the bathroom would have been closer to six were Smoke Speaker not to give up his life.

What David did know, however, was that with each shade of gray that darkened the sky, the Army of the Dead was that much closer to crossing through to the Land of the Living. Ian didn't have much time left.

"Things will never be the same now, will they, Dad?" She wasn't expecting an answer. David hadn't spoken to her since the previous night, after she cursed his beliefs, as well as his supposed love for his family. Sighing and tearing her eyes away from the precious picture, she rested her head against the wood and chewed her bottom lip.

"This is never going to end. Never. Everyone has chosen sides," she continued, mostly to herself. "Mom chose my side…the media chose Cole's…you chose the Elder." And that hurt most of all.

David considered his daughter's words. It was true, he thought. The television was covered with accusations, support, theories. Everyone had an opinion on Cole's murder, everyone thought they knew best. "And whose side have you chosen, Julia?"

The sound of her father's voice startled her, as did the question. She chose her son's side, obviously. She was Cole's mother, and it was her job to hate and despise anyone who stood in her way. And yet….

"I still love him, Dad." She laughed a sarcastic laugh of disbelief. "After what he did…I still want him back. What the hell is wrong with me?"

The revelation both pleased and disappointed him. "Julia…do you truly believe Ian is capable of murdering Cole?"

She could lie to herself, but not to her father. "No," she admitted with a heavy sigh. "I don't think I ever really thought that. But he did leave, Dad, and that I can't ignore. He just…disappeared, right along with that Whisper woman."

"That doesn't mean he left you, honey."

"Oh, right. It means he went to the Land of the Dead to save Cole from the evil Raven-Eater." The scorn in her tone was obvious, but David let it go. "No, Dad. He didn't go to some mythical place. He left his family for a younger woman. He found his way out. He's been thinking about it ever since he hired that tramp of a secretary, and finally acted on his thoughts."

Oh yes, she knew about the redheaded temptation flirting up a storm in his office. Sure, Rebecca was sweet to her face, but there was something about the way she batted those long lashes at Ian that triggered suspicion in Julia. A young woman who looked like that, dressed the way she did, was nothing but trouble. And when Ian started working later, becoming lost in thought more often, Julia had known it was just a matter of time before she came home to find them in bed. The camping trip was to be her last straw, Ian's last chance to prove his loyalty. And he had failed.

But what if her father was right? What if, on the crazy, one-in-a-million chance that there was some greater power in this world, Ian had gone to save Cole? Or had gone to save Cole truly believing he was doing the right thing, whether or not such a place existed? Smoke Speaker certainly believed in his people, and there were no doubts in her father's mind. How far would her husband go for his family?

"I have to bury my son," Julia said determinedly, a hot tear streaming down her cheek. "No matter what you believe, no matter where Ian is, this isn't fair to Cole. He deserves a proper burial. My son...your grandson, deserves that much from you."

The few seconds that passed seemed like hours, but soon Julia heard the click above her head. She jumped to her feet, feeling slightly sluggish as she steadied herself, and yanked open the door. Her father stood before her, sadness and defeat spread across his face.

"Have you lost faith in Ian, Julia?"

Pausing long enough to think about her answer, Julia hated the only reply she could think of, because it was true. She held up her left hand, where her wedding ring still shimmered beneath the lights. "I just can't bring myself to take it off."

Then she brushed past her father, setting her sights on the morgue. She had more important things to worry about than David's beliefs, Ian's whereabouts, or her own conflicted emotions toward people who would never be in her life ever again.

Whisper stood in what was to be her new room, looking out at the black smoke that clouded the Western Sun. She didn't know if Ian and Cole were still alive out there, navigating the flames, and for some reason, she didn't care. Ultimately, she didn't need them to fulfill her mission. She needed only her own self, and the power steadily building within her soul.

This was where she belonged; she could feel it deep within her heart. Growing up, there had always been something missing. Although Smoke Speaker did his best to provide a home filled with laughter, happiness, and love, Whisper had never felt like anything more than a replacement daughter. Her entire life had been devoted to training, a destiny she had no choice but to follow, as the Elder taught her the ways of their ancestors in preparation for a future she could not deny. Her fate was to kill her father, and save her mother. There was no other path.

But now she was given a choice, to go through with Smoke Speaker's training, or to join forces with a being who could literally hand her the world. She felt no connection to her mother, as she barely remembered the timid, unremarkable woman, and supposed her only loyalty to Blue Feather was the fact that she sent her daughter away for her safety. But she felt no connection with the Raven-Eater either, and cared nothing for his well-being. The one person she had ever loved was the man who saw her only as a way to save his daughter, rather than as a granddaughter. But she couldn't fault him for that. Smoke Speaker had traveled to the Land of the Dead with the intention of rescuing his daughter, being forced to return with a child he'd never known about instead. It was a sacrifice she could not imagine.

"You have become a beautiful woman, *Kanegv*," a voice said from behind. Whisper turned to see Gentle Heart standing just inside the massive room decorated with genuine articles of their heritage. Her face was shadowed with a dark bruise, a gift of hate from her husband as punishment for her deceit. "I always knew you would be." Whisper crossed her arms suspiciously as Gentle Heart took a few steps closer. It was strange to think of the woman before her as her mother, as she looked barely a year or two older. "My *uwetsiageyv*."

Whisper pulled back when Gentle Heart reached out to stroke her cheek. Her eyes filled with bitterness. "I am no woman's daughter," she replied harshly. "I was born in death."

Sorrow nipped at Gentle Heart's soul, mainly because it was true. Whisper was a half-breed, a creature that had no true stake to any one being. She was crafted of the two halves that made up the world, and as such, was more a part of the earth than she was any mother and father. For that reason, she had trouble forging relationships, a disbelief in the concept of love and affection.

"You were also born in life, *Kanegv*," Gentle Heart whispered, touching her daughter lightly on the arm. "There are two sides to every stone. Only you can decide which one faces the sun."

Whisper turned then, and for just the briefest of moments, Gentle Heart saw compassion and understanding flicker across her face. Then it was replaced by doubt and disbelief. "There are two sides, Blue Feather," she agreed, a hint of sadness in her voice, "but one cannot turn the stone alone."

"Then let me—"

"You have no power here," Whisper interrupted, the hardness back in her voice as though the stronger side of her had overcome the other. "My path is my own."

Giving up, Gentle Heart's shoulders sunk as she asked, "And the side you choose to reveal to the Western Sun?"

Her daughter's lips curled into a righteous sneer as she spoke the word that had granted her passage by the Watchmen. "...*Atleisdi*."

"Against who?"

Even when Gentle Heart gasped and stumbled back a few steps, Whisper didn't move a muscle; her back was to the Raven-Eater as she glared at her mother. He stepped into the doorway. "*Atleisdi*," she said again, drawing out the word with glee, "against the one who forced me into the Land of the Living."

From behind, the Raven-Eater shared in Whisper's evil glare of daggers and hate. He shifted his eyes to Gentle Heart, who had paled in the realization of her fate. *Yes*, he thought with a nod, *the time has come*. "Your use has run out, woman," he told her, grabbing the woman who was no longer his wife by the arm. He could find another wife, a woman more capable of meeting his demands, who would know better than to deceive him. "Tonight, you shall die by the hand of the one you bore."

Chapter 41

They were so close now, so close to the end of their horrific journey; only the Bridge of the Dead stood in their way.

Whisper hadn't prepared him for this, for this incredible sprint across the world, for the nonstop torture of searing agony that pulsed through his veins with every step. As he raced across the Land of the Dead, dodging falling fire and gritting his teeth together when sparks pierced his tattered clothing and smoldered into his skin, he racked his brain with ways to approach the obstacle that had nearly taken his life in the beginning of their journey. He was weaker now, covered with excruciating blisters that were scabbed and oozing pus. His face was charred red, his blonde hair black with dirt and grime, every inch of his body wrapped with lacerations, bruises, and tiny nicks. Cole, thankfully, wasn't so worse for the wear, but he was weak nonetheless.

Sweat poured down Ian's face and into his eyes as he neared the deadly bridge. From the distance he could see it was empty, could hear the screams of the fallen as they plunged to their deaths into a time without end. Dead souls lined the bone gate that encircled the hut of the Watchmen, waiting for the next victim to cross the Bridge of the Dead.

The fear of those three evil cats waiting for him nearly made Ian stumble to a halt before he even reached the bridge. He could take their wrath, could willingly suffer the revenge that they very well deserved, but would take his own life before letting them harm his son. So he slowed as he reached the edge, anxiously awaiting his fate.

As expected, the animals he once scorned throughout his life appeared along the Bridge of the Dead, staring at him with those accusatory eyes that demanded revenge. Sucking in a nervous breath when the hawk and pelican perched warily on the railing, Ian began his walk of vengeance.

Then something happened that shocked him into stillness.

The three cats moved to the side of the bridge, lying down and resting their heads on their front paws. The insects and mice scurried to the edges, creating a clear path, while the birds fluttered their wings and turned so their backs were to the travelers, settling in as though for a good night's sleep.

They were letting him pass, he realized, without a fight. As though he could read their minds, he understood their actions. Whisper had once said that the Land of the

Dead was a dark place because of the Raven-Eater, and that his destruction meant the dead could once again rest in peace. Cole was the key to his destruction, and so even the animals that would love to see Ian tormented were willing to set aside their grudges for a greater cause.

Preparing himself for a run just in case, Ian jogged across the bridge, casting a lone glance down at the three cats as he passed, who merely blinked and swished their tails. Amazement nearly halted him, but he kept his composure and convinced himself not to show his fear.

"Tomboy," Cole whispered when he peeked out from his father's shoulder and caught sight of the white cat. "Hi, Kitty." His aunt's cat lowered his head in response, a sign of respect for the boy.

The race across the bridge was a lot faster than Ian remembered, obviously because this time he wasn't being torn to pieces or being watched by a woman who hated him. He silently thanked whatever greater being was responsible for making the return trip surprisingly simple. The dead souls at the gate were silent, angry that their show ended with such anti-climactic results.

Ian stopped at the door that led back to the Watchmen. While the bridge may have been a breeze, he doubted that the ghoulish guards would be willing to let him pass without confrontation.

Heaving in a deep breath, Ian lifted a hand to open the door—and was violently sucked inside.

Ian tumbled to the floor as Cole landed hard against the dripping wall. Cole screamed when the brownish goo seeped across his arms and shoulders, locking his wrists in place. The child kicked and squirmed against the strange restraints, getting trapped further in the wall the more he struggled. Ian grabbed his son's arm, pulling hard, but not moving the boy so much as an inch.

"Let him go!" Ian shouted when the two guards came into view, gray and black mist swirling and forming their eyeless outlines. "You want a prisoner, you deal with me!"

The Watchmen spun around in at dizzying speeds before coming to a dead stop on either side of him. Ian's eyes took a moment to adjust. *"The unworthy. . .has returned. . . ."* they rasped, shoving Ian back a few steps with a strong, invisible force. *"The unworthy. . . shall not. . .pass."*

When Cole was pulled further into the grisly dripping wall, Ian reached out only to be slammed to his knees as the Watchmen moved closer, gaping mouths threatening to swallow them both whole. "You have to let us pass. Both worlds depend on it."

Hoarse laughter erupted from the depths of the guards. It reverberated off the slimy walls, rumbling throughout Ian's head. *"Such confidence. . .from the unworthy. . ."* One of them spun around Ian, observing their captive. *"Do you know why. . .the half-breed. . . returned?"*

"Whisper?" Ian thought back to their first trip across the Bridge of the Dead. He had known then that something had been said during her exchange with the Watchmen, but as always, she kept her true motives hidden. He was slightly surprised to hear that they had known who she was. "To. . .to rescue her mother from the Raven-Eater. To save Cole."

The Watchmen laughed again, and Cole shouted for his father when the harsh sounds pounded painfully in his ears. Ian looked over to see tears streaming down his son's cheeks, but the guards had him in a strong hold so he couldn't grab the boy in his arms and whisper that everything would be alright.

"The half-breed returned. . .for one reason. . ." The Watchmen shoved their dark faces mere inches from Ian's, and only then did he see the reflection of his own face in two cloudy makeshift eyes shared by the guards. *"Atleisdi."* The word echoed around the tiny room, the white flame of the lone candle flickering. *"Atleisdi,"* they repeated. *"Revenge."*

"Revenge? Revenge against who? The Raven-Eater?" Their death stare confused him. He already knew Whisper's goal was to save Blue Feather and kill the Raven-Eater. So what was the Watchmen's point? "I. . .I don't understand."

"Kanegv knew her destiny. . .Why. . .did you. . .make this journey?" the Watchmen asked. *"Why is your son. . .in the Land of the Dead? Why. . .did your son. . .die?"*

It was the same question Whisper had asked him several times. And still, he had the same answer. "The Raven-Eater wanted a son," he replied hastily. "He tricked Cole into his death. Ah!" he shouted when his feet were lifted out from under him and he tumbled to the gooey ground. At the same time, Cole moved further into the wall. Ian reached out, desperate to touch his son, save his little boy. All he could see were Cole's hands, face, and feet—a grim, grotesque portrait of the Watchmen's mysterious magic.

"Why is your son. . .in the land of the Dead?" the Watchmen asked again, beginning a slow circle around Ian. *"Why. . .did he. . .die?"*

"Because. . ." he struggled to think of the answer they wanted. He still didn't understand why he had been faced with this question from the very beginning, one he thought he already had figured out. "Because Whisper let him die, so she could return to the Land of the Dead and have her revenge!"

The Watchmen's spinning quickened, accusations and questions and condemnations mumbling in their draft. The faster they spun, the faster Ian became conscious of the fact that they were sucking the air from the room. His lungs began to burn, and he started to panic as he frantically searched his mind for the answer.

Why was Cole in the Land of the Dead? Why did he die? Why....Because the Raven-Eater wanted a son; because his own was brutally murdered....Because Whisper and Smoke Speaker needed an excuse to go to the Land of the Dead....Because Cole was tricked by a so-called ghost into attempting to cross the river, where Whisper watched him drown and did nothing to save him...Because Cole wandered too far away from his father on the playground, and didn't listen to orders to stay in sight... Because....

And then the truth finally set in.

Because Ian was musing over the idea of having an affair with Rebecca, instead of watching his son.

"Oh, God," Ian whispered, clutching his aching chest when the realization struck. His fault, he thought as his lungs screamed for air and his body involuntarily heaved. His own fault.

"It's my fault!" He nearly choked on the genuine words, breathing in empty air as Cole's cries faded into the background. His mouth dried and his head spun light-headedly. A curtain began to close across his vision as he clutched his throat. "It's my fault...he died."

Suddenly the spinning stopped. Ian gratefully heaved in deep breaths, surprised to find that he was crying. The guilt and grief that racked his body over the major part he played in his own son's death was almost too much to bear. His greed, his selfishness, his desire to fulfill some stupid fantasy with a woman who meant nothing to him, all led to this very moment.

And all this time, throughout the entire journey, Whisper had known. She had tried to get him to realize the error of his ways, without actually revealing the truth herself. That was what she meant, he thought, when she said he was yet to prove himself a man. It was a test of his worth as a man, as a father, as a dead soul worthy of his second chance in the Land of the Living.

When Ian lifted his head, the Watchmen were regarding him with cool, almost indifferent stares. "It was my fault," he said again, shakily rising to his feet. "I wasn't watching him, and he wandered away. If I had been paying attention to my son, he would still be alive."

Without a word, the small hut shook and Cole tumbled out from the wall, covered in sticky brown goo. He crawled over to Ian, who picked him up and wrapped strong arms around his frightened, mud-encrusted boy. "Let me make up for this," he said, his demand coming out more as a plea. "I have to make this right, and to do that I have to return to the living world."

"So. . .you. . .believe—"

"Yes, I do. I really do." That surprised him more than anything.

"Ian Daivya. . .Creator. . .is. . .forgiving."

Then the Watchmen stepped to the side, the tattered cloth door blowing wide open. Ian took one final glance at the ghastly guards then raced past them into the darkness.

Fresh from her father's makeshift prison cell, Julia squared her shoulders, stepped out of her car, and walked up to the front door of the funeral home. She felt lethargic and heavy, but attributed the sensation to grief. Not aware that time had slowed, she never even noticed that what should have been a fifteen minute drive took longer than two hours.

Before stepping inside, Julia took a moment to crane her neck and stare up at the sky. Dark clouds had crossed over the sun many days ago, and with each passing hour they thickened and moved faster throughout the sky as though on a mission of destruction. It was spooky, an ominous sign of a danger she was yet to understand.

Shaking off the feelings of trepidation, Julia shoved open the door and entered. An uncomfortable stillness instantly greeted her. The room was vacant, sparsely decorated walls making the small space seem even lonelier. Not even the bright flowers lining the windows and countertops could bring any cheer into such an empty room. The coffins didn't help either.

A man stepped out from a back office. He was tall and lean, with thinning gray hair and thick glasses that sat atop a small nose. He was dressed nicely—a white polo shirt and pressed jeans making him look more like a teacher than a funeral home director. "Mrs. Daivya," he greeted, a bit surprised to see the small, exhausted-looking woman. "I was expecting you quite a few days ago."

"I was. . .held up," Julia replied, shaking the man's hands. "I'm ready to go over the plans."

Frank Farber regarded Julia with a sad stare. He'd watched far too much of the news coverage on Cole's death, and while he had never personally experienced the loss of a child, he felt like he knew the entire Daivya family just by seeing so much of their grief on television.

"Mrs. Daivya," he began, walking about the counter. "I just want to say how—"

"I'd rather not talk about it," Julia interrupted, stifling a yawn and wondering how she could react in such a way. She sniffled while running her hand over a casket far too small for an adult. "Such a shame we have to use these," she whispered to herself, turning back to Farber. "When can we do this?"

Farber cleared his throat and pulled a small stack of papers from a cabinet. "Well, I took the liberty of putting some things together, based on when we last spoke. With the flower arrangements, minister—"

"No," Julia cut in again, this time more forcefully. "No frills, no show, no people. My son has been put through enough in his death. I want him buried now. When can that happen?"

Understanding her need for urgency, Farber shut the folder and looked at Julia knowingly. "Tomorrow."

Chapter 42

Putting aside the incredibly painful realization that hit him square on the head at the Bridge of the Dead, Ian ran as fast and hard as he could across the open land surrounded by mountains. All around him dead souls reached out and moaned for mercy or snarled in vengeance for a crime Ian never committed against them.

Dirt and grime clawed at his new eyes as his feet screamed with each step. His scraped heels and mangled toes couldn't take much more, and his shoes were now mere remnants of rubber cast off long ago. Bloody footprints made a trail from the Western Sun, a trail that left both a visual and aromatic mark for the army that marched with a quickened pace. He could do nothing but grit his teeth and suffer silent screams as he pushed through the burning agony. His arms felt like Jell-O, but held on to Cole as though the boy would disappear again were he to let go.

Ian's breath wheezed out of fiery lungs. The roar of the Western Sun had faded now, and only the pale gray light of the land Whisper called Waiting lighted his path. The trip back seemed faster, perhaps because his focus was on one thing—the lake that took his life.

When the trees that cloaked Whisper's Waters came into view, Ian allowed himself to stop. He set Cole down on his feet and grabbed him by the shoulders. "Cole, listen to me," Ian panted, his chest pleading for a break. He glanced over his shoulder when a huge rumble rocked the earth, and tightened his hold as the Army of the Dead broke through the Western Sun. For a single, incredible second, their vast line eclipsed half of the sun, shadows rising into the sky, spreading across the lands.

"Daddy, the bad guys!"

"I know! I know, Cole! Listen!" Ian pointed to the forest. "We have to go to a lake, OK? And we have to go underwater. When we go underwater I need you to blow out all your breath, OK? Do you understand?"

Confusion crossed the boy's filthy face. "But…but how will I breathe?"

"Cole, you have to trust me, and we can go home. Do you trust me?"

Cole hesitated. Clutching his hands together, he looked around, thinking of any other way to escape this scary place of zombies and ghosts. He didn't want to go back into the water. The water was why he was there in the first place, and he was scared.

He didn't even like to swim in his pool at home. But he knew he had to be brave, so he faced his father with wavering yet growing courage.

"Yes," he said determinedly.

"Good." Ian nodded and straightened, his back cracking and popping in protest. Though he too wished there was another way, any other way, he reached down and picked up his son with the last strength he had left. A rock flew past his ear, and he turned to see that soldiers from the Army of the Dead had picked up weapons and had incredible throwing distance abilities. Some had sticks and were slowly sharpening them. Ian tightened his hold on his son and fought a painful cry when a second jagged stone came flying his way and struck him solidly in the back. Soon, they would have spears, and he would be no match for their wrath. He had to move, and had to move now.

"I promise that this will all be over soon, Cole. And we'll get back to your mommy and everything will be better again."

With his promise ringing in the boy's ear, Ian began his final race into the woods.

Whisper led the way to the top of the Fire Tower, each step echoing off bare yet dripping stone walls. Her eyes were clouded over with concentration as she let her feet be guided by the directions inked into her back throughout the years leading up to her death. She had endured that pain for this very moment, the walk up those long, winding staircases, anticipating the future with each step that echoed off bare stone walls. The only light that cast their shadows eerily behind them, making their trio double in size, was from the torch Gentle Heart was forced to carry.

From behind, the timid wife sniffled and racked her brain for a way out of this mess. Escape was out of the question. Whisper stood before her, a powerful woman who could kill those who shared her blood without thought, and the Raven-Eater walked steadily behind her, a man who cared only for complete and total annihilation of the Land of the Living. For pure torture purposes, Whisper had decided to force her to endure the long walk so, as her daughter had declared with such detachment, she would have that much longer to reflect on the treacherous action that took place in the Land of the Dead eighteen years ago.

Gentle Heart didn't understand how Whisper could see her action as anything but loving. She had given her daughter, only five summers old at the time, a chance to live, a chance to be free of a father who was determined to see her put to death and had attempted to murder her himself. The fact that Smoke Speaker would later use her as a way to return wasn't something she had anticipated, and though Gentle Heart certainly faulted her father for raising Whisper to be a vessel of revenge rather than a granddaughter, she nonetheless failed to see the true source of the girl's hate.

Her heart broke as she watched the fascinating yet horrifying black lines pulse across Whisper's back as they neared the top of the Fire Tower. To be so young and have such a mark forever etched into her skin…Gentle Heart silently raged over the Elder's actions. No other hand could have done such a thing, and she knew her father's work when she saw it. It was little surprise, then, that Whisper had developed such animosity toward her mother.

Perhaps she truly is her father's daughter, Gentle Heart thought sadly, and knew then that if she couldn't escape, her only other option was to somehow reach Whisper's compassionate side, her human side. No matter how hard she tried to deny it, she still had some part of her, however buried, able to see the good in the world. As her mother, Gentle Heart had to try.

"*Kanegv*—" she started, only to be shoved in the back by the Raven-Eater. She bit back a cry of pain, pressing her lips together and fighting to disregard the sore spot now throbbing in her left shoulder. If Whisper heard her attempt to speak, she made no acknowledgement. Instead, she merely kept her pace until they reached the door that led out to her murder. Gentle Heart chewed her bottom lip, searching her soul for the inner strength her daughter had, the faith her father believed in with such conviction. When Whisper turned, a hand on the thick, rusted metal lock, she spoke out with the only thing that came to mind.

"*Kanegv*, you are better than him," she said low and quickly, staring her daughter straight in the eyes and refusing to back down when the haunting darkness threatened to swallow her whole. For a moment, she thought Whisper was considering her words, perhaps impressed by her courage not to break the visual connection.

Her hope vanished into the depths of lost souls when Whisper narrowed her eyes, shoved open the heavy door, and pushed Gentle Heart through.

Chapter 43

Today was the day her son would finally be laid to rest. When Julia woke in the morning, she felt no satisfaction that her son would be at peace, no closure that this nightmare was over. She was merely empty. Her heart had stopped beating for any and everything other than the necessity to rise for Cole's funeral.

It would be private, she had decided, only her and her son. After everything that had happened since Cole's disappearance, no one else deserved their chance to say good-bye. Not her sister, who stuck around only to flirt with the young deputies, not Sheriff Forbe, who had called the night before to inform her that Elder Smoke Speaker had died in the middle of the night. Not even Olivia, who had stood back and watched as her daughter was locked in a cold, unfeeling bathroom.

She got ready slowly, barely bothering to spruce up her haggard appearance. She brushed her hair without worrying about frizz, and dressed in a pair of jeans and a white shirt with the face of a puppy that said "I Woof You!" Cole had given it to her just last Mother's Day as his way of both expressing his love for his mother and his desire to get a dog. At first she'd thought the shirt to be ridiculous and slightly embarrassing, now she cherished it like she did every precious memory of her child. Without wasting time for breakfast, Julia gathered up her purse and keys, along with a stuffed Saint Bernard and T-Rex that had been Cole's favorites, and left the house.

As soon as she stepped outside, black clouds that tumbled across the sun met her eyes. The terrifying sight made her pause and wonder how such dark skies could be without thunder and lightning accompanying the threat of impending storms. The thought of the end of the world briefly crossed her mind as she imagined some strange black hole swallowing the earth.

Wouldn't be such a bad thing, she thought, getting into the car. As she drove to the funeral home, she saw several people along the way staring up at the heavens, some grabbing their children and ushering them indoors, others taking pictures. Some were even packing up their belongings—clothes, toys, food, and all—in hopes of escaping whatever weather was about to strike. By the time Julia reached her destination, morning was beginning to look like dusk. A storm that normally would have worried her was now met with merely irritation. It seemed that it wasn't just her father trying to prevent Cole's burial. Even nature was now against her.

As ordered, Frank Farber was ready for the funeral when she arrived. The grave had been dug early that morning, and the casket holding the boy's body was next to it. On either side stood a gravedigger who stared at the ground, saddened by the fact that they had to put such a small coffin in the earth, and even more so by the idea that the child's ceremony was being rushed by a mother who refused to allow any other family to attend. To them, it was selfish and unforgivable.

"Mrs. Daivya," Farber greeted, offering a gentle smile. "Are you ready?"

"Yes." Julia swallowed hard and tried not to look at the casket. She caught glimpses of it as she approached, despite her attempts. Tears burned as she clutched the stuffed animals to her chest and the wind began to blow, furiously whipping her unwashed hair around her gaunt face. No, she thought, not even nature would stop this day from happening. "Would...would you mind if I took a moment to say good-bye?"

"Of course not."

Pounding through the woods, fighting the thorny branches that tore their cheeks, arms, and legs apart, Ian and Cole desperately raced to Whisper's Waters. Now that the Army of the Dead had walked through the Western Sun, their pace had quickened and their screaming moans were louder than ever. Makeshift spears flew their way, but luckily for Ian the soldiers' muscles were yet to fully develop, which meant their aim was off. Only two hit their mark, and Ian had the bloody shoulder and shin to prove it.

Despite himself, Cole stared over his father's shoulders and watched as they made their way across the open plains until the trees hid them from his vision. Now, he gripped Ian's neck and prayed that the army wouldn't catch them.

"Almost there," Ian wheezed, tears streaming down his cheeks as the pain burned from his feet to head, which stung as Cole clung to his mucky, blood-matted hair. Dark clots of blood formed a path through the woods, fallen sticks and sharp rocks piercing tender flesh. But he didn't care. The pain was worth his son's salvation.

Something was guiding him to the lake, a force within his own self. Perhaps it was because that was the place of his death, perhaps it was Whisper's and Smoke Speaker's doing. Either way, he hoped with all his might that he was going in the right direction, and furiously wondered how the Army of the Dead could move so fast now that they were past the Western Sun. His own speed hadn't quickened, and he hated how everything in the Land of the Dead worked against him.

He had little time left. Cole was weak, and beginning to feel lighter, as though he was being lifted away by a higher calling. And Ian was running out of energy.

If they didn't get there soon, they would both be lost forever.

Whisper slowly circled the rooftop of the Fire Tower. The vast stone platform offered a panoramic view of the Land of the Dead, with miniature towers for defense at every corner, despite no war ever being fought. The walls were lined with jagged rock so no flying creature would dare to perch, while the ground was coated with sticky black goo that clung to her shoes. In the center of the roof was an altar stained with blood, the place of many sacrificial rites. Whisper had long been intrigued by sacrifices, but the Elder had strictly forbidden such a practice, denouncing it as work of witches and evil spirits.

"Surely it has some purpose," she murmured, narrowing her eyes as the colors in the Western Sun began to blur together and slow in movement. When the Army of the Dead crossed over completely into the Land of the Living, the Western Sun would stop spinning altogether, forever opening the portal between both worlds. To do so would mean the spirits dwelling in the Land of the Dead had free passage back to the Land of the Living, where they could take revenge on those who murdered them, live a life that was stripped from them, and take whatever they wanted from those whose hearts still beat. The passage meant chaos, fear, and destruction. It meant the beginning to a new reign of kingdom and power.

In her mind, Whisper imagined Ian and Cole's race to the lake. Were they alive, they would be close, the Army of the Dead right on their heels. The end of their journey was sure to be a test of Ian's faith, his determination, and his willpower. It was a long run through fire and forest, carrying a child who was the key to his own salvation. By now, he was likely experiencing the taste of his own blood as it dripped down his face from cuts by thorny branches, and near naked as his clothes were torn to shreds. The thought pleased her, as she was now standing atop her new home freshly washed and dressed. Her face still told a story of fists and fights, but at least it was clean.

Unlike the Raven-Eater, she preferred simple attire, pants similar to her old pair and a short-sleeved shirt made of a thin fabric only found in the Land of the Dead. On her feet was her own pair of old boots, while her wrists and throat were free of decoration. Only her hair, tucked back in a loose braid, was adorned with a single white feather. Despite her lack of show, she looked regal nonetheless, regarding her soon-to-be kingdom with an air of authority.

"Here," Whisper announced, her accented voice carrying across the Barren Plains. She turned, crossing her toned arms and tilting her chin in the direction of the altar. "An offering to the new Land of the Dead."

Chapter 44

Julia's lips moved quickly, but no sound escaped as she silently said her farewell. She'd thought there would be no words for this grief-stricken event, but now they came flooding to her in a downpour of sorrow. She remembered the moment she learned she was pregnant, how happy she and Ian were to be parents. The first time she held Cole in her arms, she knew she was in love. And watching him grow, there was nothing lovelier than that. And she remembered his first day of kindergarten, and how nervous he'd been to meet his new teacher; his excitement over Santa's Christmas present of a brand new bicycle, and how eager he'd been to take his first ride down the street; learning how to read with his favorite book about dinosaurs, refusing to put the book down even though he struggled with the big words. Even the less-than-happy moments, such as his fear over swimming lessons and the time he split his chin open after a tumble off the swing set, were special to her.

So she apologized for not being there enough, for not watching him closely enough, for leaving him in the incapable hands of a father who didn't love him enough. Her baby boy was gone, and she knew deep down that it was all because she was unfit to be a mother.

"I'm sorry, Cole," she whispered, kneeling at the base of the six-foot-deep hole as the gravediggers began lowering the casket. "I'm so, so sorry."

Father and son burst into the clearing that opened to Whisper's Waters. Ian could see the lake ahead, so close, and yet still such a run. The Army of the Dead crashed through the trees behind, forcing him to dodge fallen branches as they tumbled to the ground. The closer they got, the more the ground shook, the sky swallowing the red and purple lights and the air turning to stale dust. He prayed that the Land of the Dead was changing because the army was approaching, and not because Julia was burying Cole, thus forever trapping him in eternal darkness and allowing the Raven-Eater to consume the Land of the Living in hate and death.

"Almost there," he panted, wincing when a loose shard of black bark struck him in the back. "Almost there."

A pit of fear and desperation dropped in Gentle Heart's stomach as the Raven-Eater forced her to her knees on the altar of sacrifice. She fought back tears, determined to show a front of bravery despite her terror. Death by the hand of her daughter was something she never would have foreseen. She had witnessed many sacrifices on this altar by her husband and his guards, and never did she think that her time would come as well.

"Why?" she asked Whisper when the young woman took the blade that the Raven-Eater held out. It was the same sword used on so many other sacrificed souls, one that had been put away for some time now since the Raven-Eater began his hunt for a son. And now it would be used to destroy the one Whisper despised most. "How could we come to this moment?"

Whisper turned the sword over in her hands, marveling at the weight, the fine craftsmanship. It had been sharpened recently, she noticed with satisfaction. Deciding to appease her mother, she kneeled down, threateningly twisting the tip of the blade into the stone as she spoke. "Do you know what life is like, Blue Feather, when it is not one you chose for yourself?"

Incredulity filled Gentle Heart's reply. "Do you think I chose to be here, *Kanegv*?" she asked, sweeping an arm around to gesture to her surroundings.

"Yes, Blue Feather, you do know. You too know the burdens of a forced existence." Whisper's tone told Gentle Heart that her answer had been expected. "And yet you forced a similar life onto your own daughter, one filled with training, conspiring, and constant preparation for a fate not chosen by the one who must follow it. One where that fate was chosen instead by an Elder willing to send his granddaughter into death."

"I did what was best," Gentle Heart whispered, a tear escaping down her cheek. "I couldn't let you die here. I wanted you to live a long, happy life in a better place. You would punish me for that?"

Whisper ignored the question. "My purpose, Blue Feather, has always been to destroy the one responsible for a life of captivity. There are no words to change that fate."

For a moment, neither spoke, and the Raven-Eater gleefully took his place just behind Whisper to watch the death of the one who couldn't produce him a male heir. Finally, Gentle Heart swallowed heavily and nodded. "I understand, *Kanegv*...and I forgive you."

"There is nothing to forgive," Whisper snapped, slightly offended. "You do not understand. You could *never* understand."

"Enough," the Raven-Eater cut in, his deep voice sharply cutting into Whisper's ears. "Your sacrifice awaits our conquest."

Angered by the interruption, no matter who it was from, Whisper straightened and cocked her head to the side. "Sacrifice," she repeated quietly, eyeing her mother curiously. "What has been denied to me is now openly offered."

"*Kanegv. . .gvgeyui.*"

"Love," Whisper responded to her mother with a malicious grin, "has no purpose here."

He was just steps away. He could smell the murky water, could see the pale red and purple lights reflecting off the gray ripples. The end to this eerie land was finally near.

"Cole! Cole! I need you to blow out all your breath!" he shouted through wheezing pants as his bloody feet touched cool, refreshing water. "Do as I say, and hold on tight!"

He felt the boy do just that before they plunged into the water.

Ian gripped Cole with one hand and strong plants beneath the water to hold his body down with the other. He quickly released all the air in his lungs, bubbles flowing up to the surface and breaking through in tiny ripples. After just a few seconds, Cole's body began to jerk, and Ian's heart shattered into a thousand tiny pieces.

I'm so sorry, Cole, he shouted in his mind, squeezing his eyes shut as his lungs began to fill. He choked violently, sucking in more water. He felt Cole's tiny fingers release their grip and his own mind slip into a clouded dizziness.

In those last moments before his heart stopped beating, he saw both worlds in their final moments of existence.

He watched as his wife kissed the stuffed dinosaur given to Cole last Christmas by his grandparents. She held the animal over the grave, hand trembling as she struggled to release it. He watched as Whisper lifted the sword high above her head, twisting it in her hand so the blade faced downwards.

He saw the gravediggers pick up their shovels, casting sad looks at Julia as she burst into tears, clutching her hands together as they began to shake. He saw Gentle Heart close her eyes in acceptance of a sacrifice she could not prevent, a single sad sigh escaping her lips as she lowered her head before her daughter. And he saw the Army of the Dead as they entered Whisper's Waters, ready to take over the Land of the Dead and complete the Raven-Eater's bidding. They grabbed for Ian, bony hands grasping his legs as he fought to hold on to the plants with what life he had left.

Then, as his heart stopped pumping, his lungs shuttering with dead air and his vision blackening, both worlds pulsed for the second time.

For Ian, it meant the painful end to a life he had just realized how to truly live, a life filled with all the love and laughter he had ever dreamed of.

For Julia, it meant the black clouds swallowing the sky opened, lightening striking the earth just yards from where she sat before everything went white and completely silent.

For Whisper, it meant her moment of vengeance had finally come, had finally been granted to her after so many years of bitter hatred, and so with an evil snarl of detestation, she swung the blade down.

And deep into the gut of the Raven-Eater.

When the newly mortal tyrant collapsed, a confused look spread across his scarred face, she lowered herself to his level and pulled the sword from his stomach. Blood and guts caked the blade, and she pushed it up against the bottom of his chin so he could smell his own death.

"The Land of the Dead," Whisper sneered haughtily, "belongs to *me*."

Chapter 45

Ian awoke with a start. Sunshine and singing birds greeted him upon waking, and when he leapt up off the bench he spun around and realized he was back in the park at Big Creek Campground.

"What…" He peered around, grabbing his hair and finding it clean, frantically searching his arms and seeing them scratch and blood-free. His clothes were spotless, his muscles felt refreshed, and his feet were no longer on fire. It was over. His journey had finally, thankfully, come to an end.

"A dream?" he asked himself, thoroughly confused. "It couldn't be…."

Then he noticed that Cole was nowhere to be seen.

"No," he whispered, his heart starting to beat harder. "Goddamn it, no. Cole! Cole, answer me! *Now!*"

He knew exactly where to go, and although the thought of returning to the woods was depressing, he would suffer through Hell and back to prevent another trip to the Land of the Dead.

When he burst through the other side, he saw Cole standing on the riverbank, dazed and disoriented. "Cole!"

"Dad!" Cole spun around and raced to his father, who dropped to his knees and gathered his son into a tight hug.

"Oh, God, Cole…it worked. It actually worked. How is that even possible?"

Cole pulled back, fear flickering into his eyes. "It was real?"

Ian hesitated, asking himself that very same question. Was it real? Could they have actually spent the past month-and-a-half trapped in the Land of the Dead, fighting witches, giant worms, and evil leaders with super-human powers? Now that he was standing on the riverbank dressed in nice clothes and enjoying the sunshine streaming through the leaves, he wasn't so sure.

But he knew how to find out.

With a shaking hand, Ian reached out and lifted the sleeve of Cole's bright blue shirt. And there, just below the shoulder, were three burn marks etched into his skin. To show he was accepted by the Raven-Eater, Whisper had said.

"It was real," he murmured, dread curling in his gut. Then he looked down to see the necklace at Cole's feet, the one Whisper had pulled from Gentle Heart's throat, the one made by the hair of the Raven-Eater.

Bury it at Howling Vines, she had ordered.

"Cole, we have to go see someone," he said slowly, picking up the necklace. "Then we can go home."

The trip that took nearly two hours the first time only lasted half that this time around. Ian and Cole hurried down the path, not taking the time to talk about what happened, not bothering to reflect on what it was like to be back in the light, with sounds and colors all around them. Instead, they marched steadily until they reached Howling Vines.

"What do we do here?" Cole asked as they entered the clearing. Ian didn't answer, as Elder Smoke Speaker had already risen and was hobbling their way.

"I've been expecting you," he greeted, clasping Ian's hand with a quick shake. "Come, we must hurry." He eagerly and quickly led them to the hearth, where he had removed the hot stones and coals and dug a hole at least eleven feet deep. How he had managed it by himself was something Ian couldn't take the time to consider. "The boy must bury the necklace. Now."

"Why Cole?"

"Only one protected by the Raven-Eater can bind him to eternal darkness. Crossing into the Land of the Living made him human, now only your son can stop him from rising again."

"OK." Ian took Cole by the shoulders and placed him in front of the hole. "It's OK, just do as he says. Quick."

Cole followed orders, tossing the hair-braided necklace into the hole and quickly pouring in the dirt. When he was finished, Smoke Speaker lit a bowl of white sage and said a prayer to Creator, an offering to the sacred directions, forever ending the reign of the Raven-Eater.

The red and purple lights glittered high above the Land of the Dead, the Western Sun churning steadily in the distance. The world of dead and lost souls was balanced once again. Whisper knew the moment her new kingdom had been restored, as not only did the light return and the wind blow refreshed air, but the

Raven-Eater stopped groaning and convulsing, passing away into eternity, along with his army.

"*This is...not...over...half-breed*," he had snarled around a mouthful of blood, anger taking over any fear that may have filled his black heart when he realized he was about to die. "*You will...suffer. I...will...return...*"

Whisper had only knelt down and smirked, holding the blade across her knees so the Raven-Eater could see the weapon that took his life. "*Until then, Raven-Eater,*" she had answered, just before his eyes closed for the last time.

Only when the Raven-Eater was truly dead and vanished in a subtle burst of gray dust did Whisper release Gentle Heart from the altar. She tossed the sword to the side and stepped to the edge of the Fire Tower, looking out over the Land of the Dead fondly. *Yes*, she thought without any regard to her confused mother rising to unsteady feet on the altar, *I am home.*

"I don't understand," Gentle Heart said from behind. "I thought you wanted me."

Whisper turned. "I never said I wanted you."

"But you said you...." She was right, Gentle Heart thought as she recalled her daughter's words. Whisper never said outright that she wanted to kill her, only that she wanted revenge against the one who forced her into a life of training. "The Raven-Eater," she replied quietly. "He tried to kill you, and ordered your death, and so I had to give you up."

"Yes." Whisper walked up to her mother and touched the bone necklace around her throat. "I have never blamed you for my existence in the Land of the Living, only him. I cannot fault the Elder for wishing his daughter to be returned to him, for being blinded to any other purpose. It is only human. His grief, as was my training, was the result of the Raven-Eater's treachery. And so he had to be destroyed."

"But how...how did you kill him?"

"The boy," Whisper answered, pointing to the Western Sun. "Only a child protected by the Raven-Eater can bind his powers. When a part of him crossed through the Western Sun and into the Land of the Living, he became mortal. By burying his hair, he is forever bound to a place created for souls without a life in either world, a place where he can never exist except within his own black soul."

"And me?"

"You..." Whisper bit back a sigh and turned her attention to the Barren Plains, remembering her attack, Ian's courage. It seemed so long ago. "You are free, Blue

Feather. Free to return to the Land of the Living. I have the power to return you to Smoke Speaker, so you can live the life that was stripped away by the Raven-Eater."

"And what about you?"

Hundreds of images came to Whisper's mind. What she could do with this place, how she could rule. The possibilities were endless. "My place has always been here."

Chapter 46

Before he could return to his own life, Ian had to get answers. Smoke Speaker was willing to hear his questions, and had built a fire over the Raven-Eater's place of burial to cook a rabbit for the three of them. Cole sat silently at Ian's side, fidgeting and wishing he could go home.

"So you've trained Whisper since she was a child to kill the Raven-Eater."

"Yes." Smoke Speaker nodded and turned the rabbit. Only he, Ian, and Cole would ever remember this journey, and it had taken its toll on the Elder. Giving up his life, knowing there was the chance he would never return, acknowledging the fact that Whisper wasn't coming back, was a lot for his old heart to bear. "I gave her a choice, though. She did not have to go. She chose to save her mother."

"How do you know she's still alive? That he didn't kill her first?"

Smoke Speaker gestured to the gray tendrils drifting up to the sky. "She told me she is still alive, and that my daughter is free."

Ian looked around. "Then where is she?"

The Elder frowned and poked at the rabbit. "Blue Feather has chosen to stay in the Land of the Dead, to be with her daughter." His answer was sad, though tinged with pride. "She chose right. And one day, I will join them in the Land of the Dead, and be reunited with my loved ones."

Ian considered the old man's declaration. Smoke Speaker had trained Whisper to defeat the Raven-Eater so as to save his daughter. To be so young and be forced to carry such a burden, he couldn't imagine, and to be a mother, living for so many years with a terrifying beast filled with evil in a world not meant for a woman so kind, choosing to stay for the sake of a daughter she never got the chance to know. That was a sacrifice he wasn't sure he was strong enough to make. Yet it was one to be honored, no matter how deceitful Whisper had been, no matter the fact Cole died because of the Elder's own objectives.

The truth was, Cole was safe, and Whisper was dead. She had given up her life for them both, making her own fate a reality. He truly believed that deep down she understood the power of good over evil, and would rule accordingly.

"You're lucky, Smoke Speaker." Ian accepted the wooden plate that the Elder offered, picking up a chunk of meat. "Both your daughter and your granddaughter will be legends for your people."

The comment filled Smoke Speaker with delight. "My Whisper was born into a world she was destined to change. And now, she has the chance to do so."

Ian handed Cole a bite of meat. The boy wolfed it down and grabbed for more. He cleared his throat. "Just two things I still don't understand. The first is…well, there was this word tattooed on Whisper's back. It said *Ayohuhisdi*. I asked her a few times what it meant, but she would never tell me."

The happiness on Smoke Speaker's face faded. "*Ayohuhisdi*," he repeated, remembering the sad day he had inked the word on Whisper's flesh at her own request. "It means…Death."

"Death? As in…her death." The pieces came together for Ian, and he felt guilty for his accusations. "So…all this was never about us. Cole was just the unlucky kid in the wrong place at the wrong time. You both used us to get Whisper into the Land of the Dead and the Raven-Eater's hair here."

"Yes, Mr. Daivya. I only hope you can forgive my granddaughter for following her destiny."

Part of Ian wanted to fume, wanted to hate Whisper and the Elder. And yet, he was here, alive, and Whisper would never return. He just couldn't despise a woman following the path set before her at her birth.

"So…she knew all along that the Fire Tower would be the place of her true death. God, all this time I thought that word had something to do with Cole."

"Not at all, Mr. Daivya." Now the Elder was gloomy as he recalled the magnificent tattoo. "Those markings were meant to serve as a map, her guide. The paths led to one destiny, *Ayohuhisdi*…You have a second question?"

"Yeah." Still trying to wrap his head around the answer to the first, Ian moved on. "When we first found Cole, he had the mark of the half-breed on his back. But when we got to the RiverKeeper, it washed right off. So…who put it there? And why?"

Smoke Speaker smiled, revealing two rows of yellow and crooked teeth. "I must tell you a story, Mr. Daivya…many moons ago, I traveled to the Land of the Dead to save my little girl. It was a long time after the Raven-Eater had taken her, as it had taken a lot of work to prepare for the journey. Like you, I had to cross through the Western Sun. On my quest, I met a young warrior who had fallen. His eyes had burned, and his flesh was scorched. He lay on the earth just fingers away from the Western Sun. He was weak after an ambush by other dead souls, and could not pass through on his own. So I gathered him in my arms and pulled him through. I helped him through to the red and purple sunset, and together we faced our fate." He sat back and thought of the warrior, so scarred and ragged. His death had not been an easy one, and he had lay before the Western Sun for many years before help had come.

"He gave his word that he would return such kindness when I asked, no matter what I asked."

"So you asked him to draw the mark of the half-breed. Why? To confuse me?"

"So you would believe, even if it was in the wrong person."

"Huh." So the Elder had a few tricks of his own up his sleeve. And yet, Ian didn't mind, because it he hadn't of seen that mark, he never would have believed Whisper's outlandish tale. He never would have tried so hard to reach the RiverKeeper, and things may have turned out quite differently. "What was that warrior's name?"

"Hunting Hawk."

At the name, Ian laughed, his first true laugh in so long. *Loyalty is truly something among these people*, he thought. Hunting Hawk had the chance to leave along with the other guards with Whisper's magic powder, but chose to stay. He had the chance to return to the Land of the Living, but chose to save Ian and return to help Whisper. Whisper and the Elder had been looking out for him and Cole all along.

"Well, I know it's hard losing Whisper like this, but if it makes you feel any better, I met Hunting Hawk at the Fire Tower. And I think he had a little thing for her."

Smoke Speaker smiled. Hunting Hawk, if not a bit rough around the edges, was a good man, loyal and true to his word. "Then I pray she opens her heart."

After saying their good-byes, and after delivering Whisper's final message to her grandfather, a message that made tears brim in Smoke Speaker's eyes and his bottom lip tremble, Ian and Cole eagerly headed back to their campsite. Cole was antsy, bouncing with each step, gripping his father's hand hard with excitement. He had promised Ian not to tell his mom where he had been, because he didn't want to scare her.

But with each passing moment, the Land of the Dead felt more and more like a dream, and by the time they reached the campsite, he wasn't sure if it had actually happened or not. His young mind wasn't capable of grasping such a concept, and the Elder had whispered a chant of sorts to ensure the journey would be a mere memory in the distance to the boy as he grew older, like a faded idea, a forgotten dream. Ian was grateful for that, for he didn't want his son living with such a traumatic event.

Julia and Olivia were gathering up food for dinner when they returned. Cole raced to his mother and all but leapt into her arms, smothering her with kisses. Surprised, Julia laughed and dropped the hot dog buns, returning the hugs.

"What's gotten into you?" she asked with a chuckle.

"Nothing," Cole answered after a pause. He remembered feeling like he really needed to see his mom while on the trail, but now he couldn't remember why. It didn't matter though, for he was still delighted to see her. "I love you."

"I love you too, honey," Julia replied, thinking that her son must want something. Her smile faded when she saw Ian walking her way. His stroll was determined, though slightly awkward, like he was afraid of getting any closer.

She set her son down and regarded Ian with a suspicious frown. "Is everything OK?" she asked when he stopped, peering at her through sad eyes. "Did something happen at the park?"

"Yes," Ian answered truthfully. He saw the worry cross his wife's face when she glanced over at Cole, who was chatting up a storm with his grandfather at the picnic table. "I realized something."

"What?"

Ian frowned, closing the gap between him and his wife. "That I've been a crappy father, and an even worse husband." He tucked Julia's hair back behind her ear, tracing a finger over the bottom lip she had begun to chew. "I want things to get back to how they used to be. I don't want work to come between us, or anything else. I want us to last."

Tears flooded Julia's eyes as she listened to her husband speak the words she'd waited so long to hear. "What...well...Ian, you know that's what I want, but...what... well, what about your secretary? I can't do this if—"

"Nothing's happened," Ian cut in honestly. "I swear. And nothing ever will. She's nothing, just some redhead bimbo who thinks she can use people. Hell, she's gone Monday morning if you want. I don't care. You're the one for me. You always have been."

Julia sniffled and raised her hands to cup Ian's face. She saw truth in his blue eyes; she saw the man she fell in love with. "You're the one for me," she replied, rising to her toes and kissing him firmly, tenderly. She didn't know what caused this sudden trans-formation, but welcomed it with her entire heart. "So let's make this vacation our new beginning."

"Deal." Ian like the weight of the world had been lifted from his shoulders, though there was a small place in his heart that mourned for the woman who had died so he could realize what he truly wanted out of life.

Pushing the thought from his mind for the moment, Ian swept Cole up from the table and tickled him. The boy squealed with delight, kicking and squirming in his father's arms.

"How about a hot dog for dinner, Champ?" he asked, plucking up a pack from the table.

"How about a real doggy when we get home!"

Ian looked over at Julia, who had raised her eyebrows. "I knew that question was coming sooner or later," she said, then nodded. "I think we can talk about that and see what we can do."

"Yea!" Cole cheered. "I'm gonna name it Whisper."

Ian's breath hitched in his throat, but Julia didn't seem to notice. "Whisper?" she repeated, wondering where such a name had come from. "Well, if that's what you want."

Cole struggled to get down, so Ian set him on his feet. The boy ran to the tent, where he grabbed his book on dog breeds and began flipping through the pages. Ian watched him with a smile, not noticing as David came to his side.

"Whisper," the military man said, crossing his arms. "A good name."

"Sure," Ian agreed warily. "Strange though."

"Not so strange." David shook his head and adjusted the collar of his shirt. "After all, it's always good to pay your respects." With the slightest of winks, David patted Ian on the back then walked over to his pop-up trailer to get ready for dinner, leaving Ian standing in a standstill of surprise.

"No way," he whispered, and then had to smile. Yes, he agreed, it was always good to pay one's respects.

With that thought in mind, Ian headed over to the table, where Cole and Julia sat oohing and ahhing over puppy pictures. He would pay his own respects here, by rebuilding the family he almost lost.

Bright orange flames raged atop the Fire Mountains. At their base stood Whisper, tossing ancient relics onto the pyre as she burned everything that had once belonged to the Raven-Eater. When she was finished, no trace of his memory would remain.

She had worked hard her first six months in power. As the magic of the half-breed continued to grow within her, she learned more of the talents that lay within her heart and soul, talents that enabled her to transform the Land of the Dead into a world worthy of death.

Just weeks ago she had taken a burning ember in her hand, crafting a ball of fire in her palm and sending it up to the sky. Now the red and purple hues once lighting the darkness floated among a bright sky that darkened only at nightfall. Villages had begun to spring up in new places no longer tormented by the Raven-Eater's evil minions, though Whisper had been careful not to banish the creatures of her ancestors' pasts. It wasn't fair to them to be punished for living in their natural form.

The Land of the Dead would no longer be a place of torment and fear. She would make it a haven for those who didn't receive a proper burial. Though the Land of the Dead would never be the refuge that the Spirit World offered, she could still provide a safe place for those who crossed the Bridge of the Dead and reached their final resting place in one piece.

She thought about how she would redesign the Fire Tower to suit her own needs as she carelessly threw an old blanket onto the pyre. Thick, dark gray smoke billowed up to the sky. She was looking forward to her rule, to being the one everyone called their leader—the half-breed, coming back from the dead to destroy the tyrant and bring forth their land from the blackness.

The sound of a twig cracking in the distance had Whisper spinning around. Before she had even come to a stop, she had an arrow knocked and aimed directly at the approaching figure.

Hunting Hawk paused long enough to shoot Whisper a smirk. He continued along the path that led to the burning pyre, the red and orange flames reflecting off the round stone that hung low on his bare chest. It was the stone given to the River-Keeper, the stone that held the blood of the half-breed. Whisper had retrieved it upon establishing a new RiverKeeper, and given it to the guard as a way of thanking him for staying true to his word to Smoke Speaker. She had been surprised when, instead of using it for his own advantage, he merely crafted it into a necklace and asked to stay in the Land of the Dead.

"I received a message from *Utlav*," he announced, his accented tone welcome to Whisper's ears. "He said you wished for me to come to the Fire Tower."

"Mole was mistaken," she answered, lowering the bow and arrow. "My message was for you to stay away." Then she lifted a hand, palm facing Hunting Hawk, and shoved her arm forward.

The churning fire burst forth, burning the path and creating a scorching circle around Hunting Hawk. He was a warrior, though, and refused to show fear, even as the flames licked closer to his feet. He stood in place and watched as Whisper appeared through the flames, walking among a fire that shaped to her curves, a phoenix rising forth from the ashes in a glorious portrayal of magic and power. She broke through the blaze and entered the circle where he stood.

"It seems *Utlav* has deceived me," she said, looking over the Barren Plains, where Mole still reigned.

"And you had expected otherwise." It was not a question, merely a teasing accusation they both knew to be false. Hunting Hawk reached out and grasped Whisper's chin, turning her head back in his direction. "Who am I speaking with today? The half-breed…or *Kanegv*?"

She half-smiled then and lifted a shoulder. "Who would you prefer?"

The taunting, husky tone had Hunting Hawk grinning as he leaned over and grabbed Whisper in his arms. He kissed her firmly, feeling her hands tracing over the scars that lined his chest and shoulders. Those scars had been what first captured her interest, and she'd had many questions about them. Hunting Hawk had obliged, his ego certainly stroked by her attentive listening to his many war stories about a time before the white man. It was a battle for her attention any other time, as her souls constantly fought against one another, one side struggling to overcome the other, but the Elder had taught her well. Just as Smoke Speaker had saved Hunting Hawk from the wrath of the Western Sun, he had likewise educated his granddaughter on how to fight against the Raven-Eater's blood. It wasn't easy for her, and there were certainly moments when she failed, but Hunting Hawk was there nonetheless. He had suffered her wrath, faced the deception of a bloodline that craved destruction, and already had the scars to prove it. But Whisper's soul was strong, and he knew how to create a wall to separate the two halves of her own self.

And now she was all his, no matter the soul he would face for that moment. She had finally let down her guard and accepted the possibilities he had to offer. He was not there to take over the Land of the Dead; he was there to be the eternal companion for the only woman he'd ever met who was worthy of her own empire. Her strength, her mind, her ambitions, matched his own, if not surpassing them completely. Hunting Hawk had never married in his previous life because such a woman had never existed, and now he had his chance to start a family with the one he was proud to hold in his arms.

From her room high in the Fire Tower, Blue Feather watched her daughter open herself up to love. It had taken Hunting Hawk many moons to break through the barrier that cloaked her heart, but she had finally accepted him, and what he had to offer. Now, she enjoyed his company, as much as the half-breed could enjoy the company of another person. Hunting Hawk's devotion to her was obvious, even when he went on long trips throughout the Land of the Dead to collect dead yet willing souls for Whisper's guards, servants, and advisors. Blue Feather knew that her daughter would always be torn between the two sides that made up her soul, the good and the evil that she had been born with, but so far that dark part had been overcome.

If Whisper ever faltered in her steadfast determination to make her world a better place, Hunting Hawk would be there to lead her back to the right path. Knowing that, Blue Feather turned away when the fire faded and went back to her quilting. She was making a beautiful white blanket for the pair, which she would give to them at their union.

Not once had she regretted her decision to stay in the Land of the Dead. Giving up her child so long ago had been the hardest thing she'd ever done, and it tore her apart with each passing day to know that she couldn't be there to watch her daughter grow. This was her second chance to be a mother, a friend, a guide. Her father understood, as Whisper had used her magic to create a connection between the two so she could inform him as to her decision. Never interested in learning the art of Speaking, Blue Feather needed her daughter to make that link and hold it while she explained her choice to the Elder. Smoke Speaker, though his life's work had been dedicated to his daughter's rescue, understood and supported her. He would meet them in the Land of the Dead when his time had come, but for now, he still had important matters that needed tending to in the living world. People needed help, nature needed a voice of defense, and Howling Vines needed a powerful spell to ensure that the Raven-Eater's soul could never be freed.

Back on the cliffs, Hunting Hawk took Whisper by the hand and led her to the edge of the Fire Mountains. The heat from the pyre warmed them as a light breeze carried the smoke toward the Western Sun, while villagers greeted them in the distance with waves and smiles. They welcomed their new leaders, the half-breed and the loyal guard, grateful for a second chance in death.

Together, Whisper and Hunting Hawk watched over their new kingdom, the land of death and new beginnings that existed in all its glory, just beyond the Western Sun.

Acknowledgements

Beyond the Western Sun would not have been possible without the encouragement of my family and friends. As always, my mother, Cindy, has been my support system from the first to last word. Without her as my constant cheerleader, editor, friend, and inspiration, this novel would never have been finished. I also must thank my husband, Seth, for not only reading and editing my novel but also believing in me from the very beginning. His love, including putting up with my long hours at the computer, listening to me talk about my characters for hours on end, and debating on the best cover art design, is what encourages and drives me. He is my best friend and unwavering shoulder of support.

I would also like to extend this message of thanks to my father, Rytch, and stepfather, Rodney, who both read early versions of *Beyond the Western Sun* and offered helpful tips on how to improve the story, as well as encouragement. Along with them, I must thank Mackenzy Dodds, my trusted and go-to young reader who read this story in its first draft and provided valuable feedback from the teen demographic point of view. My family members, from my amazing Mema and Papa to my supportive aunts and uncles, have always been my number one fans, and it is their unwavering faith and love that have allowed me to pursue my dreams in writing.

I also have to thank those who took the time to help make *Beyond the Western Sun* all that it could be. Much thanks to Molly Johnson and Chris Johnson for reading and editing my novel. Their insight and advice as readers contributed to the creation of *Beyond the Western Sun*, and I appreciate their commitment to editing my novel and helping me work out all the kinks. My Aunt Debbie is also amazing in her dedication to helping me market my novels, always believing in me and going above and beyond to show her love and support.

Finally, I would like to thank my generous and thoughtful grandparents, Tom and Betty, for helping me bring *Beyond the Western Sun* to light. Without their encouragement and steadfast conviction in my dreams, this novel would still be a mere story on the computer screen.

I thank everyone for their help, and look forward to working together in sharing my stories with eager readers everywhere.

P.S. A special and promised shout-out to my "uba" little brother, Lathan!

Legends, Myths, and Lore

I would also like to take this time to share my sources for *Beyond the Western Sun*. Nearly all legends revealed in this book are part of Native American spirituality and history, though not all are Cherokee (and very few, such as the Raven-Eater and the Watchmen, are entirely fictional). Many stories and names shared were passed down from my great-uncle, Elder Anthony "Little Feather" White, though a few others were researched. Some legends came from the "Native Languages of the Americas" website and some animal references are from Ted Andrews' *Animal Speak*. For more information, I encourage you to explore my sources:

Andrews, Ted. *Animal Speak: the Spiritual & Magical Powers of Creatures Great & Small*. Llewellyn Publications. St. Paul, Minnesota, 2005.

Cherokee Culture and History. 1998—2010. http://www.native-languages.org/cherokee_culture.htm

Kristina Circelli

Stay Tuned for Book II in the Whisper Legacy:

Walk the Red Road

www.ingramcontent.com/pod-product-compliance
Lightning Source LLC
Chambersburg PA
CBHW030112180626
46812CB00002B/389